Advance Praise

"A novel-in-stories, and also a novel about stories: how, when they run up against the limits of what's verifiably true, love and empathy can still carry them across the finish line. Matthew Fox has written a family saga that's as formally inventive as it is funny and tender."
—JONATHAN DEE, PULITZER PRIZE-NOMINATED AUTHOR OF *THE PRIVILEGES*, *SUGAR STREET*, AND *PALLADIO*

"I've never read anything like *This Is It*. No secret can ultimately withstand the brilliant and unusual way this family epic unfolds, especially not when an unruly queer is looking into the genealogy. The cast inhabit a kingdom where laughing at tragedy is sometimes the only way through. Bold and unforgiving, but never without empathy—*This Is It* will take you to totally unexpected places."
—DANIEL ALLEN COX, AUTHOR OF *I FELT THE END BEFORE IT CAME*, *MOUTHQUAKE*, *SHUCK*, AND *BASEMENT OF WOLVES*

"Like our inscrutable families, like our most bedeviling love affairs, *This Is It* is a puzzle that reveals itself in bursts of insight, tender and startling revelations and self-implications, and in the everyday intimacies that form our messy, complicated lives. A wise, honest, and beautifully constructed novel."—CHRISTOPHER CASTELLANI, AUTHOR OF *LEADING MEN*

"Brimming with heart and humour, Matthew Fox's *This Is It* is an epic family drama that spans (and skewers) the generations. It's bold, clever, queer, and sexy. The novel-in-stories moves at a clip and stings with its emotional honesty. A musical masterwork that examines the boundaries of love and bravery."—CHRISTOPHER DIRADDO, AUTHOR OF *THE FAMILY WAY*

"*This Is It* moves through multiple cities, decades, and historical moments to excavate both gut-punching emotional trauma and domestic farce, as its many characters use dialogue to wound one other and to shield themselves from hurt. Fox has the rare ability to be heartbreaking and hilarious in a single line."—NATHAN WHITLOCK, AUTHOR OF *LUMP* AND *CONGRATULATIONS ON EVERYTHING*

"In the exquisitely rendered world of *This Is It*, being young doesn't mean you have a future, being old doesn't mean that you're known, and being family doesn't always mean that you're loved. Matthew Fox's novel brings us an urgent and contemporary take on the intergenerational family saga—you don't dare miss it."—MATTHEW J. TRAFFORD, AUTHOR OF *THE DIVINITY GENE: STORIES*

"Keenly observed and punctuated with wry wit, Matthew Fox's *This Is It* offers a moving meditation on queer love and loss. These interweaving, intergenerational stories are a stunning act of literary unearthing, examining the families we're born into and the ones we choose through an unvarnished, but not unkind, lens. Fox has crafted a gripping read filled with fierce tenderness and aching poignancy."
—K.R. BYGGDIN, AUTHOR OF *WONDER WORLD*

THIS IS IT

THIS IS IT

A novel in stories

MATTHEW FOX

Enfield & Wizenty (an imprint of Great Plains Publications)
320 Rosedale Ave
Winnipeg, MB R3L 1L8
www.greatplains.mb.ca

Great Plains Publications gratefully acknowledges the financial support provided for its publishing program by the Government of Canada through the Canada Book Fund; the Canada Council for the Arts; the Province of Manitoba through the Book Publishing Tax Credit and the Book Publisher Marketing Assistance Program; and the Manitoba Arts Council.

Design & Typography by Relish New Brand Experience
Printed in Canada by Friesens

Library and Archives Canada Cataloguing in Publication

Title: This is it / Matthew Fox.
Names: Fox, Matthew, 1977- author.
Identifiers: Canadiana (print) 20240396405 | Canadiana (ebook) 20240396545 | ISBN 9781773371207 (softcover) | ISBN 9781773371214 (EPUB)
Subjects: LCGFT: Novels.
Classification: LCC PS8611.O893 T45 2024 | DDC C813/.6—dc23

The creation of this work was partly supported by a generous grant from Le Conseil des arts et des lettres du Québec. Je remercie le Conseil pour son soutien et pour tout le soutien qu'il apporte à des projets artistiques vitaux au Québec.

Canada

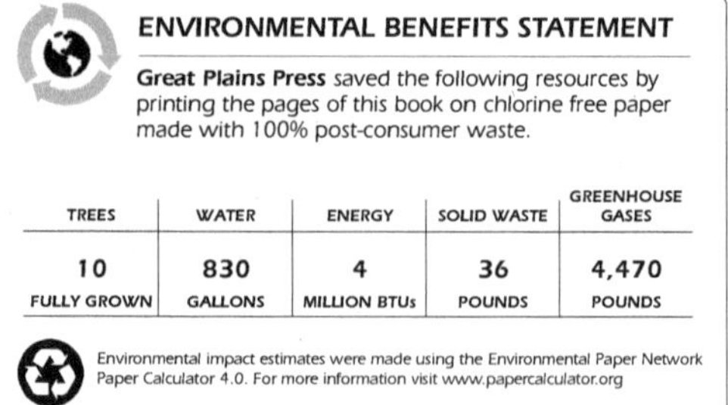

ENVIRONMENTAL BENEFITS STATEMENT

Great Plains Press saved the following resources by printing the pages of this book on chlorine free paper made with 100% post-consumer waste.

TREES	WATER	ENERGY	SOLID WASTE	GREENHOUSE GASES
10	830	4	36	4,470
FULLY GROWN	GALLONS	MILLION BTUs	POUNDS	POUNDS

Environmental impact estimates were made using the Environmental Paper Network Paper Calculator 4.0. For more information visit www.papercalculator.org

To my one and only inspiration, Brian Franklin MacDonald, who is, and will always be, younger than me, and prettier, and better in bed. And has better taste in home decor, amongst all other things. And he wore it better, too, whatever it was. He is just a better human being. Amen.

And for the rest of my family, too.

Table of Contents

1
Is This It? (Part One)

"Well?" Great-Aunt Maeve said. She pumped her La-Z-Boy.

She'd always had a La-Z-Boy. I remembered this emerald velour version from her old house in Fiona, the Ontario town that had produced us both. The tall radio, too, had been moved down here to Brooklyn from Canada. It sat in the middle of the room, dominating it, a hulking wooden creature from the '40s. It had city names on the dial instead of numbers. Roma, Wien, Köln, Gdańsk. Its bottom half was a bar crammed with whiskey bottles gleaming under a light bulb. The radio's cord was a tripping hazard, snaking across the carpet to an outlet.

Maeve's living room also contained two couches—two too many, considering they lived alongside piles of banker's boxes, a huddle of ashtray-stands, a credenza rammed with LPs and a sideboard with stacks of unmatching china. Clashing lamps sat on end tables. The TV predated my birth, and I was twenty-four years old then.

Maeve must have been eighty-two. She'd shrunk since I'd last seen her. She'd always been small, but when I think of her back in Fiona, I remember a stout, powerful, unstoppable Irish woman with authoritative gestures and a grouchy laugh. Now she was shrivelled and droopy-skinned. Her navy sweatsuit was bunchy, two sizes too big. Her red hair had gone silver and dull. Puff and pinkness were taking over her face. The motion of the La-Z-Boy was the only thing that kept her from camouflaging into the clutter.

"Well," I said. Between us sat a coffee table stacked with stale magazines. I placed my dictaphone on a *Life* magazine cover that warned of test-tube babies. I took out my pen and notebook. "It's going to be a book about the family. Our family."

"Christ, why?"

"We've been telling the same stories all these years. I want to get them down. Some of them are pretty juicy."

"Don't drag me into that mess."

"Which mess, exactly?"

My pen hovered.

"You name it," she said. "Messes all around with your bunch."

"Name one."

"Nah."

"I came all the way to New York from Montreal."

"I didn't tell you to come down here. My nurse made the arrangements."

"Why don't we start with an easy one, like how my parents met?"

"Dull as dust, that story."

"Mom loves to tell it."

"Your mother—she's the one that reckons she's a journalist, right?"

"She is a journalist."

"Doesn't run in the family. You're doing a lousy impression of one," Maeve said. She kept her haunted green eyes on me. "Betcha her version's as tall a tale as they come."

"Maybe. She tells it like it was young love. Swoony. Borderline schmaltzy."

"Don't write it like that. Wasn't exactly *Doctor Zhivago.*"

"Why not?"

"We were at my cottage, for starters. Hard to think of romance in there. Place was a dump," she said. "Was 1960. Summer of the miracles."

I wrote: *summer of miracles.*

"Miracles? Like, magic?"

"No, kid. Smokey Robinson."

"Oh."

I capitalized the M.

Smokey Robinson and Miracles were on frequent rotation during family car trips when I was a child. My parents sang along; my sister and I rolled our eyes at each other. The power of the music, or the memory of the music, was lost on us.

"That summer was a scorcher. Like this one," she said. It was the last day of August, and the room was sticky with humidity. Maeve's caregiver, Patricia, who had let me in, was cooking down the hall, making the house hotter with simmering tomatoes and peppers. "I was planting trees all up and down Lake Huron. Brutal kinda work, but I made a mint. Birches and maples and that."

"And my dad came up from the States to help you?"

"Guess he helped. Mostly wanted to get on top of your mother. Wouldn't stop screwing."

"That's gold."

fucking constantly, I wrote.

"Guess I couldn't blame them. I gave them the bed, didn't I?"

"Weren't they only, like, fifteen years old?"

"Who can remember? Don't go thinking they were anything special. He would've gone for any pair of tits. And your mother, yikes. She had a set—"

mom's giant titties

"—and she was a know-it-all, like all teenagers. Sharp as a pin, though. I'll give her that. Your mommy would've done anything to get away from her parents."

"And her mom let her go—my grandmother?"

"Crumpled like a sheet of paper."

nonna capitulated

"Really?"

"Your grandmother was a snivelling piece of work. Fiona from Fiona they called her. She was named after the town, if you can imagine. Pathetic."

I tried to square Maeve's assessment with the grandmother I knew. Before she died, Nonna was bedridden, but wasn't that different from Maeve; she was as tortured and as hard. Hated dancing, but loved food. She gave cruel advice and had nothing but judgement for her daughters and granddaughters. For the men of the family, she had only praise.

"Go on," I said. "Spare absolutely nothing."

"And don't get me started on that husband of hers—that Zappacosta."

"Papa Zap, we called him."

"Cad," she said. She rubbed her hip.

"He didn't care much for you, Aunt Maeve. Or your sister."

"Ha! Your Auntie Dot had a way about her, didn't she?"

"I used to love her outfits."

"Yeah, you're the type."

"It wasn't only me. In Fiona, she was a legend."

"She was a retard."

aunt dot = "retard"?

"I think you mean she had a mental illness."

"I think I know what I mean, kid. I took care of her for thirty years. Couldn't wipe her own ass at the end."

"I didn't know that."

"Can fill a canyon with what you don't know. Thorn in my side, keeping her from killing herself, but someone had to. Day she died was the saddest and happiest of my life."

"Is that why you left Fiona?"

"That's one reason."

reason #1—dot died

"What were the others?"

"Fiona's a shit town. A company town. General Motors. When I was done with GM, I was done with Fiona."

reason #2—quit/retired from GM

"How long did you work at the GM plant?"

"A million years. Besides, once she died, I had no reason to stay."

"She? Auntie Dot?"

"Yeah, sure," she said. "Is it four o'clock yet, kid?"

"Not quite."

"Damn." Maeve rubbed her hip, winced. "Don't get old. There's some advice. Put that in your book."

avoid aging

"Any other reasons you left town?"

"Stop harping on that one—"

reason #3—???

"—you left Fiona too. Why'd you do it?" she said.

"Similar reasons, I guess."

"Didn't want to end out at GM, eh?"

"It was more that I wanted a chance to be myself. Not so easy in Fiona."

"You're the faggot, right?" Maeve said.

faggot—hmm

"Um."

"Yeah, y'are. And your sister's a dyke, I remember. Two in one family. Your poor father."

"My parents are pretty supportive."

"Your mother's a Zappacosta. Probably too jelly-spined to say anything about it."

mom = weak—really???

"She had a lot to say," I said. "She always does."

"And you had to get away from it. You wanted to be with men."

"That's one way to put it."

"Wouldn't've happened in my day, I'll tell ya. Couldn't have."

"Different times."

"You got a lover?"

"lover." blech.

"A boyfriend, yes."

"You leave him at the hotel?"

"He's at our apartment in Montreal. He couldn't come to New York. He's sick."

"Sounds like an excuse. Sounds like he's embarrassed to be seen with ya. Ha!"

"It's four o'clock now." It was 3:58, but I wanted to move on.

"Hot damn," she said, then shouted, "It's four!"

Patricia arrived with two tumblers of ice and some painkillers in a plastic cup. Maeve produced a cane from beside the recliner and leaned forward. She started pointing at the bottles in the radio-bar, nudging them with the cane's rubber nub.

radio, booze—4 p.m.—alcoholic?

"That's why the radio's in the middle of the room," I said.

"Smart as a whip, this one," Maeve said. "The Jameson's today. Don't ever let me catch you drinking Bushmills, kid. That's Protestant stuff."

"Promise."

"How's it going in here?" Patricia chirped as she poured the whisky. She was a striking woman in her late fifties, bright-eyed and animated, with the permanent grin of a kindergarten teacher. Her jet-black hair, with one bolt of silver, was pulled up in a high ponytail. She wore a wool cardigan despite the heat. "Your aunt's not being too difficult now is she?"

"She's my great-aunt," I said.

"I'm not so great," Maeve said.

"Don't let her fool you," Patricia said. "She's tickled you're here!"

"She's always telling me what I am," Maeve said.

"I can't wait to read your book, Giovanni!" Patricia clapped her hands. "It's about our little Maeve here?"

"Not exactly. It's about my whole family."

"Is it nearly done?" Patricia said.

"I'm just getting started. Maeve's my first interview."

"Nothing but me so far? You're a glutton for punishment, kid."

"Well, I have all the stories my parents told me. Mom especially. They're all typed up."

"Then you've got less than nothing," Maeve said.

less than zero

"It's twelve pages."

"Twelve pages of hooey."

"Ignore her, Gio," Patricia said. "When you're all done, who will publish it?"

"I haven't thought of that yet."

"Why are you writing it now, then?"

"Um—"

"He wants gossip," Maeve said. "Get it outta me before I breathe my last."

"I want the whole story."

"You can't get whole stories, kid. And a good thing too, because no one really wants the whole shebang."

"I do."

"Nah. You just wanna tell yourself what makes you feel good."

"What's wrong with that? Gio deserves to feel spectacular!" Patricia said. "It's all just too exciting for words."

"It's not," Maeve said.

"Good luck," Patricia said. She winked at me before going back to the kitchen.

"No one'll read your book, you know," Maeve said, sipping. Green veins snaked under the skin of her hand. She moved the whisky around her mouth.

"The stories are fascinating."

"That's not why. No one'll read your book because you'll never finish it. You're a Zappacosta, and Zappacostas can't see anything through to the end. No guts. No stick-to-it-ivness."

gutless

"How would you know?"

"For the same reason you wanna pester me with questions. I know your lot," she said. "You haven't even asked me about the scandal. That's what you oughta write about. Your grandmother and her marriage and that."

write about the scandal

"You know about that?"

"Know about it? Ha!" She dumped the pills from the cup into her mouth and downed the rest of her Jameson's. "Whole damn town knew. She married another woman's husband."

bigamy

"I didn't realize it was such big news."

"Wasn't on the front page or anything, but it got tongues going. The priest nearly strung her up himself."

"Which priest?"

"Father Dupuis. Rest him. You met him, yeah?"

fr. dupuis knew some shit

"Unfortunately."

"Don't speak ill of the dead 'round here, kid."

"You just did."

"Dupuis was a man, OK? Did what he thought was right. More than I can say for you Zappacostas."

"What'd he do to my grandmother that was so 'right'?"

"He gave her what she had coming. The whole kit 'n' kaboodle. Dragged her right through his sermon. Not by name, but c'mon. We all knew."

nonna publicly shamed/mocked—"had it coming"

"That sounds terrible."

"No less than she deserved."

"It's hard to imagine it being such a big thing. But I guess it wasn't done back then."

"What wasn't?"

"Defying convention, I guess. For love."

Maeve laughed. It was her signature laugh—an open-mouthed cackle that flushed her face a deeper, more violent pink. As a kid, I was proud of myself if I could draw it out of her. But that reward now sounded sinister.

"You're a hoot, kid."

"I don't think it's funny."

"It's hilarious."

& maeve thinks it's "hilarious"

"My mom told me that Nonna really suffered over the guilt."

"Oh sure." Maeve was still giggling, shaking with each titter. "She was the type."

"the type"?—maeve not telling everything—ask mom

"Did you know her well, my grandmother?"

"Knew her well enough. Went to the same church and that. Butter wouldn't melt in her mouth."

"What can you tell about Nonna that I don't already know?"

"Probably everything. You don't seem to know much," Maeve said.

"You mentioned that."

"Used to see her in Fiona when I went around with the ice." She tinkled the cubes in her glass. "Be useful and pour us another."

another

I poured.

"The ice?"

"People weren't pampered like today. Had to get ice delivered right to their kitchen. I hauled big blocks of the stuff to people's houses."

the icewoman cometh

"Just you?" I said.

"I'm nothing to look at now, but I used to be hardy as a horse. Tough as tar."

"I remember."

"Robust as Roosevelt," she said. She wasn't looking at me anymore, but off towards the hall, as if the past resided among the coats hung by the door. Her laugh came through a sad, wistful smile. "Determined as a donkey."

hardy/horse

tough/tar

robust/roosevelt

determined/donkey

"Not much has changed," I said.

"Stubborn as syphilis."

stubborn/syphilis

"Are those old sayings?" I said.

"Nah, just an old game we used to play," she said. "Give me my pills and I remember this stuff—who knows what's gonna drop outta my mouth."

pankillers + booze = unreliable? extra reliable??

"My boyfriend's the same way with his painkillers."

"What's wrong with this lover of yours anyway?"

"Boyfriend," I said. "And let's move on."

"What? You're the only one who can ask questions?"

"It's a long story," I said, eyeing the door.

"Thought you came here for stories."

"Not my own stories."

ugh

"Barnburner, is it?" she said, her puffy face tilting forward. "You can tell Aunt Maeve."

"Cancer."

"Criminy. Where?"

"Brain."

"Bad?"

"We'll see."

"The poor kid, to gotta live through that," she said, "and with you to boot."

"Of course we hope he'll bounce back."

"You don't know?"

"It's not relevant to the book," I said. I swallowed hard. Since the cancer diagnosis, I'd been living with a knot in my stomach, and it now tightened, as though Maeve were pulling at both ends of the cord. "But no."

"Christ alive. What the heck you talking to me for? Get back there and take care of the bloody sod."

sod

"I have been. This trip is a little break, to get going on my book."

"Who's making excuses now, eh?"

end

"I think I should go," I said. As I closed the notebook, I saw my hand was shaking.

"Yeah, you should. Get your backside to his bedside."

"Patricia?" I called out, my voice breaking on the last syllable.

"You got a lotta Zappacosta in ya, kid," Maeve said, leaning even further. The La-Z-Boy tipped as though it might launch her at me if I didn't leave immediately. She gave me a smug nod to transmit that my escape was what she expected—that I'd lived up to such low standards.

"Done here already?" Patricia said as she came into the room.

"I struck a nerve," Maeve said. "He's spooked."

"Oh dear! Did she say one of her little atrocities? Don't mind her, Giovanni," Patricia said. "Stay! You know what she's like."

I scrambled to get my belongings in my bag.

"Look at him run, Patricia. Like a roach when the light comes on."

I thanked them from the hall as I crammed my feet into my shoes.

"I thought you wanted to take pictures?" Patricia said. "We still have plenty of time before dinner. You could even eat with us if you'd like!"

"I don't wanna eat with a roach," Maeve said.

"I should get back," I said. I reached for the door handle.

"Gotta get back to nowhere," Maeve said. "Ha!"

"Thanks again."

"And good riddance," said Maeve, the words clipped by the slamming door.

*

Maeve was right. I was a coward then. You could've filled a canyon with what I didn't know. It was 2001; this book had not yet gripped me, but it had started.

The details Maeve gave me piqued my curiosity, though not nearly as much as the details she hadn't given me. The plot points she hinted at could only be imagined and I didn't have the imagination yet. I'm not sure I have it now, all these years later, but I'm told I have no choice but to find it. At least I have help.

I am getting ahead of myself, though, and I promised not to do that. At this point in 2001, the book was merely an excuse to run away from the horror I faced in my apartment in Montreal.

That's where I'd left BF. He'd just completed his third round of chemo. Brain cancer, stage three. The doctor had said, "this time, let's hope," as if we hadn't been hoping for months. I was sick of hope. Hope had previously led to hell; good news scuppered by another scan or some turncoat bloodwork, and we were back in ghastly unknowns. The thought of renewing the hope and the horror had made me run. I found an excuse: I had to go to New York to interview Maeve.

"I'll only be gone for the weekend," I told BF.

That was two weeks ago. After the interview, I remained in my hotel in Brooklyn Heights. I changed my flight every few days, extended my room booking. I created more excuses, which I told BF over the phone. I needed to talk to Maeve again, I needed to photograph her neighbourhood, I needed to do research at the library.

I had my reasons, too, which I kept to myself. In New York, I could keep the cancer at bay. As long as I stayed here, the situation was suspended. I'd hit pause; nothing could progress. I'd convinced myself of that. BF had stopped telling me to come home, and filled our phone calls with weighty silences. I pictured his beautiful, wasted face, with the receiver on his ear below the crescent scar where the doctor had gone in for the tumour. He'd be pulling the lobe of the opposite ear, as he always did when thinking things over.

Then, yesterday, ten days after the interview with Maeve, there was a change. The doctor could find no traces of the cancer. The knot in my gut loosened. I said I'd come back to Montreal immediately, but BF said no. His voice was bright and decisive. He announced that he was well enough to travel, and had booked a flight to New York.

"I don't want to discuss it in our apartment."

"It?" I said.

"Yeah," he said.

I was dreading "it," but "it" was better than the alternative. If I lost him to my own deficiencies, I could handle the shame, but if I lost him to death, a vacuum would exist in the world, and his colour and irony would feel like they were being sucked out forever, into nothingness, and it would be my fault. That's how I thought about things then—that in some universal justice system, the pain of the break-up was an accepted trade-off for allowing him to live.

That night I couldn't sleep. Even on nights without dread, sleep was elusive for me. To nod off, I'd usually tell myself stories. I'd close my eyes and let my mind start in some remembered reality, then careen off the rails of facts towards somewhere more vivid, and I'd end out dreaming, never realizing I was asleep until I woke up. This technique didn't work that night. The rails of facts were too magnetic. I tossed my body around the coarse hotel sheets, trying to find the story that would give me peace, but thunder rumbled and rain splats kept bringing me back to my present circumstance. BF's visit would be an excoriation. I deserved to be dumped, and there was nothing I could do to avoid it. I looked at the clock: 8:47 a.m. Air Canada flight 7620, Montreal to LaGuardia, was in the air already. In two short hours, he'd be here for three long days.

The phone rang. It was cheap, its receiver light as a leaf—a plastic shell full of my mother's voice, telling me that a helicopter crashed into the World Trade Center. She was in her office at *The Globe and Mail.* She made an hour-long commute every morning to be there by 8:00 a.m. I could hear the shouts of other journalists in the background. My hotel wasn't far from the Brooklyn Heights Promenade and she wanted me to go take pictures of the crash from across the East River. I could sell them to the *Globe*.

"They might even be on the front page," she said.

"I'm still in bed."

"Mr. Lazybones. Don't you want to make a bit of money?"

"How much money?"

"Beggars can't be choosers, Gio."

"Sure they can."

"Don't be smart," she said. "You shouldn't even be in New York, but seeing as you are, you might as well make yourself useful."

"Let's not discuss it."

"When are you coming back?"

"I'll take the pictures on the condition that we end this conversation."

"BF will talk some sense into you. When's he getting there?"

I hung up.

The camera was somewhere. I tidied while I searched for it. BF would hate this hotel room, even at its neatest. It was a rectangle hemmed in by gold-painted walls, as though the designer had been told to make it look opulent on a tiny budget. The carpet had probably once been a blazing orange but had faded over the years to a rusty desert with paths of dirt pressed into it. On the ceiling there were circles of plaster puckers. I stared at them every sleepless night, these meringues greyed-over with cobwebs and dust.

There were roaches, too. I imagined multitudes of them in the walls, crawling over one another in a buggy orgy, amusing themselves until I turned the lights out. The minute I did, they poured out to feast on my remnants—toaster pizza crusts, gyros wrappers, coffee cups, Triscuits, Canadian Club. My New York diet. Back home, I loved to cook and kept a spotless kitchen. I couldn't afford a stray germ getting into BF's body and regularly berated his mother for leaving a mug in the sink or running the dishwasher on any setting other than pots and pans. But here, where life and death were paused, none of that mattered. I grew to respect the roaches' patience and determination, but I also learned to leave the lamps on at all times to keep them in the walls. I respected them, but didn't need to see them; if I could wait it out, they could wait it out. My insomnia was brightly lit.

I found the camera in the bag I'd taken to Maeve's, along with my notebook. I slipped the camera's strap around my wrist and pulled on my favourite T-shirt, a black one made of cotton so overwashed you could make out my chest hair through its fibres. My cell started ringing, then the landline started up. Competing clangors. Likely Mom wanting an update. I left the cell on the desk, wedged earbuds into my ears and hit play on my Discman. The Strokes' "Is This It?" flooded my brain; whiny guitars drowned out both phones. My Converse were cold on my bare feet.

Once outside, I saw that last night's rain had washed the city. Today was clean and bright, like I was viewing Brooklyn Heights through a lens ticked one level sharper than yesterday. The sky was a limitless ceiling and the sun was the same colour as the taxis. The subway station didn't give up a single commuter, and no one went in or out of the brick-faced triplexes down Henry Street. The only humans I saw were in the supermarket across the road, where a group had gathered around a TV. Next door, in the bakery, no one baked. In the tailor's, no one sewed. At the hotel's emergency exit, no one smoked. Among the butts on the sidewalk were three half-finished cigarettes, still burning. The air was still, and streams of smoke flowed off them, rippling as they rose.

It was only when I saw the cigarettes that I felt an alternate energy in the scene. I was very familiar with Henry Street by then, but looking at it this morning I detected a change—a downshift in speed, a creepiness. An unseen irrevocability. It was like staring at the face of someone you love, only with a new suspicion that changed everything about him. It was the difference between seeing his face and seeing his face with the knowledge that it was being eaten from behind; between trying to sleep and trying to sleep with an army of roaches out of view, but an inch away.

I pulled out the earphones. The music reduced to mouse sounds in my hand. Sirens cried, far-flung but persistent. I turned down Pineapple Street. A straight couple ran down the sidewalk holding hands. They were chubby, in jeans; they weren't joggers. Her backpack jiggled furiously. I picked up my pace, a new urgency blowing me towards the East River. I saw a slice of sky above Manhattan—blue marred by a black smear. As I approached the Brooklyn Heights Promenade, the road turned into a footpath under a canopy of boughs. At the end of it, a cluster of people were gathered at the railing. The couple arrived before I did. The woman spun to be embraced by the man, who wrapped his arms around her, protecting her from the vision that would, in the heartbeat it took for me to step out of the tunnel of trees, be seared on my memory.

One of the World Trade towers, the far one, was wounded, split on its flank by a black gash. Smoke poured from it in billows of impenetrable blackness, stacks of black roses wilting in fast-motion, one replaced by another, more and more flowers, more and more fuel for the furnace. The silvery vertical lines up the facade of the building had been severed, reduced to gnarled tines against the obscurity. The blackness grew southward, swelling but barely dissipating.

No one moved. We stared. A man in front of me sniffled up a cry. A woman in a housecoat said, "but it was such a beautiful morning." The river separated us from the disaster, but I could perceive small items falling from the windows of the building. I tried to work out what they were—desks? computers? sofas?—until the housecoat woman whispered, "bless their souls."

I hadn't thought of the people. I thought of the inferno devouring boxes of copy paper, staplers, credenzas, motivational posters, cubicle walls, desk cactuses, lumbar support pads. I thought of the progression of the smoke down elevator shafts and emergency stairs, of whole offices being vaporized, of Xerox machines melting into blobs, toilet stalls buckling in the heat. But I didn't think of the people until that moment. That's the kind of person I was then. I had to be reminded that there were people in the building, in hell, clawing at one another to get down an endless flight of stairs, or flat on their stomachs to keep from inhaling smoke.

Pushing desks through windows to let in fresh air. Jumping to a few terminal moments of freedom.

There were people related to those people, and they were screaming into phones somewhere. There were people who loved those people who were getting dire text messages. There were firemen in oxygen masks pounding into melting boardrooms. There were probably cowards too—or maybe I was the only one. I stood there, watching the smoke blow out to the Atlantic, unable to conceive what I would do if I were in that building. I couldn't even take a picture of it.

More people joined the throng at the promenade, pressing in. My Discman fell from my hand and smashed on the pavement. The CD poked out. It looked alien, pointless. A mother held her son's face to her belly. The backpack woman still had not turned around. The sun was bright; the river winked at us, indifferent. A cluster of emergency lights—red, blue, white—swarmed the Manhattan streets. Beneath us, the traffic on the expressway had stopped, and periodic horns joined the sounds of sirens. To our right, the Brooklyn Bridge reached over the water, clogged with gawkers. We must have looked exactly like them, people frozen in place, lined up to bear witness.

"Another one," the man told the backpack woman. "Don't look."

She looked. We all looked. Heads turned like a school of diverting fish, the light capturing the identical motion of their faces. It wasn't a helicopter. It was a plane, and there was another one.

The grey aircraft wobbled above New Jersey, as if it were a toy guided by the hand of a toddler. It looked dangerously out of place, out of control, out of reality. Sweat rolled down my ribcage, my tongue pushed into my teeth, and the nose of the plane pierced the skin of the building.

For a microsecond, it seemed the building had absorbed the plane. It disappeared into the wall as though it had flown into plasticine. But then the firecracker of it exploded out the opposite side, lava aloft, with ticker-tape of spinning debris. The crowd flinched, producing a garble of obscenities and gasps and screams.

An old lady jolted away from the railing. She pushed people out of her way with hooked hands. She looked into my face. She was a scorned Betty White, with furious grey eyes and a growling mouth. A few people tried their cells, a few ran. The rest of us stood there. We watched as though we didn't have a choice. People spoke to no one, to everyone.

"Are there more?"

"So it was on purpose?"

"Do you see more?"

"Is it the end?"

"There must be more."

Someone produced a radio tuned to hysterical voices. "United Airlines flight 175 out of Boston's Logan Airport," it said. I had no curiosity and felt repulsed by details. I followed Betty White's example, clawing my way through my fellow bystanders. Dozens of people had arrived after me, maybe hundreds, and it seemed as though I'd never manage to grope free of them.

Air Canada flight 7620 out of Montreal's Dorval Airport.

I gripped a woman's bare arm and she screamed. I elbowed a child in the face. "He's a bum," someone said. The strap of the camera got caught on the button of a cardigan worn by a middle-aged bald man. He looked at me, baffled, eyes rimmed in pink flesh, knowing something was wrong, but incapable of determining the cause amid every other fucking thing that was wrong.

"Are there more?" he said.

"I don't know," I said. "I don't know anything."

"Go find out."

I unhooked the strap from my wrist, and left the camera dangling off him, pulling his cardigan crooked. He extended an arm, pointing the way out. He thought I had noble intentions. He thought I had somewhere to go. He thought I wanted to know what happened. He thought I was good.

Air Canada Flight 7620 out of Montreal's Dorval Airport.

My feet directed themselves up Pineapple. In the windows of the houses there were flashes of TV screens, barely perceptible in the light of the day. CNN, Fox, MSNBC. I thought of the TV in my hotel room, a plastic box with a curved screen. It was bolted to the top of the dresser, as though someone might steal it. I used it for Nick at Night, as a background player to my insomnia, but the news could flow from it as easily as *Three's Company*. I could go there, up to my room, and open the firehose of information. The phone, too, with its receiver light as a leaf, was sitting in there next to the bed. It was probably ringing. To answer it, to know if BF was dead, to stop avoiding the thing I had avoided for months, all I had to do was turn right. Like a roach when the light comes on, I turned left.

*

The first headache I remember was eighteen months earlier. BF and I had driven from Montreal to Fiona—that small Ontario city where Maeve and I had both grown up—and I was showing him how a teenage version of myself would do doughnuts in the parking lot of the GM plant. The lot had its own brand of industrial night, a blackness cut with the orange glow of sodium bulbs. When BF wailed at me to stop the centrifuge, I braked hard and looked at him. In that artificial light, his eyes were wild and pained as he pulled the skin back at his temples. He looked like a scared, uncomprehending animal. Strands of his blond hair had escaped his ponytail and made creepy shadows on his cheeks. He said he was "peachy."

That dire face reappeared rarely in the coming months—or, at least, rarely to me. I remember one instance dancing at a gay bar, another when BF was writing his bachelor's thesis. It wasn't until he moved in with me that I knew how often it happened.

One Saturday, I woke late, and he was already in the bathroom. I read the paper and waited. I heard flushing, periodic showers. We went to the movies on Saturday afternoon, but as his bathroom session stretched on, and showtimes came and went, I flipped back through the paper to see what films were still playing. *Dancer in the Dark*, 12:30 at the Parc Cinema. *Traffic*, 1:25 at Famous Players. *Hannibal*, 1:50 at The Forum. *Snatch*, 2:15 at Loews. Finally, I heard the washing machine start up under the bathroom sink. BF emerged. He was naked, freshly clean.

"Everything OK?"

His smile was a coy crack. He'd towelled his hair and some of it was cowlicking, looking untamed and sexy. He bursted with colour and energy and health. He was shorter than me and had powerful thighs, a thin neck, fat calves, irradiant blue eyes, and wide hips. He liked to paint his nails, and that week they were black and shiny, chipped, needing attention. He had a capacious chest, and inked into its pudgy white expanse was a dragonfly tattoo that I had designed for him. The wings expanded below his nipples and ended on his flanks. The bug's head, between his nipples, had a sarcastic face, which I'd based on his own.

He pulled my chair from the table with me still in it, moved my boxers down to my ankles and straddled me. His heft and strength teamed up with his impetuousness and his unique sort of dominant submission. He spat on his hand, reached around, and slipped me into him. He pressed the dragonfly to my face. He was still warm and wet from the shower. He smelled of his overpriced eucalyptus shampoo. He gripped the back of the chair. My field of vision was bordered by his arms; his face was still coy when I looked up at it. I grew hard inside him, gripped his waist, and moved him up and down as he rotated his hips. He came the second after me. He always did. That's what he wanted: my gratification. He didn't even have to touch himself. He was a sexual miracle. In the denouement, his face changed to a satisfied half-smile. I loved putting that smile on his face.

"We could do *Crouching Tiger, Hidden Dragon* at Ex-Centris at 4:30."

"Subtitles give me a headache," he said. He pecked me on the forehead and stood up, disappeared into the bathroom.

"What's the matter?"

"We're out of Advil," he called.

My mother gave me a bottle of 120 extra-strength Liqui-Gels in my stocking every Christmas. It was February. "Are you becoming a pill popper without me?"

"Yeah, I thought we could use another expense."

"But Advil? At least take the Tylenol 3s, the ones with the codeine. At least take something addictive."

He returned in his bathrobe, tossed me a towel, and said, "We're out of Tylenol 3s."

The pain was now getting him up at night. He recounted how he'd crawl from our bed, careful not to turn on the hall light before closing the bedroom door, then sit in the office where I worked on my design projects, researching symptoms and drinking pint glasses of water until he threw up. Vomiting made the headaches go away. He'd wipe down the porcelain rim of the toilet and take a shower. Brush his teeth. Usually, he snuck back to bed and put my arm over him. All I knew is that I woke up happy, holding him.

"But this morning, it kept coming up," he said. "It came up until I had nothing left."

"Is this why we had sex?"

"That's your reaction?"

"We always have sex before you give me bad news."

"It's not the only reason we have sex," he said. "But it was this time."

"Why the sneaking around?"

"I didn't want you to notice," BF said. "Babes, you know what you're like."

"What am I like?"

"Impossible," he said.

"I think I'm quite possible."

"You're not," he said. "Maybe I should go to the doctor."

"Doctors make things worse."

"The doctor is free. Advil is $18.99 a bottle."

"How much is the generic ibuprofen?"

"$9.99."

"I feel richer already."

"Would you go to the doctor, Gio?"

"Doctors scare me."

"I'm already scared," he said. He was sitting cross-legged on the couch now, the sexiness gone. His eyes were scanning my face for signals of humanity. He stuffed his hands under his robe, into his armpits. "Fear means I should probably go to the doctor, right?"

"If you want," I said. I stood and walked to the kitchen, started making coffee, filling the apartment with noise. I shouted, "Don't do anything you don't want to do."

"See?" he said. "Impossible."

*

BF was at the doctor longer than expected. Every time I called his cellphone, it went directly to voicemail. We had tickets to a matinee at the Centaur Theatre, and I waited to hear from him until the last moment before I had to leave, figuring he'd meet me there. I was still standing in the lobby when the lights started going up and down. Maybe he was already seated? That was impossible—his ticket was in my pocket—but I wanted it to be true. I went in, found my row, and felt the emptiness next to me as the room was plunged into darkness and the play began.

A rabbi starts off, saying something about clay. BF never shut up about *Angels in America*. "Genius," he'd said when he first read it for a cultural studies class. "Soaring and necessary. It's a comedy!" I wasn't laughing. The action on stage turned to a gay couple. One of the men was dying of AIDS and the other one couldn't handle it. He was a coward, so I had a dose of sympathy for him. He couldn't take watching his boyfriend suffering, so he ran away.

I pitied him. Was this possible? To be pitied if you were pitiful?

I started to think the worst. BF was going to miss *Angels*, that was clear. The empty seat was a void of attention; BF's absence filled the theatre, filled my thoughts. The play ceased making sense. I stood, was shushed. Then I pawed down the row with apologies, and pushed out into the afternoon sun, blasting light into the theatre to hisses of annoyance. I told the cabbie to speed.

The absence chased me, kept pace. It entered the apartment with me. There'd been no phone calls, no left messages. I loaded the dishwasher, made a quiche. I tidied the apartment. Before BF moved in, the place had been bare and basic. I had a TV, couch, coffee table and bed. Nothing on the walls, nothing on the shelves. There were no shelves. Now, Wonder Woman figurines stalked the mantlepiece, CD towers lined the walls, and three different Winona Ryder movie posters loomed behind the couch (*Boys*; *Night on Earth*; *Welcome Home, Roxy Carmichael*). There were boas and nail polish bottles. There were board games and books, Adorno and Barthes slid in with Madonna's *Sex* and Joan Crawford's *My Way of Life*. I dusted them, alphabetized them. I vacuumed the zig-zag Black Lodge throw rug. It took hours; his absence stalked me. I sat at my computer to work on some of my freelance design projects, but I couldn't concentrate and instead looked through BF's search history. Symptoms, outcomes, consequences, porn.

I opened a Word document, insomnia.doc, and scrolled through its twelve pages. This was an old exercise of mine. When I couldn't sleep, I'd sit at the computer and try to write down every detail I could remember from the stories my family loved to tell. The summer my parents met. My grandfather's emigration from Italy. The scandal of the family he'd abandoned there. My eccentric Auntie Dot.

I had long threatened to write all this into a book. As the text sailed by, I thought that I should work on it again. Months later, I would tell BF that his condition made me realize that life was short, that I needed to seize opportunities, that I needed to write this book, that I needed to go to New York to interview Maeve. But I didn't think those things as I waited for him to return from the doctor. I thought of the coward from *Angels in America*. I looked at the text. It could be a project that was separate from me, above me, that had to be served. At the very least, it could act as a legitimate escape from the knot of anxiety that had been tightening in my gut all day. I thought: this is an exit.

*

After we got the diagnosis, we focused our anxiety on his hair. It was styled like blond drapes, parted in the centre, creating an M that framed his face and left a white line across his scalp. Before the surgery, a nurse came into BF's hospital room with a smock that could collect the hair while she shaved his head. It was pale green and made BF look ghostly when it was fitted around his neck. The blue of his eyes changed depending on what he was wearing, and at that moment, they were dull aqua crystals, panicky and round.

"I'm going to need you to distract me," he said. "Tell me a story."

"Which one?"

"One where my hair and I live happily ever after."

"OK, so, once upon a time, I actually did think you were going to die."

"The Easter ham?"

"Right, the ham." I paused, inhaled. My mother, a legendary storyteller from whom I stole all my tricks, always did this to build anticipation. "It was Easter, and you had just met my parents for the first time. I was so scared to have you meet them—"

"Because you're a wimp."

"—because I *was* a wimp. I thought that, once you met them, well, that'd be it. It would make us official. I'd never be able to get out of it. Seems ludicrous now, but not half as ludicrous as the car you rented us for the trip."

"I don't know cars."

"It was a Kia, and it was a piece of shit. You and my dad drove it out to pick up the Easter ham, and it started to snow. I wasn't even awake yet when you left, and when I came down for coffee, the snow really started raging. And I thought of you and Dad in that cheap Kia, fishtailing on some backwoods road. Smashes and crashes. Gory and gross."

"This is really uplifting so far."

The nurse returned with hair clippers. She asked if BF was ready, and he nodded and said "no." He winced when the razor clacked on. I held his hand under the smock, and he gripped back when the blade touched his forehead. The buzzing changed to a gargle when it started to chew the hair. I placed my lips close to his ear to be heard over the mechanics.

"And when you didn't come back, I got so worried. My other fear, of you meeting my family, looked so minuscule compared to this new fear—that you might be mangled in some accident, that you might even—"

"Croak?"

"Yeah."

Yellow hair landed in his lap.

"So I did everything I could to avoid thinking about it. I shovelled the driveway, I chlorinated the hot tub. And I designed that dragonfly tattoo you'd asked for. I thought, *He wants this tattoo so badly, that if I finally create it, then he has to come back. He'll survive for the tattoo.*"

"That's dumb."

"But I was right. You came back, didn't you? I saw that crappy car pull into the driveway, and I was so relieved. That's when I knew."

"Knew what?"

"That this was it."

"What are you going to do this time, to keep me from dying?"

"You're not dying, so I don't have to do anything," I said and kissed his ear and pulled away so the nurse could finish. The last of his blond streamers were reduced to stubble.

"How do I look?" he asked.

"Butch."

I handed him a mirror.

"I do, don't I?"

He didn't. He looked sick. He looked like a twenty-four-year-old homosexual with a brain tumour. He looked like a painting popped from its frame, with no context, no borders, his facial features floating in the world and exposed to all its elements. The white line of scalp that had bisected his skull had taken over all of him.

After the hair, more of him went away. The tumour, which we celebrated, but then the chemo stole his bulk, and, frequently, his train of thought. Chemofog, he called it. He couldn't remember which pills he'd taken or what day it was or when his next treatment was scheduled. Some days, he'd forget if he'd eaten until he threw up whatever was in his stomach into the bucket next to our bed: "When did I have macaroni and cheese?" His aim was poor. I invested in wider buckets, but they didn't help when he shat or pissed the bed. He was in a perpetual state of excreting liquified versions of my meatballs and gnocchi and Italian wedding soup, rendering them green and brown and rank—a slop that I began to regard as the essence of his treatment.

When he soiled the bed, I moved him to the couch and put on one of his tapes. BF had refused to give up the four large boxes of VHS cassettes when he moved in with me, and he was glad to have them now. As a teen, he'd taped things he loved off TV and had created detailed notes about what clip appeared at what time. The practice had only one rule. BF had to record the stuff in whatever order he came across it. He'd wait for something to come on, then hit the record button as fast as he could.

"They're like maps of my brain," BF said. "They help me remember things."

Things? Everything. A syndicated episode of *The Simpsons*—commercials removed by his rapid-fire finger on the pause button—gave way to Buddy Cole smoking in a gay bar. Then, the video for "Drawn to the Rhythm," one of Sarah McLachlan's triter ballads. Julia Child trussing a chicken in black and white. The one moment in *Blue Velvet* when Kyle McLachlan's cock is visible. Portions of *The Blue Lagoon* in which Christopher Atkins wandered shirtlessly through paradise. *Married with Children* featured prominently. The episode of *The Cosby Show* featuring The Real-World Hotel. A Heritage Minute about an epileptic woman smelling burnt toast. Toni Braxton singing "Unbreak My Heart." Alanis on *You Can't Do That on Television. Jem and the Holograms. WKRP in Cincinnati*. The controversial midnight airing of Madonna's "Erotica" video on MuchMusic, billed as *Too Much 4 Much.*

When he wasn't watching TV, he slept or played CDs. Listening on headphones gave BF headaches, so the music filled the apartment. I became an expert in his favourite albums, all of them depressing and performed by women on guitars or pianos. Tori Amos. Sinead O'Connor. PJ Harvey. L7.

Bikini Kill, Björk, Bush.

Cher, Chapman, Chapin Carpenter.

Hole, Heart, Heavens to Betsy.

Jones, Joni, Jewel.

Poe, Portishead, Patti Smith.

Siouxsie, Suzanne, Stevie.

They were moody, rough, sensitive melodies from ladies who seemed to live in a perpetual November, winter coming on, skies grey, axes to grind, traumas to describe. We agreed only on Stevie-era Fleetwood Mac, but even the biggest fan can only revisit *Tusk* a few times per week.

Sometimes, he'd call me in from the office and say, "This one." I'd pull a spiral notebook from the bedside table and write down the title and the artist on a list of songs he wanted at his funeral.

"We're up to twenty-one songs," I said, scribbling "The Fairest of the Seasons."

"That's OK," BF said. "Bonnie won't let anyone leave."

It was true. My mother adored BF. I could picture Mom with her arms folded, standing before a pair of doors at a funeral parlour, shaking her head at any escapees as "The Circle Game" went into its fourth interminable verse.

"I've never actually been to a funeral," he said. "What are they like?"

"It doesn't matter. This is the DJ set for your remission party."

I didn't permit any discussion of death. Ignorance was the only way I could keep going. BF's will, power of attorney, and insurance were never mentioned to me. I left it all up to his parents. They drove in from the suburbs to take him to chemo. They talked to the doctors. Even BF's passing mention of funerals made me think of all the ones I'd attended. My family believed in open caskets, the Italian side especially (the Irish side prioritized whiskey). My mother once declared that seeing the body was the only healthy way to say goodbye. I thought of it in more practical terms. We needed to make sure the person was dead, to know their life was irrefutably over.

I wasn't prepared to do that with BF, even while his body reminded me of the ones I'd seen in coffins. By the end of his second cycle of chemo, his skin had devolved from scaly to ashen. His teeth were see-through; I could make out his tongue moving behind them. He'd become so thin so fast that his dragonfly tattoo was wrinkled and collapsing; it looked desiccated. Between cycles, his hair returned to his head weak and crinkled, in patches, but fell out when the drugs started up again. Pubic hair, too. He was a surreal combination of a baby and a corpse. His skin was thin. His bones were evident. His mouth was full of sores. I couldn't imagine ever fucking him again.

At night, once BF was snoring in our bed, I crawled onto the couch in the living room so I wouldn't wake him. I curled myself into a corner, hugged a throw pillow, tasted rye on my breath, and did my sleeping trick. I told myself a story that started in my past, but careened off towards a better fate. Instead of getting a blowjob on the day of my grandmother's funeral, I delivered a powerful eulogy that moved even the funeral director to wailing sobs. Instead of abandoning BF with my mother on the day they first met, I swept him away to a romantic cottage somewhere safe from her intervention. Instead of plotting to leave, I cured cancer.

Those alternate versions of me permitted rest. It wasn't sleep, but a suspension of consciousness programmed to end the instant BF coughed or mumbled my name or stopped snoring. Even in slumber, awareness gnawed at me. Death was there, always, at the window, checking its watch.

None of this was a reason to leave. There were moments when I wanted it to be, when I wanted the volumes of urine and shit and vomit and hair and sleeplessness to be poured together and reach a line marked MAX. Above that line, I could be forgiven for running away. I loved BF, but had to remind myself that I didn't hate him—that it was the disease and its toxic cure that I hated. It pinned me down. It foreclosed on my choices. It dead-ended freedoms and futures—his and mine and ours. What few were left all detoured back to cancer.

These thoughts pumped me full of a shame so intense it would have made Father Dupuis, my childhood priest, call uncle in the confessional. I couldn't share them with anyone; any normal person would have judged me harshly, and with good reason.

I would have handled everything if I knew that it would make BF healthy again. But cancer doesn't work that way. At the bottom of every puke bucket, under every pissy bed sheet, were the twin terrors of cancer: the prospect of imminent death and the prospect of its future return. The idea that we'd go through all of this and that it might add up to zero, even years from now, was a prolonged torture that only got worse. I never got used to it. My threshold of tolerance only got lower.

*

BF had finished his third cycle of chemo when Mom told me about Aunt Maeve's fall.

"Right in her living room. No reason at all, apparently. Guess you don't need a reason at that age, but let's face it, she was probably three sheets," Mom told me on the phone. "Four sheets, knowing her."

"What's the prognosis?"

"A fall like that would kill anyone at eighty-two. But Maeve? She's built like a tank."

I showed BF the Word document, insomnia.doc. Twelve pages into writing my family history and I'd already gotten to Great-Aunt Maeve. She was my father's aunt and seemed to be present at key moments in the Zappacosta-O'Hara story. She owned the cottage where my parents fell in love. Her old house in Fiona had been a refuge for me; I used to go there when I ran away as a kid, and she'd let me watch movies that were too violent for my age. After that, I saw her at family gatherings, when she deigned to attend. She'd say things like, "So, kid, you're the product of this mess?" I hadn't seen her since Nonna's funeral, when she stunned everyone by announcing that she was moving to Brooklyn at the age of seventy-four.

"You want to go to New York to interview your aunt?" BF said.

"Great-aunt."

"But now?"

"In a week. I'm going to make sure you're comfortable and that your parents are here. I'm not a monster."

"Some might disagree."

"The doctor said we had reason to hope."

"*Now* you care what the doctor says?"

"I won't be gone long. It's a weekend."

"But this is the worst part of the cycle."

"Maeve's old and sick. I can't have her take all that juicy gossip to the grave."

"Oh, so you don't mind seeing *her* on death's door?" He pulled the blanket down, exposing his ashy skin and chest tattoo. It had crumpled further, in fissures, like a piece of rotting fruit. He shivered.

"You're going to get freezing." I pulled the blanket back up to his shoulders.

"If you need a break from my hideous existence, then say so. Don't make up some lame excuse."

"It's not lame," I said.

"Babes, why do you suddenly care about this book? You're a designer, not a writer," he said. "You haven't mentioned the book in aeons. And I'm still holed up in bed."

And then I did it. I disgusted myself, but I did it. I opened my mouth and lied. "This—all of this—just makes me realize that everything can just go away. That you've got to seize opportunities. You know that I've always wanted to do this."

"But now?" he repeated.

"Yes, now. 'Now' is the whole point," I said. "It's only a weekend."

Before I left, I moved our TV into the bedroom, along with his boxes of tapes. He was too weak to come say goodbye at the door, so I kissed him in the bed, his lips not responding, passively grazing my own out of exhaustion or loathing. He was propped up on pillows, remote in hand, pale as a cloud, staring into the opening credits of *The Craft.* He didn't turn to watch me leave.

"Thank you," I said from the bedroom door.

He hit pause, cutting off Our Lady Peace's butchering of "Tomorrow Never Knows."

"Fuck you," he said. "Fuck you from the bottom of my heart."

*

Now, I was back in Maeve's neighbourhood. Once I'd opted to avoid my hotel, I sought out Flatbush Avenue. I wasn't familiar with Brooklyn geography, but I knew Flatbush ran for a long while in a straight line—from the East River all the way to Marine Park—so I could march forward with my back to the disaster. Walking was the only way not to know anything. I just followed the continuum of power lines that stretched or sagged against the blank blue sky.

I'd successfully avoided information, but there were hints. Stores were closed. People cried in the street. They queued at pay phones and stood on their stoops, having intense discussions with neighbours. I noticed an increasing number of American flags. How did everyone acquire them so quickly? They hung off balconies and overpasses, and they flew from vehicles, accompanied by torrents of car horns. A couple had babushka'ed their pug with one.

And there was the smell. A shift in the wind must have pushed the smoke in my direction. I'd been inhaling it since Prospect Heights—the combustion of everything all at once, plastic, wood, concrete, flesh, metal, plaster, fuel. According to my mother, a keen sense of smell runs in our family, and right then, I felt like I'd inherited it.

The odour unlocked a memory from when I was a child, back in Fiona. My parents had given me a train set for Christmas and they helped me set it up in the basement, running the tracks through a forest of pipe-cleaner trees and past small plastic homes. This was 1985, but all the items—table, tracks, power box, houses, people, trees, train cars—were from much earlier. All the miniature cars were sleek '60s gas-guzzlers and the clothes on the human figurines were out of style. Boxy business suits for the men and, for the women, long, belted house dresses made of chiffon.

After he'd set it up, Dad had taken a marker to the dial on the power box and put a black line at the seven, indicating I should never crank it further than that. One Sunday after Mass, I got bored of watching the train move steadily around the town. I turned the dial to eight, and the locomotive jolted forward, speeding faster than I'd ever seen it before. The way the cars moved together, snaking around the curves, entranced me. I added more cars, making the train so long that the little rail-crossing sign never got a break. Its two red lights flashed incessantly; Gio Rail Lines was either passing or approaching it at all times.

At nine, the smell started. An electric burning. A warning, I realized, once I got the thing to ten, and there was a violent derailment next to the little Catholic parish (Dad also made me put in a Protestant one and a synagogue, but they were on the other side of town). The train cars smashed through the church and several adjacent houses, extinguishing many small, plastic lives. The current that had sent the train surging now had nowhere to go, and smoke began to emerge from the power box. I was too scared to touch it, so I sat frozen, staring, until it erupted in flames. I screamed. Mom found me in a ball, crying on the other side of the room. She doused the fire with flour, repeating my full name over and over again, "Giovanni Zappacosta-O'Hara!"

To punish me, my parents made me sit in the room with the burnt train set and write eulogies for the victims of my carelessness. Mom, always the journalist, told me it would run in the fake town's fake newspaper, *Giotown Today*. The smell of electric fire and melting plastic grass and scorched flour was intense, as was my child's shame at disappointing my parents. I couldn't write a thing, so I packed up my knapsack and escaped the house. I ran all the way across town to where Aunt Maeve lived at that time. And here I was again, running away, approaching Maeve's house with that smell of tragedy around me, now clinging to actual horror.

I turned down Avenue S and stopped on Maeve's block, surrounded by a menacing stillness. The asphalt here was tired and split, SCHOOL XING worn into white islands of paint. The houses were squat, each with a single window on the second floor; rows of cycloptic dwellings staring each other down. The residents manicured their cramped lawns and hearty hedges. Aluminum siding was sprayed clean. Mailboxes were painted in pastels.

Maeve's was the exception. Its wood-slat facade had chunks missing, like teeth punched out. On the crumbling concrete veranda, a walker was U-locked to the railing. A square of grass was unkempt and trapped beyond a rusty chain-link fence. The dandelions I'd seen on my first visit had evolved into puffs of seed. Neighbourhood children surely theorized she was a witch.

Why was I here? I could tell myself that I was being a responsible nephew, come to check on Maeve, but that was just another pretense. It wasn't a good enough reason to walk here. I could have called, but that would have meant returning to my room at the hotel, confronting the TV and phones, and I needed to be as far as possible from those things. No, I wanted a destination—some semblance of control—and this was the only other place I knew in Brooklyn. Now that I was here, though, I worried about what information the house contained. Maeve had a phone. Maeve had a TV. Was BF dead? The answer was inside this house, and I was too much of a coward to knock on the door. I was negotiating the edge of the fear that had driven me from BF's bedside to Marine Park. I'd walked here in a straight line, but how had I gotten here?

I didn't get to make the decision. The door swung open and Patricia appeared.

"Giovanni!" she said. "You're OK! Thank God you're OK!" She turned behind her and yelled, "It's him and he's fine!"

"I wanted to check on Aunt Maeve," I said.

"Well, get up here! I don't want to keep the door unlocked too long." I heard Maeve's grumble behind her. "Maeve says it's now or never."

I was exhausted and starving. The walk had rendered my legs numb. I put one foot in front of the other, but they didn't want to proceed. I had to close my eyes and force them, launching myself towards the only immediate thing that tethered me to my life.

Maeve was waiting in the hallway, leaning on her cane. She was wearing a ratty housecoat with a Holiday Inn Express logo stitched to the breast. Her face was identical to when I'd last seen it, armoured and ancient, pale green eyes squinting at me. Behind her, in the living room, I could see flashes of a TV on mute.

"Get the heck in here, kid," she said.

Maeve reached out a hand. I didn't know what she wanted me to do with it. Her whole existence seemed to be an argument against affection. She grabbed my T-shirt to pull me towards her. She put her free arm around me and hugged hard.

"Making an old lady do all the work," she said. Her breath smelled of whisky. "You look like a ragamuffin."

"Can I have a drink?" I said. "Don't tell me anything until I have a drink."

"Get the kid a glass. Ice, right?" Maeve said. "Pick a poison. Anything but the Laphroaig."

"Canadian Club, if you have it."

"We do!" said Patricia.

"Upgrade him to the Crown Royal," Maeve said. "It's that kind of day."

Patricia helped Maeve move towards the living room. I stayed in the dark hall, leaning into some coats that hung near the door. I heard the La-Z-Boy accept Maeve's weight. I heard the ice tinkle.

"You left your doohickey here," Maeve said.

"My what?" I shouted from the hallway.

"Your damned recorder. You left it here. Had half a mind to erase the whole thing."

Patricia came in and handed the slim device to me, its mini-tape staring out like owl's eyes.

"Why not join us in the living room, Giovanni?" Patricia said.

"Turn the TV off," I called out.

"Christ, why?" Maeve said.

"Please."

The lights ceased flashing.

"There you go, your highness," Maeve said.

"Thanks," I said, entering the living room. Patricia gave me my drink, a double. I was surprised that I could grip it. I took a gulp and it burned through me.

"I don't know anything," I said.

"That's an understatement," Maeve said.

"I mean about today. I don't know anything."

I told them about Mom's phone call, the burning tower, the second plane.

"Holy jumpin'," Maeve said.

"And then I walked here."

"So you don't know," Patricia said and turned to Maeve. "He doesn't know."

"He's not the only one. Your parents think you're dead. They've been pissing down my phone line all day."

"You should call them!" Patricia said. She went to the kitchen and returned with a white-shelled phone dragging a cord. She placed it in front of me, on the radio.

"You're putting them through the wringer," Maeve said.

"Did Mom mention anyone else?"

"Anyone else?"

"Someone named BF? Brian Franklin?"

"Nah," Maeve said. "That your lover?"

"Boyfriend."

"Fancy," Maeve said. "Your mom probably thinks I hate nancies. Didn't want to give you away."

"He was on a plane this morning."

"Oh my lord, you poor dear!" Patricia said. "What you must have been going through!"

"He's not a poor anything," Maeve said. "He coulda known at any minute."

"Yeah," I said.

"But you couldn't hack it."

"Yeah."

"A Zappocosta through and through," Maeve said.

"Yeah."

Maeve shook her head at me. Her angry pink colour intensified in her cheeks.

"There were two other planes, Gio," Patricia said.

"What airlines?" I said.

"Don't tell him," Maeve said.

"Maeve—"

"No, he's gotta call. Patricia, give him some courage."

Patricia picked up the bottle and topped me up. I drank it and placed the empty glass on top of the radio. I dialled. I held the receiver in one hand, the dictaphone in the other.

"Hello?" BF said. His voice was quick and desperate. It surged into my ear like it was putting out an inferno.

"You're alive."

"And you're dead once I get my hands on you."

"I'm sorry," I said. "Where are you?"

"Home. Montreal. They turned our plane around somewhere over the Hudson," he said. "I could see it, Gio. The black smoke in the air."

"I saw it too," I said. "Are you sure you're OK? I need you to be OK."

"I'll be fine until they send me to prison for your murder."

"Make it painless."

"No promises," BF said. "Where are you?"

"Aunt Maeve's."

"Babes, what are you doing there?"

"I don't know. I don't know yet. I don't know anything. Just that I'm coming home."

story1.12February2018.m4a

[BFM]: You're ending it there?

[GZO]: The first story, yeah.

[BFM]: Seems abrupt.

[GZO]: I thought you'd enjoy it because I come off like an asshole.

[BFM]: It has certain virtues, no question.

[GZO]: You told me to write it the way it came to me. That I couldn't get ahead of myself.

[BFM]: And you did?

[GZO]: Yeah, you made me PROMISE.

[BFM]: But babes, readers only know what you tell us, and this is all you. It's how YOU saw things. I'm just this sickly presence.

[GZO]: I don't know how you felt in these moments. I'm not in your brain.

[BFM]: Well, I can tell you. Get in my brain. Plenty of unwelcome things got in there anyhow.

[GZO]: You're hilarious.

[BFM]: Thank you.

[GZO]: Do I need a different ending?

[BFM]: No, keep going. Don't revise. I didn't say the ending was bad. Just sudden.

[GZO]: That's the moment I remember clearest. Being on the phone with you.

[BFM]: And not knowing anything.

[GZO]: Not knowing anything YET. Like, I was about to go find out.

[BFM]: And all it took was me nearly dying.

[GZO]: You nearly dying TWICE.

[BFM]: Three times, if you include the Easter ham.

[GZO]: I do.

2

The Easter Ham

Early in our relationship, BF was the only colourful thing I allowed in my apartment on Querbes Street. He still lived with his parents then, in a Montreal suburb, but spent weekends in the city, in my bed. His hair was yellow and long and unwashed. After sex, it held itself in a golden hurricane, the strands wrenched from their ponytail. The hair-tie was stuck in the chaos, a lavender squiggle of plastic like a bit of telephone cord. He was straddling me, and I looked up at him while he caught his breath. His body was expansive and plump and rosy with blood. His eyes were blue, his fingernails were green. One sock clung on. It was periwinkle, with two fat orange stripes near the top, a gay parody of a sports sock, and was bunched around his ankle.

I had just moved in and hadn't yet hung curtains. March's drab light seeped through the window making the room more bare and BF more colourful. He shot out a gratified sigh and smiled out of one side of his mouth. I loved it, that confirmation that I had satisfied him. And he knew I loved it because he chose that moment to ask to meet my parents.

"Are you embarrassed of your family?" he said.

"No, but I've told you everything I can. Every story."

"What's the house like?"

"It's all bugs and Jesus."

"Your dad keeps his crickets in the house?"

"Only dead ones."

"I thought he studied how they sang."

"He does."

"I bet they don't sing much when they're dead."

"Wouldn't matter. In that house, crickets wouldn't get a word in."

"See?" BF said. "Dead crickets! There's so much I don't know. I don't even know what your folks look like."

"They look like parents."

"You haven't put up a picture of them."

"I haven't put up a picture of anything."

There was one thing on the wall. The rental agency had left me a calendar for the year 2000—a welcome gift when I moved in a few months earlier. Otherwise, four empty white walls surrounded the bed. The mattress sat on a metal frame with exposed casters. My alarm clock was shoved against the corner, far enough away for me to see it from the pillow without raising my head.

"All I know is what you tell me," he said.

"And you think I'm lying?"

"Not lying," he said. BF tugged on his earlobe. They were chubby; everything about him was. His emerald fingernail polish was bright against his flesh. "Not lying, but filtering."

"So?"

"So, you've already met my folks. Fair is fair."

"I wouldn't characterize that as 'fair.'"

He stood up, towering over me, and lifted the calendar from its nail. I looked up the length of his thick body, trying to picture it ruined by the tattoo he wanted. As always, I couldn't. He dropped the calendar on my chest.

"We'll go down for an event. What's coming up?"

"Arbour Day."

"I mean a birthday or something." He snuggled next to me, covering us in the black sheet. "You guys are Catholic. Didn't Jesus do anything of note around this time of year?"

"He died."

"Everyone dies. I said *of note*."

"He rose from the dead, too, shortly after."

"With the Easter Bunny?"

"If you believe the scripture."

"I don't," BF said. He pointed to Good Friday. "But it's a long weekend, so it'll have to do."

"Can't you go without me?"

"Oh my god, yes—can I?"

"Over my dead body."

"Then those are your options. To die or to come."

"I already came."

"Death, then."

"You joke, but Jesus might not be the only one dead by the end of this."

"If I die, babes, I'm taking you with me," he said. He gave me that satisfied sigh-smile again, and my dread was suspended—briefly—by the notion that I hadn't disappointed him.

✷

I had met his parents; that part was true. It happened by accident three months earlier, on BF's twenty-second birthday. He always wanted to have a surprise party, but he'd been born on New Year's Day, which made this difficult, so I didn't try. Instead, I planned a dinner for him. I'd moved onto Querbes Street over the Christmas holiday, and the apartment had no dining table or chairs. BF's parents were out of town, so I lugged bags of ingredients on the commuter train to the suburbs.

Hudsonville was not a town. It had no centre, not even a mall, just a train station-SAQ hybrid surrounded by lagoons of parking lot. The walk to BF's parents' house took an hour, bringing me past dozens of identical streets, each mysteriously a cul-de-sac, lined with blocky houses, mathematically spaced, with white-door garages prominent enough to resemble buck teeth. Perhaps Hudsonville could have charmed me in the summer, when the young trees were leafy and the yards saturated with colour and the houses could be discerned one from the next. But in winter, the same lonely sapling shivered in every yard and the snow was piled so high that every driveway was a tunnel. There was nothing but white and grey, and when I found the address, I looked up at the conformist mini-mansion and wondered how I would escape from it if I had to.

Inside, the convection oven and induction stove baffled me as I eked out four courses: rosemary roast chicken stuffed with bread, bacon and chestnuts; gnocchi, prepared my Nonna's way, rolled off a fork and swimming in porky tomato sauce; sour salad with lemon dressing and fennel cut so thin it only whispered its flavour. Dessert was pecan pie, BF's favourite of my pies, topped with vanilla ice cream that was melting perfectly at midnight, pooling around the nuts and seeping into the filling. As we kissed to welcome the new millennium, his parents came through the front door screaming, "Surprise!"

BF yelped in delight—right in my face, lips still on mine—and ran to hug them in the hall. "You got me! I can't believe you got me!" he shouted. "Gio, were you in on this?"

"He didn't have a clue!" Mrs. MacDonald said. She walked in linking arms with her son, and extended a hand to me. "But this young man doesn't mind, does he now?"

"Of course not," I said, boiling with rage, shaking her hand. "Happy New Year, Mrs. MacDonald. I'm Giovanni."

"Call me Barb," she said. "That's some grip you have there. Morty, come shake Giovanni's hand. Isn't that some grip?"

"It's some grip," Morty confirmed.

"Were you even in Ottawa?" BF said.

"We came back this afternoon!" she said.

"It was a trick," Morty said.

"We've been at the club for hours, haven't we, Morty?"

"There were cocktails," Morty said.

Barb was inquisitive and upbeat as she busied herself cleaning up from dinner, tasting bits as she went. "Well, this is something else. Who knew a chicken could have so much oomph? And is that some kind of pasta? Morty, isn't that so different?" She was the same height as BF, and equally pale, but the similarities ended there. Her hair was cut close to her skull and brushed forward, feathered over her temples, and dyed a mauvish crimson that has never existed in the natural world. She had the dimensions of a bookmark, and everything about her was sharp: nose, cheek bones, jewellery and pale hazel eyes scanning the scene. "And to do the stuffing right in the bird! Don't mind gambling with your belly, Giovanni?"

Morty was avuncular, slapping me on the back with a fat hand. His eyes were as blue as BF's, and his hair as thick and as blond, only short. He had a tubby face and a welcoming smile. A Christmas sweater featuring a pattern of reindeer stretched around his gut, leaving the animals deformed, deranged. "Sorry about this, Giovanni. The missus gets ideas," he said. "Any leftovers?"

BF was bright in their presence. With his wild hair and sapphire fingernails, he looked different from his parents, but it became evident that he'd inherited his kindness and trust from these people. And they were atheists, too, so they didn't even have a religion to credit for their decency, the way my parents might. They were unruffled by his painted nails and the homosexuality underway in their kitchen. I surmised that they were good people, curious and welcoming, and that I had to get away from them immediately. As Barb pelted me with questions, drawing me into the MacDonald family orbit, I ran through the possible ways to escape. There were none.

"You come from a journalist and an entomologist. How original! Entomology—which one is that? Birds?"

"That's ornithology," I said. "This is—"

"No! Let me guess."

"Better let her guess, son," Morty said.

"Lizards?" she said.

"Herpetology," I said.

"Little fishies?" she said. "In the deep blue sea?"

"Ichthyology," I said.

"She doesn't know," Morty said.

"Clearly I don't!"

"It's bugs!" BF said. They laughed. Barb even clapped. All this unearned reward irked me further, and I stretched a flat smile across my teeth.

"Aren't my folks the best?" BF said.

"They are. It's hard to be mad about the interruption when they make you so happy."

"I'm sure you'll find a way." BF squeezed the top of my thigh. I enjoyed a brief erection, then we spent the rest of the night playing Euchre. Morty and I lost twice, then I was directed to the guest room to sleep.

My gift went unnoticed. It was tattoo-related. BF didn't know what design he wanted, or where it would go, or why, but he floated possibilities on a daily basis. A bear, a deer, a pink triangle, an angel with two faces (one of Stevie Nicks, the other of Christine McVie). BF had mythologized the tattoo into a thing of mystical importance. Like the second coming of Christ, it would certainly happen, but no one expected to witness it. I mentioned his indecision whenever he criticized my procrastination. His birthday gift was a kind of dare—a $200 gift certificate at a tattoo parlour, with a clear expiry date in six months.

"A dragonfly," he said the next morning, driving me back to the train station in Barb's Volvo.

"What?"

"Your gift. I found it this morning and I know what I want. A dragonfly. A huge one. On my chest."

"Why?"

"They're wily. Shrewd."

"They're creepy."

"They take aeons to reach maturity. It'll remind me of you."

"I'm not sure how a dragonfly will look."

"Me neither, which is why *you're* going to design it. I wouldn't trust the task to anyone else, and you're a pro."

"You're mocking me."

"Correct," he said. "I wouldn't procrastinate on this project, Mr. O'Hara. I'm a very demanding client and my expectations are unrealistic."

"Why an insect? It'll just remind me of my dad."

"He does crickets. I want a dragonfly," BF said. "I want a dozen options by the end of the week."

Three months later, the options were still half-finished. My mediocre dragonfly designs haunted a sub-folder on my laptop. They were all blue-winged creatures, very real to life, with implied shadows to make them seem three dimensional, as though the bug had landed between BF's nipples and was waiting to be scared away. The permanence of the tattoo unsettled me—my design in his skin; a reminder of me, stained forever, hugely, on his square torso. It was one of several commitments that he started to suggest. He mentioned family reunions in Hudsonville, and gay marriage rallies, and emergency contacts, and moving in, and meeting my family. I was terrified of every one of them, terrified of what I'd owe him if they were ever real. A cowardly brew of things churned in me—laziness, responsibility, and the two-pronged fear of losing and disappointing him. I'd come to know it well. It would churn for years.

*

The morning of Good Friday, BF pulled up to my building in a rented Kia Spectra. He'd burned a dozen CDs for the drive. I had to move them from the passenger seat before getting in. He had the whole trip mapped out in song. Each disc was labelled for a different stretch of the six-hour drive.

"Look at us, on the road together," BF said.

"It's exciting."

"So wipe that look off your face."

"Is my face making a look?"

"What is it? The CDs? It can't be my nails. I depolished for you."

"It's the car. It's nothing."

"It's the cheapest one they had."

"It's a Kia."

"It's a brand new model. It's a 2001. It's from the future."

"It's not a GM."

"It's not a Porsche either. Shall we list more things it's not? It's not a cereal."

"It's not going to fit in, I mean."

"It's not a disgraced clown."

"It's not very Fiona. Fiona is a GM town."

"It's not getting off to a great start."

"It's not."

BF blew hair off his face and I could sense his frustration in the fluttering strands. Everything but the Girl finished singing "Driving," and Sheryl Crow started in on "Every Day Is a Winding Road." He changed lanes with a recklessness that betrayed the music. The freeway was dense with people leaving Montreal for the holiday weekend, but BF was blind to all of them, zipping the car across the painted V of an exit lane he'd almost taken by accident. I white-knuckled the door handle until we were off the island, bordered by soggy fields, and on a straightaway to the Ontario border. Cindy Lauper was insisting that she drove all night.

"It's not one of those hard things you bite into sometimes when you eat a hot dog," BF said.

"It's not."

"It's also not the end of the world."

"It's not."

"It's definitely not one of Margaret Atwood's ovaries."

"No." I stared out the window at a passing sixteen-wheeler and imagined being under it. "It's not."

*

"This place looks like a Heritage Minute," BF observed as we rolled down Fiona's main drag. I took over the driving in Kingston, so he was free to rubberneck. Maple Street was lined with Victorian red-stone facades and curved windows and marble curbs. Rising to one side was the Catholic hill, the poor bit of town where my mother had grown up. On the other side was the more wealthy hill, topped by the Basilica with its twin belfries, grey and pseudo-Gothic, as permanent as the sky.

"It's like that church is keeping its eye on everyone," BF said.

"It's exactly like that," I said. "That's the rich people church."

"Tell me about some other landmarks."

"I barfed behind that arena once," I said, indicating the indoor hockey rink where my sister once played. "Too many Bacardi Breezers at the drama club party."

"You look like you could use a Breezer right now."

"No thanks. But I might barf."

"You'll live."

But would I? The truth was that BF was an excellent candidate for entry into the O'Hara-Zappacosta mythology, and I was panicked by how well he'd fit in with my family. Mom and Dad would love his questions and curiosity. The way he poked fun at me, with easy grace and humour, would endear him to my siblings. This trip would taint our relationship with a new legitimacy. Once my family knew him, they couldn't unknow him. I was already planning my aloofness for the coming months, during my calls back to Fiona, Mom on the dining room phone in her rocking chair, Dad on the extension in the TV room with *CBC Newsworld* on mute. There would be questions about BF, his classes at McGill, his applications for grad school. With each question, he'd be attached by another tether.

I turned the Kia down my parents' street. The houses had a vampirish quality in the dusk, which for BF, after a teenage diet of Anne Rice, was a positive thing. It was dinnertime, and kids' tricycles and toys were left abandoned on plots of lawn. The oak branches over the road were studded with green specks, harbingers of spring. Ahead of us, I could see my parents and brother on the porch. Mom was already waving like she was flagging down a plane from a desert island.

"You're the image of your mother, even from here. And your brother's like a hot version of you."

"He's sixteen," I said.

"Still."

"I guess it's too late for me to stop, drop and roll."

"You'd find a way if you really wanted to," he said. "Any last remarks? Things I should know?"

"Ask for seconds," I said. "At dinner. Go easy on your first plate so you can request more. My folks love that, so humour them."

"So treat them the way I treat you, babes?"

"Minus the sarcasm."

"Sarcasm?" BF said as I slowed the Kia to a stop at the curb. "Never touch the stuff."

He bounded out of the car before I'd cut the engine. I watched through the windshield as he proceeded up the steps to the veranda with his hand outstretched. Dad took it between two palms. Mom grabbed BF by the shoulders and drew him in for a kiss on both cheeks. Danny slapped him on the back. They gestured at me to join. I flipped the turn signal, put the car in reverse, and made as though I was returning to Montreal. I waved goodbye—*here's your replacement son!*—and pretended to pull away. Danny shook his head and rolled his eyes. Dad laughed. Mom called, "Very funny, Mr. Comedian!" BF squinted as though he was willing the Kia to explode. The fear of disappointing him once again overtook my dread and I ran from the car with a smile so forced I could feel it in my ears.

Danny was in his usual weekend tracksuit, but my parents had groomed for this moment. Dad had trimmed back his ginger beard; I could make out wax-white skin under the bristles of orange. He wore a collared gingham shirt and too-short khaki dockers that allowed for several inches of black socks above his brogues. Mom was in a loose pink blouse and navy slacks. She hugged me hard and close. The smell of her—Opium perfume, garlic, Big Red gum, Bounce dryer sheets, white wine—shot through me in an instant, like I was inhaling my whole history.

"The prodigal son returns," Dad said. "That a Saturn?"

"A Kia," I said.

"Rookie mistake," Danny said.

"Totally my fault," BF said. "I rented it."

"Yeah, Fiona's a GM town," Dad said. "They assemble them over on the west side. You'll stick out like a sore thumb around here."

"Someone didn't tell me that," BF said.

"Guess I should have," I said.

"Just don't park it in the driveway," Dad said.

"What else didn't he tell you?" Mom said. "Did he warn you about the fish? Gio, tell me you warned him about the fish."

"The fish?" BF said.

"Sorry," I said. "I meant to tell you that my parents are superstitious weirdos who eat fish on certain days."

"Like today," Danny said.

"Why?" BF said.

"Catholic stuff," I said. "Meat pisses off God."

"But only sometimes," Danny added.

"Don't listen to them, BF," Mom said. "We're fasting. It's a small sacrifice—"

"Teeny tiny," Dad said.

"—to show we appreciate what Jesus went through."

"Cod's roughly on par with crucifixion," I said.

"Bet you've already had meat today," Mom said. "What did you eat on the drive?"

"A sandwich," I said. "Tim Hortons."

"A BLT," BF said.

"I knew I could get it out of you," Mom said. "Never underestimate me."

"Go easy on him, Mom," Danny said in my defence. "That's not real meat anyway."

"Your man ratted you out, Gio," Mom said, teasing. "And we haven't even left the veranda."

"BF's an only child, so overindulged he never learned about certain things," I said. "Like alliances."

"I'm a fast learner," BF said. He smiled at me and started pulling on his earlobe.

*

"Well, this is it—" Mom was saying.

It was her favourite phrase. Her four sisters used it as well to indicate that we've arrived at the heart of the matter. I'd heard it countless times over dinners like this one. We were at the breakfast table, a six-seater at the end of the kitchen, surrounded by windows. I placed myself in BF's perspective and compared the room to the MacDonalds' ordered kitchen in Hudsonville—ultra-modern relative to our hundred-year-old mouldings, splattered countertops and brutalized wooden spoons. For the first time, I noticed the worn cupboard edges and the clusters of fingerprints around the light switches.

And it wasn't just the kitchen. In Hudsonville, the newness of the house and its lush carpets meant the MacDonalds could tread through their space like cats, unheard. Here, every footstep squeaked the floorboards, and we all knew what transpired in the washrooms, farts and plops followed by the rumbling of pipes surging with water. When the basement's washing machine was on its spin cycle, it sounded as if a vortex was about to open and swallow the house. The vibrations left every wall decoration crooked, especially Dad's framed white squares pinned with dead crickets. *Gryllotalpa major. Neoxabea bipunctata.* They lined the hall upstairs, all tilted. We had long ago given up straightening them.

To me, all of this made my family seem quaint, analogue, disqualifying. To BF, it made my family bewitching.

"—Jacko and I didn't care about the fact of it," Mom continued. "I mean, if he's gay, he's gay. That was the truth. It was the *way* we found out."

"We found out through the backdoor," Dad said.

"No pun intended," Danny said, hoisting cod.

"And his sister, too," Mom said. "We got more than our share of gay around here."

"Not that we mind," Dad said.

"Of course not," Mom said.

Danny shrugged.

"We think the Church is wrong on this one," Mom said.

"Your lips to God's ears," Dad said.

"I consider us blessed," Mom said.

"Twice over," Dad said.

"Who wouldn't want our Gio?" Mom said.

"You're blushing!" BF said.

"Yeah, because I know what's coming," I said.

"Take it away, Bonnie," Dad said.

"So, we already had our suspicions," Mom said, pausing, sighing, bringing her audience around to a familiar starting point. "Hated sports. Put on my eyeliner as a kid. That kind of thing."

"There are photos," Dad said.

"Well, the big reveal happened when my mother passed, God rest her," Mom said.

"This is Grandma Footloose?" BF said.

"Grandma Footloose!" Mom said. "Oh, is *that* what Gio called her?"

"I thought you all did," BF said. "I didn't mean any disrespect."

"We called her that, Gio and me," Danny said. "Don't lose your shit, Mom. It's just because she hated dancing so much."

"She did hate dancing, Bonnie," Dad said.

"Well, it's not part of this story," Mom said. "This one's about Gio."

"Is it, though?" I said.

"Of course it is!" Mom said. "Anyhow, we were all in a bit of a state with the funeral. Things were madness around here. I was devastated, as you can imagine. Thank the Lord for Gio's sister Tina. She organized *everything*."

"You'll meet her tomorrow," Dad said.

"She's a whirlwind," Mom said. "So, I've got a million things to deal with and I can't sleep, thinking about my mother—or Grandma Footloose, as she was known. I'm tossing and turning upstairs, but then I hear someone skulking around down here in the kitchen. And I'm thinking, who on Earth is that? We had the funeral in the morning and we all needed to be asleep or risk looking like the dead ourselves. So, I'm up like a shot to see what the heck's going on."

"And because you can't leave well enough alone," Dad said.

"You shush. First thing I noticed was that the light on the phone upstairs was blaring red, and that means someone's on the line somewhere in the house. I looked at the caller ID and wouldn't you know it! What do I see? You'd never guess."

"The number of the funeral home," Dad said.

"The number of the funeral home! Now, BF, you tell me. If *your* mother had just died and *you* knew someone was calling up the funeral home in the middle of the blessed night—"

"It's 4:00 a.m.!" Dad said.

"It gets later with every re-telling," I said.

"—wouldn't *you* want to know what the heck is going on?"

"Without a doubt, Bonnie." He was already calling her Bonnie.

"Well, this is it! I *had* to know. So, I pick up the receiver and who do I hear? Giovanni Zappacosta-O'Hara crying his little eyes out—"

"I don't think I was crying," I said.

"—and I'm thinking, did he think he'd be able to speak to his nonna? I mean, she *was* at the funeral home, only dead."

"As a doornail," Dad said.

"But no. Turns out Gio had been carrying on with the son of the undertaker! Joey Callino. Good kid. A bit squirrelly."

"You'd be too with all that death around," Dad said.

"No competition for me, I hope," BF said.

"Not by a mile!" Mom said, pausing for effect. "They'd been seeing each other for a while based on what I heard on the phone. Now, BF, I'm not one to pry—"

"This story notwithstanding," Danny said.

"—but he was being so emotional! Mr. Standoffish here had the most gorgeous things to say about his nonna. Her cooking, her affection, the way she cared for everyone in her life. And he was a teenager! Seventeen! He never talked that way with his mother. So, BF, forgive me, I couldn't resist. I listened to the whole thing. Five minutes later, Gio found me weeping on the floor in the hall, the phone beeping like crazy for me to hang up."

"Woke the whole house," Dad said.

"And Jacko here, and Tina, and Danny, all stood around and watched me hug my son. I was so sad, but I was so happy!"

BF kissed me on the cheek, saying, "Such a softie."

My family cooed.

"That's not how you told it to me," BF said.

"Mom tells it better," I said.

"Never underestimate me," she said. "Like the cod?"

BF did. He liked everything, I could tell—the cod, the old house, the close room, the family in-jokes that made him into more of a co-conspirator than a guest. He beamed throughout Mom's story, hungry for any detail that left me exposed. He was high on information.

"Tell me another," BF said.

"Oh, how to choose?" Mom said.

"Maybe you can wait for Gio's book," Danny said.

"Your book?" BF said.

"Gio's going to write the whole family history. Didn't he tell you?" Mom said. "The whole Zappacosta-O'Hara chronicle."

"And you'll be sorry when I do," I said.

"Are you going to make villains of us all?" Mom said. She gulped her wine.

"Wait and see," I said.

"But you don't even know all the details," Mom said.

"Are you kidding? You never shut up about any of it."

"Oh, there's more, Gio. You don't know the whole story."

"Fine. I'll make it up," I said.

"He'll never write it," Danny said. "He just likes to threaten."

"Gio can do anything he puts his mind to," Dad said.

"That's right," said Mom. "Now if he'd only put his mind to something."

"You should put your mind to this fine gentleman." Dad pointed his cod-laden fork at BF.

BF looked in my direction, grinning with acceptance. "Are you going to make an honest woman of me?"

I listened to my jaw work a green bean to a pulp; my non-answer filled the room; his question floated away. I let this happen. It had to be clear that I did. When they resumed talking, BF was no longer looking in my direction.

"I thought after dinner I could give you a tour of the town," I said, jumping into the clatter with a non sequitur he couldn't ignore.

Mom was standing, refilling BF's glass with wine. "Don't know *what* that has to do with my story about how you used to hang out with that old grump."

"Aunt Maeve," Dad said.

"We can drive by her house on the tour," I offered.

"She hasn't lived there in forever, Gio," Danny said.

"Oh."

"She's in New York now," BF said. He still wasn't looking at me. "By the end of the weekend, I'll know more about your family than you do."

"Maybe *you* should write that book, BF," Danny said.

"Maybe I will."

"I'll give you *loads* of material," Mom said. "Just let me get you in for a soak."

A soak. The suggestion was as inevitable as it was disquieting.

I felt the hot tub's presence behind us in the dark backyard. At full activation, it bubbled like a cauldron, reeked of chlorine and had a disarming power, like a confessional. Dad had added it on a whim, suckered by a salesman at the plumbing store. Mom was furious at the time, but now she was the one most likely to be neck-deep in gurgling water, wreathed in steam, a glass of white Zinfandel above her shoulder on the wooden deck, where a constellation of ring-stains was bitten into the wood. Over the years, she'd bought accessories: a floating bowl in the shape of a frigate (meant for pretzels, used for olives), submergible disco lights, an umbrella the size of a car.

"You told him to bring his bathing suit?" Dad said.

"No. He didn't," BF said. "One more thing he didn't tell me."

"Always rushing. No nuance. Just like his dad," Mom said. "Don't worry your angel head about it, BF. We have loads of spare trunks."

"Stacks," Dad said.

"So how about that tour?" I said. BF glared at me, likely wondering about my sudden interest in a town I'd always told him wasn't worth describing.

"That can wait," he said. "I want to have seconds."

*

Once the Kia was in motion, I asked BF what he wanted to see.

"The interior of your parents' house," he said.

"We're going to be there for most of the weekend. We need to take these moments to ourselves when we can."

"That's sweet, babes, but I'm fucking sick of you." He kissed me on the cheek. "We've been in this car all day."

"Have we?"

"And you were acting like a dick at dinner."

"Was I?"

"Are you always this much of a pill when you're with your family?"

"Maybe?"

"Don't forget that this weekend is a test."

"Not sure how I could."

"I'm grading you on performance, technique, and creativity."

"Maybe it's not my family. Maybe I'm miserable when I'm on the spot all the time."

"You're doing poorly so far, if you're wondering."

"Maybe I don't *want* to perform for my boyfriend."

"You've only scored fours in all categories."

"Maybe this is all too much pressure."

"You understand these scores are out of a hundred, right?"

I took him back down Fiona's main drag. Maple Avenue had been gentrifying in increments since I'd moved to Montreal. A café with smoothies had replaced the espresso bar where old Italian men once played briscola and screamed about taxes. The Tim Hortons had been reconstructed to take out the drive-through, making room for a tacky cellphone retailer.

"This is my school up here on the left, Our Lady of Victory." BF glanced out at the square building of poured concrete and plastic windows.

"Looks like Our Lady of Mediocrity," he said.

"It was more like Our Lady of Perpetual Tedium."

"That's just because you're Our Lady of Perpetual Restlessness."

"You wouldn't have liked it either, Our Lady of High Maintenance."

"Our Lady of Dead Horses is begging us to stop with the whip already."

I drove him past the imposing Basilica he'd admired earlier, and showed him my family's parish, which was also called Our Lady of Victory. It was modest by comparison and dilapidating towards desolation. While in that part of Fiona, we went past the Laurier Street house on Catholic Hill, where my mother grew up. It was a tiny brick square with four rooms and an attic; all in all, it was the size of my apartment in Montreal. The sidewalks here were once cracked, with sandy anthills rising from the fissures. The residents were poor then. Now, the sidewalks were seamless, the houses renovated to bourgeois standards, and the ants driven elsewhere.

"Can you believe my mom lived there with four sisters, two parents and a brother?"

"Not to mention her personality, which would have taken up a lot of square footage."

"It was all immigrants along here. Italians, mostly. Every yard was full of clotheslines, and every clothesline was heavy with diapers."

"Your kind loves to breed," BF said. "Bonnie has a brother? You've never mentioned him."

"He's dead," I said. Driving BF past Uncle Roberto's house hadn't even occurred to me. I remembered him as a WOP stereotype. He was a GM worker in a white tank top and a faux-gold crucifix nestled in his chest hair. I knew little about him relative to the rest of the family, only that he was my mother's eldest sibling, born nine months after their parents were married. He treated Nonna like a queen; she treated him like a mistake she was forever apologizing for. Mom and her sisters regarded him as a footnote in their history, though I was never told why. The most time I'd ever spent with him was at his funeral. "I can take you to his grave, if you'd like."

"You really know how to show a girl a good time."

I drove us past Exhibition Park, pointing out the pathway to the clearing where men were known to cruise for anonymous sex. I showed him Chéhab and Sons Funeral Home, famous for its phone number and swishy undertaker's son from Mom's story. I finished the tour at the GM plant, an industrial tangle of concrete with desert-like parking lots on each side. It was ugly and empty. Sensing BF's boredom, I showed him how we used to do doughnuts in the lots here, under the flashing red light atop the GM water tower. I managed to cheer him up, centrifuging him to giggles, until he screamed at me to stop, pleading a headache.

The car was dark, but in the creepy orange hue of the sodium lights, I could see his eyes were wild and pained as he pulled the skin back at his temples.

"Christ, are you OK?"

He took large gulps of air and removed his seat belt so he could put his head between his knees. I went to touch his back, but he held a hand up to stop me. I watched, attempted to help by putting his window down from the driver's-side panel. Its motorized descent underscored my uselessness.

"I'm peachy," he said, eventually.

"You don't look peachy."

"I'm approaching peachiness, OK?"

"You look like you pushed the car here."

"I'm bent over, babes," he told the floor mat. "You can't even see what I look like. I assure you I'm very attractive."

When he sat upright, he looked restored except for the flyaways that had escaped his ponytail. "See?"

"Very sexy, yes. But you had me worried."

"It's nothing."

"Are you sure?"

"One of my little spells."

"Are you *sure*?"

He pulled the purple elastic from his hair. He looked angelic again, a Renaissance cherub in a Kia Spectra.

"You actually look worried," he said.

"You scared me."

"You could use a good scare."

To fix his hair, he adjusted the rear-view mirror. It couldn't turn all the way towards him so he slipped over to my lap, making a show of it, sweeping his hair over my face. He leaned back for a kiss, and pulled my hand around his waist to his thigh. I gave him a peck, but he drew my head down further for a deeper kiss, tongue. I indulged this for a minute, then lifted my lips away. He contorted himself so he could snake a hand around to my crotch.

"I'm not getting a reading."

"Sorry," I said. "Guess I don't find this super sexy."

"Thanks."

"I don't mean you. I mean the setting."

"Let's go back to your folks'. We can defile your childhood bedroom. It'll be like a porno." I could feel the words in his breath. They were hot and disgusting, and they smelled of my mother—white Zinfandel and garlic.

"No," I said.

"Yes."

"We could get caught."

"Even better."

"We'd just give Mom another story to tell," I said. "I don't want you to be something she'll throw in my face until the end of time."

I reached around him and started the car. He hauled himself back to the passenger seat and leaned his head against the window. He was radiating disappointment.

"Your family is lovely," he said. "So, why are you like *this*?"

It was one of his normal quips; an invitation to banter. But I decided to be mad about it. He'd left me alone. He made me the sole guardian of the barrier that might keep our relationship from leaking into my family. He had sided with them—at dinner, on the porch—and even refused to see things in these terms. He wanted to be a character in one of Mom's stories. He was writing himself into the plot as I was desperate to be killed off. This argument is petty, I thought, staring through the windshield, wishing the car was a standard so I could punctuate my pissed-off demeanour with shifts in vibration and torque. Petty, but plausible.

When we got to my parents' house, he stepped from the car and slammed the door. I left, for real this time. I didn't bother looking into the rear-view mirror to see his disappointed face or to watch him shrink away. I acted as though he was, somehow, still watching my performance of not-caring. I did this sometimes when I was mad at him and alone and feeling petulant. I carried on the premise as I went on my own tour of Fiona, pretending he could still see me. I wanted him to witness my flared nostrils and wincing eyes. I wanted him to feel blamed. Guilty. Watch, BF. Watch me haunt the monuments of my upbringing. Watch me roll this car, this shitty car you picked, along the alleyway behind Cruikshank Drive, where I used to hide and read; watch me zip down Caribou Road, where I used to run away to Aunt Maeve's house to watch movies; watch me flip-off my high school; watch me stop near the forest path at Exhibition Park, where shame-filled men passed the Kia on their way to the cruising ground. Watch. Watch all of this.

*

To write this story, BF advised me to get into his brain.

It was cluttered. The tumour was small at that point—a pack of insidious cells—but fury and questions took up space. Fury that I'd driven off, and questions about how I'd represented myself to him. My family had provided more information about me, and he was now imagining me like one of my father's crickets: pinned to a white board, ready for examination.

Such were his thoughts when he entered my parents' house that night. He already felt comfortable enough to do so without knocking. He popped off his shoes and ambled down the corridor as though he were at home. Bonnie was in the kitchen, rifling around in the freezer, finding room for ice cube trays amid the pounds of brick-hard butter that were $20 a dozen last week at No Frills. She asked after me, and BF shrugged. She then asked a sly question—a trap, but he didn't know that yet.

"Is he in one of his moods?"

"I think he went to the store or something."

"Do you?"

"Not really, no."

Her face morphed from motherly to shrewd. "You know what? Let's get a soak."

"In the hot tub?"

"It's already warm. Danny was in there. He always goes in after practice," she said. "And you'll fit into one of Gio's old swim trunks."

He chose the most embarrassing pair, outsized board shorts covered in neon-green skateboards and flamingos. When he got to the backyard, Bonnie was already there, talking with Danny. She was in her black one-piece (she got the same one every year for Christmas from Dad), standing ankle-deep in gurgling water. My brother was wrapped in a towel, smoking a joint. BF tried to keep from taking too many glances at his body.

"Want a hoot?" Danny said, offering the spliff between pinched fingers. BF looked at it. It had been rolled with orange papers bearing a repeated NDP logo.

"No thanks," BF said, unsure of the protocol. "But cool papers."

"Mom got them for me," Danny said.

"We're very open-minded around here," Bonnie said. "I like to give my kids a lot of space."

"Sure you do, Mom," Danny said. Smoke escaped through his smile. "Watch her, buddy. She'll get you when you least expect it."

"Let's have none of that. This poor creature gets enough crap from your brother," Bonnie said. "Don't listen to him, BF. Here."

She handed him a wine glass full of ice cubes, then poured in some white Zinfandel. The bulb started sweating.

"The trick is to slip in all at once," Bonnie told him. "Don't ease in."

She showed him how it's done, sliding into the froth without spilling a drop of wine. "You get a real rush. Give it a go."

He did. The heat drove an ecstatic shiver up his whole body.

"Feels good," BF said.

"Forty-one degrees," Danny said.

"How long have you had this thing?"

"Do you really want to talk about the tub?" Bonnie said.

"See? Here she goes," Danny said. He pinched off the joint with licked fingers. Its musk disappeared, replaced with the reek of chlorine.

"You go be stoned somewhere else," Bonnie said. "BF and I have to get acquainted."

"Good luck, buddy," Danny said, and headed back into the house.

"Finally, some privacy," Bonnie said. "Now, you must have questions about Mr. Sulkypants."

"Gio? Yeah, I do. But I like asking them in front of him."

"Make him squirm, yes. I admire your technique."

"Has he always been this way?"

"What way?"

"Aloof. Like tonight. I don't even know where he went."

"Who cares?" Mom said. Only her head was above the water. Her eyes were closed, and she was vibrating under the power of the jets. BF stared at her, pulled his earlobe. Her mix of dominance and openness intrigued him. He could see that she controlled the narrative, moved events around to where she wanted them.

"Will he come back?" BF said.

"Oh sure. He always comes back, you'll see," she said. "Running away runs in the family, that's what I always say."

"So, that's what I'm in for?"

She sat, scanned his face. He gave her a goading smile.

"Let me tell you a little story. Some real classic family lore."

Her repertoire was boundless, each episode polished and ready to go. She assessed BF, who was still staring at her while he played a private game in which he let his arms blow up to the surface of the water on the propulsion of the jets.

"Jacko and I, we met when we were kids. Fifteen and sixteen," she said. "See, we were born during the war. The second one. That may not seem like a big deal now, but back then, it meant something. The baby boom, that came after the war, so when we were teens, most kids were a few years younger. It was slim pickings in our cohort, believe you me. Anyhow, there came a summer when I wanted to get out of my parents' house. And so I made the decision to get the heck out of there. I *ran.*"

"For the same reason as Gio?"

"No, I had a real reason. I did it because we were poor, BF. Poor as dirt."

BF stopped playing with his hands. He knew the real story—or rather, my version of it. Already there were discrepancies. Where was the belt? Where were the cruel names, the endless fights? Where was her parents' vicious marriage? The nightly episodes, when my grandmother had to sleep in my mother's bed?

"Wow, really? That's it?"

"I'm a journalist, BF. I wouldn't lie to you."

"Sure."

"We had no car, no laundry machines. We only washed our hair once a week. Mama would douse our heads in white vinegar, then dunk us in the kitchen sink."

"Different times."

"When Jacko turned up, I saw my ticket out. That poor panty-twist didn't know what hit him. He was in town for one week before going west to plant trees. I had a limited time only! But I got him. I ran away with him and we had the greatest summer of our lives."

"I'm sure you were very convincing."

"I was a minx," she said. "We grew up fast, back then. I had to be twenty by the time I was fourteen. I didn't want that for my kids. I'm a pushover, I admit it—but it's because I know the other way is worse. You can blame me if Gio's being childish."

"I think I'll still blame him."

"Atta boy. But give him some room to be stupid. I mean, look at me now, sitting in this tub, boiling my brains out. I know how far I've come." She took a punctuating slurp of Zinfandel. "But that's not the point. Point is, running isn't always bad. Gio can't help himself. It's in his genes. His sister ran off to university, his grandfather ran from Italy, Jacko ran from the States. Runaways, all! And all the better for it. If we don't find something when we run, we run back twice as fast. You'll see."

"Sounds exhausting."

"Depends on how much you care, I guess. How exhausted are you?"

"I'm dead."

"Well," she said and refilled their wine. "There you go."

*

I woke on Saturday to a spring blizzard of wet, heavy flakes that had accumulated on the lawn, trees, and pavement. Only the lid of the hot tub, heating up for Mom's soak, managed to fend it off.

"The temperature of the air is right at zero," my sister, Tina, was saying to my mother as I walked into the kitchen. I was drowsy, still in the same boxers and T-shirt I'd slept in. "That's the death zone. Snow's freezing to the asphalt as soon as it hits."

Tina was perched on the edge of one of the breakfast chairs—she seemed to occupy only the first inch of any seat—in a yellow fleece vest zipped to her chin. Her windbreaker pants had reflective piping and were tucked into wool socks, and she was illuminated by the light coming in from the windows. The whiteness of the snowy backyard glowed from every angle. As always, she looked like a more successful, lesbian version of me. The same olive skin, better moisturized; the same thick brown hair, tamed into a slicked-back helmet.

"You look like a hobo, Gio," she said.

"Good to see you too," I said. "How much police tape had to die to make that vest?"

"Oh, go hug your sister," Mom said. She was at the counter eviscerating a loaf of bread, creating chunks for the dressing. "Coffee?"

"Immediately." I bent over and hugged Tina. She crushed me like it was a contest. "What ungodly hour did you get here?"

"Eight."

"Lesbian o'clock."

"I wanted to beat the snow, but it hit halfway through the trip," she said. "I drove most of the way in the death zone. Saw a dozen spin-outs at least. Couple of crashes. Had to divert from the QEW to the Dundas Line, and take the 9a from Hamilton."

"Did you beat your PB?"

"Maybe my PBIS," she said. "Personal best in snow."

A former hockey player, Tina was always competing, even with herself. Every time she arrived in Fiona from Toronto, the family had to endure an analysis of the shortcuts and maneuvers she'd used along the way. We always knew if she'd beaten her personal best.

"I'll call the *Guinness Book of Records*. Keep them posted."

"Don't listen to him, Tina." Mom handed me a cup of coffee. "He's in one of his moods."

"Because of the boyfriend," Tina said. "I'm all caught up."

"Do me a favour and go easy on BF," I said, imagining Tina ripping into him like Mom into the bread. "None of your relentless questions."

"You're a bit late for that," Mom said. "She already interrogated him."

"He seems frigging charming," Tina said. "What's he doing with you?"

"A mystery for the ages," Mom said.

"BF's up?"

"Up and gone," Mom said. "He went to Hamilton with Dad to get the ham for dinner. I bet your father's already doing his cricket songs."

I filled my mouth with coffee, stinging my tongue with bitterness and heat. Last night, I hadn't joined BF in the spare room off the landing. I'd stayed out late, then stamped up the stairs, making enough noise for him to hear me bypassing his door on my way to my old room, where I slept fitfully, but pointedly, alone.

"But Dad's car is still in the driveway."

"He'd already taken the snow tires off, so they took that piece of tin you rented," Tina said. "Dad must like him, to get into a Kia."

"In this weather?" I said.

"BF insisted. Said he wanted to do his part," Mom said. "The snow wasn't this ferocious when they left."

I thought of them in the Kia, on Highway 9a, somewhere between Fiona and Hamilton, the wipers beating, measuring out the rhythm of conversation, Alanis belting out "Ironic." Dad had finished talking about cricket songs, and was telling him about the ham, how it's spiral cut around its bone with a taut bit of fishing line. The Kia lost traction here and there, and the two of them felt a glitch in control.

"Did Dad drive, at least?"

"Does it matter?" Mom said.

"Matters for the insurance," Tina said.

"BF drives like a madman. You should have seen him on the 401 from Montreal. He drives like he's not even aware that he's driving."

"Dad'll hate that," Tina said.

"You couldn't have picked up the fucking ham on your way?" I said.

"Don't speak to me like that," Tina said. "Mom, say something."

"What would I say?"

"So, you two let them go? Let them walk out of here into the snow?"

"We thought it'd be done by now," Mom said.

"I didn't," Tina said.

"This is partly your fault, Tina," I said.

"What is partly my fault?"

"Yes, enlighten us," Mom said.

I thought of Dad and BF again, quiet now, as though words might send the car off the road. Silence in deference to danger. The Kia was small and had a forced intimacy. I'd experienced it yesterday. The heat of an adjacent body, the shared vibration of the motor, the endless breath of manufactured heat, the amplification of every shift of leg, every tightening of ponytail. All this would be magnified by the snow, swallowing them now, reducing visibility to nothing, making their capsule seem smaller, more perilous, cut-off from visual anchors. BF was squinting, maybe fending off one of his headaches. Dad's fist was tight around his seatbelt, keeping himself from reeling off driving tips.

"You're right," Tina said as I left the kitchen. "He's in one of his moods."

This was the first time I ever had to consider BF's death, and my reaction presaged embarrassing things for the future torture that awaited me. All I wanted was distraction. Procrastination. It had never seemed more important. I brought the portable radio into the washroom while I showered. In my life, it had only ever been tuned to the CBC, but the news was reporting about the blizzard, families' disrupted Easter plans, pile-ups on the highway. I chose jazz, not willing to risk a station that may play one of BF's songstresses. Once clean, I laced on a pair of Dad's old boots and went outside with the shovel, clearing the driveway of snow, jabbing and heaving with urgency, as though I were easing the Kia's path, wherever it was. I did the sidewalk, too, and the path around the house to the backyard. The flakes were fat; they collected on my hair and melted into drips that ran down my scalp, cooling me as my body heated with exertion. I shovelled the flagstones, the deck. When there was no path left, I pulled up the tub's lid. The water steamed. I checked the pH balance and found it insufficient. The filter lid, hidden under a hatch in the deck, was frozen shut. I hammered the ice away with the shovel until I could wrench the thing open and pour chlorine crystals into the filter basket. When I got back to the kitchen, Mom and Tina were covering casserole dishes with tin foil. Except for the ham, lunch was ready, and there were no distractions left.

"I'm getting a soak," I said.

*

The juxtaposition of warm water with cold air gave me the sensation of melting to the froth. I leaned against one of the jets and watched the dots of snow drift in the air between the tub and the house. Mom and Tina emerged in identical bathing suits visible under opened parkas. Naked legs; winter boots. Tina had inherited

Mom's impatience for easing into the water. Both plopped down, causing waves.

"You should calm yourself," Mom said. "I'm sure BF and your father are fine."

"We're not talking about it," I said.

"They have the sense to pull over. Go into Tim Hortons or something."

"Topic change."

"Well, we like him, in any event," Mom said, sharing a nod with Tina.

"Please stop."

"You like him, too," Mom said.

"I came out here to be alone. If you want to stay, we have to talk about literally anything else."

"OK, let's talk about why you're screwing it all up," Mom said.

I went under the water, where there was a purgatory of senses. A droning noise, a chemical taste, a warmth. Bubbles shot through my vision, a snowstorm of its own, a TV with no signal. Nothing received. I wanted to stay down there forever. The jets turned off and I heard voices sloshing above. The remaining bubbles rose, revealing four thick Zappacosta legs. They reminded me of hams.

"—but Gio's being careful," Tina was saying in my defence, when I was forced to resurface for air.

"Oh please," Mom said. She handed me my glass. "He's being careful with himself. Not with that poor angel being bored to death by your father right now."

"Let's change the subject," I said.

"You're hilarious, Gio," Mom said. "You and your little act."

"It's not an act," I said.

"It's cute, once you get past how pathetic it is," Mom said.

"You don't know anything about it," I said.

"I know *everything* about it," Mom said. "Can I tell you a story?"

I drank half my wine, shot Tina a look. It was our gay-sibling look of unspoken understanding.

"Which one will it be, Bonnie?" Tina said. "Gio running away when he was ten?"

"You can't escape who you are!" I said.

"You two think you're awfully smart," Mom said.

"Or will it be the statutory rape one?" Tina said. "The one where Jacko swept you off to the beach when you were essentially a child?"

"Follow your heart!" I said.

"Is this funny for you?" Mom said.

"Or maybe Papa Zap leaving Italy with only a thousand lira in his pocket?" Tina said.

"Take risks to live life!" I said.

"OK, Mr. and Mrs. Know-It-All. You tell one."

"Shall I spin the cliché wheel that is our family lore?" I said.

"I heard you wrote the book on the subject," Mom said, sipping, never taking her eyes off me. "Oh wait, you never got around to that. You never got around to so many things."

"I got around to getting out of here."

"You're back, though, aren't you? In the tub?"

"She's got you there," Tina said.

"You should put this in the book—us having a soak, telling our stories." Mom said. "Introduce all the people at once."

"Sounds boring," Tina said.

"Yeah, I'll leave this part out," I said.

"What will you say about how you ended up here?" Mom said.

"Very little."

"What will you say about how you let Brian MacDonald slip away?" Mom said.

"OK, tell me your story," I said.

"Now you *want* the story?" Tina said.

"Anything's better than this."

"Finally," Mom said, sitting up for her audience. "This one starts with your Uncle Roberto."

"The dead lug?" Tina said.

"The very same," Mom said. "Well, he's not my brother, and he's not your uncle."

"What?" Tina said.

"He's your half-uncle," she said. "My father had him in Italy with another woman, another wife. Papa Zap had a whole family over there. You have three other half-uncles running around the old country."

"Cripes, Bonnie," Tina said.

"Not so mouthy now, are you?" Mom said. She did her coy trick of checking her cuticles. "Never underestimate me."

Tina looked at me, gobsmacked. My mouth was hanging open; I could taste the mist of chlorine off the water.

"Close your mouth, Gio. You look like a simpleton." I did. "It was a whole scandal at the time. But this is not a story about Papa Zap *or* Uncle Rob. This is a story about my mother. Grandma Footloose."

"Are you sure?" I said.

"Quite." She thinned her lips into a smile. "Now I don't tell this one very often, so it's going to lack my usual zing and flair."

"Just stick the dismount," I said.

"I was never sure why Nonna married Papa. I loved them both, of course, but by the time I was old enough to understand things, they didn't seem to have much left for each other."

"Judging by the birth rate in that house, there must have been *something*," I said.

"Exactly. I like to think Nonna was happy, at first. But then we came, the kids, me and your aunts. One after the other, almost yearly. Back then, you know, there were miscarriages all the time, and she had her share. Stillbirths and crib deaths. I don't know how many. Your aunts could tell you. But it was loads. And you know what they all had in common?"

"They were all boys," I said.

"Clever Gio."

"Do I need more wine for the rest of this story?"

She handed me the bottle.

"See, I like to believe that she married for love. Because if she did it for love, then it makes sense that she'd start to mistrust love. Every dead baby boy that came was whisked away to the graveyard, or the incinerator."

"Holy moly," Tina said.

"Each one left her ashamed, but she didn't know why. Why couldn't she have a son? Then, bless him, Roberto found his dad. Just walked up to the front door of their house and knocked. When he revealed who he was, that was the end of happiness for Nonna. She realized she'd married someone else's husband—and that the original wife was still alive. She concluded that God was punishing her all this time. Mocking her, dangling her husband's son before her. The next years—decades, really—every diagnosis was God mocking her. Diabetes? Punishment. Arthritis? Screw you. A stroke? Ha! She never once believed she'd die, even when doctors would give her a year, eight months, she knew she'd live. She'd live on to be God's punching bag. Remember how many times she got the last rites?"

"I counted three," I said.

"Four," Tina said.

"Four, total," Mom said. "And she lived through it all, blew away every nurse and doctor. She subsisted on guilt."

"Poor Nonna," I said, thinking of her on her deathbed five years ago, pointing fingers at her daughters, saying she'd live forever, dismissing pain and decay with a wave of her hand and a stream of Italian expletives.

"Well, this is it," Bonnie said. "'Poor Nonna,' sure, whatever. But not because she lived in pain and remorse. 'Poor Nonna' because she *chose* to live that way. She could have lived with love. She could have treated me and your aunts as people, not as non-boys."

"And Uncle Roberto?" Tina said.

"She could have seen him as a gift. God giving her a son. But she didn't. She couldn't see what was right in front of her."

"Oh, I get it," I said.

"Yeah," Mom said. She lifted her hand from the tub and gripped the hair on the back of my head the way she used to when I misbehaved as a child. It was as violent as she ever got. Feeling the hot water soak down to my scalp, and the pull of her fingers, I was right back to being a kid. A stolen can of pop, doctored report cards, lying about skipping class. "Look at what's right in front of you, Gio. Know what it is. Because otherwise, everything is just a string of dead babies."

"Jesus," I said. "You still got it, Mom."

"Never underestimate me."

"That wasn't a compliment."

"Was it an insult?"

"It was an observation," I said. "This is how she does it, isn't it, Tina? This is how she punishes us."

"I never punished you! I gave you a wide berth. A *huge* berth. I let you get away with murder."

"Well, this is it," Tina said, imitating her. "You never *punished* us, punished us. But you got it in. You got it in this way."

"How?"

"You insinuate yourself," I said. "Admit it."

"Are you two deaf as posts? Did you hear that story I just told?" Mom said. "I grew up getting punished every step of the way. I didn't want you two spoiled brats to face that kind of thing."

"Yeah," Tina said. "And now look at him."

*

I pressed my pencil hard into the dragonfly's wing. I had a new idea for BF's tattoo, one that abandoned the shadows, the cartoonish colours, the implication of life. It would be inert and stark, but icon-like; something from a textbook or an ancient religion. Something that wouldn't die. I outlined the four wings in strong black lines, then sectored them into compartments. I barbed the legs. I patterned the body. But I made the eyes humanoid and slightly sarcastic, in a way I knew BF would like.

The design was reminiscent of leaded glass, so I did the work before the only leaded-glass window in the house, in the spare bedroom off the landing. The window was long and narrow and had a view of the street. Sitting cross-legged on the bed, I could flick my eyes from my sketchbook to the window to capture the way the lead bars made an image (in this case, birds), but also check to see if the Kia was returning. Every time there was a splash or rumble, anticipation rose in my gut and I inhaled sharply. This used to be Nonna's room, and with each inhale, I thought I could still smell her—urine and A535 and denture cleaner—through the odours of Mom's lunch preparations. And there was BF's eucalyptus shampoo, too, imported from Montreal and now clinging to the pillows. Off my own skin, there was the chemical sniff of the tub's chlorine rising from under my housecoat.

BF couldn't see me sitting there, of course, but I pretended he could. Watch this, I thought. Watch me make it up to you. Watch me create this thing you want, this thing I will have to look at over and over and over. I won't mind. Come back, and I won't mind. You can't die if your dragonfly is waiting for you.

By the time the Kia pulled up to the curb, the snow had evolved into rain and the street was coated in slush. BF stepped from the passenger's seat with the foil-wrapped Easter ham cradled in his elbow. He stood out against the bleak road. Neon-blue windbreaker, bright silvery ham, dazzling blonde hair. All my procrastination hadn't saved his life, but I decided it had. I needed a small piece of this outcome to be credited to how desperately I wanted it, how forgiven I was. Faith is just fear with good intentions.

BF slipped on the ice as he and Dad walked up the driveway. I touched the leaded glass, as though this could keep him from falling. But Dad steadied him, and they continued like that, awkward but connected, my boyfriend fastened to my father's arm, on the short walk from the street to the house, as I'd done countless times with my mother and grandmother.

There was no chance BF could see me—I knew every vantage point from the house, every sightline at every point of day—but he put on his half-smile and waved anyway, assuming I was watching. There was an inevitability to it. Not the gesture, but the message it contained and the bone-deep relief I felt when I received it: I am here.

story2.05April2018.m4a

[BFM]: The banter, babes. Jeez. We don't sound like that.

[GZO]: We do to me.

[BFM]: It's schtick.

[GZO]: It's music.

[BFM]: It's dishonest.

[GZO]: But it's true.

[BFM]: You're just like your mother. Making up details to suit yourself. You WANT it to be true.

[GZO]: So? It works for her, you have to admit.

[BFM]: But you hand a lot of the story over to Bonnie and her embellished version.

[GZO]: I want that in there for contrast. Makes my version seem, I don't know, TRUER. I'll include other people's, too. Like yours—I got into your head, like you told me to.

[BFM]: What other heads will you invade, besides mine and Bonnie's?

[GZO]: Dad. Maeve. Tina.

[BFM]: Well, don't go back and put all that in now.

[GZO]: Why not?

[BFM]: We don't have time. Just keep going. Don't edit. What's Tina's angle on things?

[GZO]: On what things? Grandma Footloose? The Roberto scandal?

[BFM]: All of it. Or the coming-out story?

[GZO]: For Tina, that's a love story.

3
Our Lady of Victory

The letter was dated two weeks ago, February 12, 1993, and was printed on paper with ceremonial heft. Tina could tell it wasn't fresh. It had been concealed from her somewhere; there were creases throughout. A drop of mercury would have to run zig-zags to find its way from the top to the bottom, move along the crumples, but inexorably down, off the page, to the rubber floor of the girls' locker room. Tina imagined the silvery droplet, its descent like her control, falling away.

"Dear Miss Marisol Cruz!" Tina read aloud to The Captain. "It is with great pleasure that I offer you admission to the University of Wisconsin-Madison Class of 1997, in the Department of Kinesiology!"

She stopped. Marisol's face was tenuous, worried. Their teammates, other students at Our Lady of Victory High School, had gone and the locker room was empty. Noises amplified the silence. Water dripped from the nozzles in the gang shower. On the other side of the wall, the Zamboni growled its way around the hockey rink.

"You look terrified," Marisol said.

"'Furthermore!'" Tina read. "Lordy, Captain, there's a 'furthermore.'"

"I know!"

"'*Furthermore,* I am delighted to inform you that the Athletics Department, along with the Department of Kinesiology, offer you an entrance scholarship in the amount of USD $25,000."

"That's a lot."

"It's a full ride," Tina said. "They're '*delighted.*'"

Of course they were delighted. The team was 8-0 this season. Victory was right there in the name of the school. The players felt blessed by this, though less blessed by the name of the team—the Hornets. It wasn't as intimidating as my sister would have liked. It was left to the girls to intimidate the other team, Tina especially. Her brutality and fearlessness made the opposing players edgy. They had to keep a slice of their awareness on Tina's position. The Hornets had become experts at gliding through that slice, using the spare seconds to slap the puck ahead of their opponents' attention. The puck was usually destined for The Captain. That's what the team called Marisol because that's what she was. She had speed, precision, a C on her jersey. If Tina was the enforcer, The Captain was the goal-maker.

Tina hadn't fallen for The Captain, though. She'd fallen for Marisol, the tall, ropey, serious Filipino girl who fretted in English class, who hadn't been able to tell Sister Fran why Daisy's dock-light was green at the end of *The Great Gatsby.* "Can't it just be a light? That's green?" she'd said. Marisol's talent wasn't in literature; it was in systems. She got math, got biology. She was as meticulous on graph paper as she was on the ice, zipping through calculus equations, eyes darting down rows of symbols. "Cripes, Rain Man, show your work," Tina would say, and Marisol would go back to the top of the page, with as much patience as she once had speed, to draw out the problem with crisp Xs and Ys, unravelling it for Tina with simple language.

"I'm so effing proud of you," Tina said.

The Captain greeted this with a hopeful lift of her eyebrows.

"And it's *Wisconsin.*"

"Not my first choice."

"Maybe not, but c'mon," Tina said, and listed the school's virtues, which she had memorized. They had researched universities together, Tina thinking ahead one year to when she would be applying. They'd both agreed University of Toronto was their first choice. The Captain would go this year, Tina the following September, and they'd be only an hour's train ride away in the interim. Toronto had also accepted Marisol, but it wasn't the best. Wisconsin was the best. "It's not what we planned, but we'll make it work."

"You think?"

"How far away can it be, anyway?" Tina said, even though she knew the school was a thousand kilometres away.

"Far," The Captain said. "Like, an eight-hour drive." Ten hours.

"I can buy a car."

"And learn to drive it?"

"Maybe Jacko's ancient Oldsmobile."

Dad was in the Oldsmobile at that moment, sitting alone in the parking lot, listening to the CBC and waiting to drive the two of them home. Tina imagined herself in the driver's seat instead of him, barrelling down the ribbon of highways connecting Fiona to Madison. She'd be alone in the car, surrounded by black trees, still unsure how to keep steady at these speeds—130, 140 km/h.

"I'll be there all the time," Tina said.

"Promise?"

"As often as I can."

"How often can that be? With practices and everything?"

"Once a month." Marisol's eyes widened. "Maybe less."

"Jeez."

"Don't do that. Don't 'jeez' me."

"It's just not that often."

"Don't go wussy on me here."

"Sorry."

"Don't effing apologize." Tina frowned. She'd learned to frown in millimetres. One millimetre was a warning; three foreshadowed a weekend without phone calls; five pointed to full-blown anger, and would require days of apology. "You're reminding me of my dad. Totally defeated—that lost Catholic look."

"That's unfair."

"To you or to him?"

"To both." Marisol rubbed a coat sleeve under her nose.

"Are you crying?"

"I promise I'm not."

"Good. Zip up."

"Yeah, your dad's been waiting extra long."

"He's not why we're leaving. We're leaving because there's nothing left to say. Unless you want to make a decision?"

"Am I supposed to decide now?"

"You do whatever you want, Captain."

"Monthly?"

"At most."

The Zamboni sighed, shut down.

"OK, so, Toronto then? I guess?" Marisol said.

"You *guess*?"

"I guess I don't know. I don't know yet." Marisol turned away from Tina's screwed-up squint of impatience. "Is that OK?"

"It has to be OK if that's how you feel."

"Peck me? Before we go out?"

Tina did, on her cheek. She put her hands under Marisol's parka and squeezed her above the hip. Marisol giggled at the cold and tickle.

"But I'd miss this," Tina said.

*

Tina needed a session with Nonna. They did them regularly, in our grandmother's room off the landing, watched by the leaded glass birds in the window. The space had an Ikea presswood highboy, a deep tub chair and a single bed with adjustable mechanics Nonna never used. On the end table was the ornate rosary box that she treasured, sitting next to her hearing aid and a tumbler containing her dentures. A digital clock had outsized green numbers—5:23 p.m.—so that Nonna could read the time with her trifocals off. She'd moved in with our family four years ago, after a series of small strokes left her unable to care for herself or her house. When she first saw her new bedroom, set up so sparsely, just for her, she said, "I'll die here." Bonnie, crying, said, "That's the general idea."

At first, Nonna was determined to help around the house—or what she thought was help. She rearranged the kitchen to her liking. She ran the carpet sweeper—*click! click! click!*—across the shag in the living room. She corrected Bonnie's parenting and cooking techniques. She praised the men of the house, calling us "strapping." She was undeterred by the steep stairs, carrying buckets of lathery water from the kitchen to the second-floor bathroom, saying a fresh pail would waste "perfectly good soap."

Within months, the stairs winded her, and she'd have to pause on the landing after taking the steps one at a time. Then, she had to climb them hand-over-hand, tendons straining under the skin as she clutched the banister. The sessions started around then, when Tina volunteered to help with Nonna's care. Tina clipped toenails, injected insulin, collected and disposed of urine pads. She combed the white wires of Nonna's hair, and plucked the errant ones that shot out near the corners of her mouth.

Now Nonna was sick. She refused to see the doctor and welcomed only the priest and her family. She winced with unreported agonies. She was weak, shapeless, immobile. She had to be graduated to proper diapers after multiple soilings of the bed. Tina and Bonnie cleaned, but the smell lingered, combined with her medicinal ointments and putrid breath.

I was sixteen then, and had no idea I was learning to care for the sick—lessons I would have to apply a few years later. I loathed breaching the threshold of Nonna's room. Energy drained from me the moment I did. Not Tina. For their sessions together, my sister sat between the window and the bed with one arm resting alongside our grandmother's body so that they could touch, lightly at first, but Nonna's claw would eventually dig into Tina's flesh to emphasize key points. When the old lady fell asleep, Tina would emerge from the room exactly as I couldn't: recharged, confident, full of life.

"He might leave, Nonna."

"Heh?"

"LEAVE! HE MIGHT LEAVE!"

"Arrrg," Nonna said. "Far?"

"VERY!"

"Toronto? Toronto—blech. A dump. *Full* of temptations. Don't you let him go there."

"NO, WISCONSIN."

"Heh?"

"WISCONSIN!"

"Arrrg," Nonna said. "Get me the thing."

Tina took the hearing aid from the bedside table and clipped it into Nonna's ear. She'd refused the device for months, like her trifocals and her dentures. Asking for it was a kind of affection.

Nonna moved her unfocussed eyes to my sister, turning her head slightly, but it caused a shift in the loose skin around her neck. The folds quaked, merged together into a deflated surface marbled with veins and dotted with mushroomy skin tags. Her face was sunken and slack, with divots where her teeth should be. Each spoken phrase required a sucking sound.

"Why would he go?" Nonna said.

"It's a great opportunity," Tina said. "For university."

"There are universities everywhere. Down the road, there's a university."

"That's what I've been trying to tell him," Tina pressed her fingers into Nonna's forearm for emphasis. "But this one, it's better than the rest. It's special."

"Special," Nonna said. "Why does everyone think they're special all of a sudden? The women, the nancies. Immigrants."

"You were an immigrant."

"And I wasn't special, was I?"

"Of course you are," Tina said. "And so is he."

"Arrrg," Nonna said. "You're young."

"But isn't it mature to want *him* to make the decision? He needs to. Otherwise, it's not worth a darn."

"What the hell's the matter with you, heh?"

"What the heck's the matter with *him*, you mean."

"No. You. *You.*" Now it was Nonna's turn for emphasis, pressing dints into Tina's meaty forearm. "I tell you all the time. I told your mother. I told your aunts. Don't let go. *Don't.* Be tough as tar."

"Is tar tough?"

"Stubborn as syphilis."

"Gross."

"Arrrg, nobody listens."

"I'm trying to keep control. But there are other factors." Tina detailed the scholarship, the benefits, the opportunity; the relinquishment, the loneliness, the long drive. "I don't want to stand in his way."

Nonna laugh-sucked in her empty mouth. "You're already in his way. That's where you oughta be."

"But the guilt."

"Guilt," Nonna said. "Who is he? He's a man. He doesn't know anything."

"I told you, he's special. He can think like a woman."

Nonna gripped with all five fingers this time. "Then why would you want him at all?"

"I just do." Tina looked into Nonna's blank old eyes. "I just love him."

"Love." Nonna's eyes re-found the ceiling. "Who cares? That's not why people do things. Is he afraid?"

"I think so."

"Good. Because *that's* why people do things."

"Is that why you do things?"

"I don't do anything."

They laughed.

"You laugh with me, you hear? Never with him."

"Never?"

"Almost never," she said. "It's a reward. Don't give it to him. Never laugh, never cry. And never dance."

"Right. You've always hated dancing."

"It's too easy to get carried away, moving around like that. That's how they get you—when you're laughing, crying, dancing. All those things. Don't bother with them. Shows weakness."

They sat in the underlit silence, arms still touching. No weakness, Tina thought. Like on the ice.

"Can I ask you a question?" Tina said. "How did you keep Papa?"

Nonna farted then, her trademark long, weak horn-blow ending in a bubbly sputter. She'd dozed off, or, at the very least, pretended to. Her grip was lax, her mouth hung open. Tina was left in the dim room, the rankness building around her, wondering if this was an answer to her question.

*

Tina stood outside the nook of the guidance counsellor. Everyone at Our Lady of Victory High School called it an office, but it wasn't. The space had once been a janitor's closet, a nub at the end of the hall where the drywall had been removed and replaced by glass to give it the illusion of space. Within the transparent box, Tina could see Miss Smythe smile-talking and Marisol looking bewildered. Young adults of every race grinned down at Tina from posters next to the door, broadcasting enlightenment from distant educational utopias. They were surrounded by lush campuses and faux-Gothic buildings—what passed for august in Canada. How were they so unworried, the people in this multicultural horde?

There was shuffling, the scrape of chairs. The door swung open and Marisol stepped out hugging a University of Wisconsin catalogue to her chest. Miss Smythe was right behind her, clutching her red pack of cigarettes.

"Miss O'Hara! Waiting for Miss Cruz, then, are you?"

"Yes ma'am."

Marisol rested her chin on the catalogue, frowned down at Miss Smythe's creased, unpolished loafers. Dull pennies stared out of them. Miss Smythe was in a man's V-neck sweater—baby blue, wool, too large for her frame—and a khaki pencil skirt. Her face always had a brownish smile and shining eyes projecting helpfulness. Her voice was reassuring and deep from an adulthood of du Maurier Ultra Lights.

"Teammates stick together, I see!" Miss Smythe said. "You all must be so proud of your Captain."

"The team's behind her, whatever she chooses."

"It's not much of a choice, is it, Miss Cruz?"

"I'm still not sure," Marisol said.

"Jitters! What you're feeling is *so* natural. But you'll see!" She continued to Tina, "Already thinks she'll be homesick. Tina here will talk some sense into you."

"I'll do my best."

"Work your magic!" Miss Smythe said. "After all, I might be having this conversation with you in a year's time."

"You never know."

"I have a feeling!" Miss Smythe placed her hand on Tina's shoulder, a blessing with cigarettes, before striding away.

"Did you tell her?" Tina said.

"Of course not."

"It sounds like she knows."

Tina regarded the guidance counsellor with suspicion as she shrank down the hall and paused to talk to Sister Fran, the English teacher. Tina often found herself scanning women for traces of difference. Miss Smythe had a moderate reading. The Hornets made fun of her, joking that she watched them in the shower through a crack in the tile.

Sister Fran read as a normal. Normal and a virgin. She was among the women Tina pretended to be. Alone in her room, Tina imagined that she was as bird-boned and graceful as Sister Fran, wearing a simple tunic and complicated makeup, cooing to the students to read *The Stone Angel.*

What would it be like to be one of them? Even before she knew who they were, she wondered. When Tina was fourteen and babysitting, the curiosity was overwhelming. After she'd put the kids to bed, she'd rummage through their mothers' dresser drawers. She fondled vibrators, marvelled at condoms. She'd put on the women's scarves and earrings, sit at their desks and mimic them. For five minutes, Tina was Ms. Chéhab, the manager of the funeral home; or the Ob-Gyn; or the housewife with too many perfumes. For five minutes, she wanted to know what it was like to be undifferent.

"Put your head up," Tina told Marisol. "You look ashamed and you shouldn't be ashamed. This is all good stuff. You got early acceptance *everywhere.*"

"I know."

"You're a superstar. You heard Miss Smythe. It's a frigging celebration!"

"I know."

"So hold your head high."

Marisol lifted her head, but trained her eyes off Tina's face, towards the hall, and said, "Can I ask you a question?"

"Sure."

"Why did you make me apply to so many schools?"

"So that you'd be in exactly this position."

"I'd be happier if there was only one option."

"That—wow!—that's a terrible attitude."

"Sorry. But it'd be easier. Let's face it." Marisol found it in herself to look Tina in the face. "It's like when my dad died. It was hard, but there wasn't treatment, and that made it easier. He had to go. And he did."

"Maybe the decision is easier than you think?" Tina said. "Have you thought about what people in Wisconsin will say about people like you? Like us?"

"Don't ask, don't tell? Isn't that what they do down there?"

Marisol attempted a laugh. Tina kept herself from joining her, saying, "They could eat you alive."

"I don't think they will. Miss Smythe said Madison is a pretty open place."

"Jeez! You *did* tell her, didn't you?"

"No, of course not."

"We have a deal."

"I know."

"Not a word until we're both out of here."

"I didn't say a word, I swear."

The bell rang. Streams of uniformed students poured into the hall.

"Peck me?" The Captain said. She always asked at the wrong moment, somewhere public or before a game. At least she blushed. Tina loved when she did, because she always smiled at the same time to counteract her bashfulness. The smile was always wider on the left side and showed off the charming snaggle of her incisor.

"No," Tina said and frowned three millimetres.

*

Tina looked affronted by the fish pie. Our father's unique touch was to rake a fork across the mashed potato topping so the lines browned along the peaks and stayed buttery in the valleys. It was a family favourite, taking pride of place in the centre of the dining room table, flanked by an arugula salad and a platter of roasted asparagus. Marisol and I were already in our seats, explaining universities to Danny. Jacko was losing a battle with a wine cork. Tina put her hands on her hips and said, "Are we really doing this?"

"Yes, it's Friday," Jacko said.

"After what just happened?"

"Especially after what just happened."

"Then give me the bottle," Tina said. She rescued the white Zinfandel from our father's hands. "You always do it wrong."

"If you say so, Tina," Jacko said.

Bonnie entered with the priest. He'd been consoling her on the landing; she'd stopped crying now but was raw-eyed and pale. Father Dupuis was sniffing the meal's aromas with his veiny, purplish nose. His corpulence was responding to his breath. Strain-lines formed and unformed around the buttons of his shirt. His white collar was nearly subsumed by his jowls.

"Bountiful spread, isn't it?" he boomed. "What's on the menu?"

"Friday pie," Danny said.

"It's a pound of butter with cod and haddock," I said.

"And salmon," Dad said. "We have a great fish guy."

"Fish on Fridays! Nice that some traditions don't die, isn't it?"

"Would you like to stay for dinner, Father?" Jacko said.

"If there's enough—" Dupuis said.

"There may not be," Tina said.

"I don't have much of an appetite," Bonnie said, indicating that Jacko should fill her glass with Zin. "Stay, Father. For your trouble."

"Hardly any trouble. It's in my job description, isn't it?"

He had administered the last rites. Twenty minutes ago, we had been clustered around Nonna's bed in the netherworld off the landing. Tina had kept her gaze on Nonna's face, not even flicking a comforting eye to our weeping mother. The priest had placed a scrap of Communion wafer on Nonna's tongue, like a hit of acid. There had been incantations. His holy fingers, liver-spotted and slicked with oil, had drawn a cross on Nonna's forehead. The old lady had not reacted to the unction and viaticum; she'd merely inflated and deflated. Maybe it had been the tranquility that disturbed Tina. This had been Nonna's fourth time getting the last rites, and she'd slept through it, as if even she were bored of this rote, grim chore. She was my sister's dimming oracle. There was nothing Tina could do about that. The letter and the last rites,

The Captain and Nonna; everything suddenly seemed temporary to Tina.

And now she had to sit down with all of us for a fish supper.

Dupuis blessed the meal, thanking Christ for the flow of grace into our family. "The same grace we have shared with our sister Fiona, so close to her calling by the Lord."

"She's always been more of a grandmother than a sister to me," I said.

"She's your sister in Christ," Marisol said.

"Correct," Dupuis said, breaking the pie's crust with a spoon.

"And you're my brother, even though you're a father, Father?"

"You know the answer to that already, don't you, son?"

"And I'm your son, even though I'm your brother?"

Dupuis chuckled. "You haven't changed since Sunday school, have you Gio?"

"Yeah, you still got it," Tina said. She frowned down the table at me, a warning.

"So, if I follow, The Captain and Tina are sisters?" I said.

"Of course," Dupuis said.

"Gio," Tina said. When she was annoyed, she said my name as though it were two words. Gee. Oh. "Mom, tell Gio to behave."

Mom's mind was still upstairs with Nonna. She passed the platters from Danny to Jacko without taking any food. "What's he doing now?"

"Being himself," Tina said.

"Then you should be used to it," Bonnie said.

"I'm an acquired taste," I said. "Like Catholicism."

Jacko dipped his fork up and down in the air, signalling for me to cool it.

"Sorry," I said. "Sorry, Father. When I'm emotional, I make jokes."

"I do recall Sunday school, yes."

"Did you have to go to Sunday school, Father?" Danny asked.

"A long time ago," Dupuis said.

"Did you, Marisol?"

"Of course, Danny."

"And now you're going to a big school?" Danny said. "Far away?"

"Yes, the Captain was telling us that she got into Wisconsin," I said. "Can you believe it?"

"I most certainly can," Jacko said. "That's wonderful, Captain, although I can't say I'm surprised. Huzzah!"

"Toronto too," I said.

Tina glared at me. It baffled us both that we came from the same genetic mash. She thought her determination and power flowed from Nonna, skipping a generation like diabetes, while my creativity and quips came straight from Mom. The things we had in common—the titanic nose, the thick brown hair, the homosexuality—were incidental to Tina, relative to our disproportionate inheritance of athleticism and artistry.

Tina had insisted that we make a pact about the homosexuality. We'd confessed it to each other last year, after I'd caught her and Marisol making out on the basement stairs when they thought no one was home. It had been an easy conversation—a confirmation of suspicions, really—but she didn't want our parents to know. I thought Jacko and Bonnie had already figured it out, but Tina prevailed, saying any revelation would make it real, permanent; it would let the situation slip from her control. Worst of all, she told me, the news could make its way to Nonna, a homophobe of the highest order, who categorized homosexuality along with tarragon, Anglicanism, birth control, and aluminum siding—just another disgusting thing that non-Italians did to make themselves important.

"So many choices!" I said. "Captain, you must be stoked."

"Stoked?" Marisol said.

"The only thing we stoke is a fire," Tina said. "But yes, she's thrilled. Queen's and U-Vic, too. The Captain has her choice."

"I'm sure The Captain can answer for herself," Dad said.

All heads turned to Marisol. She'd just slid the fork from her mouth. We watched her chew.

"Just a sec," I said. "Her mouth is full of fish."

"Could you discipline him, please?" Tina said.

"For what?" Mom said.

"He's winding me up," Tina said. "Be a parent for, like, one second?"

"Watch your mouths, both of you," Dad said.

"He's not even *funny,*" Tina said.

Dupuis spooned mash to his face, rapt.

"I guess I'm excited," Marisol said, finally.

"And you should be," Jacko said. "Wisconsin's the holy grail. I hope to drive Tina down there myself next year."

"No pressure," I said.

"It's not perfect," Tina said. "It's far."

"Surprised to hear you say that. It's all you used to talk about," Jacko said. "Which school are you leaning towards, Marisol?"

"Toronto," Marisol said. "I guess."

"You *guess*?" Tina said.

"Any particular reason?" Dad said.

"No."

"Money?"

"No."

"Huh," Jacko said. "Well, I'm sure we can all agree that your success is something to celebrate."

"This isn't a celebration! It's stupid to be sitting here, eating Dad's Friday pie and talking about schools, when Nonna's dying, like, *right there*," Tina said. "Yeesh."

"Yeesh?" Jacko said.

"Yeesh," Tina confirmed.

"Yeesh!" Danny said.

We laughed; Tina didn't. She cupped her hands around her face and pulled them back over her hair to her ponytail. She scowled at our mother, who was emptying the bottle of wine into her glass.

"Don't give me that look, Tina," Mom said.

"You aren't even *sad*."

"You have no idea how sad I am," Bonnie said. "None."

"If that were you up there, I'd be bawling my eyes out."

"Aren't you a saint," I said.

"Giovanni, this is your final warning," Jacko said.

"At least he's acting how I expect him to act," Tina said. "Like a little frigging smart aleck."

Bonnie nodded at her wine in resigned agreement.

"The rest of you are just disappointments," Tina said.

"Even the priest?" I said.

"Tina, we're all sorry the world isn't exactly as you'd like," Jacko said. "But here we are."

"Disappointment is part of death," said Dupuis. "Part of grief. But it's misplaced. Faith allows us to know your grandmother will live on. So you see, child, with faith there's no need for anger, is there?"

"God doesn't mind," Marisol said.

"I beg your pardon, dear?"

"He doesn't mind that Tina's upset. He would know what Tina's going through. He'd forgive her, right? Grieving isn't a sin."

"It is without faith, because then it's worthless, isn't it? It's despair."

"She has faith, though. Tina's different. Different than what everyone thinks."

The table was silent.

"Right?" Marisol said. She tried to lock her eyes with my sister, but Tina was looking at her unfinished pie.

"Wisconsin," Tina said. It was the closest thing to profanity I'd ever heard her say.

*

Sunday mornings, the Hornets played a scrimmage game, one half of the team against the other. Tina blatantly unwatched The Captain as they geared-up in the locker room. She laced her skates with violent tugs, clipped on her neck guard with a loud snap.

The other girls must have felt the arc of cold electricity shoot from Tina to Marisol. The chatter dropped to a lower octave, a slower tempo. The room crackled with potential and fear.

This was Tina's desired effect. She hadn't slept much in the two nights since the last rites, and she needed fuel from somewhere. The previous night, the phone had pealed out a dozen rings, the caller ID showing the name of Marisol's dead father. Tina had the family on strict lockdown. Do not answer. She'd had an argument with Bonnie, who'd given her sisters an open invitation to come by and sit with Nonna, which limited Tina's own time in the room off the landing. She'd woken up early this morning to sit with Nonna, hoping for one last claw-grip—one more top-up of doggedness, a stiffening of backbone that could send her sailing through the scrimmage with brutal grace. None came.

Hockey is heat. It was easy to forget that, sitting in the stands, as Jacko was that morning, bundled in his beige parka, a Hornets toque pulled down over his ears, sipping instant coffee from a styrofoam cup. But on the ice, warming up, the players were boiling in adrenaline, locked into pads and elasticized bras and polyester jerseys, each a furnace of trapped sweat and energy, with helmets like plugs to keep the pressure contained. By the time Tina hunched at the red line, she was fevered and pulsing. The Captain took her place a few centimetres away. The pause before face-off had a tense intimacy; they breathed each other's air, the sound of inhalation amplified by their helmets.

"I prayed for your grandmother," The Captain said. "Any news?"

The puck dropped. Tina rocketted it to the right wing and pitched her shoulder into The Captain's throat. The Captain tumbled, gasped out "oops," as though this moment of violence were a mistake, and landed on her backside. Tina caught a glimpse of this on her way to her new position, left of the crease, where she awaited the puck, nabbed it, and shot it up, high, beyond the goalie, who expected the thing at her waist and could do nothing but scramble with her cartoonish gloves, raised too late and too low. 1-0.

On the next play, Tina skirted three players to come around the back of the goal. The unnecessary move confused them and they swarmed to envelop her and protect the net. Tina still had momentum and slammed through the wall of girls, throwing The Captain against the boards with a crunch of gear. Tina could feel the cold, dry air against her cheeks as she sped up the length of the rink to her own side. She registered the blue line, the red line, triangulating her location using the memorized scuff-marks on the boards. Her thighs were pistons, the meat of them surging with power as she curled to a stop with a spray of ice. She hammered her stick, beating out a signal until the puck came her way. Ludicrous to pass up the ice to one's own goal, but the other girls were in her thrall, and one of them shot the puck to her. Tina looked down the rink, zeroed in on Marisol.

She knew that The Captain was onto her. Marisol had peeled away from her teammates and positioned herself at centre ice. Smart, Tina thought. The Captain had realized that she couldn't predict Tina's next move and had prepared for anything. She had a crouched, solid stance, neither offensive nor defensive—just ready. This was how The Captain played, exploiting an honest position for the greatest gain, inspiring workable formations that could adapt to the situation. It was clean, strategic playing, even vulnerable. How could this creature, so sure on the ice, wilt so easily elsewhere?

Tina pushed off towards her. The puck stayed husbanded between rapid cuppings of her stick. At the last moment, she passed to a teammate, and collided with The Captain square-on. They were a single, tangled unit. The Captain wedged her stick against Tina's hip and stayed locked there as they glided, breathing hard, pads smashing. The puck was down the ice; Tina was blind to it, caught, and couldn't turn to the action. She elbowed The Captain in the gut so hard she felt a phantom pain in her own stomach. They split, regained independence on their blades, as the coach's whistle screamed out. Tina had gotten the assist. 2-0.

In opposing penalty boxes, they were adjacent, but split by a plexiglass divider. The Captain took off her helmet, squirted water in her mouth and all over her face. Tina was hunched forward, stoic, though her instinct was not to be. She had to fight the urge to look through the plastic, assess the damage. She'd know the extent of it from one glimpse at Marisol's face. She didn't dare look. She set her face like Nonna would, unbothered by the surrounding drama or the precedent of expectations. The Captain tapped her stick on the divider, once, twice, then in a series of hard bangs, to make sure the situation was clear. Tina had chosen this and wasn't going to indulge communication until they were back on the ice.

The game continued in this vein. After more penalties—two cross-checking, one elbowing, all against The Captain—Tina was sent alone to the locker room. She ignored the coach's command to report to his office, as well as the showers, and instead slipped from her gear and headed for the exit in a stink of sweat. She kicked the arena door open and stomped into the winter. The fresh-fallen, powdery snow escaped from under her boots before the soles kissed the pavement.

The windshields in the parking lot had shimmers of frost—all but the Oldsmobile. Dad was warming the car for her. She could see him following her with his eyes, twisting the rusty hairs of his beard. He didn't break his stare when he popped the trunk. The rear hatch opened ominously through exhaust that was thick and blue in the cold.

Tina stored her duffle and sticks, and settled into the passenger seat, looking straight ahead at the arena's exit. "Let's go."

"The Captain needs a ride too."

"Let's go."

"Not yet."

"Can't you let Bonnie punish me?"

"You'd like that. Get off the hook."

"Darn right."

Jacko turned the car off. The key chain swung and jangled.

"So, let's go. Let's get it over with."

"We're waiting for The Captain."

"No, we're not. The whole point is that we're not."

"I'm waiting for her, then."

"You're such a sucker, Dad."

"If you say so, Tina."

"We're just going to sit here?"

"That's right."

"In silence?"

"I can do some cricket songs, if you'd like."

Tina pressed her palms onto the glove compartment. Her pulse hadn't dropped since the game. She could feel it in her wrists.

Jacko imitated a cricket, "*riiiiiii, riiiiiii, riiiiiii.*"

"Dad, shut up. You don't understand what's going on."

"You'd be surprised."

"I'd be shocked. I'd frigging *die* of shock."

"And I thought you could handle anything."

He put a hot hand on her shoulder.

"Don't touch me."

"Things are about to get harder." His voice sent calm, subtle tremors down to his fingers. She could feel them through her coat. "People go away."

"Only when they choose to."

"That's not true. Look at Nonna." He gripped her harder. "Most times, there's nothing you can do about it."

"You still have to try," she said. "You try, even if you're pretending."

"I don't think you have to pretend. But like you said, I don't understand," he said. "Take me and your mother. We love each other, right—"

"Gross. Please don't."

"—and we simply say it. And it's fine. Can you imagine what it would be like if we didn't have a way to say it? If those words hadn't been invented?"

"Maybe you'd shut up from time to time."

"Yeah, that's right. We wouldn't have a choice. It'd be hard. We'd have to make jokes or speak in code, because it's harder when there are no words for it. You know the story of your mother and me at the beach. It's a beautiful story."

"It makes me barf."

"That's only because we're your parents. We met when we were young—younger than you are now—and it all unfolded in a way that was new to me and to her. But we were ready for it, you know? Somehow. We had, I don't know—information. Emotional information. We knew how to say what we felt because it already existed around us. We were trained for it. It's not always that way. It's not always that easy to tell the story. Are you listening?"

"You had it easy. Lucky you."

"Yeah. Lucky me. Because for some people, the story is underneath everything else. You have to sneak it in."

The doors to the arena opened and the girls started exiting. One of the younger players was helping The Captain limp towards the Oldsmobile. Marisol waved at them as if saying "halt!"—as if they might peel away and leave her there.

"I just realized," Tina said, watching Marisol approach through the salt-splattered windshield. "You're completely inadequate in every way."

"If you say so, Tina," he said with a chuckle. He popped the trunk for The Captain. "If you say so."

*

Nonna died; Tina missed it. It happened the night after the scrimmage, while my sister was sleeping in the tub chair. When she woke at dawn, she could see Nonna's breathing had stopped, but it seemed that our grandmother had merely been switched off or that there was some small technical error that, once solved, would reboot her. Tina puzzled over the problem, knowing at once that there was no solving it, but feeling sure that she could. It was only when Bonnie came in with a cup of tea that Nonna's death became real.

Our house, already a constant churn of aunts, uncles, friends, children, neighbours, and Hornets, became twice as bustling. A supply of casserole dishes and Tupperware continued unabated for days, all containing the reheatable, freezable, family-sized meals that every local Catholic had in their cooking repertoire in case of death. In the living room, Bonnie and her sisters took weepy shifts on the couches, retelling every story of Nonna's life. Acquaintances arrived, departed; they moved through the folding chairs that we only deployed for brushes with the divine: births, deaths, baptisms, confirmations, Easters, Christmases, the series finale of *Cheers*. The phone rang as though Nonna were running for Parliament.

Tina didn't play that week. She funnelled her energy into making funeral arrangements. She assigned roles to each of us. Danny collected wads of tissues from the living room and kept the snacks circulating. I was assigned food organization, labelling every container that arrived with the contents and the giver's name—"Danish puff, Gladys O'Brien"—using a Sharpie and masking tape. Dad was sent to the den to write the eulogy. Mom and her sisters were told to go through the photo albums to find a picture of Nonna so that the funeral director, Ms. Chéhab, could prepare her body for the open casket.

Tina flipped through the Yellow Pages, making snapping sounds with each sheet, licking her finger every fifth turn. She ordered flowers in a curt, clipped manner on the kitchen phone, then dictated the obituary to the Fiona *Spectator* and called the Canadian-Italian Club to arrange the reception.

"That's unacceptable," she said. "Orecchiette, not penne. Romaine, not iceberg. And you always do the salads with too much oil, not enough vinegar. These people are grieving, they don't want to eat greasy salad. My grandmother always commented on that. Everybody does. The whole town thinks so. It's not flipping brain surgery. It's salad. And only red wine vinegar. No white."

My aunts and mother, listening from the living room, responded like a Greek chorus.

"Oh, hasn't she got a mouth on *her*?" Isabella said.

"And why *shouldn't* she?" Filomena said.

"Runs in the family," Lia said.

"Truer words!" Teresa said.

"Remember Mama taking on Papa?" Bonnie said.

"She could give as good as she got!" Isabella said.

"It's the kind of lesson every girl needs, growing up," Filomena said.

"Lord knows we learned it!" Lia said.

"You give 'em hell, Tina!" Teresa said.

"Is there more sherry?" Bonnie said.

They turned their attention back to the stacks of photo albums, reviewing each tiny window into our family history with scrutiny and tears and giggles.

"Oh, *this* one! Remember that chiffon?" Isabella said.

"Moths have *gorged* on it by now." Filomena said.

"She wore it to Danny's christening. Downright *elegant*!" Lia said.

"*That* was the baptism with the chicken supreme?" Teresa said.

"Tough as *nails*, it was," Bonnie said.

"No *flavour*!" Isabella said.

"Who'd want to remember *that*?" Filomena said.

Tina sat with The Captain in the breakfast nook, their fingers intertwined, but hidden under the table.

"Listen to them all," Tina said. "Cackling when they should be crying."

"They're crying, too," Marisol said.

"It's disgraceful."

"No it's not. Not everyone's going to do this like you do."

"Bet you weren't laughing when your dad died."

"We did, a bit," Marisol said. "Sometimes it's all you can do."

"Laughing shows weakness. Have any other ideas?"

"Spend some time with the body," Marisol said.

"That's dumb."

"No really. The soul is gone and you see that it's for real."

"Sounds like hocus-pocus."

"I want to help." Marisol squeezed Tina's fingers. "But I'm not sure I'm helping you."

"Just don't leave."

"You mean tonight? Or, like, in general?"

"I'm not even sure," Tina said.

"Wow, there's a first time for everything," Marisol said. "I'm still not sure either."

Another swell of laughter came from the living room. Tina jumped up, stamped out of the room and up the stairs. Her footsteps shook the house. She grabbed a photo of Nonna that she had wedged in the frame of her bedroom mirror, carried it downstairs, and slapped onto the coffee table at the centre of our aunts as though it were a royal flush.

*

Tina arrived an hour before the viewing. Joey, the undertaker's teenage son, hadn't even put on his tie or jacket when he unlocked the doors for her. He compressed his face in sympathy as Tina hustled past him into the empty funeral home.

"Tina, it's good to see you again. I'm only sorry it's under these circumstances," Joey said. He had a slight lisp; "circumstances" set off an alarm in Tina's brain. Thircumthtanthes. She wondered how many times this kid and his family members had said that in their lives. *I'm only sorry it's under these circumstances.* The words had always seemed kind, but this time they felt abstract and bloodless, implying affection and remove all at once. This family breathed those words like oxygen; "these circumstances" were their livelihoods.

"Yeah, same," Tina said.

He walked ahead of her towards the viewing room. His gait was what Nonna would call "squirrelly."

"You're not working the door, right? When the people come?"

"My mother will be doing that."

"OK, great," Tina said. "No offence, Joey."

"Of courth."

He showed Tina to Nonna, then closed the door behind him. Silence. The Rose Room had the clean, boring quality of a hotel suite with its grey couches, ivory wallpaper, beige rugs and ochre drapes. On the wall hung pictures of dusty pink roses framed in goldish rectangles that hinted at opulence. Every element was aggressively inoffensive and vacuumed within an inch of its life.

The only hint of personalization was the corpse. Morticians try to make bodies look peaceful—something Nonna had never been—but Ms. Chéhab had failed. Nonna looked like herself. Below the trowelled foundation, Tina saw the lupine awareness and weary knowledge in our grandmother's face. Her hands were on her chest, folded, with her rosary slid between the fingers—the one she loved, that had always been in its ornate box by her bed. She was in a blue satin dress that had filaments of silver threaded through it in squiggles. It had been Tina's choice, after a long argument over a black, shapeless garment that Bonnie preferred. The victory paid off. Nonna looked immortal.

"I got you the Kleenexes you like, the three-ply," Tina said. "We never told you this, but they're super-expensive. You know, for tissues. We knew you'd never let us buy them if you knew they were $3.99 a go."

Silence. Tina opened her backpack and unloaded her haul. She placed the premium Kleenex under the decorative box-covers—white plastic with gold piping—and pulled starter tissues through the pre-cut slits on top. She hid the provided, down-market tissues in a cupboard. She changed her footwear from boots to flats, and went to work rearranging the flowers, giving the lilies pride of place around the body.

"I'm going to downgrade these carnations to the end tables. I'll make sure the cards are visible so everyone can see who cheaped out. You'd like that?"

Silence. Tina went on, describing the schedules and arrangements she'd set. Obituary, orecchiette, Offertory hymn; priest, pallbearers, Prayers of the Faithful; embalming, Ecclesiastes, eulogy.

"Dad's writing it, so it's bound to be cheesy. I mean, the things he comes up with! You should have heard him the other morning in the car. He's going to tell the story of how your parents named you Fiona after the town before they even came from Italy. Their hopes and dreams and all that."

Silence.

And then, noise. The Rose Room doors opened, and crowds surged through them. I only did an hour in the receiving line, but Tina stood there all day with Bonnie and our aunts. Neighbours and second cousins and parishioners moved through, squeezing Tina's hands, looking in her face with sadness and concern. It was hagiography by assembly line, concise memories of Nonna's virtues, delivered in such a random chronology that Tina gave up stringing them into a story. Up and down the line, she could hear the snippets of our aunts' reactions.

"She could be tough, but always *fair*."

"She was *pushing* us."

"She *loved* us."

"She could *never* say."

"She *showed* it."

"She was *proud*."

"She was *hard*."

"Hard is *good*."

The town's professional mourners were out in force—local Italians we saw exclusively in this building. Efficient in nothing but the realm of death, these hunched men and their Aqua-Netted wives zipped down the line of relatives at a shocking speed, skipping chatterboxes who had stopped to reminisce, and jabbing out "*mie condoglianze*" to each of the bereaved. Their fingers were already slipping away from Tina's hand when she went in for a shake. "And how do you know my grandmother?" Tina asked them. They took a moment of indignity, then coughed out "*per rispetto,*" out of respect, and moved on. They had other cadavers on the schedule.

Marisol and the Hornets arrived late in the day, appropriately in a swarm. They were energized after practice, giving hugs instead of handshakes. Aunt Maeve, caught in the middle of the melee, found them hilarious.

"Kinda circus your granny would've hated. Ha!" she said.

"Did you come all the way across town to say that?" Tina said.

"I got nothing else to do. Good a time as any to say goodbye."

"How kind."

"And not just to this old battle-axe. All of you. I'm moving off to New York in a few months."

"Jeez, at your age?"

"I'm not so old, kid. I have the Brooklyn house to settle up. JJ left it to me. Your grandfather had a sick sense. Some joke, eh? Might as well take advantage before I end up like Fiona from Fiona over there," Maeve said. "But listen, kid, I don't mean to be cheeky. Your granny, she was trapped. Trapped by worry. And all that worrying she did? All her life and that? It's over now."

"She never worried. She was never afraid."

"Sure she was," Maeve said. "Gotta think about these things."

"Do I?"

"Yeah. It's good, see? She's gone now. Free as the wind."

"Who's *that*?" Marisol said when her turn came. She tipped her head at Maeve, who was now bending before the coffin, clasping Nonna's hand, whispering something.

"My dad's surly aunt. I don't know what she's doing here," Tina said. "I don't know what half these people are doing here."

"They're paying their respects."

"Yeah, but why? They didn't even know her."

"I think it's more for you than your Nonna. You and your family," Marisol said. "I won't ask for a peck—"

"Keep your voice down."

"—but I'll call you later."

A wake at Aunt Lia's followed this juggernaut of condolence. Tina didn't go straight away; she wanted to set the room right before the pre-burial blessing, scheduled for the following morning. After the crowds left, Ms. Chéhab asked Tina if she needed anything.

"I want another moment with my grandmother, if that's OK."

"We do the prep at this point, so we don't allow—"

"At these prices?"

"Right, very well. I suppose a few minutes couldn't hurt," Ms. Chéhab said and closed the casket lid. "I'll see you at the wake. Give Joey a knock on the office door when you're ready, and he'll start the prep."

After hours of circulating mourners and the distant click of Ms. Chéhab pulling shut the main doors, The Rose Room was silent again. The textured wallpaper and soft drapery sucked up even Tina's own noise. It reminded her of her babysitting days, when the kids had been put to sleep, and she could lurk through the home, violating all its codes and secrets, or pretend to be the woman of the house. Here, she tried to be Ms. Chéhab, walking with the funeral director's professional elegance across the carpet. She ran a finger along the wainscotting, checked the sconces for spiderwebs. She picked up some fallen lily petals. Last, she lifted the coffin lid to check on the body. Glancing at the unmoving woman inside, Tina said, "It's good to see you, Nonna. I'm only sorry it's under these circumstances."

Silence.

"Do you remember that funeral—I think it was Aunt Dot's—when I asked you and Mom why we had to call Ms. Chéhab 'mizz' instead of 'missus,' even though she was married to Mr. Callino? And before Mom could explain the whole kept-her-own-name thing, you said, 'because she's on her high horse, that's why.'"

Neither of them laughed. My sister leaned in and pecked my grandmother on the cheek. The act reminded her of Marisol, and Tina felt a flash of weakness. She didn't want Nonna to see it, so she pulled the coffin lid down on its quiet, expensive hinge, and wiped imaginary fingerprints from the handle.

✷

Moments later, Tina approached the funeral director's office. The laughter was loud enough—that must have been why Tina looked so angry when she entered, caught sight of us, and upgraded her face from outrage to annoyance. Joey was on his knees; I was in the office chair. Our ties were over our shoulders, our belts were flopping. Porn aside, suits are terrible for blowjobs.

I locked eyes with Tina, gave her our gay-sibling look. An exchange of homosexual data. My blood was reassigned to my face, which reddened with embarrassment. Joey sprung from the floor, overflowing with apologies as I turned to the wall to zip up.

"You cannot, *cannot*, say a word. Not a *peep*," Joey said. "I'm really, really thorry, Tina."

"I'm not your babysitter anymore," Tina said. "Get your things, Gio."

"I don't have things."

"Then get my things."

I collected her backpack from The Rose Room. When I returned to the foyer, she was standing by the exit with her gloves and coat on, hood up, ready for the cold. Joey's terrified sniffles floated in from the washroom.

"You want to check on her?" Tina said. For a second, I thought she meant Nonna. "Little Miss Vacuum?"

"I should, shouldn't I?"

She shrugged.

"Joey we're going," I yelled.

"OK," came his muted croak through the door. "Probably, yeah, you should."

Out in the biting dark evening, we walked a block without speaking, listening instead to our different paces, squeaked out between our boot soles and the snow.

"How long?" she said.

"A few months."

"Who knows?"

"You."

"Ah."

"I should go back, shouldn't I?" I stopped walking, letting the frigidity wrap around me.

"Don't bother."

"He's terrified."

"It'll do him good. Let him cry in the toilet."

"Is it cold out here, or is it just you?"

"That's not your best, Gio." She put her hands on her hips, the motion repeated in her long shadows on the snow in front and behind, cast by street lamps. "That was weak. And so are you, if you go back."

"That's your advice?"

"Trust me."

"You mean trust Nonna," I said. "Grandma Footloose. What did you get from her, anyway?"

"What, you didn't love her? Your own grandmother?"

"Of course I did."

"You have a screwed-up way of showing it. Joey Callino, for god's sake. What would Nonna say if she saw what I saw?"

"Who cares?" I said. "This is all super-sad and everything. I'm sadder than I thought I'd be. But isn't there a tiny part of you that's glad she's going to take her opinions to the grave? A teeny-tiny part? She hated people like us."

"At least she wasn't afraid."

"Everyone's afraid," I said. "Though I guess Nonna's not anymore."

"If everyone's afraid, why were you laughing? I heard you two giggling away."

"Well, the situation was pretty hilarious," I said. "Objectively speaking."

"How can everyone laugh at a time like this?"

"Because we can't help it," I said.

"Yes you can," she said and squinted at me. It was a face of genuine miscomprehension, lost down the puffy tunnel of her parka's hood.

*

Tina spent that night in Nonna's room. The gigantic green numbers glowed 1:18 a.m. The leaded glass birds were rendered flat by the moonlight. There were still wrappers from the coroner's medical supplies on the floor and teeth in a glass by the bed. The rosary box, of course, was gone. The space felt like what it was, the setting of some freshly over drama, but with nothing yet put back in order.

Soon it would be. The nether-time between the death and the funeral would end, and all of this would be gone, Nonna's presence along with it. Tina shoved her face into the pillow again and again, filling her sinuses with Nonna's medicinal smells until her synapses fired off a holistic idea of the woman she was inhaling, a glut of indistinct memories conspiring to conjure the entirety of a person in a single sniff. It was Nonna, delivered to her brain in particles, as Tina had always known her, with her hardened truths and angry advice.

Tina registered a series of steps and creaks elsewhere in the house. She guessed it was Danny going to the washroom or Bonnie getting a glass of water. But then there was murmuring somewhere downstairs, and then a creak and a shifting noise and a sharp intake of breath upstairs, near the bedrooms. And then a peal of Bonnie's laughter. Tina rose, opened the door and padded up the stairs to the hall, where our mother was sitting on the floor next to the phone desk. Bonnie was giggling, one hand over the input end of the receiver. Jacko and Danny joined the scene, standing in the doorframes of their rooms.

I arrived late, climbing the stairs. I'd felt guilty and worried about what Tina had witnessed at the funeral home and had snuck down to call Joey and reassure him that it would all blow over.

"Oh, it's a riot!" Bonnie said, now crying from laughter.

"What is?" Jacko said.

"Have you finally lost your mind?" Tina asked.

"It's so much better than that," Bonnie said.

"Were you listening to me?" I said, though it was clear she had been.

"Gio, yes, but, oh my God. Please forgive me!"

"Mom, I—"

"Don't! Gio, please. It's fine. We knew it anyway."

"Knew what?" Tina said.

Mom looked at me.

"It," I said.

"No no no, you have to say the words," Mom said.

"I do?"

"Yep. Out loud."

"You don't have to say anything," Tina said.

"Come on, Gio," Mom said. "You might as well now."

"Do it so we can go back to bed," Danny said.

Tina shot me our gay sibling look—a panicky version, as though she'd reach into my throat and grab the words away before they were real.

"Fine," I said. "I'm gay, OK?"

"And he's in love with that undertaker's son!"

Tina shot me a look of panic.

"Well, 'love' is a bit strong," I said.

"So, I got up to pee," Mom said, "and saw that the light on the phone was on. Who could be on the horn at this hour? The caller ID said it was Chéhab and Sons! And, Gio, again, I'm sorry, but I thought the worst. I thought something had happened with Nonna, with the funeral. But it hadn't! It was you comforting that Joey kid."

"Joey Callino?" Jacko said. "That boy with the lisp?"

"Yeah, *theriouthly*," Bonnie said. "At least he's Catholic."

"And rich," Jacko said.

More laughter.

"I'm glad you all find this so funny," Tina said.

"Well, this is it!" Bonnie said. "I'm so relieved!"

"So now you know," I said.

"We always knew."

"Told you," I said to Tina.

"Shut up," Tina said.

Bonnie jerked a thumb at Jacko. "This one called it when you were ten and wanted to hang out with your wild Auntie Dot, God rest her soul."

"Bonnie, we *agreed*," Jacko said. "In their own time."

"I'm sorry. I know this isn't about me," Bonnie said.

Tina looked like a female mirror of me with her wrinkled T-shirt, boxers, baggy under-eyes, slack jaw, and visage of creeping comprehension. The words had weight; they altered the balance of reality.

The phone started blaring its warning to hang-up. Bonnie stood, replaced the receiver, then came over and hugged me hard, deep and tight. It was a full embrace of all of me. She did the same to Tina, who stared at me over our mother's shoulder. When I realized I was smiling, I amped up the grin so Tina could share my reaction.

Tina looked at my smile. I don't know what it seemed like to her, but to me it felt involuntary and foolish. A smile of alleviation. She wasn't feeling the same relief I was. For her, Bonnie's hug squeezed out something different, though it was akin to relief. It was permission.

Finally, Tina laughed. Laughed and cried, all at once. It was as though her centre had crumbled, and she put her arms around our mother to keep from collapsing. She wailed intensely—like a siren, like an emergency—and convulsed with a powerlessness she could only interpret as love.

*

"She doesn't look peaceful," Marisol said. She was in The Rose Room with Tina, hovering over Nonna with a face like an inspector, someone deployed to confirm the fatality.

"Not at all," Tina said.

"More bothered."

"Yeah. Death is pretty inconvenient, especially for the corpse."

The Rose Room was empty, even emptier than yesterday. The flowers had been packed up, moved to the church. The skirt below the coffin had been removed, exposing the wheeled metal frame that would roll the body to the hearse.

"This is it," Tina said. She gripped Nonna's arm. The sleeve was rough on her skin, and there was no heat coming from the body—no reaction, no flicker of life. Yesterday, she'd wanted one, but for their last session, Tina was hoping for stillness. "Before you go, I want you to meet The Captain. This is The Captain."

"Hi," Marisol said.

"Wisconsin. She's going to go," Tina said.

"I'm looking forward to it," Marisol said.

"And I guess you can tell she's a girl. A woman."

"It's true," Marisol said.

"Don't give me that look," Tina said. Nonna's face stayed unsettled, annoyed, worried. Disappointed. It's the face she'd worn all her life, and would for the rest of time, Tina thought. There is no changing that. "Wish I had the words to explain it to you. I'm not sure they even exist. Or if you'd understand them. But you don't have to understand. Or approve. Maybe you'd do both, if you knew what I knew."

"You would," Marisol said.

"It doesn't matter," Tina said. She gave Nonna's arm one final squeeze and kissed her on the forehead. A dot of wetness stayed on the skin, biting into the makeup. My sister decided to leave it there, a little imperfection of her own, that would go into the grave.

"They're all waiting to come in for the blessing," Marisol said. "We should get going."

"Yeah, it's going to be a long day. And I'm tired. Mom had us up all night, talking and talking. I'll spare you the details, Nonna, but you know Bonnie—it's going to be *months* of talking now. Bet you're glad you're dead."

"That's not funny," Marisol said.

"Yes it is," Tina said.

story3.11May2018.m4a

[BFM]: Tina's going to kill you.

[GZO]: I know.

[BFM]: And you'll deserve it.

[GZO]: Hey, you TOLD me to get into people's heads.

[BFM]: And you're getting better at it. Keep going.

[GZO]: Felt weird to do it to Tina.

[BFM]: Did you learn to think like a lesbian?

[GZO]: I'm far too masc.

[BFM] [ROLLS EYES TO THE POINT IT'S NEARLY AUDIBLE]

[GZO]: Not masc enough?

[BFM]: I don't think it has to do with masc. Or femme. Or whatever.

[GZO]: I don't want it to read like I'm appropriating.

[BFM]: You're trying to understand her point of view. Those aren't the same thing.

[GZO]: It wasn't easy. Tina and I are so different.

[BFM]: [EXTENSIVE LAUGHTER—THAT PURE JOY RINGING LAUGHTER HE SAVES FOR LAUGHING AT ME WHEN I AM AT MY MOST UN-SELF-AWARE]

[GZO]: You think that's funny.

[BFM]: Yeah, because you and Tina have the same trait—it runs in your family.

[GZO]: Smouldering good looks.

[BFM]: You all think you can control things by just TRYING to control them. We've already seen it from Bonnie. And Grandma Footloose, too.

[GZO]: Nonna was more effective, though. She wins the award for that.

[BFM]: Along with Outstanding Achievement in the Field of Homophobia.

[GZO]: It's weird that Tina thought that Nonna's room was a safe place, even though she had to tell lies in there.

[BFM]: The rink turned out to be unsafe too.

[GZO]: Especially for Marisol.

[BFM]: Marisol's interesting. You got how she ended up as the safe place for Tina.

[GZO]: I told you it was a love story.

[BFM]: You did. So, what was your safe place? And don't say me.

[GZO]: Why not?

[BFM]: Because that's where you are now. What was it when you were a kid?

4
Aliens

"Why, this is persecution!" Aunt Dot said. "I won't live with this negligence."

"Who the heck's neglecting you, girl?" Aunt Maeve said. "I have to look at you every minute."

"*I'm* neglecting *them*."

"Oh, 'them.' The Hollywood crowd."

"They're my *set*."

Maeve leaned forward in her La-Z-Boy and pointed out the picture window. "You think Whoopi Goldberg is out there wondering why you haven't called?"

"You treat me so poorly. I'm deprived."

"It's a matter"—Maeve rubbed two fingers against her thumb—"of cash."

"Always money with you. It's downright miserly. Money, money, money!"

"Must be funny," Maeve said, "in a rich man's world."

The sitting room smelled of adults, of cigarettes and Revlon Charlie. I was ten years old, a periodic visitor on their sofa, and even I could tell Auntie Dot's fantasies were becoming stranger. They were becoming more inconvenient for Maeve; more difficult to confine within the safe space of their bungalow. When the delusions arrived, they temporarily but thoroughly became Dot's reality. Omar Sharif, Julie Christie, Sissy Spacek, Clint Eastwood.

Celebrities were always on their way over in Town Cars to collect Dot and bring her to parties. She had proof in the form of invitations that she had forged, forgotten and re-found among the cosmetics on her vanity. The notes sparked a flurry of what she called "gussying-up." Around her neck at that moment was a half-smock made of paper to protect her clothes while applying makeup. She'd been halfway through putting on her face for tonight's "shindig" when she came out for a cigarette and another argument about their VCR.

Dot lit a Benson & Hedges and exhaled the smoke up and down, producing plumes articulated by the sunlight. She sat in her throne-like Bergère with her legs crossed, explaining to me that all the new movies were being released on tapes called VHS. They wouldn't play in their VCR, which was called Beta. This injustice was why she hadn't yet seen *Romancing the Stone*.

"How am I to speak with Michael and Kathleen about their work?" Dot said. She was on the move again, coming to perch next to me on the armrest of the couch. She leaned in, confiding to me that "they're both *dolls*, by the way! Dolls down to their souls."

"Pretentious so-and-sos," Maeve said. She carried the ashtray tower from the Bergère to Dot's new location. "They're probably screwing each others' brains out."

"You think everyone is fornicating."

"Aren't they?"

"What do *you* think, Giovanni?" Dot said.

"Yes?" I said.

"Kid knows a thing or two," Maeve said.

I relished the validation, smiling at the sisters as I sat in my church clothes. My family went to morning Mass; Maeve and Dot went in the evening. Getting gussied up was the only thing I liked about Mass, and I was feeling sophisticated in a navy polo shirt, beige shorts and the ultramarine suede loafers I'd begged my mother for at Eaton's. Maeve was in her sweatpants. Dot wore a faux-silk dressing gown with a pattern of moustachioed Japanese cartoon figures that bordered on racist, even in 1985. Leaning next to me, Dot looked martyred, staring out the picture window at their rock garden, their Bonneville, and the bungalows on the opposite side of Caribou Road. Her hair looked painful. It was streaked with peroxide, cemented in hairspray, and strangled around curlers.

"You two are conspiring against me. Why, I don't have to endure it! I'm going to gussy up," Dot said. "But you won't run off on me, will you Giovanni? You love me enough to stay?"

"Yes, Auntie Dot."

"I'll only be gone a spell!"

"And good riddance, too," Maeve said as Dot left the room. I could hear her descending to the basement, taking the stairs one at a time. "Can you believe that one?"

"No?" I said.

"Your parents know you're here, kid?"

"Yep."

"You liar," she said.

Back at my house, across town, I could go unnoticed for hours, disappearing between Tina's pee-wee hockey career and Danny's screeching infancy. That morning, I'd felt bored and ignored, and decided to crank my train set to its maximum speed. The toy had crashed, and the power console had burst into flames. Bonnie had put out the fire and punished me, but then had to drive Tina to the rink. I didn't get the attention I wanted, so in defiance and shame, I'd decided to run away and go on one of my adventures.

I went on such adventures from time to time. I'd pack my knapsack with cereal bars, RC Cola cans, a sketch book, and Laurentien coloured pencils, then sneak out the back door without telling a soul. Those adventures were my first real taste of freedom, and they frequently brought me to my great aunts' bungalow.

"Are you going to call my parents?" I said.

"I'm no rat," Maeve said.

"Very gracious," I said, using a word Dot had taught me on a previous adventure. Aunt Maeve laughed her laugh. She had many facial expressions to show disdain, but only one for happiness. It, too, was sinister; a toothy laugh-smile through which I could see her tongue undulate. Two years ago, it scared me. Now, I was proud to draw it out of her.

I'd also grown to appreciate the bungalow. "Disordered" was Mom's word for it. There were unwashed dishes, cigarettes, swearing, junk food. Dust in the sconces, weeds in the garden. Everything I'd been told to avoid was right here. It had once repulsed me, but now I felt safe in the bungalow. The adults treated me like one of their own. I could pick a grown-up movie to watch from the cassettes in the bookcase. I could help Dot with her nail polish. A briefcase hid a backgammon set. A gun was a lighter. The aunts had a hutch with a trap door that revealed a turntable and record collection.

And then there was the radio, a wood-panelled, hutch-like contraption that was as tall as me. I would see it again and again for the rest of my life, but I didn't know that then. When I was ten, that radio was new and held mysteries. It had city names on the dial instead of numbers—Roma, Wien, Köln, Gdańsk—which seemed exotic and promising to me. Its bottom half accommodated a bar stocked with an assortment of glasses and boozes. The bottles huddled together in various shapes, sizes and colours, most with crazy-sounding names that I practised rolling around my tongue as though I were drinking them—Crème de Menthe, Tia Maria, Galliano, Angostura, Smirnoff.

"Your aunt'll be back in a jiff," Maeve said. "Wanna drink while we wait?"

"She's my *dad's* aunt. She's my *great* aunt."

"She's not so great," Maeve said. "Want your usual?"

"Yes please. But I want to pick the glass."

"No ordinary glass will do, eh?"

I crouched before the radio and looked at my options, wondering which liquids were meant for which vessel—especially my "usual," fizzy water, which I was training myself to like. I chose a champagne flute.

"Interesting choice, kid."

When Maeve returned from the kitchen with my water, she offered me liquorice allsorts from a wooden bowl that looked like a concave parquet tile, then collapsed into her La-Z-Boy. I took my pencils from my bag and asked if I could draw her.

"No one needs a picture of this old mug. You can draw Dot. She loves that kind of garbage."

"Oh, OK." I already had drawings of Dot, but she never remembered that I had done them. "Aren't you going to ask me about the baby?"

"What baby?"

"Danny. My brother."

"Babies are all the same. Tell him to call me when he's interesting."

I laughed. By process of elimination, I was interesting.

"You were right. My parents don't know I'm here. But they know I'm OK."

"Running away again, eh?" she said. "All the boys run to me. Your daddy did the same thing, way back when."

"I know, you told me."

"You let me know when you're ready to head home. I'll take you."

"Not soon."

"Now who is that you're talking to, Maeve?" Dot called from basement stairs. "Is that Master Giovanni O'Hara?"

"Here we go," Maeve said. "You know the drill, kid."

I nodded gravely. I loved knowing the drill.

Dot burst forth. At first, her mint-green balloon trousers appeared to be a skirt, but it became evident as she danced across the carpet, showing off, that it had discrete legs. The pants had an ornamental gold chain affixed to a front panel; it jingled as she moved and caught the sun, as did her elaborate gold and silver blouse, which had monstrous, rigid shoulders that minimized her neck to a toothpick. The sleeves fanned when she raised her arms. The whole get-up seemed to depend on a small, straining bow tie around her throat. It was sewn into the neck of the blouse, even though it was a different colour and fabric—lustrous red satin.

"A gentleman caller in the middle of the afternoon! What could be more of a treat?"

"Hello, Auntie Dot!"

"When did you arrive, you handsome devil?"

"Now," I said. "I wasn't here before."

Maeve nodded.

"Your footwear is dazzling me, Giovanni. What do you call that gorgeous colour?"

"Ultramarine."

"It's sublime!" She leaned in and kissed the air next to my cheeks. Up close, I saw her nicotined teeth between bubble-gum lips. Her eyelids were now orange. Her eyebrows were ghosts of themselves.

"Two kisses, Giovanni," Dot said. "Two is customary. If you greet people with two kisses, they'll be yours forever."

"All people?"

"Everybody."

"Even boys?"

"Everybody! Worldly. That's what they'll say about you. So European. Do you know Europe at all?"

"It's a continent."

"It's a frame of mind!"

"My grandfather came from there on a big boat," I said. "From Italy."

"That's not the kind of Europe I mean," Dot said. "Are those *your* fancy pencils?"

"Aunt Maeve said I could draw you."

"What a thing to ask! Did you hear, Maeve? He loves me enough to draw me!"

"I ain't deaf," Maeve said.

"Are you famous for drawing, Giovanni?" Dot said.

"I want to be."

"I'm sure you are. We're all *known*. Even Maeve!"

"What are you famous for, Aunt Maeve?"

"Never you mind," Maeve said.

"The women all gossip about her, believe you me," Dot said. "Master O'Hara, I'd be honoured for you to draw me. Aren't you glad I put on my face, Maeve?"

"Thrilled," Maeve said. "Don't you have enough pictures of this one?"

"I'm his muse!" Dot raised her arms for emphasis, letting the sleeves fan out. I thought of a flying squirrel. "How do you want me?"

I told Dot to sit in her Bergère, in the light from the window. The sun made her makeup brighter, more clownish. With deliberation, I chose pencils and opened my sketchbook. I asked her not to move.

"I won't twitch a muscle!" Dot said, and grandiloquently lit a cigarette. Maeve carried the ashtray stand over to her sister, commenting that the "buggering thing" weighed a ton, before coming around to see my progress. Dot was talking and moving fluidly, telling us of a recent awards show. I found myself looking at her less and less, drawing from memory to shape her face and only looking at her to catch today's variations. The sequins shimmered and danced; I couldn't quite get them.

"Kid's got talent," Maeve said, looking over my shoulder. "But don't go easy on her. Those earrings are much uglier."

"You are plainly sadistic to me," Dot said. "Isn't she sadistic, Giovanni?"

"I'm not sure what it means," I said.

"It means realistic," Maeve said.

"It means cruel! Cruel and *loving* it!" I kept drawing, going in for a new pencil to match Dot's eye shadow. Sarasota Orange. "She keeps me deprived!"

"Not this again." Maeve sat back down in her La-Z-Boy. It was the only thing in the house that suited her. It was like she wore it—wore it like her sweatpants. "You never forget the right things, Dotty."

"Maeve would cut a penny in two, Giovanni, I swear." Dot was up now, lamenting this by the window. "It's the tiniest little thing, and it would delight me."

"You're plenty delighted."

"What else am I supposed to do? When you go to work and *abandon* me? Sit here and go screwy?"

"You know what I do all day, kid?" Maeve said.

"You put cars together."

"Bang on. And I should've retired by now. But oh no, I can't. All 'cause of this one."

"You shush," Dot said. "You love my movie cassettes, don't you, Giovanni?"

"Yes, a lot."

"Well, your aunt wants to rob me of them!" She was getting flustered. "Wouldn't that be heinous?"

"Heinous," I said.

"Don't get her going," Maeve said. "It's not worth your breath. And we still gotta get to church."

Sensing this hint at departure, I said, "Can we put one on? A tape?"

"Of course, lovely! While we still can!" Dot said. "I've fallen behind on all the premieres, all the new films, all the new stars. Why, I haven't even seen *Splash*!"

"That Darryl Hannah is such a phoney," Maeve said. "You're better off without."

"Darryl is divine!"

"Nothing to her. Skin and bones," Maeve said. "Not worth a $500 upgrade, that's for sure."

"You'll be sorry when *you* want to see something new." She opened the glass panel of the bookcase and clawed cassettes out onto the carpet until she found a specific one. She shook it at Maeve, who said,

"Easy there, girl."

"Here!" Dot was almost screaming it, rattling the tape. "What will you do when they release the new version of *this*? And you can't see it because our machine's a relic?"

"I can see it at the Famous Players down on Exhibition Street. Four dollars. And I won't take you if you keep carrying on."

"You wouldn't dare!"

"Can I come?" I asked.

"No!" Dot wailed. "It's far too much!"

"I'm big enough."

"It's not about *big*. It's a matter of *delicacy*. It will be violent. Just like *this*!"

I needed—desperately, suddenly—to see the film in Dot's hand. "Can we watch it?"

"Under no circumstances! It's a man's movie—just vicious. Not for you! You're a gentleman!" The distinction exhilarated me. "It'll poison your sweet little mind!"

"Can I see the tape, then?"

Maeve grabbed the cassette and handed it to me. Its sleeve was black, with a sinister orb on it with a green light glowing through a crack in its surface. There was foreboding steam. Above the image was the title, *Alien*.

"Alien," I said.

"And there's a new one coming out next year. A sequel! Only there will be more than one alien this time, so the movie will be plural." She spread her wings to illustrate the vast number. "And Sigourney Weaver is coming back for it and everything!"

"She'll make that Darryl Hannah look like a mouse, that's a sure bet."

"Can't we watch it?" I said.

"Absolutely not," Dot said. "So macho!"

"Let's queue it up," Maeve said, giving me her laugh. "We have time before church."

"Sadistic! She's being sadistic to *both* of us, Giovanni!"

Maeve pulled the curtains over the window, giving the room a gauzy, underwater feel.

"Oh, what you *do* to me! I can't have *anything* my way!"

"We'd all be dead if you did," Maeve said.

"How aggressive you are," Dot said. She pulled a cassette from the shelf and threw it at her sister. *The Children's Hour* clanked on the burgundy carpet. "And all before I have to go out. I'll be wound-up. Grotesque!"

Sweat was beading at Dot's hairline and she wasn't looking at either of us anymore. Her eyes were twitchy. Maeve didn't look at me, but said, "Go put the tape on, kid. Your auntie and I are gonna take a walk."

"Are we going to my room?" Dot said.

"Good idea," Maeve said. "Why don't I take you down?"

"But I have places to *be*."

"Get watching, kid. I'll be back in a jiff."

Maeve hooked her hand onto Dot's arm and drew her safely from the room. The affection was so unexpected, it amazed me.

✷

A distress call woke the astronauts in *Alien*. They were not like the astronauts I'd seen on TV, on the *Challenger*, Marc Garneau in his big orange space suit. These people were like the GM workers I met in Fiona—rough and tough, but wearing underwear. Everything seemed dangerous in *Alien*, but the astronauts didn't seem to notice at first. They just swore and joked in an adult manner I found titillating.

I was so engrossed, I didn't hear my great-aunts trying to make their way down the stairs. I had to imagine it later: Dot's body feverish with excitement, her weight crushing Maeve's shoulder.

"Why you wanted the basement room, I'll never know."

"Peeping toms! I don't like people ogling me."

"The hell you don't."

This will be impossible in a year, Maeve thought, coming through the tight squeeze of the bedroom's doorframe. When she lowered Dot to the mattress, she could feel sweat under the sequins and polyester of the blouse. She unclasped the bow tie and pulled the garment open at the neck.

"There you go. You've gotta breathe, for Pete's sake."

"I confess that's better. Perhaps the tie was a bit *de trop*?"

"You think?" Maeve was gathering pillows against the headboard. She kept most of the bungalow's pillows here to pack around her sister. Dot was safest when she was walled in.

"It was a flourish."

"It was choking you half to death."

"How *morbid*. You're positively macabre."

"Stop whining and lean back."

She tipped Dot into the wall of pillows, then went to work removing her shoes. The flesh of Dot's feet puffed in relief. Maeve held up the black patent leather pumps, dangled them on her finger.

"If I'm a sadist, you're a masochist."

"Are you putting me to sleep?" Dot asked, packed in her pillows. "I'm not ready to retire for the night. I have to be places later."

"You mean church?" Maeve said.

"I seem to remember talk of a drinks party?"

"Of course you do."

"I have to start getting ready!"

"You're going to relax first, hear me?"

"Beauty rest, you mean?"

"Sure." Maeve put a hand to her sister's forehead, assessed her eyes. "I'll get you some water."

"You're not leaving me, are you?"

"Just for water. Pay attention."

In the pink-tiled washroom, Maeve ran the faucet. She pumped a finger in the stream, waiting for it to turn cold. She clutched a water glass; she was still catching her breath. One day soon, they'd have to switch rooms. Maeve thought of which co-workers from the GM plant she'd ask to help her haul the furniture up and down the stairs. How much pizza she'd have to buy, how much beer.

She filled the glass. Avoiding her reflection, she opened the medicine cabinet hidden behind the mirror. Pill bottles stood like soldiers, each with its own talent, each telling the story of a previous upheaval. This episode merited none of them. Instead, she pulled out the aspirin and shook out a tablet.

"Is that rattling I hear?" Dot yelled.

"You don't miss a trick, do you?" She re-entered the bedroom, handing her sister the pill and the water.

"And what do we have here?"

"Powerful stuff," Maeve said. Dot downed it, burped. "So ladylike."

"Don't be sour."

"Bit late for that."

Maeve took the glass from her and returned it to its place next to the sink.

"You're not leaving me, are you?"

"Nah." Maeve stopped in the bedroom's doorframe. It was a bit early in the year for air conditioning; the room was only mildly warm. Dot seemed cooler now anyhow, calmer, drifting away on the imaginary effects of the pill.

The stars watched them. Dot had Scotch-Taped celebrities' headshots in a grid on the wall facing the bed. There was overage now; a dozen or so had invaded an adjoining wall. Dot spoke of these luminaries often, yet Maeve could rarely put a face to a name. They all looked self-aware and made the room feel smaller. They were a fire hazard, too, which is why Dot's cigarettes were limited to the sitting room.

Maeve checked the vanity. Amid the tubes of lipstick and palettes of blush were two rectangles of paper. They were simple notecards from Shoppers Drug Mart—eighty cents for a pack of one hundred—but Dot invested much more into them. Her berserk cursive had written out invitations to a pair of non-existent parties. Maeve folded them into quarters, then eighths, and slipped them into the pocket of her sweatpants. She settled into the threadbare La-Z-Boy in the corner. It had once been upstairs, but she'd carried it down here when she'd bought the new one. Dot disapproved of its appearance and had covered it in a satin sheet that made it slippery.

Maeve was beat. Yes, they'd have to change rooms. Dot would object. Change baffled her. She needed anchors, and when Maeve was forced to take an anchor away, she did it with dread and strategies. The new VCR was the obvious concession for swapping rooms. Maeve would start on the next paycheque, putting aside $30 a week.

"You're not leaving me, are you?" Dot said. "You love me enough to stay?"

"Sure, why not."

"You can't say anything normally, can you?"

"Go to sleep for Pete's sake."

In the silence and dim light, Maeve could hear a muffled scream from *Alien*. A creature made of fingers had squeezed a man's face. She figured I was fine and remained downstairs to keep an eye on Dot. She played her usual game to pass the time, scraping her eyes across the stars' clueless faces, seeing how many she could recognize from here—Sigourney Weaver, of course, but also Dusty Springfield, Katharine Hepburn, and that far-away one was what's her name, the mother from *Family Ties*.

✷

The Bonneville reeked of Dot's Revlon Charlie. Maeve let me sit in the front seat. She always did, after my adventure was over and I was being ferried back home, hoping to slip into my family's house unnoticed. I felt more adult up here, like a mom. Dot, energized from her nap, declared that she preferred the backseat. She believed she was being chauffeured.

I was looking for traitors. Traitors was a game Maeve invented. I counted all the cars we passed that weren't GM models—Volvos, Fords, Toyotas, Mazdas, Volkswagens, Hondas. I shouted the number out as we went.

"Twenty-three!"

"Twenty-three, my stars," Maeve said. "Twenty-three traitors all around us."

"What a world!" Dot said.

"Not us, though. Eh, kid? Dot's Bonneville here is tried and true."

"It's Auntie Dot's?"

"Dotty, you want to answer that?"

"Why, I *chose* this car, of course. A Bonneville! It's French!"

"It's not," Maeve said.

"Isn't it luxuriant? With the deep seats?"

"It's a tank."

"But I've never seen you drive it," I said. "Can you drive, Auntie Dot?"

"Not in this reality," Maeve said.

"Don't listen to her filthy rumours, Giovanni. It so happens I *can* drive. But I prefer to be driven."

"Ain't that a fact."

Maeve asked me what I thought of *Alien*.

"I loved it!" I said.

"Kid's got taste."

I hadn't understood it, but I'd felt it. *Alien* had me bolted to the floor. My parents didn't have that kind of movie in the house. Watching it, I had felt like I was getting away with something as monstrous as the beast on the screen, and any minute someone would realize the mistake and switch the movie off. Not Maeve, though. She'd come up halfway through and had watched with me, making little comments—"look at her go," "my stars." She hadn't explained it to me. She'd just let me gawp at the space travellers as they were plucked off one by one by the alien, a creature afforded no sympathy, and whose behaviour I ascribed to loneliness. There it was, deprived and alone and surrounded by alarms. An insect in a world of human tunnels, thinking it could hunt its way back to safety.

Dot had emerged from the basement as the credits began,

dressed for Mass. She'd opted for a purple caftan, its polyester cinched by a plastic belt the width of my thigh. Above and below the waist, the thing ballooned, giving her the billowing motion common to many of her getups. It responded to her movement with dramatic surges of fabric. She'd been asleep, she said, and her hair was "a fright," so she'd hidden it under a royal blue turban-hat that sprouted a tall feather. Her makeup stayed the same as earlier, perhaps a little smeared from the nap, but she'd changed her earrings from gold hoops to jet half-spheres—clip-ons that tortured her lobes. She was suffering now, with the sun pouring into the back seat of the Bonneville, and she asked me to retrieve her hand fan from the glove compartment.

"I wish I didn't have to go home. Not yet." I was anticipating my parents' street, five blocks ahead, and their disappointment at my departure after I ruined the train set. "My adventure doesn't feel over."

"Wanna come to Mass with us, kid?"

"I'd love to make an entrance with a gentleman on my arm!" Dot said.

"But I already went. I don't want to go again," I said.

"I can drop you somewhere else if you'd like."

"Exhibition Park?" I said.

"Bit dangerous over there," Maeve said. "Oh, I know—what about granny's?"

Nonna's and Papa Zap's house was the opposite of the sisters' bungalow. Everything in it served some purpose. There were expectations, but no flair, no mystery and no interest in me in particular. Children were all considered the same, from the babies to the bullies. When I was at the Laurier Street house, I performed the role of "cousin" or "grandson," and sustained it until I could go home.

"I guess," I said.

"Oh, come on. Granny'll be happy to see you. Give her the thrill of a lifetime."

"OK. I guess it'll be OK."

Maeve made a turn, changed course. The Bonneville climbed the Laurier Street hill like it was anxious to get there. I hoped no one would be home, and when we pulled up to my grandparents' brick square house, I thought my wish may be granted. It looked sleepy. Maeve cranked the parking brake to keep the car from rolling back down to a more prosperous neighbourhood.

"Stay put, Dotty," Maeve said.

"What in heavens are we doing in this neck of the woods?"

"We're dropping the kid off."

"I shouldn't be seen here. Why, it's so grimy."

I kneeled on the bucket seat to face Dot, who looked like she was posing in the back, fanning herself while trying to make sense of the low-income scenario out the window.

"Bye, Auntie Dot. Have fun tonight."

"Thank you, my lovely! Where am I going, though?"

"You said a party?" I looked at Maeve, who gave me a nod.

"Oh yes! Are you sure you won't come?"

"I have to go to my grandparents' house now."

"A previous engagement!" She leaned in for a perfumey hug and two contactless kisses. "We're all so busy these days."

Maeve and I slammed our doors and approached the house along the concrete walkway that split the front lawn. Last summer, my dad, uncles, and a bunch of my more terrifying male cousins, had replaced the old dirt path that used to be here. The kids got to write their names in the cement before it set. There were rows of boys' names leading up to the porch, all but mine, as I'd gotten bored and had gone inside to help my aunts bottle tomatoes.

"Let's get your granny out here," Maeve said. She checked her watch and then Dot, who was smiling at us from the car. "Think she's home?"

It had not occurred to me until that moment that only Papa Zap would be home. I was afraid of him the way I was of my cousins. They all exuded a gruff, masculine surety that I didn't understand and was terrible at imitating. I felt like I had made a miscalculation early on in my adventure, like the crew of the mining ship in *Alien*.

Maeve rang the bell twice and no one came.

"Maybe no one's here?" I said.

"One more try, OK, kid?" This time she knocked and raised her voice to yell, "Fee! Come on out!"

Papa Zap came around the side of the house, dragging a hose. He must have been working in his garden out back. Allergic to bee stings, he always covered his skin as much as possible when he was gardening: black canvas jumpsuit, work boots, filthy Blue Jays cap. When he pulled the handkerchief from around his face, I could see that his fingernails were packed with dirt. He sprayed mud off his boots before he even acknowledged us.

I stuck close to Maeve as we descended the steps.

"Where's your wife?" she said.

The lack of formality amazed me. Papa Zap didn't respond and didn't stop walking towards us. His face was volcanic. He wrapped rough fingers around my upper arm and jerked me towards him. Then he hugged me hard, like he'd pulled me out of the path of a speeding locomotive. It was visceral and surprising, loving and angry. I had never figured that he cared for me one way or the other, but there I was, enveloped in his earthy smell, his coarse jumpsuit sanding my cheek.

"Whatch'you do?" he said to me.

I didn't know what to say, so I looked down, hoping a performance of shame might save me from his next impulse of fury or affection. My suede ultramarine loafers looked pathetically elegant facing off against his dirty boots.

"Look up. Here, here." He knocked my chin with the top of his fist. I looked into his face, which was as big and as cratered as the moon. All his blood wanted to escape through his head; his eyes were bloodshot, his bulb of a nose was violet. He had a lightning bolt vein that zig-zagged from his brow to his temple, where it disappeared under a thick carpet of black bristles. His eyebrows were overgrown and inquisitive. The warmth of his embrace was unfindable now. I didn't know what he wanted to hear, so I said nothing.

Papa Zap shook me by the shoulders. I made cartoonish yelps with each jerk.

"What the heck's the matter with you, Brutus? You're going to give the kid whiplash," Maeve said.

"Where you go?" he continued. "Bonifacia, she call! Your aunts, they call! Everyone worries!"

"Don't blow a gasket there, tough guy."

Papa Zap sniffed the air and shot two flat hands up into my armpits, then lifted me up to his face and buried his nose in my stomach. It tickled horrifically.

"Like a girl, you smell."

"It's my sister's perfume," Maeve said. "Put the kid down, for Christ's sake. He was with me all day. Not that you give two shakes."

"You—who are you?" He bunched his fingers together to a point, gestured at her head.

"You know who I am."

He spat a gob of mucus to her feet. My mind was swimming in fear. This was not like a movie, and it was not like Maeve and Dot arguing over the VCR.

"Go get in the car with Dot, kid."

"You stay." He cuffed his hand back around my biceps.

"Where's your wife, eh?" Maeve said again.

"You get outta my business."

"Somewhere better than this, I bet," Maeve said. "Bet she runs away whenever she can."

"Go back! Leave him and go back."

"You bet I'm going," Maeve said. "But let the kid be."

"The boy, he stays."

A car door slammed behind us. Both adults found the noise with their eyes. I smelled Revlon Charlie.

"Shit," Maeve said.

"It's frightfully lonely in there," Dot said. "To *abandon* me like that! It's an absolute crime."

She walked up and stood between me and Maeve. Her purple caftan stood out like blood on snow. Her turban was crooked. She lit a cigarette and the smoke raced away on the breeze as fast as it could. I envied it.

"Get back to the car, Dot," Maeve said. "Take the kid with you."

"He stays," Papa Zap said.

"I needed one little cigarette. I was gagging for it." Dot thrust out some bent fingers to Papa Zap. They were adorned in plastic gold and costume rubies. Her sleeve puffed and flounced. "I don't believe we've met. I'm Dorothy, but these wondrous people call me Dot. Everyone in my set does. Charmed, I'm sure."

Papa Zap took in the three of us, foreign objects inserted into his world.

"A terribly uncouth welcome," Dot said. Her eyes gave a twitch of recognition. "Why, I remember you! You're hardly a gentleman at all!"

Papa Zap's lip went up as though caught on a hook. I understood that he wasn't angry anymore, he was repulsed. He was threatened. A new fear overtook me. Maeve must have felt it too, because she pulled Dot towards the Bonneville. She gestured for me to join. Papa Zap had to let me go in order to reach for the hose.

My instinct has always been to run—just hours before, I'd escaped to the bungalow—but I didn't do it right then. I wanted to take off and get soaked with my aunts on their dash to safety. Yet I stood there, watching them go away. I could still smell Papa Zap's hug on me, feel the validation and authority of his arms. It wasn't a lapse in instinct; I had a choice.

I ran. The water from the hose landed on the top of my head. It was cold as it ran down my back, into my shorts. I focused on the Bonneville's passenger-side door. Maeve threw it open for me as I approached and she cheered when I made it safely into the car.

Later, my parents picked me up at the bungalow. They weren't even angry, and they didn't punish me any further. Maybe they had heard what happened. They didn't say one way or the other, but they did make fun of my suede shoes, which were wet and ruined. They never asked why.

story4.03June2018.m4a

[BFM]: I love Dot's outfits. They sound positively Zbornakian.

[GZO]: With a dash of Mrs. Roper.

[BFM]: It's cute how Maeve undresses her, how you take us into the basement with them. Much better than retelling the plot of the movie.

[GZO]: I wanted to give them a moment.

[BFM]: Dot sounds a bit like me, in the dialogue.

[GZO]: She does. And she did. She was really like that, but I wanted a connection between her and you.

[BFM]: Because we're both wildly stupendous creatures?

[GZO]: Because you both allowed for the same thing—I felt most like myself around you both. That safe place that we talked about.

[BFM]: Dot couldn't punish you, though, if you misbehaved.

[GZO]: When have I ever misbehaved?

[BFM]: Well, I can't help but notice you wrote another story that justifies running away.

[GZO]: That's not misbehaviour.

[BFM]: It certainly was when you did it to me.

[GZO]: Ouch.

[BFM]: The problem with you is that Bonnie and Jacko never really punished you. They went easy on you.

[GZO]: Jacko could hardly punish me. He was a runaway himself. That's how he met Mom—running away from home. The mythical summer of 1960.

[BFM]: That's just how Bonnie tells it. Two kids at the ice cream shop or whatever. It's so Archie Comics. I never really bought that story the way Bonnie tells it.

[GZO]: Blasphemy.

[BFM]: You don't buy it either, babes. But you think Bonnie's stories are gospel, even when you don't believe them.

[GZO]: I hope I'm moving away from her.

[BFM]: I'd love to hear Jacko's version of events. We've barely heard from him.

[GZO]: He wouldn't dare contradict Mom.

[BFM]: So do it for him. Give him what you gave Dot.

5
Messages in the Air

Jack once thought of Canada as a feral place: houses incidentally built among colossal Douglas Firs, hawks swooping down to devour beavers, white bears batting salmon from rivers. Noble Aboriginal men, draped in feathers, killing themselves for love, like in that Johnny Preston song.

The reality, or at least the reality he observed from the bus window, was narrow highways cut through rock or fringed with ordered fields of corn and tobacco. Towns grew up around the highway, turning the asphalt into a main street for five slow blocks. Then the buildings shrank away, leaving more farmland. The towns had few variations. Each had two brick churches, an IDA Drugs and a gas station that sold live bait. When his destination materialized, Jack barely noticed. Night had fallen, and Fiona appeared to be the same as the other towns. It was disappointingly similar to the United States, the country he'd come from and was so keen to leave. Union Jacks instead of Old Glories; IDA Drugs instead of Woolworth's. A banner that read DOMINION DAY 1960 billowed over an intersection. It might as well have said "Fourth of July."

But it's new, he told himself. Newness was the point. He'd wanted out of his house, out of Marine Park, out of Brooklyn, out of the US. It wasn't that he disliked any of it, but he was sixteen years old. He was restless and, like all teenagers, he thought he knew best. When the news came from Canada that his aunt was taking leave from her job at the GM plant in order to make "a mint" over the summer doing work for the government, Jack sensed an opportunity. He asked Aunt Maeve if he could do the work too, and she consented, with the warning that it was going to be tough.

The set of responsibilities she described—transporting trees, digging holes, planting, watering, pruning—seemed minuscule compared to his roster at home. In Marine Park, Jack wrangled his siblings, who were fourteen, eleven, a set of Irish twins that were then both nine, a set of real twins that were six, a four-year-old terror, and the baby. Jack had basketball practice at 7:00 a.m. and worked at the school council after class. He picked up his sisters at their grammar school by four. He shovelled the driveway, cut the grass, made dinners. He washed diapers, lunch boxes, toilets. He'd recently received his driver's license, and now had to drive everywhere. Swim lessons, Girl Scouts, Mass, Key Foods. In Canada, all he'd have to do was plant trees. He obtained a work permit, packed some back issues of *Boy's Life,* and boarded the Greyhound.

Fiona didn't have a bus station then, so Jack was deposited on top of a hill in front of a stone church with two matching belfries. The Canadian air contained pollen and cricket songs. A solitary woman stood with her legs apart on a patch of lawn, holding a photograph. She wore an impassive face and a sweatshirt of overlapping roses that was too large for her frame and ballooned out around the waist, where it was tucked into slacks. Her hair was permed into tight springs close to her skull. It was brassy, but not as red as Jack's. She approached as the driver freed Jack's duffle bag from the luggage hold.

"This you?" she said. She held up the black and white image. It was him, smiling in a suit. His hair was shorn at the sides, with the longer bit on top set into a series of waxy lines made by a comb. His parents and siblings stood around him, looking solemn—faces befitting the seriousness and expense of getting their photo taken at Martin's department store on a Saturday outing to downtown Brooklyn.

"You're John, then? Another John?"

"I go by Jack."

"Too many Johns in this family."

Every first-born son in the family was named John. Jack was "Jack" to differentiate himself from his father, "JJ"—John Junior. Before him was "Jay." Jack's great-grandfather was the last John to be called "John."

"There are a lot of us."

"You're the one that was born during the war?"

"That's me. At your service."

"You're hard to miss. Haven't seen you since you were a whiny little creeper. And now you're an Irish giant," she said, looking up at him. "That's no compliment. Car's this way."

"Yes, ma'am."

It wasn't a car, but a black pickup truck with a chrome grill and filthy whitewalls on the tires. Maeve executed a heaving maneuver that propelled her into the driver's seat. She looked like a child playing grown-up, gripping a steering wheel that was wider than her shoulders and stiffening her spine so she could see over the dashboard. The bench seat was so high and pulled so tightly to the glove compartment that Jack had to sit on his foot.

"Great truck," Jack said.

"She's a beaut. Not mine originally, but I bought it to haul the plants. We'll be putting trees in the ground up west of here, at Cobble Beach."

"How far west?"

"Couple hours. The township there is trying to replant its trees, so there's lots of work to be had." She rubbed two fingers against her thumb. "Ka-ching."

Maeve had recently moved into a subdivision that could have been lifted from Fiona and attached to any town in the US. The bungalow on Caribou Road had a bay window and fat, multi-car driveway. Out front was a rock garden, which made it look forlorn and out of place on its street of grassy yards and baby maples. The interior had new appliances and smelled of paint. The rooms had little more than boxes and lonely mattresses on metal frames. In the living room, a La-Z-Boy sat in a sea of new burgundy shag carpet.

"Did you just move in?"

"JJ told you squat, eh?"

"Dad didn't say much."

"My brother, such a prig," Maeve said to the ceiling, to God. "Your Aunt Dot's away for a stint. Thought I'd move to the new place while she's gone. A clean break. She's a bit of a retard. Sensitive, you know?"

Jack knew not to answer. The family didn't talk much about "Dotty" Aunt Dot, but when they did, it was in a nomenclature Jack didn't fully understand. Dot was often "away for a stint" or "in the booby hatch." She had "episodes" or "one of those bouts" or "got into one of her pickles." Jack's mother noted that she was "at it again" and needed to get "screwed tighter," "head shrunk," or, even more baffling, "zapped." Dot was "slow," "special," "scattered." She had "a basket of nerves," was "beyond repair," "off-colour," "short of a dozen."

And now he was assigned Dot's room, in the basement. It was square, muted, beige, and it was as charmless and as unlived-in as the rest of the house. It was not what he'd pictured for his Canadian odyssey. The only bit of nature was outside the window, some grass and a few inches of sky. He was relieved that Dot hadn't yet spent a night there, though. There were no traces of her eccentricity. He'd heard that Dot kept everything, and he was expecting stacks of old newspapers or Depression-era polio braces to be on display. Jack eyed the boxes piled against the wall and wondered what they contained, if Dot's tchotchkes and possessed dolls were sitting in there, waiting for her to reanimate them with her mad-tinged attention.

"We're leaving at the crack on Monday, no dilly-dallying."

"Yes ma'am. What time is curfew?"

"Kid, if it mattered to me when you went to bed, I'd kill myself."

*

The following morning, they didn't go to Mass at the stone church where the bus had stopped. That was the Basilica, Maeve explained, and it was full of "ponces."

"There's more than one show in town," she said. "We go to Our Lady of Victory. Father Dupuis's my guy. We go way back. Fastest priest in Fiona. The other parishes dawdle, take over an hour. Dupuis gets us in and out in forty-five minutes, blessing and all."

Our Lady of Victory was newer than the church on the hill, but also more dilapidated, with a sagging roof and a cement cross above the main door that was missing a chunk, so it looked more like a capital T. The windows didn't open, and held abstract patterns made of coloured glass, making the nave somber and hot. The pews were too closely spaced for Jack's legs, and he was relieved when they had to stand or kneel. Parishioners stared at him. He was a foot taller than most of them and wore a suit that had fit when he got it last Christmas but now showed too much ankle and wrist. Maeve nodded at her neighbours but was unperturbed by their lingering glances. To those who said hi, Maeve jerked a thumb towards Jack and said, "This here's my date while Dot's away."

During the service, Jack scanned for girls. Most of them were far too young—born after World War Two—but there was one family across the aisle, in the row behind him, that had kids his age. Jack stole quick glances with a turn of his head. They looked Italian and took up a whole pew, with the spindly mother on the end followed by her children. With each turn, he took in the next girl. Most had spouses at their sides, but the youngest daughter was alone, staring at him, lips pursed, head cocked and shaking. He jolted into self-consciousness. He forced himself to stare at the back of Father Dupuis, whose Latin phrases were muttered at a speedy clip, filling the air. But even so, the image of the girl dominated his mind. She was striking, if not quite beautiful. Pronounced black eyebrows against dark olive skin, mahogany hair pulled back in a hair band. A face with so much in it. It was bored and coy, knowing and innocent. He wondered how many sisters had worn the girl's pink dress before her; it was outdated by a decade. Her bust was too big for her frame, the way Jack's limbs were too long for his.

"She's one of those blasted Zappocosta girls," Maeve said on the ride back. "Don't ask me what she's called. There's too many of them, and they all have the same name, more or less. Pink dress, right?"

"Yes, right."

"Don't let the bust fool you. She's only fourteen."

"Fourteen?"

"Or fifteen. I'm not a bloody records clerk."

"Can you introduce me to the family?"

She cackled and pounded the steering wheel. "Nah, nah."

"Why not?"

"Gossip's the devil, kid," she said. "But they have a cruddy little story, that lot. The father's a jackass. The whole town knows it. He's wrecked the mother. Used to be a pretty thing, but has worried herself down to a hag. Did you see her? Skinny as a rail."

"You said you didn't know them."

"I said I couldn't introduce you. Pay attention."

"Why not?"

"You don't need to know what you don't need to know."

"What do I need to know?"

"Nosy little thing, aren't you?" she said. The truck bumped into the driveway. "You like ice cream?"

"Not really."

"Go get ice cream at the Dairy Fairy. They make that Italian kind. She works there."

"The girl?"

"Sure. Down on Princess Street. Walk towards the Basilica until you get to Maple Street." She handed him a key to the front door. "Tell her Maeve sent you."

*

Walking to the Dairy Fairy, Jack decided he liked Canada. It wasn't the same as the States, as he'd thought earlier. Now he saw little differences. Canadians moved as though they had no place to go. They didn't shout or honk in impatience, but in greeting. He watched a train pass above him, on an overpass. Even it seemed different from an American train. The cars read CANADA next to a logo of a wheat stalk. It moved without hustle, clicking along as if content to get the wheat to its destination at its leisure.

Along Maple Street, men were hanging Union Jacks and bunting off the street lamps. There was the Dominion Day banner again. A squat obelisk on a boulevard was encircled by a wreath of copper laurel leaves. It was etched with OUR GLORIOUS DEAD and a list of names. Jack found an O'Hara—a Sean, possibly a relative—and felt connected to the town. Yellow gladiolas, not more than a day old, sat at the base of the monument in bundles bound by elastics. Someone had thought to place them there, just so, sixteen years after Normandy.

Jack couldn't escape World War Two. Everything in his family was measured as before, during, or after it. His birth was during, a rare thing for a family like theirs. His father had been sent home on account of losing his foot to a grenade. By Jack's calculation, JJ must have sired him within days of returning from France. Growing up, Jack's friends were all younger by two or three years. The discrepancy didn't bother him until he found himself tall, teenaged and horny. Most of the kids of Marine Park were still in bed by nine and spending their weekends at the King's Highway cinema with their parents, watching *Ben-Hur* and *Please Don't Eat the Daisies.* But I'm not like them anymore, he thought. I'm in Canada.

The girl was standing behind the counter at the Dairy Fairy, spinning an ice cream scoop around her thumb. She'd changed from her Sunday dress into a white uniform, which made her look like a nurse. Her brown waves of hair were tamed under a hairnet.

"Congratulations," she said.

"For what?"

"You found me."

"I did. I'm Jack."

"Hello, Jack. Want anything?"

"I don't like ice cream."

"It's not ice cream. It's gelato."

"Is there a difference?"

"It's Italian. It doesn't have eggs."

"Does it taste different?"

"It's thicker."

"That's not the same thing," he said. He looked at her name tag, attempted a pronunciation.

"That's not my name," she said. "It's Boni*fa*cia. But that's not my name either. Call me Bonnie."

"But I like the first name. It's musical. Bonifacia Zappacosta."

"So you know my family name, too," she said. "Do you have a last name, Jack?"

"Yeah."

"Last names are everything," she said. "You're an O'Hara?"

"Yeah."

"Explains the hair."

"My aunts live here."

"Dot and Maeve. I know."

"Everyone knows Dot, huh? Dotty Aunt Dot."

"You shouldn't say that. I like Dot. She comes around sometimes."

"I don't think you'll see her this summer. She's away."

"Away," Bonifacia repeated. "Fancy."

"Dot's at—I don't even know what to call it."

"It's a sanatorium. Everyone knows."

"Do they?"

"They just don't say it out loud."

"Did you enjoy the service this morning?" he said.

"Is that a real question?"

"Sure."

"Does anyone like Mass?"

"I didn't think we were allowed not to like it."

"I don't like it," she said. "Father Dupuis moves so fast. I can't process Latin that quickly. And isn't it boring? I mean, staring at his back like that for an hour?"

"Forty-five minutes."

"Even one minute is too long."

"My church in Brooklyn is the same."

"Brooklyn, as in New York? Like in *I Love Lucy*?"

"Not quite. That's in Manhattan."

"Still. It's cool."

"Is it?"

"Yeah."

"I mean, it's cool here, too. I've only been here a day. Aunt Maeve's the only person I know in the whole town."

"Huh." Bonnie smiled. "New York."

"But I'm getting away from it. Aunt Maeve and I are driving somewhere wild to do work for the summer. Planting trees."

"Oh, so you're leaving?"

"Disappointed?"

"Not if you take me with you."

"That's funny," he said. "You're funny."

"Yeah, I'm a card."

"We only go up for a week at a time, then come back to Fiona on weekends. Maeve even took time off from her job. We're going to make money." He rubbed his thumb against his fingers. "Ka-ching."

"I guess it's not cheap."

"What?"

"The sanatorium."

"Oh. I didn't know that."

"Everybody knows."

Bonnie looked past him at two girls who were standing in drab Sunday dresses about ten feet from the counter. One of them was holding a dollar. Bonnie's face changed; it became open, smiling, welcoming. She waved the girls towards the counter.

"You're scaring them."

"I'm not doing anything."

"You're new. That's enough. Go over there," Bonnie said. "C'mon ladies, it's OK. The big red man is leaving."

From a few feet away, Jack watched Bonnie coax the kids into smiles as she prepared their treats. He couldn't hear her, but was pretty sure that she was imitating him, making herself oafish, doing a lurching walk, crossing her eyes. The girls left laughing.

"You're bad for business, Jack," she said when he returned. "You're going to have to see me somewhere else, other than here."

"Are you asking me out?"

"I don't go out, not with boys. My father's strict like that."

"Maybe I can walk you to work when I'm back in town next weekend?"

"You can be a bit more gutsy than that."

"You like me enough for me to be gutsy?"

"I like you as much as I'm allowed to like you," she said. "And that's not very much. I'm only allowed to have one kind of date. You have to come to my family's house for dinner."

"With your parents and everything?"

"Mama has a rule that she meets any boy who even looks in my direction."

"OK, sure."

"You'll have a terrible time."

"I doubt that."

"Dinner's how boys learn to stay away from me. Only the strong survive."

"I can handle it. I have a big family too."

"But we're Zappacostas."

"I don't know what that means."

"Yeah," she said. "It's your best feature."

*

The following morning, and every Monday for the rest of the summer, Jack and Maeve drove up to her cottage in Cobble Beach and spent the week planting trees along the dunes. Jack was pale compared to the team of sun-browned labourers. Maeve was not officially in charge, but she was in practice. She stood in dungarees on the flatbed of her truck, ordering the crew to lift down birch saplings. Jack lasted one morning of modesty before he started working with his shirt off, tossing it onto the passenger seat with the other men's clothes. He wished Bonnie could see him like this, with his legitimized shirtlessness, ramming trees into the ground, streaks of mud on his narrow chest.

The government was paying for this. It was a replanting campaign to protect the dunes from wasting away. A storm had destroyed the beach in the spring, and the local members of the team—"the chain gang," Maeve called them—spoke of it like it had been an apocalypse. The storm had ripped homes to wreckage. The dunes were once a mountain range, if one was to believe the locals' exaggerations, and had been reduced to hillocks with wisps of grass poking through.

"They say it was no hurricane, but it was," Carla said. She'd worked these jobs every summer for a decade and had the leathery face to prove it. "It didn't have a name or anything. Not like Hurricane Hazel. Remember her?"

Jack didn't.

"You missed a show. She was a brute. Took half the town with her. That was, what? Fifty-five?"

"Fifty-four," Maeve said.

"Fifty-four. Took out the whole place, that one. The whole town."

"Town" was an exaggeration. Cobble Beach had two paved roads: High Street, with seasonal surf shops and a tiny Presbyterian church, and Lakeside Drive, which ran along the beach. All the other roads were potholed clay alleys with cottages set on cinder blocks. They looked temporary, waiting for the next storm. Maeve's was no different. It was a red clapboard rectangle with no basement and no attic. And that's not all there wasn't. There was no phone, no driveway, no running water, no TV. There was electricity, but it came from a propane generator with valves and dials Maeve policed obsessively.

The cottage was rammed with bric-a-brac. Magazines were stacked on every surface, and the furniture was packed in close. Jack had to move sideways between his bed and the dresser, between the couch and the coffee table. Maeve, or more likely Dot, had push-pinned photos to the wall panelling. They depicted movie stars. Burt Lancaster, Ruby Dee, Marlon Brando. Lucille Ball and Desi Arnaz were portrayed together, him smiling behind her as she did her surprised face, lipsticked mouth in an O. All the pictures were signed "with love" to Dot in the same childish handwriting.

"Did these stars really sign these?"

"What do you think, kid?"

The most memorable item was a radio the size of an upright piano. Crafted out of solid pine, it looked new, with a shiny finish and strong woody smell that cut through the must of the cottage. Its dial had city names on it instead of numbers. Jack could only make out "Roma" and "Paris," as the rest were in languages he didn't understand, decorated with accents. The radio also had a cove with a tiny light bulb illuminating thin shelves. Upon arrival, Maeve filled them with whisky bottles.

Every evening, after Kraft Dinner with ketchup and wiener segments, Jack met the chain gang down on the beach. This was an unpopular rocky stretch of shore, well beyond the last changing station, where they could pull Carla's Datsun close to the waterline. They lit a fire, drank cans of 50 and turned up songs on the car's speakers.

Carla said Canadian radio stations were shit. "All la-la-la," she said. "No feeling." Her radio was tuned to WXYZ 1270 out of Detroit, which specialized in musicians Jack had never heard before: The Miracles, Mable John, Eddie Holland.

"Water brings the music," Carla told him, pointing to the lake, where the moon's choppy reflection glittered in the waves. "It's Black music, this. Detroit's the only city that'll play it. We're lucky to be by the lake. The water carries the signal all the way from there to here, especially at night. We can get it on the beach. Even a quarter-mile from shore, this'd be nothing but static."

Back in Brooklyn, radio stations were still rotating soulless singles like "Cathy's Clown" and "Alley-Oop"—both the Dyno-Sores' and the Hollywood Argyles' versions. It was all frothy and thin; idealized puppy-love stories. This new music was embracing, with rich voices and emotions, blunt and melodic. Jack resisted the songs at first on the grounds that they were from the USA, the country he was trying to escape. But WXYZ won him over after a couple of boozy nights, barrelling its melodies across the watery border. It was American, but it was an America he didn't know; it spoke of things he didn't understand, but wanted to.

*

Jack sweat into his suit, walking up the sloped sidewalk of Laurier Street with yellow gladiolas cradled in his arm. They bounced as he hurried, hitting him in the face. He closed his mouth to keep from tasting pollen. Women watched him. They sat on porches in rockers as teams of children played hockey with balls on the road, trying to compensate for the incline of the street. Between the houses, Jack saw backyards with dozens of diapers fluttering on lines in the sun. Catholics, he thought.

The Zappacostas' place was at the top of the hill. Like its neighbours, the house was a perfect square, one-storey tall, and had a single window poking from the roof. Behind the house rose an acre of plants growing in patches. Jack could make out potatoes, basil, tomatoes. In the picture window, between the pane and lacy curtains, were placards to alert delivery men, BREAD MILK EGGS. The odour of garlic cooking in olive oil hit him before he reached the door, along with sounds of laughing and sizzling and chatter. Music, too: a bright lady's voice, like Connie Francis, only in Italian. Through the door he could see down a short hall that led to a second door at the back. Two girls dancing together spun into view.

"Bonnie?"

She was gone again, twirled away behind a wall. A woman's voice admonished them, telling them to stop dancing, that it only leads to trouble.

A man appeared in a white sleeveless undershirt. He was short and hunched forward in a way that reminded Jack of his own posture. Standing straight, Jack extended his hand and said, "Evening sir, I'm Jack."

"Jacko!"

"Yes, sir."

The man smiled and yelled in Italian. Jack understood none of it. A flattened hand either shooed Jack away or beckoned him deeper into the house. Bits of spit flew from behind the man's teeth.

"*Avanti*! In! Come in! In, in, in!"

Bonnie came running down the hall. "You made it," she said. "And you've already encountered Papa."

"*Si*, Jacko, Jacko," the father said, and led them down the hall, releasing a further river of Italian. There was cheer from unseen people.

"These aren't for me," Bonnie said, pointing at the gladiolas.

"Yes they are."

"No, they're for my mother," she said.

The rooms off the hall were cell-like. In the parents' bedroom, a double mattress took up almost all the space. A living room held two couches, both suffocating under a plastic film and aimed at a huge TV with a tiny screen. The kitchen was full of women and music.

"Everyone, Mama, this is Jack."

"*Vino*!" the father said. "For Jacko!"

"This is the gentleman I was telling you about," Bonnie said.

She pointed around the small kitchen. Jack strained to remember all the sisters' names. There were four of them, all engaged in some kind of food preparation. Isabella, the eldest, was rolling parsley-flecked balls of meat and tossing them into a cauldron of red sauce. Filomena sliced fennel. Teresa grated a hard cheese into a bowl. Lia dredged cutlets of veal in bread crumbs. Bonnie was the youngest; she took slices of dough from her mother and rolled them into snakes, then dusted them with flour.

"Jacko got a dose of Papa," said Bonnie.

"Ran the gauntlet, eh?" said Isabella.

"Brave boy," said Filomena.

"Bonbon's found a trooper," said Lia.

"He's earned a drink," said Teresa.

"Good evening?" Jack said. "Mrs. Zappocosta, these are for you."

"Look, Mama, they're glads. Aren't they your favourite?" said Bonnie. "I'll put them in water."

"They're nice," the mother said without looking at them. She left her pile of dough and tottered around the table to kiss Jack on both cheeks. She was skinny and worried-looking, as Maeve had said, with thinning white hair and frowny wrinkles. Her bifocals were splattered with pinpoints of tomato sauce. She looked at him as though trying to map his features onto future grandchildren. "Jacko, yes?"

"Jack," he said.

"You're staying with those O'Hara sisters."

"My aunts."

"Is Maeve even feeding you? You're too skinny. And fancy. Too fancy for this." She indicated the kitchen. Pots were bubbling and steaming on the stove. Pans hung under white cupboards, a fridge rumbled and gasped. The same Jesus, sculpted in brass, suffered on wooden crosses above every doorway. Next to the attic stairs hung a picture of John XXIII. He looked dreamy in his regalia, idealized, like something the Soviets would produce of Stalin. He was fat, bald, benevolent, draped in a Santa-like red cape with white fur and gold detailing. His fingers were raised and crooked in blessing.

"Seriously, take off your jacket," said Bonnie. "And your tie, too."

"You'll stain it for sure," said Isabella.

"Or get it smelly," said Filomena.

"Or die of heat," said Lia.

"Or of embarrassment," said Teresa.

Bonnie handed him a juice glass of red wine. "Papa makes it, so say you love it."

"I love it," he said without taking a sip. The women laughed.

"See, he's quick. I told you," Bonnie said. "And American."

"God, what next?" said Mrs. Zappacosta. "American."

"Yes, ma'am," Jack said.

"Ma'am. Bonifacia, who have you brought over? He thinks he's a gentleman. An American gentleman in my kitchen."

Thirsty from the walk, Jack took an enormous gulp of the wine. Its vinegar burn seared down his throat and went to work on his stomach, spreading heat and looseness to the far reaches of his limbs. When the record stopped, Bonnie flipped it and started it back up, leaving floury fingerprints on the vinyl.

"You're distracting Bonifacia," Mrs. Zappacosta said. "Look, she's rolling the gnocchi uneven. Jacko, go outside with the men. There's more wine out there."

Jack looked out the window at "the men," presumably the girls' husbands. This was what men were here: slouched creatures in sandals and undershirts, loafing at a weatherbeaten picnic table, rearranging hands of playing cards, poking at dust gathered at the bottom of a promotional GM ashtray. Jack did not want to join them. He was not used to being idle when work was underway.

"Is there really nothing I can do to help?" he said.

"What's wrong with you?" Mrs. Zappacosta said. "Go outside."

"Actually, Jacko, you can fill that giant pot with water and lift it to the stove," Bonnie said, saving him, smiling big and broad. "Cold water only. And toss in a handful of salt."

Mrs. Zappacosta watched in agony, hand on her heart, as Jack approached the shelf. "Give him the steps!"

"Don't trouble yourself," Jack said, reaching.

"Well, he's tall. That's useful," said Isabella.

"But gangly," said Filomena.

"Catholic, though?" said Lia.

"Irish, for sure," said Teresa.

"Arrrg. American *and* Irish," said Mrs. Zappacosta.

"Bonbon, you'll end out like Mary the Virgin!" Lia said. "Knocked up at fifteen."

"I won't!" said Bonnie.

"You better not," Mrs. Zappacosta said. "Or else."

"The Irish—oh, they always hit the mark, don't they?" said Filomena.

"How many in your family, Jacko?" said Teresa.

"We're nine kids, plus parents."

"See? I told you, Bonbon," Lia said. "Mary the Virgin."

"Who?" Jack said. "Like *Mary* Mary?"

"No, a different Mary," Bonnie said. "Don't confuse the poor guy."

"She went to our high school," Isabella said. "Irish too."

"But then she got up the duff," Filomena said.

"Would never happen to one of my girls," Mrs. Zappacosta said.

"One day, she stopped coming to class," Teresa said.

"And *we* all thought she was just getting fat," Lia said.

"She was the size of this table if she was an inch and a half," Isabella said.

The breaded veal hit a bath of oil, releasing a ripping sizzle and a nutty smell.

"Never saw her again," Filomena said.

"Parents had to move out to Fergus," Lia said.

"Fergus, they say," Isabella said. "But I heard Toronto."

"Doesn't matter where. Point is she left," Filomena said.

"And this one's Irish too!" Teresa said.

"He'll just have to *look* at you, Bonbon," Lia said.

Even Mrs. Zappacosta cracked a smile.

"Look how red he's getting!"

"Like a fire truck!"

"Like the sauce!"

"Like a beet!"

"Like an O'Hara," Mrs. Zappacosta said. She was done with the pasta now, counting them. "Get me the thing."

The women all held up their hands, some family code to show their fingers were mucky. Only Jack, palms around his glass, was unoccupied.

"Jacko, could you?" Bonnie said. "Come around here, behind me. In the fridge door. There's a thing of Tupperware. Can you grab it?"

"With pleasure," he said and stood behind Bonnie as she portioned out the remaining slices of dough. The fridge was short, crammed with stuff. He had to bend down to search through the items on the door shelves. He could feel Bonnie behind him, her legs brushing against his back. She lifted her foot, rubbed it under his bent bum.

"Got it?" she said. Her toe crept up, tickled the bottom of his back. "It's white."

"Um." He had it but kept rummaging.

"Square?"

"Yeah."

She gave him a final tap and pulled her foot away, saying, "Does what he's told!"

Jack was sure his smile was stupid-looking as he handed the container to Mrs. Zappacosta. Seated now, she didn't seem to notice. She was pulling her dress up and her stockings down, showing him a thigh with a nebula of blue veins.

"So, Jacko, tell us, then," Mrs. Zappacosta said. She opened the Tupperware. It contained small bottles and syringes in plastic packaging. She took one, bit the end off and ripped it open, plucking the item out of the pack with a deft hand.

"Tell you what?"

"About something." She filled the syringe with clear liquid from a tiny bottle. "Your family."

"Dinner at our place is different than this," he said, watching her jab herself and press the plunger. Her face didn't change at all.

"No one giving themselves shots, eh?" Isabella said.

"Might be a queasy boy!" Filomena said.

"He's gone from red to white!" Lia said.

"In no seconds flat!" Teresa said.

"It's insulin, Jacko," Bonnie said. "Mama does it every night before dinner. Keep going."

Jack stuttered an explanation of the O'Hara system. The chef on the rota was assigned a helper, one of the younger kids, and they were sequestered to the kitchen with one of his mother's typed recipe cards. The rest of the household was not to disturb them until the meal was laid out on the table: discrete bowls of meat, potatoes and something green. "The idea that a dish can have more than three ingredients is a foreign concept to me."

"Irish," Mrs. Zappacosta said, crumbling up the syringe packaging.

"Sounds strict," Bonnie said.

"My dad was in the military," Jack said. "He and I, we wash and cook as often as we shovel and mow. He says it'll make me a good husband some day."

"Thought you'd slip that in, did you, Jacko?" Bonnie said.

"Smooth as apple butter, this one," Isabella said.

"Helpful *and* clever," Teresa said.

"Not like our slobs," Lia shouted, loud enough to be heard out back.

"How's that wild aunt of yours?" Mrs. Zappacosta said. With one hand, she righted her stocking, with the other, she dropped the pasta into boiling water. She did all this with bravery and care, but also, Jack detected, a trace of victimhood. She stared into the pot, armed with a slotted spoon held near her face.

"She's getting better, thanks for asking," Jacko said. "We all hope Dot comes home soon."

"Not her. Maeve."

"Oh. Maeve's the same," Jack said. "I'd never describe her as wild."

"She's tough as tar," Mrs. Zappacosta said. "She and that priest still thick as thieves?"

"You mean Father Dupuis?"

"I see them chattering. I know what goes on."

"Sure you do, Mama," Bonnie said. "She doesn't."

"Never changes," Mrs. Zappacosta said, still reading the pot's contents like they were tea leaves. "OK, get the men."

Isabella yelled that dinner was ready, and then there were twice as many people in the kitchen. Jack was asked to drain the pasta into a colander in the sink, and when he turned back, the table was piled with dishes and scattered cutlery. Everyone grabbed. As soon as the centre was clear, platters of food were slid before them: pyramids of breaded veal, bowls of meatballs, pasta swamped with sauce, and a salad in a cavernous wooden bowl.

Bonnie sat across from him. As she blitzed through the words of grace, he felt pressure on his shoe. It was Bonnie's foot, and it fled, unfamiliar with the presence of someone so tall under the table. When it returned, it stayed, and when Bonnie finished prayer, she lifted her head from her fingers and she stared right at him, as she had at Mass. Jack had to slouch to ensure their touch didn't stop. He was growing aroused as everyone reached forward to grab their dinner, with no pretence of letting the guest go first.

"Jacko! *Mangia*!" Mr. Zappacosta said.

Jack copied what the other men were doing, assuming they didn't also have erections. He mopped sauce from his plate with a hunk of veal and one of the doughy balls. The notes rung out on his tongue, a balance of acids and fats. He'd never known the depth of a tomato's flavour, the lilt of basil, the potential lightness of pasta. That tastes could arrive in sequences, in one bite. At home and at Maeve's cottage, food only landed in him. It was ballast.

This was a chord of flavours, played masterfully as Bonnie's toe moved over his. Everyone else seemed unfazed by this miracle, but it was new to him, and he had seconds and thirds.

After eating, he praised Mrs. Zappacosta's talents as he helped clear the table. The men chuckled in his direction and went to the living room to smoke and watch hockey, a game Jack could never follow. He insisted on helping with the dishes.

"No, go smoke," Mrs. Zappacosta said.

"I don't smoke."

"It's OK, Mama," Bonnie said. "He's washing up OK. Look at him go."

"Not like Ricky—remember? And Fred?" Teresa said.

"With the rice everywhere!" Filomena said.

"Chicken on the ceiling!" Lia said.

"Men," Mrs. Zappacosta said.

"Did you watch *Lucy*, Jacko?" Bonnie said. "We love it around here."

"Sometimes," Jack said. "That was a real shame, what happened with them. That divorce."

"Worse than shame," Isabella said.

"Appalling," Teresa said.

"A sin, through and through," Filomena said.

"They'll see each other in hell," Lia said.

"Americans," Mrs. Zappacosta said.

"But *he* was stepping out on *her*," Bonnie said. "*He's* the cad."

"Ah, she didn't know what to do with him," Isabella said.

"And *he's* the real Catholic, too," Teresa said.

"That's *his* soul on the line," Filomena said.

"She's got some nerve," Lia said.

"I bet she was doing what she could," Bonnie said.

"*I* bet she's fast," Isabella said.

"I bet she's *rich,*" Teresa said.

"That show's worth a pretty penny," Filomena said.

"*He* invented it," Lia said.

"He didn't invent *her,*" Bonnie said.

"I always thought they looked so happy on the show," Jack said.

They all laughed at him.

"Jacko, the show was nothing like it *was,*" Isabella said.

"You got a sharp one here, Bonbon," Teresa said.

"But sweet," Filomena said.

"Means well," Lia said.

"He's alright," Bonnie said.

Jack blushed, drying a chipped plate. Isabella fetched a juice glass from the window sill and placed it on the table. The women reached in, fingered out their wedding bands. Over the clinking of gold on the glass, Jack risked a meaningful glance at Bonnie, but, as always, she was ahead of him. She was shaking her head. Jack gave her a grin and she smiled in return, but it was a sad kind of smile. Jack saw evidence of Mrs. Zappacosta in Bonnie's face, as though she'd inherited worry along with the big ears and massive tits.

*

Jack went to bed late, in a symphony of crickets. Starfished on Dot's bed, he could taste the salt of dinner on his tongue. When he closed his eyes, he felt tipsy again. The image of the Pope he'd stared at all through the meal came back to him, only with Bonnie's breasts and worried eyes. The Zappacostas had kept him on Laurier Street until ten, and sent him home with plastic tubs of veal and gnocchi. Mrs. Zappacosta filled a third container with fried zucchini flowers and wrote "Mae" on the lid in shaky cursive. "For your *zia*, for sending you over."

At one in the morning, he tiptoed up to the kitchen. He stood in the light of the open fridge and pinched gnocchi from the container, popping them in his mouth. Next to the phone, amid a pile of mail and stamp rolls, he found a box of stationery—creamy pages, blank save Maeve's name and her former address. Jack uncapped a Bic and sat at the table, its surface slicked with moonlight, and wrote a polite thank-you note to Mrs. Zappacosta. He sealed it and placed it away from the pasta to keep it clean. A blank sheet stared up at him.

"Dear Bonnie," he wrote. "Your house is special."

He pinched another gnocchi, ate it, and stared at what he'd written. This is shit, he thought. I don't know what I'm doing.

Headlights swept through the adjacent living room. He heard the crank of the truck's parking brake and the door slamming shut. His instincts upped his heart rate. At home, he'd be in trouble for being up at this hour. His father would make an appointment to sit and talk this over the next day—why Jack thought he could break the rules, why he should know better, how he needed to set an example, "Your mother and I are counting on you," and so on. Jack's week with Maeve left him unsure if she would punish him. He closed the Tupperware with a press of his thumb and placed it back in the fridge. When his aunt came in whistling a tune, Jack took a gamble, saying, "Your mother and I were worried sick."

"Ha!" she said. "Don't worry, I wasn't out with a boy."

"Next time there will be repercussions," Jack said.

"Don't let JJ hear that imitation of him." She flicked on the main light and moved past Jack toward the cupboard, leaving a wake of whisky fumes and cigarette smoke. "Like the way I got tarted up?"

She wore a denim blazer over a white blouse and had her curls pulled away from her temples with hair pins. Pale pink lipstick took some of the meanness out of her face.

"Very hip," he said.

"How'd you know? You dress like a square," she said. "Nightcap?"

He said no; she poured him rye. The whisky's smell ripped up Jack's nose. He frowned and sipped, working it around his mouth, sweet and unpleasant.

"How was the big dinner with the Italians?"

Jack described the food as miraculous and gave a generous review of the house.

"Sounds dull."

"It was anything but, Aunt Maeve."

"How was *she*?"

"Beautiful," Jack said. "A remarkable young woman."

"I meant the mother."

"Mrs. Zappacosta? I think she was a bit unsure about me at first, but she warmed up."

"She was probably worrying herself up into a froth, having a new man in the house. She worships men. I guess old Italian ladies do."

"She called me Jacko all evening."

"Italians and their vowels," she said. "What was she wearing?"

"Wearing? An apron, I guess? She gave herself a shot right in front of me. Did you know she's diabetic?"

"Yeah, she's been through it, I'll tell ya. But that's what you get."

"Is it?"

"Always been too fancy for a poor girl, that one." Impossibly, Maeve was done with her drink and already refilling it.

"She sent leftovers for us. Gnocchi, it's called."

"Got a little Italian vocab lesson along with your erection, eh?" Jack blushed and put all his attention into his glass for another nauseating sip. "Sorry, I'm a little tight. We tied one on tonight."

"Where were you?"

"Down the city," she said, leaning into the fridge. She took out the tub with her name on it. She smelled the fried flowers, smiled at them, then squinted at them as though trying to decode them.

"Which city is that?"

"Toronto. There's only one city." She placed the food back into the fridge. "Well, I guess there's Hamilton. But no one goes there."

"Why did you go?"

"Dot's not away that often. Gotta take advantage, kid. It's just an hour's drive and the bars are open until one and that." She was flushed and loose, back against the fridge door.

"Got a mash note on the go?"

"I guess."

"Don't send it."

"I don't know what to write."

"You don't know squat," she said. "Doesn't matter what you write. Don't send it."

"Why not?"

"Say it some other way. Don't put it on paper. Don't make it something someone can find and read and that." She stood up straight and stretched her arms towards the ceiling. "Hitting the old hay. You best go too. We're up with the lark." She clicked off the lights and shut her bedroom door, leaving Jack to find his way to the basement in the moonlight.

*

There was a phone box on the beach, near one of the changing stations. Every night after Kraft Dinner, Jack walked two blocks to the shore with a roll of dimes in his hand. He dialled the Zappacostas' number, watched the sun descend and turn the clouds an intense pink, then orange, then red, before kissing the horizon and getting swallowed whole by Lake Huron. He described all this to Bonnie and told her about the work, Maeve, Carla, WXYZ.

"Wish I could be there."

"Me too," Jack said. "We need to get you here."

"Mama wouldn't like it."

"She's met me enough times now. I can charm her into it."

"You think so, eh?" she said.

"I'm very convincing."

"She needs me during the week. I'm the last daughter left." He sensed a quickening in her voice. "You only get to see us on Sundays, Jacko, when we're all around the table. It's a different story on a Tuesday."

"You don't want to come?"

"Of course I do. I'm sick of only touching your toe."

"Me too," he said. "We're in the same boat."

"We're really not."

"I love my family too, but I had to get away. And here I am!"

"Yep," she said. "There you are."

They'd known each other three weeks at that point—three Sundays, three meals—long enough for all the songs on WXYZ to be about Bonnie. That night at the bonfire, "Come to Me" jangled along with Marv Johnson's bum-bum-bum vocals urging Bonnie out of Fiona. "Way Over There" described her trip to the beach. Jack hated "Spoonful" and "Shop Around"—they were cruel to Bonnie—but during "I Heard Church Bells Ringing," Jack heard church bells ringing.

Maeve was still up with her nightcap when Jack returned to the cottage. He'd already had four beers with the chain gang at the bonfire, but he accepted her offer of rye.

"You had to pick a Zappacosta girl, eh, kid?"

"That means something, right?"

Maeve shrugged, sipped.

"She hasn't told me what."

"Girl's got to keep some secrets. Can't say I blame the poor miss."

"Oh, it's mystique. I get it."

"Nah, nah. You don't."

"So, can she come?"

"You think I care?"

He described his plan. He'd buy Bonnie some beach gear, turn up unannounced, and convince her mother.

"That's pretty stupid, kid."

"Why?" he said. "I think it's gutsy."

"It's not."

"I'm doing it," he said. "Tell me why I shouldn't do it."

Maeve reached behind her, to a sideboard covered in scratches and dust, and produced a pack of Benson & Hedges. She lit one, inhaled, and released the smoke slowly, so the cloud hung around them. She tossed the pack to Jack. "They're Dot's. I don't usually touch them."

"No thanks."

"Suit yourself. Bonfire's got you smelling like an ashtray anyhow," she said.

She chewed the smoke in her mouth and looked as though she was putting the words together in her mind.

"So?" he said

"So what?" Maeve said.

"So, are you going to tell me or do I have to guess?"

"She's a bastard."

"Bonnie? You can't say that."

"She's a bastard, kid. All those girls are. Their monster of a father had a whole other family in Italy. A wife, four sons, the whole kit and caboodle."

"He's divorced? How—how could that even be?"

"Divorced? Nah, nothing that bad. He abandoned them. Turned up in Fiona and started a whole different life. Got a brand new family for himself and didn't think anyone would ever know he still had a wife in Italy."

"How do you know all this?"

"Everyone knows. There was a doozy of a scandal." She refilled her glass. He'd barely touched his, but she added to it anyhow.

"Yeah, but *how* did it get out?"

"Roberto. You met him at the house, I bet. Short, hairy bumpkin. He's one of the real kids—from Italy. He works with me over at GM. Nice guy, but dumb as a post."

"There were five guys there who fit that description."

"Roberto lives there with them. He's older than the girls. Just turned up one day. 'Boo! How's it goin'?' They tried to lie about it and that. Some hooey about Roberto being a nephew. But it didn't stick. Father Dupuis, gotta love him—he's wily. He figured it out. Word spread like butter. It was hell on Fiona."

"The town suffered?"

"Nah, nah. The mother. Her first name is Fiona. Her parents named her after the town because they started a new life there. Some immigrant malarky. Funny to think about it now, isn't it? After everything?"

"I wouldn't call it funny."

She shrugged, finished her whisky. "I think it's a hoot."

"That poor mother."

"Poor? She married a married man, kid."

"Did she know he was married?"

"I'm not a bloody mentalist. I don't know what goes on between that beast and his missus. I guess if you wanna tally up the sins, the father's worse off. In the eyes of God, I mean." She put her elbow on the table and pointed the cigarette at him. "That's God. I couldn't give a toss. But you better bet JJ's not going to love it if you bring that piece of work home to Brooklyn."

"But they're such welcoming people, the Zappacostas."

"Welcoming's a weak virtue. They're a bunch of cowards," Maeve said. She brought the cigarette to her face, leaving only her eyes above her fingers. She looked like she was reconsidering this, staring at a point way past Jack. "I'll give Fiona this. She goes to Our Lady of Victory every Sunday. She parades her family in front of the parish like it means something."

"Bonnie has to live in that house. With that man."

"You gotta feel for the girls," Maeve said. "They didn't do squat to deserve this."

"I should call her."

"Aren't you seeing her tomorrow?"

"So?"

"She already knows this stuff, kid. She's living it." Maeve stood. "You finding out doesn't count for much."

"But it's important."

"Nah, it ain't." She dropped the cigarette into her whisky glass. It hissed. "You're probably the one thing in that girl's life that has nothing to do with any scandal. You think she likes you because of your physique?"

"Image of Brando." He downed his whisky in one shot. He was learning that this was the way to do it.

"Just don't do anything stupid."

Jack lurched towards the payphone in a cacophony of crickets, strangling his dime roll in his left hand. He had never been so drunk; he had never been in such darkness. Not a single cottage light was on. He was the only person awake for miles. He was lonely in the way only a sixteen-year-old can be lonely, with desperation pushing him down the street towards an immediate solution—the only kind of solution he could conjure.

At Lakeside Drive, the air changed. Cold currents hit him off the water and the caws of seagulls joined the crickets. He couldn't find the path to the beach, so he scrambled over the dunes, his shoes full of sand. A haze of light came from High Street, and it was bright enough for him to make out the changing station to his right, far from where he expected it. He ran over the sand and was out of breath while spinning the numbers. The dimes were gritty. He put too many into the phone, dropped a couple on the concrete. The receiver on his ear was cold at first, but warmed as the intervals of tone multiplied. He could see the Laurier Street house in his mind, all dark. The kitchen cleaned for the night, the giant pasta pot upturned next to the sink. The bedroom doors were all closed. The refrigerator wheezed. The bell of the phone cut through the tension of the rooms. The father turned in his bed, annoyed. His wife, with her ironic name, was wide awake, looking at the brass Jesus, not daring to get up and face the wrath of her husband. Roberto, alone in the room off the kitchen, was frozen, hoping it would end. In the attic, Bonnie was above the sheets, listening as the phone continued to scream. He couldn't fathom what she was thinking. His imagination ended there.

*

"Did you call my house in the middle of the night?" Bonnie was in her Dairy Fairy uniform, standing on Maeve's porch with her arms folded.

"Don't be cross."

"You can't do that."

"Sorry."

"You going to invite me in?

"Maeve's not here. It's Saturday. She's visiting Dot."

"So?"

"Don't we need an adult?"

"If you think we're going to neck, you've got another thing coming."

Bonnie pulled the screen door open and swept past him, slipping her loafers off without breaking her gait. He followed her into the living room, where she stopped in the middle of the burgundy carpet.

"Lush," she said. "I can feel it between my toes."

"It's brand new. Everything here is," Jack said. "I've never been in a house like this. It's so modern. You should see the fridge."

"It's not suited to Maeve, is it?"

"She said she's getting it ready for Dot."

"Dot'll love it. She'll never want to leave," Bonnie said. "Guess that's the point."

"Is it?"

"You're sweet," Bonnie said, without a trace of affection. She was looking at him with an implacable face. It wasn't the face of a teenager. "Maeve told you, then?"

"I made her."

"Sure you did."

"She did it to discourage me. Stop me from doing something senseless."

"A roaring success."

"Did I wake up the house?"

"Did you ever," she said. "I got the belt, Jack. Mama tried to stand between me and Papa. It was a mess. She cried most of the night."

"I'm sorry," he said, and reached for her hand. She took a step away from him.

"You know about Roberto now, and you think you know everything."

"I don't. I don't think that," he said. "But I want to know everything."

"You say that, but you don't," Bonnie said. "Mama sleeps with me, in the attic, in a tiny bed. It's not even big enough for me, but there she is, every night, in a ball. It's ever since Roberto turned up. She won't even look at Papa. Some nights, he stands at the bottom of the stairs and he knocks on the door and yells that Mama should come down to bed. He used to do it every night, but it's better now, these past few years."

"Years?"

"Years," she said. She pointed her defiance at the window, at the rock garden. "I can't make it good. I try, but I can't make it any better for my mother."

"Or for yourself?"

"For anybody," she said.

"I want to take you to the beach," Jack said.

"Who cares what you want."

"Don't you want to come?"

"Who cares what *I* want."

"I do."

"My knight in shining armour?" she said and turned back to him. She stepped forward and kissed him. She was decisive about it. Determined. It was awkward at first—lips smashed, teeth rubbing—but they found their way. The kiss melted into an act in concert, and Jack put his arms up her back, drawing her in, and every part of her loosened. He was aroused, but she didn't seem to mind. She kept going. She shaped herself into him.

"I want to," she said when they'd stopped kissing and she held his head in her neck. Jack could feel the blood in his jugular. He felt as drunk as he had at the cottage.

"So come."

"I can't." She let go of him and retreated. The inch of space felt like a defeat. "Your aunt would never allow it anyway."

"She might. She doesn't care about anything."

"Well, don't say a word to Maeve. Don't tell her about what goes on at my house, all those details. I don't want her involved."

"You almost sound like you want me to."

"You think so, don't you?"

"Why is this so confusing?"

"Because you're spoiled, Jack. You don't even know it. You're a tourist, and you're going to leave."

"I'm here now."

"You're not even here when you're here."

"Tell me what I can do."

"Don't come to Sunday dinner tomorrow. Don't say hi to me at church. Don't do anything stupid."

"I meant tell me what to do to help."

"I just did," Bonnie said.

*

That night, Jack lay awake in Dot's room. The crickets sang. They were everywhere in Canada; he couldn't escape them. Their ghostly whistles swelled and receded, over and over—signals they were sending, dialogues they were having. What on Earth could they have to say to one another? Why send all this information into the air, night after night?

The conversation with Bonnie ricocheted around his mind. He wondered if Mr. Zappacosta was knocking on the attic door, if Bonnie was in bed with her mother. His mind went back to the kiss, the embrace, the breasts against him, the responsive slackening of her body, the flow and duet of it all. He thought he couldn't jerk off again, but then he did.

Around midnight, Maeve arrived, walked overhead, flushed the toilet and marched off to her bedroom. His eyes kept landing on his duffle, sitting near the door. He'd packed it with clean work clothes for the coming week, which took up a third of the space. Jack felt a twinge of loneliness on their behalf. He didn't want to be in this room, this room that could exist anywhere. The crickets seemed louder than before, the coverlet itchier. The walls were whiter, shorter, more oppressive. Aunt Dot's cartons were more mysterious.

He opened the topmost box. Records. Their multicoloured lines were pressed together like music staves. Mozart, Bizet, Bach. But also Peggy Lee, Jo Stafford, Frankie Lane, and several he didn't recognize. Who the heck is Lolita?, he thought. Jack pulled a few records from the box, all women, then re-sealed it and moved it aside. In subsequent boxes, he found bizarre ceramic creatures and votive candles with various saints depicted on them. There was a Saint Christopher's medal and headshots of celebrities, similar to the ones at the cottage, only Dot hadn't yet marred them with her forgeries. One of the boxes contained costume jewellery in a tangle, with loose buttons gathered at the bottom.

The boxes in the closet all contained clothes. Dot was a tall woman, and most of the items were tent-like dresses, flowing and shapeless, and designed to be pulled on over her head. One stack had shirts with wild patterns of fruits; they seemed unsuitable for a woman or a man. In another, square ladies' underwear, greyed and threadbare from years of wear. Jack blushed digging through to the bottom, where there was a pre-war girdle and bras stiffened with wire. There was also a modest slate swimsuit—a one-piece with a bow between the breasts—balled up and shoved in the corner.

Jack filled the empty part of his duffle. By the time he was done, dawn was throwing a celestial blue into the room, but the crickets hadn't yet shut up.

*

On the drive to Mass, Jack held out for two blocks before he blurted out Bonnie's whole tale. He spiked it with dramatic verbs. Nonna didn't cry, she "wailed;" Papa Zap didn't knock on the attic door, he "hammered."

"The poor so-and-sos," Maeve said. She didn't seem saddened by the story. She seemed angry—teeth clenched as she stared through the drizzle-slicked windshield.

Father Dupuis was halfway to the altar when Bonnie and her family arrived at Our Lady of Victory. Heads turned to watch Mrs. Zappacosta remove a plastic rain bonnet. The sisters kept their eyes down, embarrassed. Bonnie entered last, finding Jack with her eyes. He smiled; she didn't. She took her place with her family and Jack felt them there, torturously, until Communion. After taking the Eucharist, he didn't return to his seat for the blessing. He went outside and waited in the spitting rain. The Zappacostas were the first people out the door.

"If it isn't our midnight caller," Isabella said.

"Our heavy breather," Teresa said.

"Making an ass of himself," Filomena said.

"Again," Lia said.

"I'm sorry," Jack said to Mrs. Zappacosta in his full American accent. He scanned her face for any compassion or forgiveness. She betrayed nothing; it was all armour. "Mrs. Zappacosta, I am sorry for any trouble I've caused you. That was not my intention."

"I told you not to talk to me," Bonnie said.

"I'm not talking to you," he said.

"Ooooo, watch out, Bonbon, he's trying to grow a spine!" Isabella said.

"That's when they all go bad, isn't it?" Teresa said.

"Thinks he can carry you away," Filomena said.

"He's got it bad, that's a fact," Lia said.

Parishioners were pouring out now, pooling around. Jack took off his suit jacket and held it over Bonnie's head.

"We look ridiculous," she said. Jack's white shirt was becoming sheer in the wetness. "I can see your freckles though the fabric."

"Connect the dots."

She smiled, and said, "You look like death warmed over."

"I didn't sleep."

"Serves you right."

"Maybe," he said. "Probably."

"Go back to the beach, Jacko."

"With you. You can come," he said. "You can have Dot's room. I'll sleep on the couch. Come for a week or day. Or an hour. I won't even touch you!"

"You're kidding, right?"

"About touching you?"

"About everything."

"I'm not. We can go right now, in front of everybody. My aunt's bringing her truck around, and we can drive straight there. I even packed you some clothes, and some beach stuff. A bathing suit—"

"Jack. *Jacko.*"

"—and records, too, that I think you'll like." He bent down to match heights with her eyes. It was the moment that would define my parents' marriage; her decoding him, making decisions about which of his dreamy ideas to indulge; him romantic, jumped-up, gambling, racing to outcomes. "You said you wanted to come."

"Don't be simple," she said. "I have a job, a mother."

"Bring her."

"My mother in a bathing suit," Bonnie laughed. "You're out of your depth. It's adorable."

Maeve pulled the truck up to the sidewalk. The crowd had thinned, but a few people remained, talking with Father Dupuis. Jack couldn't make out their mutterings, but figured they were talking about the scandal. *Roberto this* and *Roberto that.*

"These people are waiting to see what my family gets up to next—some disgrace."

"Let's give it to them."

Maeve honked. Jack stayed in place. His arms ached from holding the jacket. His hair was soaked. He could feel his eyes straining with hope.

"No. No, off you go," Bonnie said and moved from under the jacket towards her family. Mrs. Zappacosta looked ruined in her boxy blue polyester dress. It may as well have been made of lead, the way it was crushing her. Both women were on the edge of crying as they embraced. Nothing showy or uncontrolled, no tears, but rather something practised. They wore wrenched faces of steely resignation.

Jack dropped his arms to his sides. The jacket scraped the cement. He backed away towards the Chevy, thinning and stretching the invisible tether between him and Bonnie. He felt the vibrations of the motor when he collided with the truck. The metal chassis jolted when the driver's side door slammed shut. The tableau of women stared not at him, but at Maeve, who joined them on the sidewalk.

"Enough of this hooey. We gotta get on the road," Maeve said. She turned and addressed Bonnie: "You come too, dear, if you want. I'll bring you back the minute you say the word."

Mrs. Zappacosta's mouth hung open.

"Fee, don't you worry," Maeve said to the old matriarch. "I got the message. Let the girl go for a bit. You know you can trust me to keep the boy in check."

Mrs. Zappacosta's face did not change, but she muttered something to Bonnie in Italian. Jack didn't understand what they were saying, but in the tenor of the sounds, he heard tones of hope. The tether started to thicken again.

Bonnie hugged her mother and turned to Maeve, thanked her, then walked towards Jack—or rather, not towards him, as she didn't meet his eyes, but towards the truck. She opened the door and installed herself in the passenger seat.

"Fiona," Maeve said, voice raising with each syllable. Jack was struck by the unusual sound of adults calling one another by their first names. These two women looked like a before-and-after photo, separated by a narrow, but very deep, canyon of time—one full of marriage and regret and guilt and pregnancies and worry and scandal—that had aged Mrs. Zappacosta like a curse.

Maeve took Mrs. Zappacosta's hands in hers, gripping them so hard that their fingers turned white. One of the sisters gasped.

"Fee, you can squeeze in too, if you want," Maeve said. "We'll make room. I'm just a little thing."

Mrs. Zappacosta couldn't manage words. Jack knew she would not accept this offer, even before she shook her head—a barely perceptible motion that cost her all her energy.

"Yeah, I figured," Maeve said. She turned her back on the Zappacostas and muttered "you drive" to Jack as she walked back to the truck and heaved her tiny bulk in next to Bonnie.

Pulling away, Jack felt the women beside him. He could smell Bonnie, garlic and cooking oil. Somehow, he'd gotten what he wanted. He wasn't sure how. He'd missed some vital, invisible message. What he felt for Bonnie, that overwhelming wave of desire, was very small in comparison to what he'd just witnessed. The scale of what was unseen, unsaid—that was even greater. Insurmountable for him, but not the women.

He looked ahead into the time beyond the truck's windshield. This was the first time he'd driven in Canada, and he saw a perfect summer at the end of this new road. He and Bonnie would swim at night, forget their socks on the sand, listen to The Miracles, and fuck in the Chevy—no, I suppose they made love in the Chevy—but that's not where this memory would begin.

Jack checked the rear-view mirror and saw the Zappacostas still there, shrinking away. It would be there that the memory would begin, outside the church in the rain, year after year, in reality and in the stories he'd tell, in his studies and in his teaching, in his courtship and in his marriage, until he understood the messages flying around him through the air.

story5.11July2018.m4a

[BFM]: Did you talk to your dad about all this?

[GZO]: I called him a couple times when I knew Mom would be in for a soak.

[BFM]: Clever.

[GZO]: And I got some details from that old interview with Maeve. The New York one.

[BFM]: It rounds things out. I like getting this from your dad's point of view.

[GZO]: Well, it's really my point of view.

[BFM]: It's good. Bonnie wouldn't tell it this way. You've made her a bit wild. I like this Bonnie.

[GZO]: I like that she got out.

[BFM]: But it damaged her a little. It cost her something.

[GZO]: Right, but it was for the best.

[BFM]: You <u>WOULD</u> say that.

[GZO]: I would. In fact, I just did.

[BFM]: Yeah, because it produced you.

[GZO]: It? The relationship with Dad?

[BFM]: No. <u>IT</u> it. The damage. The scandal.

[GZO]: Oh.

[BFM]: Don't do that. Don't pretend you don't know. You're finally getting to the juicy part. Keep at it.

[GZO]: I do know, I guess. But do I have to admit it?

[BFM]: You do. In fact, you just did.

6
The Last Son

From the cellar, Bonifacia followed her parents' footsteps on the map in her head. They were in the kitchen, creaking their way to the master bedroom. Mama was quick for a pregnant lady. Bonifacia could make out her mix of shuffling and hurrying, like she was running a race in slippers. Papa clomped behind her, barking in Italian. Mama barked back. Bonifacia understood more of their dialect than they suspected. She made out "cold" and "crazy" from Papa, "shame" and "money" from Mama.

There were daddy-long-legs in the cellar. They creeped out to judge Bonifacia in her musky, dirt-floored crucible. Papa had sent her down here as a punishment because she'd told off Roberto—she can't remember why—and now she had to clean all the wine jugs with a pair of her father's retired underwear, dipped into a tin bucket that contained water and a drop of bleach. The jugs stank of mould and sour booze. This was her fourth hour with that toxic mix. She wrung the underwear over the last jug and watched soapy tears roll down the glass surface, cutting paths in the grime. She hated the work, but at least she didn't get the belt this time. And she liked being isolated from the scandal—from the house's hot core of anger.

School, too, was a refuge. Bonifacia was allowed to walk the two miles on her own now that Lia had graduated to the high school, which was in the opposite direction. Each day at 3:30 p.m.

she pushed open the school's doors and considered turning right instead of left. But then she'd imagine her mother an hour later, staring down Laurier Street between a crack in the lace curtains, rubbing her pregnant belly, worried face floating above the MILK EGGS BREAD signs in the window. Once this image was in her mind, Bonifacia knew she had no choice. She'd turn left and climb the hill home.

Her parents were moving apart now. Papa was still yelling in the bedroom; Mama in the washroom. She was in the washroom a lot lately—for refuge, Bonifacia thought—but Papa couldn't even give her peace on the toilet. He said something about deserving better. She said something about deserving more for the $15 they sent back to his family in Italy every month.

Bonifacia imagined what $15 could have bought them, if it hadn't gone to Italy all these years. Better mattresses, a stronger lock on the bedroom door, insect poison. She let a daddy-long-legs come up her forearm to the elbow, then flicked it off. It somersaulted through the air and landed in the pail of water, appendages up and kicking. She wondered what it might be thinking—I wish I could scream, perhaps? She wondered if it knew it was dying. If I were a spider, I would scream, she thought.

"Oh, go to bed!" her mother screeched, above. Mama moved to the living room, Papa sat on the bed. The mattress squeaked under him. This signalled a detente, but nothing was resolved. It would all pick up at a later provocation. Mama always snarled the command in English, dismissively, oh, go to bed!, like it was a catchphrase on *I Love Lucy*. Something the audience was waiting to hear.

The audience had grown small. Three of Bonifacia's sisters had married and moved out, leaving only her, Lia, and Roberto as witnesses. And Roberto was useless. His arrival had sparked the scandal. No one told Bonifacia the details, but, like everyone at their church, she'd worked out the story based on the available clues. Roberto was a relic from Papa's life in Italy, one of the four sons he'd left there when he came to Canada. He'd had them with his first wife, his real wife, the one God would recognize. Roberto was his real child.

Bonifacia and her four sisters were something else. She often turned over the possibilities in her head—orphans, sins, bastards, mistakes, mongrels, counterfeits—but none seemed right. The closest she could come up with was "stains." That's how it seemed at church, when the heads turned towards the Zappacosta girls. They were obviously, but invisibly, marked.

"All clean," Bonifacia announced when she got to the top of the cellar stairs with the bucket. "Hello?"

"Keep your voice down," Mama said from behind the washroom door. "Papa's in bed."

"It's four in the afternoon," Bonifacia said.

"So what if it is?" The door swung open and there she was, pregnant and exhausted. She'd lost weight everywhere but her belly. She was sallow but carried herself with determination. Her hair was pulled back and tucked behind her ears. She was going grey in streaks. As she shuffled towards the kitchen, Bonifacia saw her bald spot reflecting the hall light.

"Come look at this meat," Mama said. From a tub on the table, she lifted a drumstick out of a pool of buttermilk. "Look. This chicken is no good. It's not even taking the milk."

She poked a drumstick in her daughter's direction. Bonifacia looked at it, plump from its night in buttermilk.

"What are you talking about? It looks great," Bonificia said.

"What do you know?" Mama said. "Don't you empty that filthy water in the kitchen. Take it out back to the garden."

Bonifacia tipped the bucket into the sink. The cloudy water circled the drain. The daddy-long-legs, now certifiably dead, plopped out at the end.

"Oops."

"You girls. You girls will be the death of me."

"You'll live." Bonifacia didn't follow this up with an apology, but she wiped the sink clean.

"An answer to everything. You always have something to say."

"It's better than having nothing to say."

"So what do I do with this chicken, then? Huh, loudmouth?"

"Fry it up!"

"An answer to everything."

She helped Mama with the batter: flour, egg yolks, salt. It smelled like cake until they added a half-bottle of beer, making it yeasty, fizzing up to a sputtering froth. Fried chicken was the only reason that the family bought beer. Bonifacia hadn't even known where to buy it when it appeared on the grocery list. Now, the man at Brewer's Retail always laughed at her—"The little WOP girl that can only handle one bottle of Labatt's"—before ringing it up for her, even though she was underage.

In a deep pan, Mama spun a white square of lard that skated around the iron surface until it was drowning in itself. These are the things I'll miss, Bonifacia thought. She kept a tally of them in her mind. The smells, for example. The batter and the beer, the garlic on her fingers, the basil in the garden, her brother-in-laws' cigarettes, the wine's putrid sharpness, the musty basement, the porcine wafts from the pan, and the pan itself, which released its odorous compilation of meals gone by: rosemary, suet, peppers, eggs, onions, fennel, cod, olive oil.

There was no list of the things she wouldn't miss. If there were, it would itemize everything else. Bonifacia was indifferent to nothing. She was already prepared to hate or love the baby that her mother had spent the last seven months laying a hand upon, separated from the child by a layer of flesh and muscle. That hand on that stomach. It was Mama's nervous tick whenever she was pregnant, as if checking to make sure the child was still there. Bonifacia and her sisters had seen it before. This was Mama's third pregnancy since Bonifacia was born, but none of those babies—all boys—came to anything but a surge of rage and a small coffin. Bonifacia pictured her brothers in limbo, ineligible for heaven, curled-up balls of wrinkled skin, one indistinguishable from the next, floating in a white sky.

"Papa won't want chicken," Bonifacia said. Fried chicken was the one Canadian dish Mama tolerated. The girls loved it; Papa rejected it.

"He's getting penne," Mama said. "Get me some of the sauce from the freezer. The one from last Sunday."

"He won't want frozen sauce either."

"He can't tell the difference."

"He thinks he can."

"He can't."

But he could. Bonifacia knew that he'd cause a scene at the table, when the food was slid in front of him. The frozen sauce, the dried noodles. She poked a finger in the buttermilk, predicting the argument to come.

"Stop playing with the food," Mama said and drank down the remaining half of the beer. She guzzled it like she'd been thirsty in the desert for a million years. Bonifacia watched the muscles in her throat work the liquid down. When Mama burped Bonifacia caught a glimpse of the strange whiteness of her tongue.

"*You* were playing with it."

"Again with something to say. Why do you have to be so wild? This is what gets you into fixes," Mama said, grabbing the drumsticks away. "Talking back."

"Oh right."

Bonifacia now remembered that "talking back" was what had put her in the basement all afternoon. She'd told Roberto that she could never marry a man like him. Papa had yelled that she should treat him like a brother. "'Stranger' is closer to the mark!" she'd replied. Bonifacia had called him so much worse in the past—ape, she recalls, and gorilla—and it had come to nothing. Maybe her parents agreed with these epithets, or maybe it was the reference to the scandal that they hated. She wasn't sure.

"What do you think of the name Bonnie?" Bonifacia said.

"For who?"

"For me. A short form, like a nickname."

"It sounds *mangiacake*." This was her term for all things non-Italian, all things Canadian, Protestant, tasteless, boring, or stiff. "You have a beautiful name."

"It was your favourite? That's why you gave it to your fifth daughter?"

"It suits you. It means good omen."

"I know what it means."

"And that's what I had in my head, when I saw you at first. You were my lucky charm."

Bonifacia looked at her mother's hand on her bulging belly, remembered her dead brothers. If she was a charm, she wasn't lucky enough.

"You should use it right, being a good omen. Don't get ideas. Don't let me catch you running away or dancing like some fool. You'll get yourself in more fixes than you'll know what to do with."

"Bonnie," Bonifacia said, exploring it. "Like Connie. Connie Francis."

"Who's that?"

"A teenage singer from the States."

"Does she dance?"

"She plays the accordion."

"Arrrg. That's the last thing we need in this house. More noise. Is she a *mangiacake*?"

"She's Italian."

"Good."

"But she was born over here. Kind of like me. I listened to her on the radio. She changed her name, just like that." Bonifacia snapped her fingers.

"Who does she think she is? Bet her mother is dying of shame."

"Maybe her mother doesn't mind."

"What was the girl's old name?"

"Concetta."

"I'd never name a child something so ridiculous." Mama put her hand on her belly, spun a chicken leg in the batter to keep its layer thick, then dropped it in the lard. It sizzled and popped, smelling of doughnuts. "Even if it is Italian."

*

In the attic, Bonifacia and Lia dressed for bed. They each had two nightgowns hidden under their pillows, flannel for winter, cotton for summer.

"Should we go flannel already?" Lia said.

"It was cold today, but isn't it too early?" Bonifacia said. "It's not even November."

"Cold is cold."

Bonifacia scanned the small window for an answer. Autumn had ceased being colourful or interesting. The weather was grey now, rainy and nippy, a harbinger of winter. The churned garden stretched away, ending with their property at a line of grapevines grown around a fence. The grapes were wrinkling and needed to be picked before they froze. Probably by her; a punishment for whatever she does next.

"You look like a frump in the flannel, though," Lia said.

"Who do I have to impress up here? Mama? You?"

They pulled the thick garments over their heads, keeping their arms cloaked inside so they could remove their bras and underwear, and pulled them from under the hems. Bonifacia had learned this ritual from her older sisters. Once, there had been four of them in the attic. Isabella slept in the room off the kitchen, a space that always belonged to the house's eldest sister. Filomena inherited it when Isabella married; Teresa inherited it when Filomena married. Now, it was Roberto's, when by all rights it should be Lia's. And Bonifacia, she should have the attic to herself.

Despite the parade of sisters, the attic was devoid of femininity. The sloped walls were bare; parallel planks of wood painted the same hospital teal as the kitchen and the living room. There was an electric heater, a wooden hamper, and an armoire where dresses and skirts hung above a mound of shoes.

There were two beds. One was tucked in a corner and had a divot in the centre that drove people together if they dared to share it. Lia and Bonifacia called it The Canoe. Mama liked the other bed, by the window, farthest from the stairs. Bonifacia and Lia preferred it as well. It was newer, firmer, and it smelled less musty. The Good Bed was most appealing on hot days because it sat in the draft that blew in from the adjacent storage space, beyond an old shower curtain made of crinkled white plastic that swayed in the subtle movement of the air. It looked spooky in the moonlight. If Bonifacia woke up in the dark, dreamy and unfocused, she thought the curtain was the ghost of one of her brothers pointing her to a world beyond—a purgatory without souls, that had once terrified her, but had lately started seeming attractive.

"I hate this green," Bonifacia said.

"I thought you liked it."

"I don't anymore."

"You're always changing your mind."

"It looks radioactive." Bonifacia pushed her arms through the sleeves, placed a hand on the wall. "We're all going to grow extra heads."

"We'll be freaks."

"More so."

"I want The Canoe tonight."

"You had it last night."

"I know, but I want it again."

"She's not that awful, Lia."

"Then you do it." Lia threw her round body onto The Canoe, back first. "Like it or lump it."

They crawled into their beds, snuggling into the arresting bleach smell of the sheets.

"Ten or sleep?" Bonifacia said.

"Yeah."

It was a game they played. They let each other be alone with their thoughts for ten minutes before they could speak again, unless one of them fell asleep. When there were four sisters up here, it was harder to maintain. "Ten or sleep" was more of a joke or a dare. Sooner or later, one of them would laugh or toot or ram an elbow into her bedmate. That was before Roberto, before the scandal. Now, they allowed their thoughts to unspool into the dark, unconcerned with each other, parents, chores, school, daddy-long-legs, the oncoming brother. Thoughts built on thoughts, logic-free and all their own.

"What do you think of Bonnie? You know, for my name?"

"It hasn't been ten minutes yet."

"How do you know?" Bonifacia said.

"I can count, Bonbon."

"I hate that. 'Bonbon.'"

"I know. Why do you think I call you that all the time?"

"I like Bonnie."

"You're Bonbon forever."

"Only to you."

"Mama will never call you anything but Bonifacia."

"Well, she doesn't have to."

"Forget about Papa, too."

"Yeah."

"And Roberto."

"I don't care about him."

"Yeah," Lia said. "It'll be a bad one tonight."

"I know."

"The second bottle of wine."

"I know," Bonifacia said.

As predicted, Papa hadn't approved of the fried chicken. He'd complained that his penne was made from frozen sauce, claimed he could tell. Mama had disagreed. His tumbler had never been empty. A second carafe of wine had to be poured, reluctantly, by Mama, who'd known that once it had been served, it would be consumed. Bonifacia and Lia had locked eyes from across the table. Mama had kept getting up, avoiding the tension, getting herself glass after glass of water from the tap. Roberto had tried to keep them talking but had found he was talking to himself.

"Why did she even make him that frozen sauce?" Bonifacia said.

"To get back at him, dummy. For the fight," Lia said. "Grow up, Bonbon. Sometimes it's like you don't understand anything."

They stopped chatting. Dread filled the silence, along with the ticking seconds of their alarm clock. Bonifacia had trained herself to detect the squeak of the doorknob at the bottom of the stairs. Then, the bolt's click. Finally, the jingle of the lock. "Lock" is what they called it, but it was more rudimentary than that—a simple loop of metal screwed into the door and a corresponding hook on the doorframe. Bonifacia had installed it herself.

Mama's progress up the stairs was slower than usual. She took them one at a time, sliding a slippered foot against each step, making a sandpaper sound. Bonifacia scooched her body towards the wall. The Good Bed absorbed Mama's weight without complaint, but Bonifacia had to grip the frame to keep from tumbling towards her. They lay like that for a while, waiting, Mama on her back, radiating heat, pushing putrid air through her mouth. The flannel was a mistake, Bonifacia thought, staying on her side, sweating, with her knees close to her chest. Pretend to be asleep. She didn't understand why she had to, but knew it was required.

There was mumbling downstairs in Italian between Papa and Roberto. The men were tipsy and laughing. Mama cringed. This is what bothers her the most, Bonifacia thought. That they're friends.

More footsteps. First Roberto's, to the bedroom off the kitchen, then Papa's. Bonifacia could follow his movements on the map in her head. He walked first to the kitchen, then to the master bedroom. He paced there, and then marched back to the attic stairs.

He knocked five times on the door, not with his knuckles, but like a hammer—blunt and loud, the grace notes of each strike jingling from the metal hook in its loop.

"Fiona," he mumbled. "Fiona, *bella*. Come to bed."

Mama did not move.

"Fiona, it's not right." He was speaking in Italian.

Mama curled towards Bonifacia, a hand finding her daughter's shoulder under the blanket.

"You're scaring them!" he yelled.

Mama came closer, the curve of her stomach in Bonifacia's back. Bonifacia pulled her mother's arm tighter around them like a scarf, thinking this could protect her. It was the only thing she could do to protect her, protect all three of them.

"What will they think a wife does? Huh?" He switched to accented English. "Girls! A wife, she sleeps with her husband!" Mama linked her arm with Bonifacia's. She didn't cry the way she did last month, when the scandal was still fresh. Now she merely shot hot bursts of air from her nose into her daughter's hair. The reek of her breath intensified.

More banging.

"I will tell them! Every night, I'll tell them!" Bonifacia could feel the baby now, as if he was being kept awake by the commotion.

"The baby is kicking," Bonifacia whispered.

"He's getting comfortable. Babies don't kick. It's just a thing people say."

"If I were a baby, I would kick."

Papa yelled, "Hell! Hell is where you'll go!"

"Oh go to bed!" Mama shouted. Her mouth was so close to Bonifacia's ear that her famous catchphrase felt like it was tearing into her. The smell from her white mouth was overpowering.

"You go to bed!" Papa said. "Our bed!"

He knocked again, but his heart wasn't in it. They all knew he'd given up. When his footsteps diminished from the staircase to the hall, Mama said, "We'll sleep now."

"The baby is hopping mad," Bonifacia said.

"Don't be stupid," Mama said.

*

Car doors slammed, waking the girls. Bonifacia was alone in the bed. Mama's side was cold. Lia was already sitting up in The Canoe with messy hair and creases on her cheeks from the pillow. Muted light came in through the window and wind whistled at the panes. The ghostly shower curtain swung deeper into the room than usual. Bonifacia looked at the top of the dresser to check the time, but their alarm clock, the one with the ticking second hand, was missing.

"Again." Lia said.

Bonifacia shrugged and said, "Don't dress for Mass."

"It's Sunday."

"I know."

Downstairs, Roberto smoked, creating an acrid haze in the kitchen. There were dishes unwashed in the sink and the espresso maker was on the stovetop, surrounded by scalded coffee splatters full of grounds.

"Where are they?" Bonifacia said.

"Left," Roberto said. "They left."

"Where?"

"Me, I stayed for you."

"Oh, *Bob*," Bonifacia said. "We don't need you to stay. We're fine."

"I want to stay. I stay."

"Tell us where they went. Is Mama OK?" He looked at Bonifacia, then Lia, confused.

"Just say it in Italian," Lia said.

She did. Roberto looked relieved.

"She will be fine. You don't worry. Don't think about it." He put out his cigarette and lit another. "It's not for you to worry about. Your mother wants you to stay here."

"You're a liar," Bonifacia said.

"Bonbon, don't. Don't go on one of your attacks."

"But he's lying!" Bonifacia said.

"He's doing his best."

"I don't even know why he's here in the first place." The girls were rushing through their sentences in English to keep him from understanding. The alarm clock was on the table next to Roberto's ashtray. Mama must have been timing the contractions. "I'm going."

"But they want us to stay here. Let's at least call Isabella or Filomena. They have cars."

"I'll bet they're all together. We're the only ones who aren't with them."

"You don't know that."

"Yes I do. Look at him! He's baffled!"

"Give him a break," Lia said. Roberto was blushing. His single eyebrow was crinkled in the centre, trying to assess the situation. He pulled on his cigarette in short intervals, which made the red-hot tip intensify and dim, like he was sending out Morse code. "It's his first."

Bonifacia took their coats from the hooks by the back door and began bundling up. Lia put her coat on but hesitated before approaching her shoes.

"No, please," Roberto said in pleading Italian, coming at Bonifacia as if to hug her.

"Don't do that," she said and slapped his hand.

"I can help. Let me help," he said. "You don't want to see all that."

"You don't know what I want," Bonifacia said. "You don't know anything."

"He knows that Mama and Papa don't want us there," Lia said.

"I'm going. Lia, are you coming with me?"

Lia slipped her saddle shoes on.

"No," Roberto said. He abandoned his cigarette in the ashtray and stood in front of the back door with his arms crossed over his white T-shirt. Bonifacia could detect yellow patches growing from his armpits. "Don't go see it. It's not for little girls."

"Who are you, anyway?" Bonifacia said. She was getting hot wearing her coat indoors. Looking at him there, determined to help in all the wrong ways, he no longer seemed like the malignant surprise that had upended their family and had put the stains on their skin. He was a clueless stranger, trying to tell her what to do. She could see Papa in his face, in the confused forehead. The wiry hairs at his throat, poking from his shirt, reminded her of the appendages of the daddy-long-legs. She was small, but knew she could shoot herself at him, like a bullet, and go straight through to the garden. "We don't know you. You're just in the way!"

"It's not his fault. We'll go through the front," Lia said.

Bonifacia took her sister's hand and tugged her along the hallway. Going past the table, Bonifacia took the smouldering cigarette from the ashtray. She needed to wound him in some way, however small, and she'd seen Lucy do this to Ricky once, in their apartment in New York City, after winning an argument or getting something she wanted, had begged after, cried over, or blackmailed for. It's the sort of thing a grown-up woman might do to punctuate a triumph. When they got outside, she puffed on it and coughed, declared it revolting. Bonifacia dropped the cigarette on the ground and stamped on it, twisting her heel until it was nothing but brown pulp on the sidewalk.

*

They found the rest of their family at the end of a long sterile hallway. They'd been to St. Joe's Hospital before. Usually, the four-bed room was full of women, but today Mama was the sole patient. The other beds were dark, made with sheets pulled snug and tucked tight. The walls were painted the colour of every room in the Laurier Street house, as if this was a continuation of their home, a room that was always there, but hidden—unlocked only for one sad purpose.

The window afforded a view of the parking lot behind the silhouettes of Filomena and Teresa embracing. Isabella sat on an empty bed playing with the gold cross at her neck. Papa sat in a chair, immobile as a statue. He didn't even blink. His eyes bored into the middle distance. Mama was under covers, skinny now, and asleep with her mouth open, its white frosting evident to anyone who looked.

No one seemed surprised to see the two youngest daughters in the doorway. Swept in here on the wind of her defiance, Bonifacia now found herself without nerve. She wanted to rush in and rewind whatever had taken place—the details were irrelevant; the outcome was clear—but she didn't know how to do it.

"You girls can come in," Isabella said. Lia rushed in and put her arms around the waist of their eldest sister, who touched her head and kissed her hair.

Bonifacia took two steps into the room. Papa's head snapped towards her. He sniffled, shot a flat hand out in his brusque way, waved for her to approach. His raw, wet eyes were alert now. There was a tremble in the skin near his mouth. It was chilling to see him so vulnerable. She went to him and hugged him around the neck. He placed his hands on her back, squeezed. She could feel his callouses through her coat.

"Go show Mama," he said. "Show Mama you're here."

She left his embrace and went to Mama, took her hand. It was bony, dry, unresponsive. "I'm here," Bonifacia said. She saw that her mother was old, with skin loose at her jowls and papery on her forehead. Her hair was pulled back, and it was clear that it was receding. Her pulse was sluggish in Bonifacia's fingers, her breathing was shallow.

"Can I see him?" Bonifacia said.

"You girls shouldn't see him, no," Isabella said.

"I saw the others," Bonifacia said.

"Just mind me," Isabella said.

"This one isn't the same," Filomena said.

"This one had complications," Teresa said.

"He doesn't look like a normal baby," Isabella said. She explained that the boy had been born premature—"teeny tiny"—and was dead before he even breathed. He had marks on his body.

"Were the rest of us born with marks?" Bonifacia said. She ran her hand down her arm, following with her eyes, but saw no remnants.

"No, Bonbon," Isabella said.

"Not even the other boys?"

"Not even them. It was only this time. And the marks told the doctors something sad." She cast her eyes to the sisters on the window sill, some transmission of adult information. Teresa nodded. Isabella sighed to the ceiling. "I guess you'll know soon enough. The marks mean Mama is sick. She has diabetes."

"It's a disease," Filomena said.

"Something awful in her blood," Teresa said. "It made her mouth all white, see? And made her thirsty. But worst of all, it hurt the baby."

"In a way, we're fortunate," Isabella said. "Mama didn't know all the signs. And now we understand."

"Heh?" Papa said. "*Fortunado*?"

"In a way, Papa. Now the doctors can treat it."

"Why do you say these things?" he said, standing now, hunched over, weak. "The baby is dead!" He continued on in a blistering stream of Italian of which Bonifacia understood *defunto, ragazzo, ingrate, mammina,* and *cara*. Dead, boy, ungrateful, mommy, dear. He was pink-faced, spitting and sweating, slapping at the air.

"Don't you yell at her," Bonifacia said.

He pointed at Mama. "You speak back to me and your mother lies here sick!" he said, in Italian.

"She's alive, isn't she?"

"She'll outlive the stars, this one!"

"I hope she does!"

"And the boys all die!"

"What do you care about boys? Where are your boys, Papa?"

"You keep your mouth closed!" He squeezed her face at either side of her lips, the callouses now scraping her. She could feel the lining of her mouth rub against her teeth.

"Oh, go to bed!" Bonifacia had to slur it, force it out between her teeth, because he was holding so tightly.

Lia chuckled at this, having heard it from their mother so often. Bonifacia cracked a smile too, in spite of herself.

"You're your mother's daughter," Papa said.

She folded her arms and felt victory in the gust of air that trailed him as he moved towards the door. He turned his anger to the hallway, bellowing that he wanted to see his son. The sisters stared at him there, framed by the door, as he continued his gesticulations. To Bonifacia, all this animated rage made him seem reduced. She felt sorry for him.

Papa re-entered after the nurse. It was Mrs. Garlito, prim and sour, with her white cap pinned in her hair. She pushed a rolling crib, but also carried into the room a sense of judgement—from all the horrors she'd seen, from all the blame she'd laid—bound up behind her starched nurse's scrim. They knew her from church; she was one of the parishioners who had stopped speaking to the Zappocostas after the scandal, so disgusted was she by the bigamy and deceit. But now, she had to say something to them.

"Ladies," she said. "This business of seeing the child. I don't recommend it."

"We know," Bonifacia said.

"I like to be professional. I like to be certain." Mrs. Garlito eyed Lia and Bonifacia, then served a questioning look to Isabella. Bonifacia felt a Papa-like rage build in her.

"We're very certain," Bonifacia said.

Mrs. Garlito pulled the sheet away.

The boy had an outsized head. Threads of black hair descended almost to his eyes. His skin was purplish, as though every inch of him was bruised. His legs and arms were pudgy, and his eyes, nose, and lips were engulfed in bloat. The marks were boils, bright red and ridged with crust.

Lia let out a trembling sound, the beginning of a crying fit that would last days. She buried her face in Isabella's stomach.

Bonifacia forced a stoniness. She knew the child was dead, but still expected him to wriggle, to cry from his painful sores. Papa must have thought so, too. He scooped up his son—his fake son. The child was tiny, but Papa cradled him anyhow, in the crux of his elbow. Bonifacia could see he was an expert at it, he'd done it so many times before. Knowing only one thing to do with a newborn, Papa rocked the tiny dead boy back and forth, back and forth.

"What's his name?" Bonifacia said.

"Mama and Papa didn't give him a name, Bonbon," Isabella said.

"Babies should have names," Bonifacia said. "Can I give him a name?"

"No, Bonifacia. That wouldn't be right."

Bonnie gave the child a name anyway, silently and privately. She beamed the gift to him with a loving stare. She lifted her eyes to Mrs. Garlito, who was staring back at her. Bonnie registered embarrassment and smugness on the nurse's face. This woman knew everything about their family—the rumours, the curses, the sins, the dead boys—and she was disgusted with them all.

Bonnie checked her arms again. There were no boils, just the blank, tan skin of always. Maybe, for Bonnie, for all of them that are alive, the marks were imperceptible, but still there. She and her sisters were all marked in the same way. Her parents, too. The chronic condition of being themselves. The stains were invisible, but everyone could see them.

In the rare instances when my mother told the story about the baby boys, she'd end off by saying that, right then in the hospital, it seemed her father was right—that my mother and my aunts were the unfortunate ones, that maybe the babies were lucky after all. But that it only seemed true, and only for a moment. It only remained true if she decided it was.

story6.31August2018.m4a

[BFM]: I don't think I've ever heard Bonnie tell that one.

[GZO]: Like I say at the end, she doesn't tell it often.

[BFM]: Her dad isn't as bad as you made him out a few stories ago.

[GZO]: He wasn't.

[BFM]: Yeah, so you have a problem now. You just gave me this whole new side of Papa Zap—like, he's not just a beast. He's a tender beast. I want to know more. Keep going.

[GZO]: I can't end it here? Why not?

[BFM]: Because I'M not satisfied. Don't avoid the hard part.

[GZO]: But I'm so good at it.

[BFM]: No you're not.

[GZO]: And there's no material left. Bonnie's stories end there.

[BFM]: That's not my problem.

[GZO]: Where would you take it?

[BFM]: Do I have to do everything around here?

[GZO]: You don't do anything around here.

[BFM]: I'm reading your bloody book. That's plenty.

[GZO]: Give me a hint.

[BFM]: All these knock-on effects must've started somewhere. Some first domino had to fall. Did Papa Zap tip it?

[GZO]: Maybe, but it must have been before Bonnie's stories began.

[BFM]: In Italy, then. You and I did that big side trip in Italy to see your grandfather's town. Try that.

[GZO]: Worst trip of my life.

7

Kingmaker

The letter had arrived. He saw it in Signora Marotti's gouty fingers as she hobbled towards him with her healthy hand on the wall. He was sweating in anticipation, she was sweating from exertion.

The whole village was sweating. It was mid-September and the summer hadn't broken. There was no moisture in the air or the soil, and dust billowed down the streets of Biletto coating every surface in a fine sepia veil. No heat wave had lasted this long, although the eldest villagers offered competing memories of worse Septembers, hotter suns, thicker bee infestations, more ruinous crops, more decimated vintages. No one believed them.

Signora Marotti read his name off the envelope—"Alberto Zappacosta!"—and looked up to confirm his identity, scrutinizing him through milky eyes as if she hadn't known him her whole life. She slid the letter across the counter. Restraining his own eagerness to look at something so hungrily anticipated, Alberto folded the thing in two and slid it into his pocket.

To distract her from the letter, Alberto asked about her grandchildren, a proven Italian diversionary tactic. Predictably, they were gifted, clever, and beautiful.

She asked if he'd been lucky with the bees.

"Yes."

"We can't have another Sister Gina."

"No."

Sister Gina was the nun who died of bee sting. Like Alberto, she was allergic. When the bug got her, the doctor was attending to patients in Gardi—a bigger town, many miles away. The priest attempted to save the nun by taking her there on horseback. Despite his prayers and skilled riding, the horse's gallop was too slow. Sister Gina was dead when they arrived.

Since then, Alberto dressed in black armour to protect him from the bees. He stood in it presently: rugged overalls, chunky boots, thick cotton shirt, gloves, scarf, and cap. His face was his only visible flesh. He apologized to Signora Marotti for smelling of manure. He'd been working in the fields all morning.

She waited until he turned to go before she said, "Fiona, huh? From another Zappacosta?"

Letters from Fiona were common in Biletto. They passed through this post office with money and news from the other side of the Atlantic, from those villagers who'd left. But this was Alberto's first letter from Canada, and she knew it. She had bored little eyes, lost in her face, but when her instincts picked up anything out of the ordinary, they doubled in size, thirsty and theorizing, creasing her forehead and flattening out her fan of crow's feet. Her pearly left iris shone.

"An uncle," he said.

"Franco, huh? Cristoforo?"

"No." He reminded himself that he was distantly related to her.

"Guillermo?"

"No," he said

"Huh."

He cauterized the conversation with a stiff "thank you" that hinted that the letter was bad news, and definitely private. He walked with purpose from the counter to the door, seeing into the future, to a moment when Signora Marotti would describe this whole encounter to other customers, her moustache moistening in excitement.

*

This was 1936, the summer of bees. The infestation was total, intentional, biblical; it was a message from God. The bugs arrived in mid-July and grew sturdier in ranks as the heat poured on, swarming all along the squat buildings that lined Biletto's main street—the doctor's office, the post office, the church. Bees gathered around crevices and corners, crawling over each other in wriggling black-and-yellow orgies, multiplying, swarming, socializing, conspiring. You could see them from a distance, huge continents of insects on the grey stone, changing in size and shape. You watched people strolling along with intense and intentional normality until one of them spasmed and jerked, hands in the air, flapping an insect away. Hitting one would come with a satisfying kiss of contact, and the bee would go hurtling through the air on the energy of the swat, until it regained control of its own momentum and zipped back in its tormentor's direction.

The villagers believed the bees could communicate with one another. If one was wounded, it called other bees to come help it. If you killed one, it gave off a scent or a noise, undetectable to humans, that signalled its brothers to exact revenge. They knew it was you from the smell of your skin. Everyone was terrified of flowers.

The view of the sunrise was now marred by bulbous hives dripping from the plane trees, each surrounded by a cloud of bees. Children had to be stopped from throwing rocks at the nests. Those that disobeyed paid with a sting or two. You could smell the recent victims when they passed you on the road because everyone believed vinegar was the only treatment.

The bees were inside and outside. They were in the parched fields with the sheep and in the spindly olive trees south of town. They loved attics, and wives refused to go up there for fear that the bees had taken it over. They got trapped in the lard, so soft in the heat, buzzing in distress as their legs maneuvered out of the goo. Their wings made a wet sound as they tried to fly. They were in the sugar and the oil, in the outhouses and the bedrooms.

They surprised you, bolting from your shoes seconds before you slid in a foot. You could spy one in your lemonade, just as you put the glass to your lips. If you were lucky enough to have cream, you found bees in the pot. Every decanter in Biletto had a saucer over it. God forbid you set down your espresso cup; it was soon enveloped by a blanket of writhing legs, wings, and pumping striped bums. The bees banged their heads in frustration on every window in town, trying to get out, trying to get in. They mistook coloured laundry for flowers, flocking to socks hung on the line, only to find they'd been duped. They dove down chimneys, they danced around the mules. They sat on kitchen tables and preened their antennae.

The bees practised their own traditions. They were born from queens and went on to lives of labour. They foraged pollen and went home to their vast families to put their earnings to good use. They swarmed to socialize, surged together like the crowd bottlenecking at the church door after Mass. They gossiped about the townspeople, what they wore, where they'd been. They passed stories down to their kids. Here's how our nest ended out on a tree instead of a gargoyle; here's how your cousin died, banged off the window of a locomotive. They mourned their dead and they prayed for their missing—uncles trapped between windowpanes and half-brothers drowned in coffee. For bees, the traditions were all automatic, inherited. They happened naturally. The bugs knew nothing else. No bee rebelled against its instincts. In many ways, Alberto was jealous of them.

Everyone had a theory about what they had done to deserve the bees. Was it the grocer's flashy new Fiat, the only car in town, and the biggest marvel of that year? Was God fed up with the doctor's transgressions, how he smuggled contraband from town to town, or how he performed abortions on the sly? Or was it the new money that had come to the landowners? But that money came from Rome. It seemed unlikely that Il Duce was to blame. The general consensus—and Alberto agreed with it—was that bees were sent because of one of the town's women. Sister Gina, perhaps. She'd been unfaithful, unrepentant; she'd thrown herself down the stairs after missing her period; she had lust in her heart. After all, the bees were everywhere. The bees could see them sin.

*

Alberto watched through his kitchen window as his wife pushed the pram down the lane. It contained two babies, vegetables, and, he hoped, coffee. Whatever else was in the carriage, it was heavy. Sofia struggled getting it over the creek's bridge, where the wheels got stuck in the rotted wood.

She'd adjusted her dress for the heat. Her sleeves were rolled up, the collar was unfastened, and the skirt was hiked up so its hem was tucked in the belt. When she got over the creek, she wrapped her hair around itself—it stayed piled there by some feminine trick—so she could cool her neck with a handful of water. She then stood on the bank, unmoving. Alberto willed her to do something horrible, something he could point to later. But she did nothing. She didn't even swat at the bees. She was so still, the tableau looked like a painting of a pastoral landscape featuring wheat fields, a bridge, a path, and a harridan. There was a barn and a farmhouse, too, nestled on the horizon, a mile closer to town.

Years ago, all of this land had been Alberto's. His parents had died in the 1918 flu and had left the land to him. He couldn't inherit it until he was done with his military service, so he was excited when he put on his uniform for the last time and left the army base in Sicily. He boarded a new boat from Il Dulce and sat on a long wooden bench in its belly with dozens of other soldiers. Each had a story to tell about what they'd do once they were home. Alberto told his story in dialect, using his inland patois for the first time in two years. Few other soldiers understood, but he didn't care. He spoke of his cousin, Sofia, the most beautiful girl in Abruzzo, whom he loved. She had a buxom shape and was ready to marry him. Her family was taking care of his farm while Alberto was in the army. He used his hands to illustrate the gentle hills of his land, the size of the farmhouse, the swell of his woman's breasts.

He was disappointed when he arrived at the farmhouse. It was more ramshackle than in his memory. The land was yellower, the sheep more emaciated. Sofia was sadder, hidden under a drab brown dress with no shape. She complained of problems both real and imagined, and was explicit in hideous ways he thought unbecoming of a sixteen-year-old woman. Gory periods, gutted lambs, threatening Blackshirts. Her father had gone broke on some bets and had been missing for two months. Her teenage brothers had no clue how to operate the farm and brought in very little money. She'd made no plans for the wedding, not knowing how they'd pay for it or if Alberto would even take her now, with no dowry.

Alberto told her to be happy. Her father was a bum anyhow. Good riddance. Alberto would take care of Sofia and her mother; he'd allow the brothers to stay at the farmhouse until they went into the army themselves. A wedding would solve the problems she bawled over. "I'll marry you," he growled at her as she scraped together overcooked bowls of maccheroni in the cobwebby kitchen. "So stop your complaining." She mumbled unsure consent as though she didn't understand the concept of marriage at all.

She didn't, and neither did he. The ceremony was joyless, and took up one of the last weekends they spent at the farmhouse. Sofia's father's debts were insurmountable. Alberto screamed his fury at her and her mother, the old lady blubbering about her sons, Sofia throwing herself into her mother's defence, trying to absorb Alberto's temper. When the officers came to collect his uncle's debt, Alberto knew who they were straight away. Before Il Duce, they had been the Strong Men; now they were the Blackshirts.

Alberto transferred the farm to them on the condition that he and Sofia could stay across the creek, in the farmhand's cottage. Alberto sent his aunt and her sons to the shore, where they had other relatives. At the end of Sofia's third pregnancy, a new landowner took over and accepted Rome's money to change the farm from grazing lands to wheat fields. He shared some of the funds with Alberto to help him make the change. Alberto took the cash and buried it in the field. He didn't even know why, at first. He simply desired something that was his alone.

Now, Sofia was on the move again. When she appeared outside the window, Alberto could see the oncoming fight on her face. She ploughed the pram through the chickens, which scattered like cowards, and she screamed up the hill to their two eldest boys, Roberto and Carmine, telling them not to get dirty while they played.

Sofia hated the view from the kitchen window. She said the farmhouse mocked them—that they should be living there, in the brick structure with the two storeys, not in this wooden shack so much farther from town. They had four boys, who all slept in one room she considered "squalid." The two older ones had a hay mattress, deemed "sickening," raised off the dirt floor by empty crates. The babies' crib took up almost all the remaining space and had to lean against the wall to keep from collapsing. "A death trap." Alberto and Sofia shared a bed off the kitchen. It had a frame that was quiet under their exertions and never woke the boys—"small mercies"—but was only separated from the kitchen by a sheet nailed to a beam. They went to bed every night surrounded by the odours of dinner. "Revolting," she said, "they give me the worst dreams of my life, those smells." The kitchen was dominated by a large dining table, surrounded by highchairs and wooden seats, all worn shiny. It was the only room in the house with proper flooring, a green linoleum Alberto had unrolled, cut and hammered down himself. Sofia disliked how broom bristles snagged on the nails. The sink was "shallow as a puddle" and the countertop was "scarred." The cupboards "gaped" and couldn't seal against mice.

She came in without greeting and moved the sleeping newborn and the one-year-old to their crib. Next emerged her bag of vegetables, which she went to work on. She was halfway through peeling an eggplant when, without looking up, she said she'd been to Doctor Futti. Alberto continued to say nothing. There was a bee on the table, its leg stuck in wax, and it struggled and buzzed in frustration. Sofia didn't look up once. She told the eggplant she was no longer pregnant.

"You did it," Alberto said.

She frowned at the naked vegetable, saying to it, "Don't worry, Alberto. No one will know. You're still the Kingmaker."

In town, people used his nickname—earned by siring four sons in six years—with demure smiles. Not Sofia; she lofted that first syllable into another octave, making it into a kind of sarcastic song that she had spit out.

He reminded her that all children were gifts. She reminded him there was no money. He said it was sin. She said he should never take her, then. He said it was his right. They were yelling. The newborn started to wail in his feeble way. On her way to the crib, she pointed the knife at him and bellowed, "so go to Africa!" as if it were the most obvious option before them.

"Always Africa with you!" he yelled into the next room. He could hear her cooing to the baby, calming it. When she returned, she whisper-screamed that "Africa would solve all your problems" and noted that "the country needs you more than I do." She pointed the knife at the wall, where the two adornments seemed to make her point: a drawing of the Holy Father and a photo of Il Duce. There was a king, too, somewhere in Rome, but they didn't have a picture of the king.

"Dead, that's how you want me!"

She moved the knife back to his face and came two steps closer. Sweat cut passages through the dust on her face. Hair had escaped its knot and frizzed out, haloing her head. Her black eyes glistened, her narrow nose flared. She looked beautiful and sad, excited and exasperated, even aroused by the fight. He made a sudden grab for her breast. He could barely feel its weight through his glove. She was used to this molestation and the angry, sweaty, half-dressed tussle that could follow. That was how their fights ended, so she didn't pull away. She leaned onto the insufficient sink, crossed her arms, and said, "Never mind." Women always have terrible answers, he thought. "They need *men* in Africa."

"Cosimo Futti!" he yelled. "Cosimo Futti! Cosimo Futti!" And he continued to squawk the name until it became an incomprehensible, shapeless noise. The baby started crying again, and his brother joined him. Sofia threw the knife into the sink, abdicating dinner to a later version of herself. The Kingmaker sat down with his erection and leaned deep into his chair. He counted the number of bees in the room and waited to be fed.

✷

Cosimo Futti, the doctor's brother, had been to Africa. His stories of the invasion differed from what the villagers believed. They believed Italy had secured the colony by overwhelming the locals, rolling through the streets in inspiring, orderly ranks, with an efficiency never before seen on that continent. They believed that the Italians could do it better than the French or the English or the Dutch. They believed the campaign still needed men. They believed the soldiers were treated as superiors, with respect, as they laid down the codes for this new piece of Italy. They still believed this, even after Cosimo returned from Africa blind and unable to smell, with a body of shiny scars.

Alberto did not believe the legend. He believed Cosimo, who would unbutton his shirt to show his chest, the cracked, crisp, scalded relief of it. He still wore his uniform when he left his apartment. It allowed him to collect the respect it offered. "Might as well get something," he'd told Alberto.

The Abyssinians were tough bastards, he said. They were not scared, and had to be made scared. Cosimo was part of what they called the Fear Offensive. The generals picked a village—some conquerable enclave of sheds and families—and cut off what little it had, until its children were starving and bloated. And then the Italians tightened their circle. Cosimo was in the first rung. He approached the village with canisters on his back. He didn't understand the language of the men and women who ran to him, blathering, but he saw the desperation in their faces as they held babies up as arguments. "Tears are tears," he said, "children are children." The whites of their teeth and eyes were stark and human, their pleading instinctual. They were everything Cosimo had been told they were not. He told them to run, to get out of their homes, to take their children and crouch in balls in the road. They didn't understand.

At a captain's command, Cosimo pulled a trigger and fire roared from the nozzle in his hand. There were small bursts of flame at first, giving the gas time to leak and spread before more ignition—fire chasing after itself to cause the most damage, until a whole house raged like a furnace. The Abyssinians threw rocks when they saw the flames. Rocks were all they had. One dinged Cosimo's canister, still on his back. He smelled the gas before he felt it. He scrambled to get it off, soaking the fuel further into his uniform. He was not sure where the spark came from, there was so much fire, chaos, and screaming. The last thing he ever smelled was his own charred flesh. He was the only casualty of the Fear Offensive. The Africans were not considered casualties.

*

Alberto hated the pig shit the most. It was looser and shinier than the pulpy cow variety, and it stank worse than the heavy loads from horses. In the heat, odour steamed out of the muck: rotting eggs, decomposing flesh, yeasty bread. Swine will eat anything. In the corridors of the wheat fields, Alberto shovelled and hoed the manure, got it trapped in his black costume. The gloves reeked and the scarf around his face added sweat to the bouquet of odours.

Il Dulce wanted wheat, so the landowner planted wheat. When the crops didn't mature with the right density, he was told to use manure. Alberto worked for him, so he dispensed the stuff, but knew it wouldn't take, especially this late in the summer. These were the wrong manures and the wrong crops for this rocky soil. This was once his family's land and he knew it was best for grazing. But now the money came from Rome, and Alberto had no say in the matter.

At the lowest dip in the field, where he couldn't be seen from his shack or the farmhouse, Alberto crouched in the lines of shade projected by the wheat stalks. He drank from his canteen and tipped over the log he'd placed here months before so he could sit and rest. Bees commuted overhead, dots against the sky. They had no reason to stop here, although sometimes one was curious enough to zip down and inspect him.

His body heaved with exhaustion. He could feel the water run down his throat and into his stomach. Could Africa be hotter than this? Smell worse than this? Could it be as pointless as this? He remembered his own time in the army, in Sicily. There, he listened to orders, fulfilled them. He cleaned artillery and dug trenches near the sea. He resigned himself to having no freedom, anticipating being his own man once he was home. He was going to learn to read and write. He was going to have children and send them to school. Now that he'd failed at that, he thought honour might be somewhere else.

Roberto's voice came sailing over the wheat, the anguished wail of a six-year-old, likely over some imagined pain. Roberto seemed to get those often. Alberto considered remaining still, unfindable in the maze of grain, but the child was getting louder and closer. Alberto raised his shovel above his head so the boy could see it, and soon enough, Roberto was parting the stems like a curtain. He'd been stung by a bee on his arm, and he gripped it with his opposite hand.

"Sit," Alberto said. The log wobbled under the child, he was so afraid. Alberto squatted, grabbed his son's hand away and showed Roberto how to pinch the skin, squeeze out the stinger.

"Can't you do it, Papa?"

"You're a big boy. You can do it."

It took him three tries, but Roberto managed to pull the stinger out. Alberto told him to keep pinching, to squeeze so hard that it hurt more than any sting. "Count to five." They waited, staring at each other in the pig shit. Roberto's face was as brown as his mother's. They looked so alike—the black eyes, the huge lips—that Alberto was tempted to smack him. "Now take your hand off it. Don't you feel better?"

"Yes," Roberto said.

"You could do it."

"Yes."

"See? You're a big boy. And you're lucky."

"But I got stung."

Alberto conceded the point, but went on to tell the story about how he, too, had been stung by a bee when he was younger than Roberto. "I came close to death. I turned into a balloon-boy and went purple all over. My nose turned into a grape! And the place where I was stung? It turned into an apple! My feet turned into eggplants! My eyes closed all by themselves. My throat became the size of a piece of thread. I was like that for hours, until the nurse was found. She had to give me a shot. She had to dip me in vinegar and had to squeeze the sting until blood came out."

"Like Sister Gina?"

"Yes, but I didn't die like Sister Gina."

"Did you cry?"

"Never! Because I would have drowned in my tears." Roberto had gone slack. "And I didn't run away, like you did."

"I'm sorry."

"If you run after a sting, you bring the problem with you."

The child apologized again and stood up. Alberto could tell he was trying hard not to touch the site of the pain. He asked his son why he didn't go to his mother, and Roberto said she'd gone back to the doctor.

"Again?"

"Yes."

"OK, go home. Put vinegar on it. But don't run. Big boys don't run."

Once he was gone, Alberto unearthed a waxy canvas bag from its burial place, a few inches below the log. He transferred a ball of cash from his pocket to the bag. Even with this latest addition, he knew the amount was paltry. He wanted to leave as much of it in Biletto as possible. He would have to find some way to cut costs.

The bills reeked of shit, the bag reeked of shit. The letter from Canada, also in the bag, reeked of shit. At least it was still safe, with its six postage stamps, each with some king on it—a row of identical portraits in profile, all staring off the edge of the envelope. The last thing in the bag was an old ledger, bound in cardboard, he'd taken from the rubbish heap near the farmhouse. Inside, the page had inscrutable words and grids of numbers, all of which Alberto ignored. He wrote over them, filling one page every day with the only two words he knew how to write. He iterated them again and again, training his fingers to conduct the pencil. *Alberto Zappacosta, Alberto Zappacosta, Alberto Zappacosta, Alberto Zappacosta, Alberto Zappacosta, Alberto Zappacosta, Alberto Zappacosta, Alberto Zappacosta, Alberto Zappacosta, Alberto Zappacosta.*

*

Doctor Futti's house loomed over the main street, opposite the post office. It was a stately building of stone, though it looked like it was decaying due to the patches of bees coagulating around its eaves and sills. A line of patients stood out front, trying not to swat around their faces. The doctor was only here a few days per month, so people were taking their chances with the bees in order to cure their ailments before the doctor left again on his endless medical circuit of the region. One week in Fossacesia, one week in Gardi, then back to Biletto in his carriage.

The patients had dressed up. The women wore versions of the same black dress, with minor variations in buttons and collars. The men stood without slouching, trying to project dignity in their rumpled church suits—long grey trousers, half-boots, white shirts with the top buttons undone, frayed at the cuffs. Hats. Alberto did not understand the pageantry. The effeminate doctor had them fooled with his education and northern accent, but he was nothing but a wisp. Alberto knew more than he needed to about the man. Certainly enough to visit his house in the most disrespectful clothes possible—his work clothes. In a month, the bees would be gone, and so would his black armour. Alberto could put on his own suit and be a normal villager again. He could so easily see himself among them that he felt nauseous.

Alberto sailed past the queue. The patients waved at him, told each other he was pitiable. They all knew the Kingmaker's story. He waved back, more of a dismissal than a greeting. He even waved at Signora Marotti, who was standing in the door of the post office surveying who was in line, who passed by, who was out of place. Alberto wasn't out of place. He came down here every Wednesday afternoon whether the doctor was in town or not. He went straight around to the right side of the house where he had to make himself small to walk the gamut of overgrown rose bushes that were heavy with blooms and bees.

"Your brother should be arrested for those roses," Alberto told Cosimo once he was inside. The nurse who helped Cosimo was not there. She was assisting the doctor with patients in the office at the front of the house, leaving Cosimo in the rear apartment to fend for himself. He was wearing a robe that was open at the chest. His whole body was a scar, a lumpy landscape of healed fissures, now pink and waxy and hardened. And Alberto couldn't even see the worst of it—the great, violent galaxy of purple on his back. Cosimo stood at the stove with his head down. He seemed to be looking at the blue flames licking the bottom of the espresso boiler, but was, in fact, listening for the tell-tale sounds of readiness.

Alberto did not offer to help, merely described his motions to his blind friend until he was seated at their usual placc by the back window, where he removed his hat, scarf, and gloves.

"I closed the windows for you, to keep the bugs out," Cosimo said.

"You're lucky you can't smell, then. I'm ripe with shit today."

Cosimo held a finger to his mangled lips, so he could hear the coffee. In the ensuing hush, Alberto could make out the up-down cadence of chatter between the doctor and his patient in the office behind the door. Soon, the coffee pot began coughing and steaming, the sound rising to a hissy climax. Cosimo killed the flame and swept a hand over the burner to make sure it was extinguished, then waited for the denouement of boiling to stop before feeling for the handle. Once he was confident of his grip, he carried the pot to the table and pawed about until he'd found a cup. He fingered the rim and poured the coffee until it touched the digit's tip.

"Still good at something," he said. He said this every week, with pride, before they exchanged updates. Cosimo described visits from the priest, arguments with his brother, the recalcitrance of the nurse. Alberto sang his usual chorus, telling of the indignities of the wheat field, the latest bee stings, gossip from around Biletto. He got heated when recounting the Africa argument with Sofia. Cosimo was the only person in town who would abide Alberto's disloyalty, his reluctance to fight. Alberto was shouting by the end of the tale, making gestures that Cosimo couldn't see. His friend nodded. His blank, unfocussed eyes were pointed to the side of Alberto's head.

"And will you have another son, Kingmaker? I know she was here." Cosimo cupped a hand around his ear and pointed in the direction of the doctor's office door.

"Not this time."

"Three appointments, she had."

Alberto sneered at the door. He felt the black weight of this news on his shoulders. It was unsurprising information, which made the weight all the heavier.

"Three," Cosimo repeated.

"I thought only two."

"It takes three."

"It's a disgrace."

"Everyone else, I hear chatter. Sometimes screams and crying. When she is here, I hear silence," he shrugged. "Silence is how I know it's happening."

Alberto checked his cup for bees. Seeing none, he threw back the coffee, then banged the cup against its saucer. He was hoping it would smash into pieces, but it didn't.

"It's what you get for marrying a beautiful woman," Cosimo said.

"You remember what beauty is?"

"I remember what it should be." As quietly as possible, Alberto placed the backs of his fingers against his throat and scraped his nails up his neck and off his chin. *Fuck you.*

"Say it," Cosimo said.

"Not yet."

"Say it. Where's your honour? Say 'damned.'"

"No."

"Say 'killer.'"

Laughter rose from the office behind the door, followed by the doctor's tenor. It was indecipherable, but authoritative and instructional.

"Zio Davide, his letter came."

Cosimo nodded, made a hum.

"From Fiona, it came."

"Fiona. With all the runaways." Cosimo flicked his hand, as if batting away Zio Davide and all those that had emigrated. "We don't talk about them."

Everyone who had left Biletto had gone to Fiona, and the Canadian town had a mythological resonance. It was a place spoken of with reverence and derision. Fiona was populated with the traitors and cowards who had excised themselves from here. They never came back, potentially making Fiona a mirage. You had to believe in it. And even those who did believe in it debated whether Fiona was worth the energy and money it took to get there. Fiona could be poisonous—a lure for the stupid or the desperate—and those that remained in Biletto had no way of knowing for sure, for those who moved overseas were not spoken of. They existed as mysterious sources of money, whose descriptions of automobiles and snow and Protestants were distrusted because of their authors' abandonment. Zio Davide was one of the traitors. He'd left a year ago, carrying with him Alberto's request for the letter that was now in his pocket.

"You won't read it to me?" Alberto joked.

Cosimo laughed. He was one of the few people in Biletto who had learned to read, but, now, could not.

"Do you have it with you, the letter?"

"Yes."

"You shouldn't go through the roses on the way out, then. Why don't you go through the front door?" Cosimo pointed towards the office exit. "Even that gossip Marotti would think it's normal. My brother leaves tomorrow, after all, and won't be back for weeks."

Alberto stood at the door separating Cosimo's apartment from the doctor's office. He catalogued his duties—something he did before acting against them. The army, his parents, his children, his wife; the land, the payments, the landowner, the wheat; the bees, the village, the church. He then tabulated his honour. There could be no formula to compare them, to calculate them against each other, but if there were, his honour would be in arrears. He'd be left with a result that would justify opening this door.

*

"Cosimo?"

Doctor Futti was seated at his heavy wooden desk at the far side of the room, turning over mimeographed pieces of paper. The room smelled of medicine—of what Alberto considered medicine—like freshly cut paper, sterilizing liquids, ink, and rubber. On the wall above the doctor was a spray of framed documents and letters and credentials, interrupted here and there with photographs of family members, rendered in shades of grey. Il Dulce and the Holy Father also made an appearance. As at home, there was not a picture of the king. An examination chair sat to Alberto's left, under a jointed metal arm ending in a magnifying glass. It looked like it was used to torture answers out of captives. The doctor himself was running his fingers along his moustache.

"Doctor," Alberto said.

The man looked up and said, "Oh!" Alberto thought he saw a breeze of fear blow across the doctor's features, the slightest darkening and widening of the eyes. It lasted no longer than the flutter of a bee's wing. The doctor leaned back in his hinged chair and smiled, his legendary composure restored.

"The office is closed, my friend, but, please, come in."

"I know it's closed."

"I see you're adhering to my instructions! You won't end up like Sister Gina. You're in your armour."

"I hate it."

"It's all necessary, as you won't take any other precautions. You should stay out of that field."

"My family would starve."

The doctor considered this and nodded. "In any event, you come see me the minute you're stung. No time to waste! Sofia knows to come to me directly?"

"And she's told the whole of Biletto."

"It's for the best, Kingmaker!" the doctor said. "Even if I'm out of town, someone should get you to me. If it's less than a day's journey and the bee gets you below the waist, you could still be saved."

"You leave town when?"

"Tomorrow, first thing," he said. "I'll be up with the bees." He went on to explain that he had excesses of paperwork to file before this departure, and his brother to dine with, and could Alberto's ailment wait a month, until he returned?

There was nowhere to sit, except the examination chair, so Alberto approached the desk, enjoying the disgusted flare of the doctor's nostrils. Alberto reached into his pocket and withdrew the letter in its Canadian envelope, folded in two. He found his hand shaking, so he tossed the document onto the desk.

"It cannot wait."

The doctor looked curious, then concerned. His cheeks were perpetually clean-shaven, and he never had hairs in his ears. He wore a crisp white shirt, laundered by someone else's wife, and buttoned to his Adam's apple. He had light brown eyes, very expressive, and a strong chin that was on the edge of being a deformity, in Alberto's view.

"What's this now? For me?" He was making a show of unfolding Zio Davide's note, smiling at it before even knowing what it was.

"Not for you," Alberto said, "although I'd like for you to read it to me."

"That's not one of my usual services, my friend. Why, Signora Marotti across the street would do it with a smile—for ten lira."

"Do you think it's beneath you to read me this letter?"

"Why not take it to Father Corsetti? He charges nothing at all. Just a donation in the box!"

"Read it to find out."

The doctor leaned back in his leather seat, picking up the letter but reading Alberto, who had no ability to pretend. If his face was angry, he was angry.

"It's directions," the doctor said, "instructions."

"Go on."

"Well, it would seem your uncle is well. He would be happy to receive you in Canada." The doctor looked up. "Alberto! Are you thinking of making the leap to Fiona?"

"I might be."

"All of Biletto would miss your clan terribly. You're the Kingmaker, after all. Our local legend."

"I wouldn't miss you."

There was a slow shift to the doctor's features—a softening of the eyes, but a hardening of the grin. He said, "Shall I read on?"

"Every word."

The letter explained that Alberto would need papers—his army discharge and baptism certificate, at least—and how those could get him a passport at the Interior Ministry in Naples. Davide wrote of how difficult the journey is, how sick the ship makes you, but how it's worth it. He described the Canadian cold, how it gets into your nose and eyes and seems like it will never stop. He said there were girls in Fiona, from an earlier wave of traitors. "All thirteen, fourteen, just about to ripen!" the doctor read, giving his own emphasis. The letter told of the cost, and how Davide managed it, and how the ship leaves from Naples, and how there was only one train from their region to the city. It left from Gardi, a half-day's carriage ride from Biletto. The letter ended with a hearty "good luck!"

"So. I must get to Gardi then," Alberto said.

"Gardi." The doctor leaned back in his chair once again and opened his knees as though trying to take up as much space as possible. Alberto had to restrain himself from yanking him forward. "Rather far for a family of six. Two babies. The expense would be enormous."

"Only me, then."

"Alberto!"

"I would send for them, of course."

"Of course."

"Once I'd established myself."

"Kingmaker," the doctor said. "Have you ever even left Biletto?"

"Sicily." Alberto winced; a section of upper lip twitched up, as though snagged on a hook. "Some of us were in the army."

"Ah yes! Then you know the trials of travel. I go to Gardi at the end of every month, and I'm telling you it's a hard journey. Up the hills, down the hills. How would you even get there, with no carriage? Do you have money for a hire?"

"There are other ways," Alberto said. "You'll be there at the end of the month?"

"What difference does it make if I am there? You'll have much bigger worries. You'll need a passport, documents. There will be forms to read—to fill out! And to sign and process."

"I'll just need to get the train to Naples."

"But you can't even write your own name!"

Alberto straightened up. "End of the month?"

The doctor was assessing him, tipping his head back, unafraid. Alberto smiled then—a forced, menacing smile of crooked brown teeth, with the tan lines along his jowls making it even creepier.

"Gardi, then. At the end of the month, killer?" Alberto said. He kept his stare fixed with the doctor's, freezing himself this way until his opponent looked away, first to the side, then down to the desktop. The doctor collected the letter, folded it back in two, and placed it atop the king-laden envelope. He stiffened the papers between his thumb and finger, pointed them at Alberto, and said,

"End of the month."

✷

The bees got slower, stupider. By the end of September, the villagers had stopped running from them as it had become easier to smack them through the air, to trap them under upturned water glasses where they'd buzz furiously, confused. The days became shorter, but the sun kept its heat. The dust still hadn't settled, the rain still hadn't fallen.

The roses had gone, though, making Alberto's departure from Cosimo's apartment less of a gamble. He strode with pride through the tunnel of branches, impervious to the thorns thanks to his armour. On his shoulder hung his shitty canvas bag, now lighter. He'd left most of the money, tucked in the ledger, with his friend, along with instructions about getting it to Sofia in a week's time.

"Tell her I've died," Alberto instructed Cosimo. "She can tell who she likes." He hoped he'd astound his wife with this news as she stared into the piles of lire and the pages of his repeating name, evolving into a sophisticated autograph.

Getting espresso at the café would normally be frivolous, but he went today. It was an investment. He took a seat outside, near the grocer's fabled car. Pietro parked it here to show it off and was presently wiping it clear of dust, grinning to passersby. Everyone knew that the Fiat was evidence of corrupt sources of money. It even looked sinister. To Alberto, it was robotic but humanoid, with headlights like eyes behind circular spectacles. They stared at Alberto over a nose of a grill and a line of shiny chrome lips. The cabin rose behind its mechanical face, like a hunchback. It shone like it was from the north, from another planet. It was showy; even the doctor didn't have one. The only roads fit for the car led out of town. Alberto didn't trust it, but knew the thing had speed. He waved at Pietro, who waved back.

"Isn't she a beautiful thing?" Pietro said.

"Beauty? Who cares," Alberto said. He added a teaspoon of sugar to his cup—way more than he'd normally take. "That doesn't matter if she's faster than a horse."

"Much faster, Kingmaker."

Alberto raised the cup to the merchant, and said, "To Sister Gina." Pietro looked confused.

The espresso went down in a single gulp. Alberto stared into the little mug. Undissolved crystals of sugar sat in the residual brown glop. There was only one answer in the cup—something fixed, fated. Or, at least, it would be soon. Have I arranged it that way? he thought. Have I sliced away every other possibility, have I done it on purpose, rendering this inevitable? Have I been that miserable? That afraid? That pathetic? That cruel?

He stretched out his legs before him, helping his pants rise up enough to show a thick sliver of flesh above his socks. In less than a minute, a bee had found the sugar in his espresso cup. The creature started at the lip, tasting and grooming, yanking its antennae. It then crawled deeper, thrilled by its luck, yellow back pumping with excitement. Alberto put his gloved hand over the top of the cup. He heard the thing buzz as he lifted the cup and moved it to his leg. He turned it over and sealed the bug in against the flesh of his ankle. My grandfather was sick of waiting to see what would happen to him next, so he pressed the cup harder and jiggled his leg until the bee was as angry, and as bereft of options, as he was.

story7.12November2018.m4a

[BFM]: Wow. How long did he have?

[GZO]: Long enough. I'm here, aren't I?

[BFM]: I always thought you died within minutes of getting stung, if you're allergic.

[GZO]: Not everyone. Not Papa Zap. You got stung that time we were in Biletto on vacation.

[BFM]: Yeah, but I'm not allergic.

[GZO]: But you believed it, in the story?

[BFM]: I did believe it. Can't say the same about all this straight sex, though.

[GZO]: That's just because I've been inside you.

[BFM]: Well, yes. And you can't write convincingly about tits. Those paragraphs don't work.

[GZO]: Fine, I'll cut them back.

[BFM]: The paragraphs or the tits?

[GZO]: The paragraphs. The tits are untouchable.

[BFM]: That's not what I heard.

[GZO]: I've made her a bit of a tart, haven't I, my step-nonna?

[BFM]: I'm glad you gave her SOMETHING to admire. Otherwise, she'd just be a shrieking harpy.

[GZO]: And you'd prefer to be the only shrieking harpy in this book?

[BFM]: AND the only tart.

[GZO]: Well, she'll have to stay the way she is unless you let me go back and change it.

[BFM]: That's against the rules.

[GZO]: Good, because I like her. She gives Papa Zap a pretty good reason to leave—and a reason to lie once he got to Canada.

[BFM]: Oh right. The big bad scandal everyone talks about. Now that we're here, it doesn't feel that scandalous. Bigamy. Who cares?

[GZO]: You're not Catholic, you don't understand. And people would have cared a lot more back then. We're looking at it with modern eyes.

[BFM]: I just think there would have to be more to it, for it to have affected your family so much. Why would your Nonna go sleep with her daughters? And why did she marry him in the first place?

[BFM]: Yeah. Maybe there's something missing.

—RECORDING ENDS—

8
Is This It? (Part Two)

"Why did you stop recording?" BF said.

"They're coming back," I said and nodded towards the open door, where a cold November wind pushed into our apartment.

BF handed me the laptop with the book manuscript on the screen. He nestled into the corner of the couch, pulling his Pointer Sisters blanket up to his neck. All afternoon, these drafts had preceded the appearance of the movers. There were four of them, all young and sexy and fit enough to haul furniture up the tricky half-helix staircase to our front door. They banged snow from their boots before carrying veiled items into the kitchen. Every time I watched one of them pull away a protective blanket, I'd hope for a jolt of recognition—a lamp or a chair that I remembered, or a story that I'd forgotten.

The shortest mover was my favourite. They all wore the same navy uniform from Callahan Movers/Déménageurs, but the short one filled it out spectacularly. His backside ballooned into his cargo pants and bowling-ballish shoulders rolled under his sweatshirt. He had a sweet, agreeable smile cut into a trimmed black beard. His English was the strongest, so he'd been nominated by the crew to ask me questions. I gave flirty answers and searched his eyes for hints of homosexuality. None came.

"Mister?" he said. He was trying to make the awkward turn into our apartment with an oak hutch. "Where to?"

"Oh, the kitchen with everything else. However it'll fit."

"Yes, just cram it in," BF said. "That's what he prefers. Any old way. Don't think twice if it hurts. Really force it if you have to."

We watched him carry the monolith into our kitchen and lower it onto the scuffed white tile. In his squat, the full glory of his ass emerged, curving hard and round then returning to its upright perfection—a fender of perky solidity.

"Do you need a better vantage point, babes?" BF said. "Am I getting between you and that teenager's rump?"

"You are," I said. "But don't move. Stay comfy."

I twisted the bristles of my beard. What did these straight movers make of us and the zone of campy irony we inhabited? I'd long ago given in to BF's love of the ludicrous, and our apartment became a repository of eclectic, repurposed oddities. A velvet painting of Elvis faced the couch, rendered as a sad clown. The sizeable kitchen looked small thanks to our collection of rarely used, but hilariously presented, minor appliances—a greaseless deep-fryer; a gun that could be loaded with a potato then shot to make fries; a sandwich press that toasted cartoon images onto slices of white bread; a raclette set endorsed by Dolly Parton; a snow-cone maker shaped like Snoopy's doghouse; Shroud of Turin tea towels; something called an "Eggstractor." What would the dreamy mover think of the framed photo of Paul Lynde opposite the toilet? The feather boas accumulating like flamboyant snow on the bookcase? The ceramic bust of John Paul II that BF bought at Value Village because he thought it resembled Justin Bieber?

And there were the two of us, lounging on a Tuesday afternoon on our Naugahyde couch. I was wearing an imitation of Papa Zap's head-to-toe anti-bee uniform, forcing myself to experience it so that I could write about it. I was showing BF how my grandfather could make himself be stung by a bee on the ankle, launching his plan that would bring him to Canada. BF watched me, reclined, with the blanket pulled to his neck. The faces of the Pointer Sisters were glamorous, alert, coke-addled; BF was dozy, with half-closed eyes, powdery face, and bald head. A crescent scar hung like a moon above his right ear, marking where the doctors went in seventeen years ago. We spent many days like this, discussing the book. He'd speak his feedback, and I'd record it on my iPhone.

Maeve's La-Z-Boy entered the living room over the head of the mover, upside down, as though it had human legs.

"This in the kitchen, too?" the dreamboat said.

"Everything."

"There's not enough space for everything."

"I guess that can go in the living room, then, in the corner." I helped him uselessly, pretending to guide the recliner next to the *Dynasty* nativity scene BF had set up. "How much is left?"

"You'll have to find more space," the mover said, surveying the apartment. "You won't be able to open your fridge if we keep putting stuff in the kitchen. Want us to clear some areas?"

"I can do it."

He flicked his eyes to my paunch. "You sure, mister?"

"He's so butch, just let him do it," BF said.

"I thought your roommate was asleep," the mover said.

"He's always awake when you least suspect it," I said.

"Boo," BF deadpanned.

I started dismantling the *Dynasty* crèche to make room.

"Do you have to? Linda Evans makes such a breathtaking virgin."

"You heard the dreamboat. We need more room."

The movers did the best they could, Tetrissing the furniture together. They fit Aunt Dot's throne-like Bergère into a ridge of boxes, then packed a few clocks and walking canes around its upturned legs. They brought in the radio. I'd been waiting for the radio. It had barely changed since the last time I saw it in Maeve's living room on 9/11. The band of stations, with its foreign city names, was darkened and scratched and dusty, and the glass panel over the mini-bar was missing.

"That can go here," I said, indicating the space I'd prepared in the living room. "Look, BF, it's the radio."

"The one that got you wasted on 9/11?"

"Yeah."

I remembered it as larger, so it seemed lost once the movers placed it against the white wall. The clutter of the rest of the apartment gave the thing outsized importance, floating like an artwork given its own room in a gallery.

"How much shit did Maeve have, anyway?"

"Lots. You've read the stories."

"I thought you were exaggerating. You *are* prone to exaggeration, babes."

"I've never exaggerated in my entire life."

✷

The remission was long. I considered 9/11 its starting point. Calling BF that day from Maeve's house in Brooklyn, with the smell of Crown Royal bouncing off the receiver, we confirmed that we were both alive. We felt the same relief—a relief that came from somewhere deeper than my cowardice, deeper than his disease. It was foundational. Solid enough to anchor our partnership.

We bought our Montreal apartment from the landlord. BF handled the decor, stuffing the rooms with nostalgic artifacts we found at garage sales and second-hand shops—other people's pasts crammed into our present, re-contextualized with the histories we made up for them. The fifty-year-old virgin who hoarded Paul Lynde merchandise until she learned he was gay. The despondent teenager in Ottawa who taught himself to read tarot cards with a pornographic deck. The retired piano-tuner with a feeder fetish who needed kitchen gadgets to make food compelling enough to keep his wife on-board.

BF finished his master's and kept going. His doctoral thesis was about Stevie Nicks, how she was the ultimate figure of '80s desire—a sex symbol of corroded, flighty, unreal, ethereal, adulterous, narcotic, misunderstood witchcraft. A publisher in Toronto put out a redacted version as a novelty book, and it sold well next to cash registers at

Urban Outfitters and Indigo. Two dozen copies of *Wouldn't You Love to Love Her?* now lined the bottom shelf of our bookcase.

I gave up freelancing and took a job as a designer at a marketing agency. It specialized in travel magazines for airlines and hotels. They ran stories about skiing odysseys in the Alps or the cuisine of minor Japanese islands. "That's not journalism," Mom said. "But I suppose we're still proud of you." When I became the agency's art director, I travelled frequently for photo shoots, leaving BF with frozen meals in Tupperware as I racked up frequent flyer miles.

I cashed some in last year, buying tickets to Italy for our anniversary—a Roman holiday, with a sidetrip to Papa Zap's hometown. We walked the streets of Biletto with an implied heterosexuality, coughing in the dust. I didn't know it then, but I was absorbing the details I'd eventually write into my story about that village: the fields of sad wheat on the outskirts; the prominence of bees; the slow, cataracted, moustachioed woman at the post office who told us where the remaining Zappacostas ran a bakery-café; the waitress who served us there, who was impatient and loud, but voluptuous. Her impressive cleavage quaked when she barked our order to the chef. I didn't know if she was a Zappacosta, but she would later stand in for Papa Zap's first wife.

Our Airbnb was on the ground floor of a stately home on the main street, behind a doctor's office. The path to its door was hemmed in by rose bushes, red and pink, attended by bees. One found its way into BF's T-shirt and stung him near the armpit.

"I never thought they'd attack the queen," he said.

"There's no accounting for taste," I said.

In our charmless Italian apartment, I searched for a first aid kit. The Airbnb was utilitarian, used only to house tourists and turn a profit. It was a facsimile of a real living space, as though a computer had been asked to guess at what humans might need for a city break. It had fifteen maps of the town, but no mirror in the bathroom; a cupboard full of wine glasses, but no mugs or tumblers; a huge bed with one pillow. No first aid kit.

"It's like ten thousand spoons when all you need is a knife," BF said as I opened and shut the drawers of the bathroom. I got on my knees and moved around bottles of cleaning products below the sink. I looked up at him to say it was hopeless. But I didn't say it. I stopped myself when I saw his head bend as he twisted his body. His arm was up and his shirt was off. He fingered the sparse tuft of pit-hairs, playing with the lump there and attempting to remove the stinger. With no mirror, he couldn't see it. He could only feel it.

"Isn't the sting on the other side?" I said.

"Yeah," he said. "I'm comparing sides. There's a lump on both sides."

The light from the window hit the ridge of his cheekbone and made shadows of the sinews in his neck. He looked down at me. His eyes were wide and no longer wincing in annoyance. They were wet, shocked, terrified. His bottom lip drooped and his eyebrows came together. I knew that look. I hadn't seen it in seventeen years, not since he was sick. He could see the recognition in my face, too. Desperate concern. Eyes staring into a future of ghastly unknowns.

*

This time, the chemo didn't work. Nine months, maybe a year. That was the prognosis.

After we left the doctor's office, we said nothing. I held his hand as we walked out. It was a clutch of twigs. BF's was skeletal, weak and clammy from the chemo. His sky-blue nails poked into my flesh as the news rolled over us, a wave of facts followed by an undertow of numb panic. No words in the elevator or in the lobby or in front of the hospital as we waited for the Uber. The only sound I remember is the whistle of an ambulance, an angry signal full of indecipherable information. I looked at the Uber app, which was full of maps and systems and icons and none of it meant anything. It was January, and our breath came out in feathers. Signs in the street—"stationnement interdit," "Jewish

General Hospital," "Urgence Emergency," "rue barrée," "Second Cup," "ostie de grosse manif contre le gouvernement Couillard," "zone free wifi zone"—were trying to communicate something but failed.

BF broke the silence in the Uber, telling the driver to pull over at the look-out. The car was coming down the eastern slope of Mount Royal. Rockfaces rose on either side of us, but ahead was a paved outcropping with a couple dozen parking spaces. From here, we could see a panorama of the city. With no leaves on the trees, we could make out all those straight Montreal roads that don't end, that continue on and on between the triplexes until they become indistinct where the Olympic Stadium gropes the sky. The driver parked, and we looked out at it, over the front seats, through the windshield, between the few, brave, parka'ed tourists who had nothing to worry about save the cold.

"If you're going to leave, leave right now," BF said.

"BF—"

"Shut up. I'll tell the driver to take me to my parents' house. I'll leave you here on top of the mountain, and you can do whatever the fuck it is you do when you run away—"

"That was seventeen years ago."

"—but if we keep driving, if we go home together, then you can't leave until it's over. You're going to be scared shitless and you're going to think you can put everything off and you're going to deny that it's happening. And you can do all of that, but you can't leave."

"This is it?"

"This is it." The slack skin around his mouth bunched up at the corners, like curtains pulled up on a cord. "And if you go now, I'll forgive you. To me, it'll just be proof that you're the shitty coward you were the first time around. That you never grew out of it. And I'll think that. I'll think, 'that's a shitty person, deep down. It's who he is. It's in his bones, in his cells. I can forgive that person because he can't help it.' But if you leave after this car moves one centimetre, with both of us in it, I'll never forgive you. And I'll hope that God exists and that there's an afterlife so that I can continue not forgiving you after the end of time."

"You're rambling."

"Of course I'm rambling," he said. "Because I legitimately don't know what you're going to say, and I'm terrified that I'm a coward, like you and everyone else on Earth, and if I keep rambling, then it means you haven't answered yet, and the concrete hasn't set, and things can still change. If you stay, you'll have to deal with a lot of this kind of thing. Like, a *lot.* It's going to be way worse than last time. What happened before? That part of your life that you thought was the worst thing you'd ever experienced? Well, that was LOLs. That was a rom-com, OK? It was *Moonstruck*. It was *Mermaids.* It was fucking *Witches of Eastwick.* What's coming is going to be *Silkwood*, OK? It's going to be some real *Mask* shit. It's going to be *Burlesque*—it's going to be unwatchable, unbearable."

"I'm staying."

"Oh god!" BF burst out in wild crying, the kind of open-mouth, heaving weeps that are out of one's control. He wrapped his arms around me and I held that slight version of him, barely there, but more present than ever.

"Just no more Cher, OK?"

He laugh-cried into my neck, sniffled up some strength, and said, "Fuck you. Fuck you from the bottom of my heart."

*

Life got deceptively better. I took a sabbatical from the agency. BF quit his professorship, halted the chemo, put some weight back on. He decided that there were things he wanted to do while he still could. Some were easy—concerts, dinner at Toqué, a week in Berlin, a weekend at Dollywood—but others were more difficult. He was never a contestant on *The Price Is Right,* but we managed to get his copy of *Gender Trouble* signed. He got into a screening of *The View.* Fran Lebowitz and Marianne Faithfull were both gracious when, on separate occasions, he ambushed them at stage doors. We overpaid for Broadway tickets to a revival of *Angels in America* to make up for missing it back in 2001.

"And then there's you," he said to my back. I was at the counter, cutting chicken into cutlets. He sat behind me at the kitchen table, poking at my laptop. "We need something for you to do."

"I have plenty to do."

"Not now. I mean, you know, afterwards."

"We're not talking about afterwards."

"I don't want you sulking around going 'Boo hoo hoo, I don't know how to live without him.'"

"Yes you do."

"'I can't make sense of anything,'" he persisted. "'What does it all mean?'"

"That's uncanny."

"'Why am I such a loser?'"

"OK, that's enough."

"How about this?"

I turned around, hands up, covered in chicken blood. He had the Word document of my family history open on the screen—my chronicle of the stories we told in the hot tub, over Friday fish dinners, on car rides. It was no longer twelve pages long. I had added a transcript of the interview I'd done with Maeve all those years ago, back when I used this book as an excuse to run away to New York. I hadn't touched it since.

"Insomnia.doc," he read. "Catchy title."

"That document's not real."

"So why is it still on your desktop?"

"It's just there."

"You've moved it from computer to computer for years, and never thought of it? Babes, it's still a .doc. It's not even a .docx." He was scrolling. "There's some good material here. The 9/11 stuff. And this interview with your aunt."

"Great-aunt."

"Look," he said, typing. The homepage of the Saint George Hotel appeared. "It's that hovel you hate. Where you were staying when you ran away. You could go back there and write about it. We're planning on going to New York anyhow to see *Angels*."

"No, BF. We're focused on you."

"This *is* for me. I want to know that you have something. After *you know*."

"OK, I simply don't want to do it, then."

"Permit me to remind you that I have cancer."

"Permission denied."

"$179 a night. Single occupancy."

"Single? You wouldn't stay with me?"

"I'll be at the Plaza," he said. "I have cancer *and* standards."

"And unrealistic expectations. I don't even know what I'd write."

"I'll help you get started. I'm an expert. Don't forget I managed to publish a book before you did."

"How could I ever forget?"

"Just get it down as it comes to you," he said. "Keep going, that's the best advice. Get used to doing it every day. That way, you can keep going after *you know*."

"I don't know anything."

"Don't hide behind that. You know a lot more than you used to," he said. "Promise me you'll do this."

I shrugged and returned to my chicken cutlets.

BF persisted. He made a list of Bonnie's stories, and on our next trip to Fiona, we interviewed her about them. We talked to Jacko and Tina and Danny. We visited the house on Laurier Street, intruding on the curious, but bewildered, couple who now lived there. We went to the Hornets' arena for a skating lesson with Tina and her daughter. We crashed a funeral at Chéhab and Sons. We drove up to Cobble Beach and pretended it was 1960. It was April, so we sat on the beach in giant coats, feeling tiny pellets of rain on our necks. I tried to get Detroit radio stations on a portable radio, but they didn't come through, so we streamed an early Motown playlist on BF's phone and cuddled for warmth like teenage lovers, like my parents once had. The phone bill, when it came, had $300 in data fees.

"Should I pay it, or?" BF trailed off.

"Or," I said.

I humoured him. I added ideas to the Word document, trying to describe all the experiences. He read them and criticized them, made edits. He told me to take it seriously, to connect the stories, to find some sense in it. He'd highlight big passages and use the commenting tool to write: "Why?" I didn't know why; I didn't want to know. The book was not the distraction BF had promised. It seemed to be hastening the inevitable. Everything I came up with led back to our immediate, truncated time, and I'd slap the laptop closed. "Keep going," BF would yell from the couch.

Why would I keep going? If I made progress with the book, it meant that I was fine and that he had permission to die. I wasn't and he didn't. All the same emotions from the first cancer episode crawled up inside me, became me, wore my skin like a costume. The notion that it could all be deferred indefinitely was so comforting that I pursued it. I chased this nothingness as though uncertainty itself was a destination. I'd driven the road of my life to a roundabout and decided to keep spinning there. It wasn't that I hadn't learned anything in seventeen years. I now knew that this mental trick was the only way I could stay put, and the only way I could give him what he needed. I could deal with each detail as it came up, solve it, and remain, as long as I believed that the inevitable would never materialize.

*

Then Aunt Maeve died. She'd made it to ninety-eight, and appeared to time her demise to throw the notion of mortality in my face.

The funeral home in Brooklyn made Chéhab and Sons seem, as Aunt Maeve might have said, fit for Pharaohs. It was on Flatbush Avenue, two blocks from Maeve's house, and looked like any normal storefront. Crumbling yellow bricks surrounded a window displaying tacky urns, two of which were elevated on plastic pedestals shaped like Ionic columns. Gold chintz was wrapped around their bases for an air of luxury, but it only underlined how cheap the place felt. A black board had ridged plastic grooves with white letters slid along them to spell the names of the dead and the dates of their visitations. There she was, MAEVE O HARA.

"The apostrophe is missing," I said.

"The place is pretty old," BF said. "Maybe they lost it."

"There's a gap. Like, an intentional one. As if they're admitting the apostrophe is missing."

"It's better than nothing."

"It's literally nothing. It's an empty space. It *is* nothing. By definition."

"Let's go in."

I didn't move. I stayed focused on the window. BF and I were reflected there, laid over the decor of death. The grime on the glass softened our edges. I was middle-aged, hollow-eyed, but well groomed and expensively outfitted. BF looked handsome in his single-breasted black suit, the pleats straight, the collar sharp. He looked as he would in his own coffin. Muscles in my neck swelled around my breath, and I started to cough and swear without even the pretence of control. BF hugged me, as if throwing himself on a grenade. I crushed him back, not caring if anyone objected. In fact, I hoped that some passing homophobe would have something to say so I could direct my fury at them instead.

"Let's not bury me in a suit, then," BF said.

Once inside, I got angrier. Aunt Maeve had the smallest room. It was tacky and inadequate, with two dozen folding chairs arranged in a half-ring around the coffin. The maize carpets were overtreaded and dotted with cigarette burns. Maeve was laid out in the dress of a headmistress, something she never would have allowed in life. Her nail polish was cheap and poorly applied, crawling over her cuticles. I knelt in faux prayer before the corpse and focused on the buckle of her belt, where my own stupid face was reflected, stretched out and brassy in the curve of the metal.

"Fuck," I said.

BF put his hand on my shoulder and said, "I know. That belt."

"This funeral's a pantomime."

"Then at least her makeup's on point." Her cheeks were reddened like brake lights, her eyes circled with black lines. The foundation was salmon-hued and cut off in a line under her chin. "It's all a bit Baby Jane, isn't it?"

"It's farcical."

BF dislodged me from the kneeler, giving other mourners an opportunity to make fools of themselves. We milled around with the sparse crowd at the back of the room. Every person annoyed me. I saw each of them as interlopers, unworthy of being present—myself included. The wake lured in uncles hoping for an open bar, aunts hoping for gossip, and cousins with no evident hope at all.

This was the American branch of Dad's family. I hadn't seen any of them in years. The elder crop were Catholics to their marrow and dressed in fabrics lifted from a three-star hotel: thick-knit wool bedspreads sewn into double-breasted suits; nylon drapes, barely cinched, restraining elephant-ish décolletage; black plastic cushions moulded into shoes, masquerading as leather. The dozen-odd cousins were like before pictures of their parents. They were bored, growing too fat for their funeral outfits, with six DeVry Institute certificates and two drug convictions between them. Each suffered a twinge of revolted understanding when I introduced them to BF, which I enjoyed. Tim, the youngest of the bunch, had grown into a giant. He was muscled in a porn-starry way and crushed my hand when he shook it, smiling down at me as though he were about to sell me a car. Athletic and graceful, busting with energy, he exuded the kind of master-race sexiness that typically eluded my family. When he walked away from us and lifted his arms to hug an adjacent crone, I took in a guilty eyeful of his backside. He's so healthy, I thought. The notion cut through my mind, leaving ripples of guilt in its wake.

"Are you cruising the funeral, babes?"

"Sorry."

I disgusted myself. Lately, my gaze was wandering to the kinds of men I'd never before found attractive. I thought nothing of it at first, these new muscled distractions—young, bulgy boys who looked as though they were coming from the gym or on their way to run a marathon. That kind of vigour and robustness was everywhere in gay clubs, on hook-up apps, in the Village. I'd always been repulsed by its implied vanity. And now, I was paunched in front and sagging behind, patchily hairy on my back, scooped out under my eyes. I could never attract them but wanted them so thoroughly, with a thirst for their healthiness that grew deeper and more daunting the closer we got to the worst part of BF's disease.

"Giovanni, look at you in your beard!" It was Patricia, Maeve's caregiver who I'd met years earlier. Her black eyes were still alert and alive, and her bolt of silver hair had thickened. "A bit of O'Hara red in it, I see."

"Patricia, you haven't aged a day," I said.

"I've aged a hundred years this week alone."

"I'm so sorry for your loss. You were dear friends."

"Oh, Maeve would never put it that way, but, yes. Yes, we were, weren't we?"

"This is Brian. BF."

"Oh? Oh yes?" They shook hands while Patricia scanned him. As a nurse, she may have been able to read the illness on him, some visual code only those in the medical profession could decipher.

"A pleasure to meet you."

"Did you know Maeve long?" BF asked.

"Gracious me—what has it been? Twenty years!" She landed the line beautifully; she'd been practising it all afternoon. "Of course, I could never replace Dot. They had a deep bond, those sisters. The stories!"

"Dot was quite a character," I said.

"Maeve had another word for it!"

"Eccentric?"

"Much ruder. But they adored each other, didn't they? She gave her life!" Patricia said. "Did your parents not come?"

"Their plane is delayed. They'll come straight from LaGuardia to the church."

"So good of you to come all this way! Maeve would have been so embarrassed. She'd have hated *all* of you for this fuss!"

"Speaking of fuss, I wondered if I could take one last look in Aunt Maeve's house," I said. "Just to remember it."

"Remember it? Heavens, why?

"Gio's writing a book," BF said.

"Oh yes, your *book*!" she said. "I never received my signed copy."

"I'm still writing it."

"And it's about Maeve?"

"Not exactly."

"She'd *hate* that!" Patricia said with a smile. "A book about her."

"If history's any hint, it'll end out being about himself," BF offered.

"All the same," Patricia said. "No, I can't imagine!"

"Imagine me paying a visit?"

"The whole shebang, I'd say. The book, the visit. Everything!"

"I think you're being a bit unreasonable," I said. "It would be a quick peek."

"Really, no."

"A glimpse? A glance?"

"Gio—" BF said.

"A gander, then?"

"So good of you to come all this way," she said and turned from us.

"A peep?" I called to her back.

"What are you doing?" BF said.

"She's a total bitch."

"She's really not."

"It's not fair. You wanted to see the inside of Maeve's house. For the book."

"Oh, you suddenly care about the book?"

"So what if I do?" I said. I said it like a child, to mask the fact that he was right. "When I write it, I'm going to make her into a total asshole."

"OK, tough guy. Let's go before you punch someone," BF said. "Although that would be a delicious detail for the book."

*

We didn't need to get into Maeve's house, in the end. She left no will, and several months later, every item she owned was automatically bequeathed to her next of kin—her eldest brother's eldest son, just another John O'Hara, my father. With one phone call to the probate lawyer, the delivery address was changed from Fiona to Montreal, and once the hunky movers left, BF and I were surrounded by every souvenir of her life.

BF sat in the La-Z-Boy as I pulled items from boxes. They seemed to have been packed in chronological order. The oldest ones were from the '30s and the newest ones from last year. Inside, they were a jumble, as though chapters of Maeve's life had been sealed away, and the next one started with all new memorabilia. Some of the contents had belonged to Dot. I recognized them from the bungalow on Caribou Road, where I'd once watched *Alien* and sketched Dot's face. One box contained their old movie cassettes. Another, stacks of celebrity headshots, scribbled over with Dot's forgeries. A third: just wigs.

I sat on the floor with my shoulder against the La-Z-Boy. I was half-facing BF as he leafed through the headshots. They were all the same dimensions and sticky from old Scotch Tape.

"Who did she think she was fooling?" BF said.

"Herself, mainly."

"The messages are so personalized, like she was writing in

their voices." BF held one of Katharine Hepburn over his face. "REALLY!" was scrawled over her white blouse and houndstooth jacket. "Really!" BF said. "I think I would have liked her."

"Katharine or Dot?"

"Both."

"Dot would have loved you," I said. "Katharine didn't like anybody."

"Spencer Tracey."

"You're no Spencer Tracey. More Tracey Ullman."

"Tracy Lords?"

"Tracey Gold if you're lucky."

"I think we've established that I am," he said. "With some notable recent exceptions."

"We should watch *Alien* tonight," I said. "We can fire up your old VCR."

"Can't we stream it?"

"No. I want the original tape from Maeve's house."

"The quality will be shit."

"It's not about the quality of the picture. It's about the quality of the memory. It's research."

I found the box of video cassettes and yanked out the movie in its creepy black-and-green sleeve.

"This is on Beta," BF said.

"Oh shit," I said. "That's right. They used to have the VHS-Beta argument all the time. Dot always wanted to upgrade."

"Very sensible."

"I doubt her reasons were very sensible."

BF held an *Arthur*-era picture of Liza Minnelli to his face. "What a most strange and extraordinary person!"

We worked backwards in time, box after box, until there were only three cartons remaining. Their bases were water-damaged and the cardboard threatened to dissolve at the touch.

"Shall we do the last ones? Or do you need a rest?"

"I'll sleep when I'm dead."

"I told you to stop saying that."

"It's an absurd statement, Gio. It means nothing."

"It reminds me."

"You're unpacking a corpse's flatware. *Two* corpses. Death is literally surrounding us. You're writing a *book* about death. And I'm still not allowed to talk about it?"

"The book isn't about death."

"Oh lord. Don't tell me you think it's about life."

"Well, lives."

"Babes, I've *read* it."

"It's not done yet."

"But it's not a pot boiler, is it?"

"Maybe it should be."

"And it's not a love story."

"Maybe it should be that, too."

"But it's not."

"Not yet."

"Babes," he said, and placed his hand on my shoulder, "it's a fucking elegy."

I quieted him by opening the next box. A desiccated odour emerged. It was a combination of dust and must, like an old book. The contents had been jammed in the box. I had the sense that the last person to glimpse inside was whoever had packed it in the '30s. On top was an old Eaton's bag containing a wrinkled red velour dress, bunched up and mashed in, brown in the places where it had come in contact with the water.

"Tack-o-rama," BF said, peering over my head. "Dot's, you think?"

I lifted the gown between pinched fingers and it hesitated before unfurling to reveal lacework around the neck and cuffs. The sleeves looked as though they'd once been puffed, but had now deflated like a week-old balloon.

"Too small to be Dot's," I said. "But too dainty for Maeve."

"Yeah, it's a bit Anne of Green Gables for her."

"Judging by the date on the box, Maeve would have been nineteen."

"Everyone makes criminal fashion choices at nineteen. What if we unearthed some of your sartorial crimes from that era?"

"Plaid shirts and fat jeans."

"Exactly."

"Yours would be what? Goth chokers? Doc Martens?"

"Actually," BF said and fingered the velour. "Mine wouldn't be too far from this."

Beneath it in the box were matching high-heels of red patent leather. They were uncreased, the soles pristine. I handed one to BF.

"I'm holding out for that *L.A. Confidential* sequel," he said.

"They're way more Dot than Maeve."

"They're brand new," BF said. He sniffed inside. "Still smells like poppers."

The remaining items were a pell-mell collection of souvenirs from a bar or tavern. There was an ashtray with ash still clinging to the bottom, and a stack of cardboard coasters with ring stains of red wine on them. Each coaster had the same Art Deco drawing. A woman leaned on a skinny arm, gloved to the elbow, hair pulled back into a bun, lips coy and big. She faced a man in a tuxedo, hair also slicked back, face also coy, only with a manicured moustache. They looked ready to kiss, but perhaps hesitating because of the cat depicted in the triangle formed by their arms. The coasters advertised a party at a place in Toronto called the Orange Cat. "Kitten Ball. August 7, 1937. Formal attire."

"Maybe Maeve was a party animal."

"I can't see her ever going to something like this. Formal attire? As far as I know, she only ever wore sweatpants, except to Mass."

"Give her a break. She was young. Maybe looking for a suitor."

"Now that I really can't see."

"Didn't you say she'd hooked up with that priest for a while?"

"Father Dupuis? That was only a rumour."

BF googled the bar.

"All I'm getting is pictures of orange cats," he said.

"Add the year."

"OK, now all I'm getting is black and white cats. Presumably both orange and dead."

"Add Toronto. Add the address and the date."

"I've googled before, babes. There's nothing. It was probably some kind of dance she attended."

"A nubile young Maeve, dressed to the nines?"

"And hating every second of it?"

"Dupuis, the dashing young divinity student on her arm?"

"It's hard to believe."

At the bottom of the box, the items were even more damaged. Water must have leaked around it at some point. There was a red-and-gold clutch, dusty with mould, and a pair of lace-fringed gloves that BF slid on. Four black-and-white photographs sat on the bottom. They were all the same: a young man, maybe twenty-five years old, distorted here and there where the water had forced the photo-paper to bubble. The man was in a tuxedo, posed full length in front of a curtain, flanked by potted plants with wide leaves. His face was water-damaged, but I could tell he looked infatuated, as though the camera was his beloved and there was nothing more natural in the world than smiling at it.

"This is the priest?" BF asked. I squinted at the images and tried to find Father Dupuis in the water-wounded features, but these were full-body shots—the faces were tiny and marred by deterioration. "I suppose he would have been pre-priest at this point."

"It's hard to square the blowhard I knew with this person. This person seems more happy than smug. He was always pretty pleased with himself."

I remembered Dupuis best from around the time he gave Nonna the last rites. He was in a puffy phase then, with droopy cheeks and a purplish nose grown gnarly and truffle-like from years of drink. The photographed man had the tight face of youth, smooth and shaven, blurry from the idealized photography of the time. He wore his top hat tipped forward, creating shadows and grading that made it impossible to determine his head shape. But he had less tangible qualities that made him a worthwhile subject. His stance made him appear bold; his smile lent him the patina of a man in love.

"Why are there four of them?"

"I don't know."

I turned them over, handed one to BF. On the back, there was handwriting; clean, teacher-like cursive, with the ink faded by time and water. They all had dates from 1937.

"Same year as the coasters. The Orange Cat," I noted.

"'I can't write,'" BF read from the back of the photo. "'I don't know how to make words mean things.'"

"This one's different, but it's in the same ballpark. 'I am not good at this. I don't know how to write about feelings. But maybe that's good? Maybe there are no words for feelings. Words like that haven't been invented yet. Words for how I feel about you. Who are you? How did you do this to me? I think it's impossible that anyone normal could do this to me.'" I tipped my head back to look at BF. "It's a mash note."

"They all are. She got four of them."

"They're all pretty terrible."

"They're better than the love letters you sent me, babes," BF said.

"I never sent you a love letter."

"Exactly."

"'Who *are* you?'" I said. "'*How* did you do this to me?'"

"Magic," BF said. "And sex."

I picked up the third photo, flipped it over. "'It's scary. I'm scared. It's like Mass. All that Latin. No one in the church understands it, but everyone feels it. They know it's all holy. I didn't know you could feel that outside of God. It's unholy. It's unholy to feel it about a person.' He wasn't Shakespeare, was he?"

"He wasn't even Shakespeare's Sister," BF said. "He wasn't even Bananarama."

"These are more articulate than some of his sermons. And twice as long, too," I said. "Maybe someone did love old Maeve."

"Maybe these were for Dot."

"1937? Dot would have been a child."

I looked at the man again. Having read his words, he now seemed scared, intense and full of inexpressible emotions he was experiencing for the first time. The black dots of his eyes were only visible on one of the four cards—they were round and wild. I knew that look. It was the look of someone with new power, a driving force he couldn't understand, but that was empowering and terrifying.

"I bet he broke her grizzled little heart," I said.

*

Barb and Morty let themselves in. She jingled her keys, the way she always did to announce her arrival. I couldn't make out her words from the bedroom, but the lilt of her voice was enough for me to register her disapproval of our new stuff. It rose in aghast declarations, then dropped an octave into judgement.

I forced myself to leave the apartment regularly so they could spend time with BF. When we got the prognosis, Barb's and Morty's suburban house had been on the market for a year. They dropped the price to a steal and used some of the proceeds to buy a condo six blocks away. They gave the rest of the money to us. They tolerated no thank yous. "When I'm on my deathbed, I'm not going to be thinking, 'Gee, I wish I hadn't given that money to my son when *he* was on *his* deathbed,'" was Barb's reasoning. I loved them for it, and giving them time alone with BF was a way of showing my gratitude.

"Morning morning morning!" Barb chirped at me when I emerged from the bedroom. She'd changed her hair again. Her fire-engine phase was over. Spiky triangles were now in effect, coloured shoe-polish black with streaks of plum. Morty was already fingering the bacon I'd left for him on the counter. "How's the patient?"

I gave them the rundown: heart rate, pill amounts, pain complaints, sleeping hours.

"Like our new interior design?" I said as I bundled up for my walk.

"It certainly is a curious choice, isn't it, Morty?"

"It's crowded," said BF's father, a master of the obvious, as he chewed.

"There's a quiche in the oven, Mort."

"Outstanding," he said and crouched to look through the oven window. "Leek?"

"And Gruyère."

"You spoil him something rotten," Barb said. She was rearranging our footwear, wiping fingers on her peach slacks, eyeing the wall of Maeve's boxes. "I guess I don't *get* it. I mean, the place was difficult already, wasn't it? In terms of getting around? And now, well, what is all this stuff? It's unique, if nothing else!"

"She disapproves."

"Hush, Morty."

"It's from my great-aunt," I said. Barb watched with horror as I plucked my boots from the line of footwear she'd arranged. "Full of key items for the book."

"This will be some book! With all this *research* cluttering up your house!"

"She hates it," Morty clarified.

"I don't *hate* it," she turned up the heat on the thermostat, making a show of having to reach around the boxes to do so. I grabbed my coat. "Such strong language."

"It's not forever, Barb, don't worry. We'll go through it all and organize it. Throw out what we don't need." I toqued and zipped myself. "See you in a few hours."

"Can Morty at least move some of this around?"

"Kind of you to offer, but don't go to the trouble. I'll do it this week."

"Thank god," Morty said.

"Ciao, guys!" I kissed Barb on the cheek. "And I love the new hair colour. Don't think I didn't notice."

"What a thing to say!" Barb said.

"Fetching as hell, isn't it Morty?"

"It's purple."

*

"The pictures stink," Tina said. I'd emailed her snapshots of the tuxedoed priest. Her voice drilled into my head from my noise-cancelling earphones. "I can't see any detail, even when I zoom way in."

"They're old-time-y and water damaged. But imagine Father Dupuis going to some studio in Toronto to get it taken. A trip to the big city for a young, thirsty kid, deciding if he wants to be a priest."

"Thirsty?"

"Oh, thirsty as *fuck*," I said. "It means oversexed, Tina."

"Horny?"

"Yes, if it were 1998, not 2018."

The cold was bracing, but the topic warmed me up. I'd left at 6:30 a.m. so I could be enveloped in the freeze. Dark when I started my walk, the skies were now a crisp, light blue, and the air was thin and frigid. The wind was light, but stung my face and drew the moisture from my eyes. The tears froze as I walked. I closed my lids for ten paces at a time so the ice would melt out of my lashes. I could taste the salt. Mount Royal soared up my right side, its trees naked, looking like stripes against the snowy incline. I turned left, where the street sloped between the Victorian stone houses plagued by their McGill University designations. ZOOLOGY, POLITICAL SCIENCE, ANTHROPOLOGY. The muscles of my thighs squeezed to give me balance.

"I'm picturing a whole set up. Accordion camera, photographer under a sheet. That kind of thing."

"Wrong," Tina said. "Those box cameras are from the Victorian era. This picture is from the '30s, right before the war. It could have been taken at home."

"Even better! Picture a young Father Dupuis, not yet priestified, just a kid in the seminary. He was so hot to bone Aunt Maeve—"

"Gross."

"—that he sets up this whole thing in his house, with the curtain and plants, and he rents a tux and everything."

"Gio—"

"And he takes a hundred pictures to choose from so that he looks fuckable. He sends them to her one after the next, with love letters on the back."

"Listen to yourself," Tina said. "You sound like Mom. You're filling in all these details that never happened."

"So?"

"So, think about it rationally."

"Why don't you want this to be true, Tina?"

A fuzzy blare came through the earphones as she exhaled her frustration into her phone. I thought of her in her minivan, in the parking lot of the suburban Toronto chiropractor's practice she owned with her wife. She held her old Blackberry to her ear as she stared into the whipping traffic of Mississauga Road.

I was under the freeway now, where the sidewalk was clear but the wind came up the hill. My coat and I absorbed everything: the cold, the conversation, the exhaust-infused drips of meltwater from the roadway above. The city around me was grey and brittle. The concrete was cracked all the way up the buttresses. The underside of the highway was bleeding rust.

"How's BF?"

"He's with his parents. I'm out for a walk."

"No, I mean how *is* he?"

"Oh." Answering this question still felt like being pushed off a cliff. "He's been sleeping more. He's over the flu. Temp stable. Vitals almost all back to normal. Well, normal for him."

"You have to watch what you drag into the house. Are you washing your hands?"

"I have no skin left."

"Are you taking off your boots?"

"Yes," I said.

"And I bet you left him food, too?"

"Of course. For him and his folks."

"Watching the salt? Nothing too rich?"

"Fuck, yes, Tina. I was feeling so good. I didn't even care that it's -20 out here. Now I'm freezing because you had to go and change the subject."

"I didn't change the subject. We were talking about the same thing the whole time. We were talking about how you want everyone to be happy. And you run away whenever it becomes too much."

"No, we were talking about Aunt Maeve, then we were talking about BF. Now we're talking about—Christ, I don't even know what we're talking about."

"You want Maeve to have been happy at some point in her life. You're willing to revise history to add a little love for her."

"So?"

"So, how do you know it's honest?"

"Does it have to be honest?"

"Yes!" she said. "You're writing it into the book. You better be writing it honestly."

"Truth and honesty are different. That's what Mom always says."

"Well, this is it!" Tina and I said together, imitating Mom.

"What does BF say?" Tina said.

"He doesn't care one way or the other. He just wants it to be fabulous."

"Has he read it?"

"Every word. But his eyes are getting weaker and his hands shake, so he can't type comments anymore. Sometimes I have to read it to him. I always record his feedback on my phone so I can listen to it later."

"And he doesn't mind it being a pack of lies?"

"Listen, I have to go."

"Cutting me off. Classic Gio."

"Bye, Tina."

"Classic Bonnie!"

I hung up on her. I'd arrived at the canal and turned west. Around me, healthy masochists were jogging beside the frozen corridor of ice. The landscape was barren until some light industrial buildings rose on my left. I had to jam my legs knee-deep in the snow to get to Pitt Street, where there was a stretch of low-rises with chipped stucco and dusty windows. Panel vans grumbled past. Parking lots made islands out of the buildings they served.

I was the only pedestrian. I had not planned for this. Swathed in my bright blue parka, head covered, face wrapped, I was both conspicuous and unidentifiable. I marched past my destination to make it appear as though I was aimed elsewhere and had to circle the block until I'd worked out a plan. The sign at Callahan Movers/Déménageurs was old and clearly used to say CALLAHAN'S, but the apostrophe-S had been painted over in deference to the language laws. It was as winter-beaten as the place it advertised, collecting blown snow in patches and swinging on chains. Below it, four large trucks were parked in a row. One of them had probably delivered Maeve's possessions to my apartment.

I went around the empty for-rent building across the road. From here, I could see through the back window, across an abandoned office, and out the front. I saw human shapes moving around at Callahan's. I decided they were my four movers preparing for a thankless day of hauling items for jerks like me. I decided they were making the best of it, maybe poking fun at their list of assigned stuff and creating stories for their assignments, the way BF and I might do. And maybe, I fantasized, they were making fun of me. They remembered the faggots of Querbes Street, and the preposterous campscape in which they lived, now heaving with the estate of an old lady. They remembered me, and my vain attempts to help them shift items too heavy for my body. They had some sorrow and theories for BF, too, and wondered if he was frail from AIDS or some other gay disease. The three others poked fun at my Adonis, having picked up on my flirtations. They were repeating those jokes now, for the millionth time this week.

I was a teenager again, with the same giddy thrill-fear of passing by a crush in the hallway at Our Lady of Victory High School. I had nothing to say to my Adonis. I simply needed to see him, confirm for myself that his robust beauty still existed. I thought of him whenever I was alone, which wasn't often. I wondered if he'd like my quiche, my tomato sauce. Hidden in the shower, I ejaculated volumes inappropriate for a man of my age, as I imagined the mover bent over Dot's Bergère, his eyes rolling back in his head, transported to bliss by my sexual momentum.

The sweat in my chest hair and armpits had chilled, but the breath in my scarf was warm on my lips. My fingers were numb and my cock was hard. I was uncomfortable, but I stayed a little longer. I felt like Papa Zap in the wheat field. In an existence full of demands and sadness, I'd found a moment that was entirely mine.

✷

Christmas is inexorable, though I would have argued the point that year. Now that I'd taken down the *Dynasty* crèche, our apartment gave no hint of festivity. I resented the Advent candles in our neighbours' window. Markers of time had become my enemy; I'd stripped the apartment of calendars and refused BF's request to get a tree. When he asked if I'd found the pink lights we typically hung from the balcony railing, I pleaded that they were buried under Maeve's avalanche of stuff.

I'd shuffled some of the items around to make the place more livable, BF directing me from a reclined position on the La-Z-Boy. Our apartment was a zone where time had become garburated. Lamps from the '50s sat before a mirror from the '80s; the soundtracks from three of the four *A Star is Born*s (Garland, Streisand, Gaga) were propped on the radio-bar in three distinct formats (LP, 8-track, and a screenshot from Spotify that BF insisted I print out). A rubber Ursula figurine from a Happy Meal was half-submerged in a bowl of American and European coins left over from our trips. The four photographs of Father Dupuis took pride of place, pinned below Elvis on the wall facing the couch.

For the first time, I wouldn't spend Christmas with my family in Fiona. BF was deteriorating. He was now gaunt, bony, sharp. His flesh had given up on tightening around his muscles, and the skin bunched into folds when I helped him in and out of bed, on and off the toilet. The painkillers were growing ineffective, and he complained of aches in his backbone and teeth. The apartment smelled of decay. Every time I walked in, the odour punched me in the face, as did the heat, which was turned up to twenty-eight to keep BF from shivering.

"The birth of your Saviour is right around the corner," he said.

"Jonnie Walker's birthday is in May."

"I meant Baby Jesus, who I understand your people worship."

"They're not people," I said. "They're my family."

"Whatever they are, you should go visit them. Barb and Morty will come stay with me."

"I cancelled Christmas this year. It doesn't exist."

"You can't cancel Christmas," he said, rolling his jaundiced eyes as he sat L-shaped in our bed.

"But I did. It's just Tuesday now."

"Contrary to whatever power you think you have, you can't cancel a capitalist holiday. Babes, who do you think you are? Amazon.com?"

"I'm just me," I said, pulling the splotchy sheets from the bed, working around him. "I'm Giovanni.com."

"You're an idiot.org. And you're being stubborn.ca."

"I have new pages for you."

"You're caught in denial.net."

"I'll show you the new stuff after I put the laundry in."

"Are you going to ask if I want to do something for Christmas?"

"Dot?"

"Dot F-U."

"Ah." I walked out, arms full of linen, leaving him small and alone on the stripped mattress. I yelled, "Christmas is hereby cancelled.gov—"

"We'll see."

"—and that's the last word on it."

"Dot?" he yelled back.

"Dot nothing."

On the morning of December 25th, I went in to check on him, take his temperature, feel his pulse, and turn him, as I did every morning. He typically slept through this process or moaned in half-awake pain, signalling for me to bring him an Oxycontin. On this day, though, he was awake when I went in. He'd managed to open the curtains to let in the dawn light. I pulled my glasses from my hair to my nose. BF leapt into focus, a desiccated angel, something excavated and preserved by archaeologists, bleached and skeletal, presented on Care Bear sheets. He smiled, and his eyes were alive in the old way—a way I hadn't seen in weeks. I grinned back, jolted from my morning grumpiness by the thought that he was on an upswing. He had energy and spark.

"Merry Christmas," he said. His voice had become rough, but in its croak I could hear an old flamboyance.

"Happy Tuesday," I said.

"Did Santa come?"

I stood in the doorframe, feet apart, as if he might make a run for it. I crossed my arms across my bare chest. He was suppressing a smile, giving him an air of mischievousness.

"Do you need the washroom?" I said.

"Is my stocking stuffed?"

"Any accidents through the night?"

"Were you visited by three spirits?"

"Your joints OK?"

"Did you see how the world would be if you'd never been born? Did Donna Reed scream when you grabbed her in front of the library?"

"How's your spine?"

"At least I have one." His face dropped. "Did you pick the shittiest tree, but then Linus somehow made it awesome by wrapping a fucking blanket around it?"

I uncrossed my arms and sat on the corner of the bed. I started a light massage on his toes. They felt like birthday-cake candles.

"I always thought of myself as Linus," I said.

"You're clearly Charlie Brown."

"And you're Snoopy, I suppose? Joe Cool?"

"I think it's pretty obvious that I'm Lucy," he said. "Can you do my ankles?"

I moved up his foot and pressed a thumb into the soft divot near the tendon. He sighed. "Better?"

"Much," he said. "Your gift is in the top drawer, behind you. I'd get it for you, but I have cancer."

I picked up his other foot and repeated the massage. "Are you hungry?"

"Never."

"Thirsty?"

"Always. You know me, a Kardashian at the Soul Train Awards."

"I'll get you more water."

"Open the drawer first."

"No."

"I'll let you be Linus."

"This isn't fair, BF. I told you Christmas was cancelled. I didn't get you anything."

"I didn't get you something, in the literal sense. I already had it. And I had my parents embellish it. I was the ideas man. Barb was the legs man." I reached further under the comforter, delivering mini-squeezes up his calves and then cupping his kneecap. "Stop. Drawer first, then knees."

The gift was a hard, ridged rectangle, poorly wrapped, with Scotch Tape spun around paper so crinkled that it made the repeating Santas look skinny. I returned to the bed and placed it on the sheets. I didn't want to touch it further. I didn't want to undo anything he'd done.

"Can you tell I wrapped it myself?" he said.

"Yes."

"I couldn't focus, but wanted to contribute to it somehow. I think I did a great job."

"You did." The gift sat between us, a dare. He leaned forward and pulled the glasses from my face.

"Now you can see it like I do."

"I can."

He put my glasses on his face and said, "Looks better, no?" He didn't let me answer, rather launched into his imitation of me: "Humbug! Humbug! Christmas doesn't exist! I'm the master of the universe! I can out-Linus you!"

"Are you finished?"

"I will be soon, so fucking open the gift."

He always gave macabre gifts. I got a Victorian post-mortem photo collection for my thirtieth and a seven-slotted, gold-gilded pill case for my fortieth, with the days of the week engraved above each compartment. I pulled away the layers of tape and Santas to find a slip of paper in a frame, covered in fuzzy type. He slid the glasses back onto my face. The gift ticked into focus. I was looking at a boarding pass, Montreal-YUL to New York-LGA, September 11, 2001. Its creases were flattened under glass, all contained in slim wooden borders.

"That was it," he said. "That was when our story started for real, just like in your book."

"Our book."

I stared at the boarding pass. The fact of it was grotesque; an item so mundane, elevated from rubbish to monument, packed with horrible, wonderful outcomes. I hated it; I would cherish it.

"Now, I know you think you didn't get me anything," BF said. "But, oh boy! Do I have a surprise for you."

I stared at the date, at the Air Canada logo. Seat 16B. No smoking. Snack served.

"You've been *very* generous this year. My parents are coming over and they're bringing Christmas lunch. And you're going to eat it! And you're not going to complain or anything. You're going to shut the fuck up and savour every morsel of turkey and chunk of Barb's sugary turnip."

Gate 14. Departure 0755. Arrival 0920.

"And your generosity doesn't end there! You outdid yourself. On Friday, you're going to stand still, in that way you think is super masc, and you're going to say nothing while a pair of medical professionals take me to the hospice."

"Nice try."

"Thank you."

"But you don't need to go anywhere. We're handling it."

"No, we're not," he said. He tapped on my hand. "You don't even know what the 'it' is."

"We'll get help in. A nurse. A hot male nurse."

"Sounds like more of a gift for you than for me."

"We'll manage."

"What? What will we manage?"

"It."

"Say it."

"We both know," I said. In my mind, I was already in the living room, googling nurses. I was looking at their thumbnail pictures. I was making a shortlist of the attractive ones, scanning every piece of information to determine if they were gay, if their English was good enough. "Cancer."

"No! We're not managing cancer anymore, are we? We're not managing pain anymore. This is the last encore! Final curtain call!"

"BF—"

"But you're right, we're not even managing my death. I'm croaking, and we're managing *you*! For too long I've been tip-toeing around *you*. You believe that you can delay the inevitable, and

I've let you think that, but you can't. I'm too weak to keep up the charade. I can't stay this way for you."

"You don't know what you mean."

"Babes. There's no stopping it. There's no pause button. There's no extending the intermission. There's no long walk to the punch line. I have no more similes. I have no more energy. I have no more excuses."

"This conversation is over."

"Damn right it is."

"You're not going anywhere."

I left the room.

"You're a shit Linus!" he screamed after me.

I crashed into the La-Z-Boy. I opened the laptop and put on my noise-cancelling earphones. I found Spotify, loaded a playlist to which we both added songs, "Music BF Hates," and hit random, and his voice disappeared under the insipid strains of "Despacito." I mashed the keyboard until I'd successfully searched for nursing services.

"gaiy male ynglish nurses maontreral"

"Did you mean: gay male ***young*** nurses ***man on man***?"

I opened the Excel sheet with our monthly budget breakdown. The cells, once so orderly, now seemed to disintegrate. The digits were indistinguishable; they toppled out of focus, slid down their lines. I'd find the money, if only everything on the screen would behave. Another tab on the browser, this time to the Ministry of Health website to see how much home care was covered by the province, but those pages were only in French, and my brain couldn't process French right then. The terms seemed more dire in my second language. And so another tab. There were always answers. I just needed the right search term. The cursor flashed in its fat white box, waiting for me to come up with the right query—the keyword that would solve all of this, maybe even give me the right apology to smooth it over, once I'd won. I simply needed to know how to find it. Why didn't I know? And why was all this stuff in the way? Why had I allowed all this? The cartons, the clocks, the repeating pictures of Father fucking Dupuis, tarted up like a dandy? The mirrors, the canes, the ashtrays—everything was encroaching now, and for the first time, I was aware of the weight of it all, of how many extra pounds were pressing down on the floor, on me; and not only Maeve's stuff, but all the freight we'd accumulated. Why had I ever ceded a millimetre to it? The apartment was once clean, orderly, nearly empty, and now we possessed relics, histories, souvenirs, shards from lives that weren't even ours. I faced the radio-bar—a thing I once loved—and wondered why I'd let in here, wondered what difference it would have made if it had gone to some estate sale, thousands of kilometres away, where I would never have to see who bought it, or think about why it had survived so long, or travelled so many distances, or what would happen to it next, after everything, after we'd both died, and it was carried away from here—to where? To the unknown.

The centre of gravity had shifted. I was no longer stable. I tipped back for support and the La-Z-Boy reclined under my weight, its foot-rest absurdly popping up as if it were an answer. I was falling. My eyes were closed and the music was piercing—"¡Ay, Bendito!"—and I dug into the armrests to steady myself for whatever came next. The music evaporated. The earphones were lifted from my head, and I opened my eyes. Barb was in front of me, fists on her tweed hips, keys still clutched in her grip. Morty was behind me, in a cable-knit sweater, red and green, entirely unflattering, holding the earphones.

"Isn't this a sight?" Barb said. She still had her coat on, a red wool trench, thick for winter, undone, and held open by her arms. She was in a cinched pantsuit and her elaborate fur hat was still on. She'd gotten dolled up for Christmas but looked bulletproof, ready to take on anything. Her face betrayed her stance, betrayed the judgement in her voice. She was pale, her jaw was clenched, and her smile was thin, pulled across her face. The slack wrinkles at her eyes trembled. She swallowed, visibly.

That did it. She was swallowing her urge to cry at my pathetic display, and I couldn't stand it; I couldn't do that to her, so I cried for her. There was no swallowing it for me. I'd been swallowing for so long, but now, the sadness was unstoppable. It took me over. I was liquid. I shook with a powerless grief so violent, the chair's nuts and bolts screamed in strain. Morty put his arm around my bare shoulders and tried to steady me. I wailed, a sound I'd never made before, heaving in great loud breaths, inhaling every molecule in the room.

"It's hit him," Morty said.

✷

On New Year's Eve, BF slept through midnight. It was his birthday and he didn't even know it. Morty, Barb, and I stood around his hospice bed, forcing smiles at each other before darting our eyes back to BF's wan body in the sheets. I expected him to wake up as the countdown ticked by, like there was some force that would align my expectations with his birthday and his consciousness. When midnight came, we said nothing, having agreed with the doctor to let BF continue if he was sleeping. I held up my phone, screen alight, and waved its ominous message, 00:00.

Barb held up an empty plastic champagne glass, as if everything had gone according to plan. Morty nodded. He'd lost weight, and the accordion of his neck turned from one slack-bag of chin into three folds of flesh, then back again. The foil-circle balloon we'd tied to the bed frame with ribbon—"You're 40!"—drifted soundlessly.

BF spasmed. He slept more violently now. Within seconds, he was slick with sweat, but shivering, kicking at his covers, and blurting out tiny moans that were cartoonish, even porny.

"He always did that when he was sick, didn't he, Morty?" Barb said. She pulled the covers back over him. "Those tiny coos and sighs."

I nodded as though agreeing, but they only reminded me of his sex sounds, the crescendoing almost-groans that preceded orgasm.

We were on parallel tracks, me and his parents. Everything BF did reminded us of some element of our life with him, something we hadn't thought about in a while, but the memories were utterly different. Where Morty remembered BF's childhood ramblings, I remembered his drunken theories about *Twin Peaks*. Where Barb saw a face from his graduation photos, I saw his thumbnail from the dating site where we'd met.

I liked the hospice. It was stripped back to essentials. Bed, lamp, chair, TV, vitals monitor, IV drip. BF had his own room, courtesy of Barb and Morty, which was like planes of minimal whiteness set one before the other. The walls were mother of pearl; the chair, beige; the patient, waxy. The space was a visual break from the chaos of home, and I was reminded of how much I once loved the bachelor blankness of my pre-BF apartment. That thought—a world without him—was followed by a stab of guilt. How could I even conceive of life without BF, when I was so close to losing him? In response, I brought some of his cherished items to the hospice room. He now had his Care Bear sheets, his pink cosmetic bag, his framed picture of Angie Dickinson with a pistol.

The days were interchangeable. I was at the hospice by 8:00 a.m. I ran errands or went on walks during his afternoon nap, then returned and stayed until he got his final dose of morphine at 10:30 p.m. Then, I went home to whack and knead pasta dough, roll it out, sauce it lightly. I refused to allow him to eat the food at the hospice, bland piles of goo and triangles of dry toast spread with some tuna-scented pulp. He couldn't handle anything too acidic or spicy or rich, so I explored new sauces and light oils; flecks of salmon clinging to hand-cut fettuccine; walnut pesto caught in dimples of orecchiette.

The pasta gave me something to do—something BF declared "one of the only reasons to keep breathing"—so I was regularly at the Italian import market to get the sandy flour it required, hauling sacks of it from Barb's Audi up to our apartment, forking it together with eggs and salt, punching at the resulting dough, loving its resistance, the way it fought me. I sliced it, cranked it through my pasta rollers and carved out ribbons, or twisted bow ties or pressed divots with my thumb.

I also worked on the book. BF had made me promise to do something with the manuscript every day. Mostly, I just re-read the stories we had written together, correcting a word or two. It felt wrong to add anything new without BF's advice and encouragement. I jotted down questions to ask him when I went to the hospice, as well as little observations about my current life—about this phase of dread and exhaustion.

I did all of this before bed at 1:00 a.m. Bed; not sleep. I got a different kind of rest at that time. It was more like sensory deprivation. I'd close my eyes, but a river of thought thundered through my skull.

What surprised me most about this phase of the ordeal was how I relented on everything. I was shocked by how much I could let go, but shocked even more at how easily it slipped away. I watched him sleep, I listened to the machines measuring his body's activity. If their pattern of beeps was interrupted, a flood of adrenaline shot into my veins. Once I established he was alive, I cried in relief and apprehension, knowing at some point, he wouldn't be. This happened so often that I'd stopped wiping the tears away. I let everything flow. Somewhere between 2018 and 2019, the theme of my existence shifted from "this will never happen" to "this will happen any second."

BF was mostly placid. He had resigned himself to the facts long before I did, and he'd done it with such flair that I was envious. His pain had stopped coming in waves. It was a constant sensation and needed constant management. The morphine made him weak, blurry-eyed, constipated. He found joy where he could and considered it a personal triumph that I could talk openly about his funeral.

"Have you decided on a T-shirt?" I said.

"The PJ Harvey. The green one."

"Which green one?"

"Where she's in the red dress, from the To Bring You My Love Tour."

"I'll get it dry cleaned."

"No, wash it yourself. I want to be buried smelling like those cheap Provigo dryer sheets you always get."

The funeral was becoming hilariously, impossibly, but characteristically, absurd. I'd sit with my notebook and pen and take down his endless specifications.

"And I want a dress code. No black. If anyone wears black, they aren't allowed in."

"No black. At a funeral."

"*My* funeral, babes."

"No black at all?"

"Belts and shoes."

"Socks?"

"No. Colourful socks. I want you to be strict about this."

"I'll have to hire a bouncer."

"Good. Write that down."

I wrote it down. I wrote everything down. I wanted all of it. I wanted a record of every detail, no matter how mundane. Like the pasta and the book, the funeral gave me something to do—the way Nonna's funeral had once served my sister. Sometimes, BF would insist I bring my laptop to the hospice, and we'd sit together discussing where the book should go next. I'd turn on my Voice Memos app, and record our conversations as we expanded on our theories about the photos of Father Dupuis, or laughed at some of the early passages about Tina playing hockey or BF in the hot tub with Bonnie. He got nit-picky about the punctuation and requested I read passages out loud so we could see if they flowed. Part of me believed he was being demanding just to occupy my mind. He was leveraging my penchant for distraction.

BF cracked only once. When we discussed the songs that would play at the funeral, I produced the list we'd written during his first bout of cancer. He opened the ruled page, creased into quarters and rough with busted holes from where I'd torn it from a spiral notebook seventeen years ago. Both sides were marred with my handwriting.

"It's like a playlist on an oldies station," I said, and continued in a mock-radio voice. "103.2! Playing your favourite funeral hits from the '60s, '70s, '80s and '90s!"

"103.2! Death march radio! Songs so familiar you'll sing them in your grave!"

"C.U.N.T.! 103.2 on your FM dial! Reminding you that your taste hasn't improved since the '90s!"

"You're listening to 103.2 FM! If you're not dead already, you will be soon!"

"103.2—" I began, but noticed the paper shaking in his hand, and an intense concentration on his face. The joke was over; he was somewhere else.

"I can't read it," he said. "My eyes can't do it. Read it to me?"

"'Songbird' by Fleetwood Mac," I started. "'Love and Affection' by Joan Armatrading. 'Dance This Mess Around' by the B-52s."

"You have it memorized?"

"I looked up the songs last night and added them to a playlist. Not everything is on Spotify, but most of it is."

I took his phone, loaded the app. He had the font size set so large that many of the words broke in unnatural spots.

THE FAIR

EST OF T

HE SEAS

ONS

NICO

I slid the noise-cancelling earphones over his head. He looked like a child in his father's earmuffs. I hit play. He leaned back into the excess of pillows I had brought him, his pale head taking on the yellow of the pillowcase—his favourite pillowcase, with

Funshine Bear standing, smiling, hips thrust out, sunlight ejaculating from his stomach. I sat back in my chair and watched him. I spent so much time looking at him now. This is a feature of the hospice scenario. You never stop staring at the sick. My expensive earphones sealed in the music so well that I couldn't even hear a whisper from them. As the minutes passed, I had no idea what song he was listening to, but it didn't matter. He mouthed the words, lips creasing and uncreasing, and I watched as tears rolled out of the corners of his closed eyes. They disappeared, one after the next, into the kitsch, sunshiney fabric. There were four hours and thirty-four minutes of music on that playlist, the entire soundtrack of his life up to 2001—that year that neatly divided our lives between "maybe" and "yes," between "ante up" and "all in," "dithering" and "definitely," "cowardly" and "committed," "is this it?" and "this is it."

*

This time I had a plan. I turned off Pitt Street and inserted myself between a chain-link fence and the grills of Callahan's moving trucks. The tunnels between the trucks provided poor sightlines, but just enough cover for me to come around the back of the building, where I'd be exposed for fifty metres until I could blend in with some cedar bushes. It was a bold, stupid strategy, but I made the walk with the confidence of a man with nothing to lose.

I crouched in the cedar branches and assessed my view. The window on this side of the building was blocked by venetian blinds. The only other feature was a monolithic black door with graffiti across it. I felt idiotic. The sun was blazing, the pavement was white with salt. I could have been spotted. All this risk, and I'd accomplished nothing. I could make out the vague outline of humans behind the blinds. Like last time, my objectives were hazy to me. Did I hope the mover would see me? Talk to me? Could I create some business reason for me to be here, first thing in the morning? Would the Adonis know why I was here? And if he figured that part out, would he beat the shit out of me? Or blush? Or scream? Watching that impenetrable door, I concluded that I wanted all those possibilities, even the most harmful, to come true. I craved some fuel for my fantastic, pornographic, lusty scenarios. I was exhausted, under-slept, and full of dread. I'd take anything.

I shuddered in the wind and in disgust at myself, but still, my embarrassment was all mine. It was the only part of my life that was untouched by the existential drama playing elsewhere. I invented it so I could have a place to go mentally—and, apparently, literally—where I was alone. It could have been anything, but I had chosen this. Chills of shame ran through me, but I didn't leave. I needed to be rewarded for all my revolting actions. I needed to make it worth it.

And then, it was. The door swung open and the Adonis stepped out, driving a spike of desire through my shame. I stayed squatted and still. Any motion would have given me away. He was wearing the same uniform with the Callahan's logo stitched over his heart. He was too far away for me to discern anything beyond the structure of his face (high-boned, power-jawed), but my imagination filled in the details. Boyish, perky, healthy, strong. Everything BF wasn't. He winced at the wind, teeth visible in his scruff. He turned to lean on the door while rummaging in his pockets. I took in the adorable smallness of his nose in profile and tried and failed to get a sense of his bum. He turned from the cold, cupping his hand over his face, and when he turned back, a cloud of smoke poured around him, got caught in the shifting air, and then dissipated towards the sky, taking my desire with it.

The thought of smoking—carcinogens compromising his body—crumbled the foundation of my fantasy. The funk in his beard, the yellow patches on his fingers, the fetid breath, they all repulsed me beyond any reasonable level. It was nauseating. It was as physical as my craving had been. It was just as unfair, too. I had thought of him as only a body, a machine. The cigarette drew a line from BF's cancer to the mental compartment into which I had put the mover. He was connected now. Everything was connected.

I had nothing left but shame. I stood in protest and walked back across the parking lot, not caring if I was identified. I didn't look back, but could hear him calling after me, "Toi là! Toi là! Kess tu fais là?" *You there! You there! What are you doing there?*

I smiled into the wind, remembering BF saying the same thing to me, on 9/11, over the phone at Maeve's house. What are you doing? What are you doing there?

*

"It won't be long now."

Doctor Singh was poised, making eye contact with each of us—me, Barb, Morty—as we sat before her desk like three teenagers sent to the principal's office. She stretched the O in "long"—*lawwwwwng*—while nodding in slow motion. She wore no makeup, as though she didn't want this announcement to be anything more than what it was. It worked; her face was placid and serious, with huge brown eyes beaming the right amount of sympathy. Her hair was pulled back and folded in on itself, held with a no-nonsense metal clip.

"Yes, but *how* long?" Barb asked.

"Not long," the doctor replied. That term must have performed well in focus groups.

"You're speaking in code," Barb said.

"I'm sorry I can't be more specific," Singh said.

"What a thing to say!" Barb said. "Morty, isn't that a thing to say?"

"He will die soon," Morty said.

I said nothing. I understood the code; I'd lived in my own world of euphemism and non-specifics. Dr. Singh was telling us to make the calls, get everyone around, book florists. She was instructing us to move our mindsets to the next stage. She was ordering us to be prepared. She was telling us to say goodbye.

At that point, I was lucky to get two or three hours of BF every day. He'd arrive at lucidity and pick up a conversation from hours earlier, sometimes baffling me, forcing me to scramble to remember what we'd been discussing.

"A little convoy, just for me," he said, surfacing from the drugs.

"What? Where?"

"On the highway. Raffi in the minivan, Smokey Robinson in the Impala. I can see it perfectly."

"Oh, my family." An hour earlier, we'd been talking about my parents driving to Montreal with my brother, and my sister and her family coming separately in their minivan. "Yes, they'll all be here tonight."

"A race to the finish line," BF said.

"Tina will win."

"Tina always wins."

"Bonnie said that she's bringing us a surprise."

"Are you trying to bribe me to stay alive?"

"Yes."

"Giovanni Zappacosta-O'Hara. Still thinks he controls the universe."

"Got me this far."

BF yawned and said, "Pretend this is a stinging zinger," and fell back asleep

Half an hour later, I awoke to him saying, "Get up, babes, this is important."

I turned to him, dizzy in a transition from a dream. "Are you OK?"

"My nails."

"Your nails hurt? Can nails hurt?"

"Only when they're this colour." He extended his fingers.

"I thought you liked the burgundy."

"I'm having one of my trademark changes of heart. This is too poser-goth. Too depressing. If I'm going to die, I need something wild. Campy, but timeless. Thoughts?"

"Does my opinion matter?"

"Not really," he said. "Let's go full pink."

I fetched the mini-duffle that doubled as his cosmetics bag and started pulling out the bottles of nail polish. "Valentine Valour? Candy Coat? Salmon Seduction?"

"Alliterations abound."

I spread the options on the bed. "Pick a pigment."

"Are we out of Conjunctivitis Couture?"

"Yes, but we have loads of BF Buffoonery."

I cracked open the bottle of nail polish remover and pressed a cotton ball over its opening, tipping the chemicals into it. The sharp, toxic smell filled my sinuses. I put his right hand in mine. It was hot and light; he had the bones of a sparrow. He'd grown sensitive to any kind of pressure on his skin, so I proceeded delicately.

"Gentle Gio," he said.

I'd painted BF's nails many times, but I still enjoyed the process. It always felt new. A new colour, sure, but it was also an act of difference, a ritual that set him apart. First, the removal of the old, faded colour, stripping him to a blank slate. The burgundy coating seared off by poison, each nail resisting the cotton wipes until Cabernet Classique was entirely off, marring the virginal balls.

"You always press just hard enough," BF said.

"Does it hurt?"

"Just enough."

"I don't want it to hurt at all," I said, and I tweaked my pinch on his thumb. "I never know how sensitive you'll be."

"Think of it like sex. I'll let you know when the pain's not worth the payoff," he said. "This is the closest we're going to get to sex anyway."

"You say that like I mind."

"Of course you mind. Who could stare at my busted carcass all day and not want to ravish it?" He swept his fingers from his stomach to his head, showing me what I was missing. He did it with the hand I'd already stripped.

"You're different without the polish. It's like part of you is missing."

He examined the bare nails, saying, "You're right. Nature sure is hideous when left unadorned, isn't it?"

"Preach."

"Don't let anyone else do my nails, OK? And don't let them put me in the ground without my nails done. Imagine?"

"Clearly I can't."

His skin was rough, parched; it felt like birch bark. Atop each joint, the wrinkles were canyons. I could feel the mechanics of the bones moving as I squeezed the fingers into place, steadied them for my work, not wanting the remover to make things worse. His cuticles were sharp as blades.

"There," I said once I'd finished.

"Thank fuck," he said. "Now cap that bottle. The smell is making me want to puke."

Before I did, I pretended like they were poppers, sniffing the opening with one nostril pressed closed. I gave a fake shudder, a pretend visage of ecstasy. He rolled his eyes. "Like you'd know what it's like."

"Do you need a rest? Before I open the next bottle of toxins?"

"Always trying to procrastinate."

"You sure you don't want a walk or something? A little intermission?"

"I don't have the energy. It's taking everything I have to make sure you don't ruin my nails. Besides—" He lifted the small button the nurses had given him. He was permitted to press it every two hours to release a shot of morphine. "—I want to be loopy when your family gets here."

"Your wish is my reprimand."

"Don't ever forget it, even when I'm not here to remind you."

"Promise," I said. BF slid his right hand in my direction. The fingers were shaking the way they always did when he'd been up too long. I knew better than to argue with him, and pressed my palm over his hand until the vibrations stopped. "I'll even write it into the book."

"Good, good. Posterity needs this stuff," he said. "Start recording. Get this down."

I moved my phone from the nightstand to the bed, opened Voice Memos, and hit record.

[GZO]: Go for it.

[BFM]: I want the dedication to be ridiculous. Like, REALLY cheesy. Fully extra.

[GZO]: To my one and only inspiration, Brian Franklin MacDonald.

[BFM]: Who is, and will always be, younger than me.

[GZO]: And prettier.

[BFM]: And better in bed. And has a bigger cock.

[GZO]: And better taste in home decor, amongst all other things.

[BFM]: And he wore it better, too, whatever it was.

[GZO]: He's just a better human being all around.

[BFM]: Even in death.

[GZO]: Amen.

[BFM]: AMEN.

[GZO]: Can I leave your dick out of the dedication at least?

[BFM]: Nope.

[GZO]: [GROANS]

[BFM]: The dedication is the beginning. Have you given more thought to the ending?

[GZO]: Not yet. I'm stalled at the scandal. It's all bees and bigamy. It doesn't feel like an ending.

[BFM]: Just keep going. You're going to have to keep going once I'm gone.

[GZO]: I do have one idea for an ending.

[BFM]: You can't end it when I die.

[GZO]: How do you know that's what I meant?

[BFM]: Because you're too predictable. And so is that ending.

[GZO]: But there's a kind of justice to it. It's natural.

[BFM]: When have I ever endorsed something natural?

[GZO]: True, but you'll be dead, as stipulated. So you don't have much say in the matter.

[BFM]: Oh, I'll be haunting you.

[GZO]: Looking forward to it.

[BFM]: Howling in the attic, that kind of thing. Making sure you end the story properly. It's not about ME. It's about your weird family.

[GZO]: You're part of my weird family. Some might say you're the weirdest part.

[BFM]: It's hard to stand out in that crowd.

[GZO]: Ready?

I lifted the bottle of Bubblegum Bounce between my thumb and forefinger. He mirrored the gesture to me, showing that he wasn't shaking anymore.

[BFM]: Ready.

The thumb was easiest. We started there, the digit resting in the nest of my own fingers. I held it below the joint and spread the bristles of the brush wide, fanning the pinkness into a stripe along one cuticle, and then the next, commanding each micro-bristle into the valley where the nail ends and emerges as skin. The pink was thick and obvious; it allowed no mistakes. The thumb was an easel, relatively speaking. It was a rehearsal for the rest. The index and ring fingers were much tougher. They required me to squint, concentrate. I kneeled on the floor next to the bed.

> [GZO]: Push my glasses up?
>
> [BFM]: Here you go. I need you to see so you don't fuck it up.

I looked up from the work to give him a glare over the rims. He was blurry, but I could make out that he had closed his eyes and leaned back into the cloud of his pillow, doing his part, not moving, trusting me as I approached his ring finger with the intensity of a watchmaker.

> [GZO]: When have I ever fucked up?
>
> [BFM]: Oh, constantly.

He was drifting now, the morphine taking him over as his hand started its predictable quiver.

> [BFM]: But I forgive you for everything because you're getting to the pinkie and you need all the confidence in the world.
>
> [GZO]: It <u>IS</u> the hardest. It's the lightning round.

I guided his pinkie into place. It felt like it could shatter. I leaned in. I made it my whole world. The tiny plateau required one motion—a slow, clean, noxious sweep. It was perfect.

> [GZO]: There.

But he was dead. He didn't lift his hand and fan his fingers, he didn't critique my performance. He had no quip on his tongue. He had no approval to give. No exchange of reassuring intimacies followed. None of those looks and nods and shapeless sounds that make up love. I'd crave those for the rest of my life, but he was excused from all that now. I knew this before I pulled back and looked at his face. I knew it before I noticed that the machines were silent. I expected him to look at rest, but when I did lean back and take in his whole body, he didn't look peaceful at all. That's something an undertaker adds later, in some sterile room of chlorine and concrete. No, he looked simply dead. His mouth was open with a hint of lifeless tongue against his teeth. His eyes, too, were half open, showing slivers of white where the blue once danced. He isn't in pain, I thought. For the first time in a year, I didn't detect anguish from him. I wasn't sad. Like the facsimile of peacefulness, sadness came later. Right then, all I felt was relief.

I rested his hand on his chest so the polish could dry. I should get his parents, I thought. I should notify the nurse. But the nails of his left hand were sitting there, unpainted. The asymmetry was a betrayal. It didn't matter anymore, but it was forever. I allowed myself one last futile act of procrastination. I shook up the bottle and finished what we had started.

—RECORDING ENDS—

*

"Sweet Jane" by the Cowboy Junkies

I remember the scene after the funeral in fragments, in songs. The funeral itself could only accommodate four of BF's chosen tracks, so I tried to play the rest afterwards for my family. At first, the music came out of my phone because I couldn't get the wireless speaker to work. The strains were thin and insubstantial, barely noticeable in the Airbnb. My parents had rented an apartment for a week to house Tina and her family, my brother, and, because Bonnie always thinks of such things, me. The rooms were spare and clean, each with the same plastic yucca in the corner. The kitchen was straight from an Ikea catalogue. The living room walls were smog-coloured and there was a framed Warhol-like print of Audrey Hepburn above the mantle—standard issue in Airbnbs. The apartment had everything, but there was nothing to it. No personality, no humanity, no charm. It was an airlock, a netherworld; a transitional space in which I could adjust to my new reality.

"The Man With the Child in His Eyes" by Kate Bush
I remember Danny coming in smelling of pot and Barb having something to say about that. He took over from Tina, who was trying to get the wireless speaker to work. A robotic voice said "HRH Brian's iPhone," a device that Danny fiddled with and then handed to me. When I thumbed through Spotify, I noticed that BF had changed the name of the playlist from "BF's Funeral Music" to "What Becomes a Legend Most." Danny attached a cord, and Kate Bush's voice leapt from tinny whine to full ring.

"Pretty Good Year" by Tori Amos
I remember Morty's ill-fitting suit. It was grey wool and finely woven, but loose, made for the fatter version of himself. It bagged up around his midsection when he sat down. When he stood, he was shapeless; there were no contours at the waist and the shoulder seams made lines around the tops of his biceps. The cuffs came to his thumb, the crotch drooped, the wool gathered at his ankles. Watching his son disappear had eroded him, too. Grief is hungry, and it fed on Morty, made him less of himself. All of it made him look younger, inexperienced, and his face bore this out. His blue eyes, identical to BF's, swam in bruisey pits of flesh. The scenario was new and devastating to him. His observations of the obvious, once so trite, were now comforting.

"Brian's nails will always be pink."

"He looked like himself."

"He isn't suffering."

"It's over now."

"It's over."

"You Said Something" by PJ Harvey

I remember Tina and The Captain telling their four-year-old daughter to "go cheer up Uncle G." Joan marched at me like I was a chore to be done. I sat on the couch, the panels of my jacket pointing to the carpet as I leaned on my forearms and knees. She behaved just like my sister, even without a scrap of our genetic material. I saw Tina's determination and curiosity in Joan's face as she confronted her pitiful uncle. She was uncomfortable in a loathed green skirt with a high waist and too-thick tights that she kept un-wedgieing.

"Are you still sad, Uncle G?"

"Yes, pumpkin. I'm very sad."

"Were you crying?"

"Yes, a lot."

"It's OK to cry. Mommy said it's OK, if you need to. But Mama always says to buck up."

"Your mothers are very smart ladies, like my mother."

"Nonna?"

"Right."

"Do you have a Nonna?"

"I did. I shared a Nonna with your Mama."

"Was she smart?"

"In her own way, yes."

"Do you miss her?"

"Sometimes."

"Do you miss Uncle B?"

"Very much."

"Because he's not coming back?"

"That's right," I said. Her head tipped to the side as she examined me. "You're a very big girl for understanding that."

"His body didn't work anymore so he had to go away forever."

"That's right, pumpkin." Her face beamed with pride, impressed with her own understanding of life's central hoodwink. "What about you? Do you miss Uncle B?"

"I guess," she said. "It's weird. When people leave, they always come back. But not this time. Mommy said he's in heaven, but Mama said that heaven is dumb."

"Oh yeah? What else did my sister say?"

"She said you paid too much money to put him in the ground."

"Maybe they're both right," I said.

"You're smiling. Did I cheer you up?" She sounded bright, excited about ticking this off her list.

"Almost. To really cheer me up, you have to give me a hug. But not any kind of hug. It can't be small or medium-sized. It has to be *huge*."

Joan flung her arms around my neck and tightened until she was strangling me. Nothing by halves, exactly like Tina. Competitive affection.

"So, are you going to cry or are you going to buck up?"

"A bit of both, I think."

"Roads" by Portishead

I remember oceans of tea. The tick-tick-tick of the electric spark on the stove, the swoosh of the flame catching the gas. Counting to two hundred—almost always two hundred—before the rumble of the boil started low and rough, then crescendoed to a whistle. I remember its insistence. Then, the clinking of mugs, the splash of poured water. The silent steeping, three hundred seconds. The #canada150 mug handed to me, my fingers wrapping over its patriotic red surface and white drawings. A trip across the country in icons. I stared at them, memorized them: totem pole, mountain, wheat stalk, buffalo, Niagara Falls, fleur de lis, lobster, lighthouse, the Bluenose, puffin.

"More tea?" I said.

"Just drink it," Mom said. She looked down at me with a face of pride and concern, lips unable to decide if they wanted to go up or down.

"Why?"

She shrugged. "It's something to do."

This is how I measured the hours, by songs, by cups, by trips to the washroom.

"Unravel" by Björk

I remember that Barb wouldn't shut up.

"That officiant was unique, wasn't she? Brian picked her himself, from this website. Funny they have a website for this kind of thing, isn't it? There were dozens, if you can believe it! I made my recommendations, but you know Brian, he had his own little plans. He kept saying, 'Well, if Alanis isn't available, this is the next best thing.' So different, our Brian. That whole ceremony was so *him*. He would have eaten the whole thing up, like a beast at a buffet."

And on she went, sitting opposite me on the loveseat, alone, tiny, but somehow taking up the whole thing. Her arm was over the back panel, so she could address everyone in the room. She was a bolt of white on the navy fabric, looking pulled-together while the rest of us were defeated and rumpled. BF had picked her funeral get-up. It suited her, though she'd never have worn it unprompted. Wide white slacks and a mohair sweater with thin tendrils of fabric that reacted to the static of the couch, all electric with her gestures.

No one wore black, as BF had requested. Bonnie was in a long tan polo dress, belted with a thin strip of gold. Tina and The Captain were more sensibly outfitted in pantsuits, one brown, one maroon. Morty, Jacko, and Danny were all in shades of grey. I was uncomfortable in my Grace Jonesian purple suit, with ninety-degree shoulders and sharp, pleated legs. Again, BF's pick. One of his closing acts of mischief.

"And look at us! More likely to have come from a costume party than a funeral. Why, Brian would be giddy to see us here like this. I can hear him laughing at us. He always loved every minute, didn't he? He didn't get enough of them—not enough minutes—but he loved every last one. And to think that someone so special, so *him*, could go. Go! Just like that! What a thing to happen to a spark plug like him."

We stared at her.

"I mean, it's impossible to imagine!"

She stood, objecting to the injustice, a lawyer in an existential court.

"It's impossible, isn't it?"

She was coming to the conclusion again. I'd come to it. We all had, again and again, for weeks, for months. I couldn't move. I wanted her to break down. I wanted the catharsis of watching it, so that I wouldn't have to do it again. It was Barb's turn. She was trembling, looking at the ceiling. Mom swooped in, embraced her at the last minute. Barb wilted and hugged back.

"There's no one like him," Barb said.

"Well," Mom said. "This is it."

"Guided by Wire" by Neko Case

I remember someone pointing out that it was after midnight. Danny, Joan, and The Captain were already in bed. Dad offered to drive Barb and Morty to their condo.

"Take your time," Mom said.

She handed me the #canada150 mug and settled in across from me, where Barb had been, one mother replacing another. Tina had changed into sweatpants, pulled her hair back into a tight ponytail, the one BF used to call a "lesbian facelift." She was drinking one of Dad's Labatt 50s and slid in next to Bonnie. I was not surprised to find my mug full of white Zinfandel.

"How's the book coming?" Tina said.

"He doesn't want to talk about that," Bonnie said.

"BF would want us to," I said. "He got me into the book on purpose. Said I needed something to do, you know, afterwards."

They looked at me.

"There's a lot of BF in it. I don't know. The book's been good. It forces me to put things in order, you know? We worked on it together, and I didn't want it to end, because if it did, that would mean BF was gone. But here we are. He's gone and I still don't know how the book ends. I don't know if I can face ending it."

"Then don't," Mom said. "You don't have to do anything you don't want to do."

"I think you do," Tina said.

"Tina!" Mom said.

"What? He should. You were always too frigging easy on him."

"We just buried the poor soul. Give your brother five minutes to catch his breath."

"Honestly?" I said. "I wouldn't know what else to do."

"At least take the time you need," Mom said.

"Or jolt yourself right out of mourning. Dive in head first," Tina said.

"Come in From the Cold" by Joni Mitchell

"I'm not talking about that. I'm not talking about grief. I'm talking about how, every day, we had stuff to do. Especially when he was sick, I had all kinds of tasks and errands to do for him. I *had* to do them. I did them, and they were never done. But they are now. Now, there's nothing to do. I have nothing to do."

"Well, you've never had trouble finding something," Mom said. "Some distraction."

"That's the problem. You were always bolting," Tina said.

"Yeah, the first time he was sick? This was all I wanted—to do whatever I desired. The minute I had permission, or even the smallest excuse, I'd run off somewhere, do something. And there's no bigger permission than this. And I've been given it. And I don't have anything to do."

"Except the book," Tina said.

"Hell, the book was my excuse once—and here we are. How did I get here?"

"How much have you written so far?" Tina said.

"Lots, but it's unfinished. I have all these recordings on my phone of BF giving me feedback. I'll go back through them, I guess. Transcribe them. And there's a lot to research, too, from all that junk I got from Maeve."

"God rest her," Mom said.

"She had a bunch of coasters from a place in Toronto in the '30s. I think it meant something to her. Have you ever heard of the Orange Cat? It was an old dance hall or bar maybe?"

They shook their heads.

"Really, the only thing in the book that I'm sure of is the dedication. And that's because BF dictated it to me."

"I hope it's about how much he loved you," Mom said. "Or you loved him."

"In a manner of speaking," I said. "He didn't talk about things in that way."

"Don't make it schmaltzy like that," Tina said. "Mom's a sap."

"Why? Because I say things out loud?"

"Just certain things," Tina said.

"Like what?"

"'Love.'" Tina made air quotes.

"Love?" I said.

"Love!" Mom replied and threw her hands up as though she'd discovered love oozing from the ground like oil.

"Yeah, love," I said. "All those different kinds of love. That's what I wanted to capture, because I was about to lose it. I wanted to trap it so it wouldn't go away."

"That's beautiful," Mom said.

"It's dreck," Tina said. "Cut that part."

"I might. Turns out that it was the actual writing part that made me feel better."

"Of course it did! Because you did it together," Mom said.

"More because it was a release. It was like exhaling—exhaling for months."

"And when do you run out of breath?" Tina said.

"I'll keep you posted. Like I said, I don't have an ending. BF believed there was something missing. Some detail."

"Up the Ladder to the Roof" by the Supremes

They exchanged a look.

"What?" I said. "What are you two concocting?"

"You remember the surprise, right?" Mom said.

"It's been a long day, Mom," I said. "Can you be more specific?"

"Sorry." She picked up her old, outsized purse from the floor and hugged it to her chest. "The day BF died, we were driving up to Montreal. I told you I had a surprise for you both. I'm sorry we didn't make it in time to give it to him."

"Oh yeah."

"Well, it's a special thing."

"Uh huh."

"Maybe for your book."

"Why not tell him before we're *all* dead," Tina said. "Cripes."

Bonnie dug into her bag and pulled out something small—small enough for her to keep concealed in her hand.

"First, let me tell you a family story."

"Oh god, no," I said.

Tina groaned.

"What?" Mom said.

"Haven't I been through enough today?" I said.

"It's a short one, I swear."

"Mom, you recycling some story about my childhood is not a surprise," I said. "Nothing could be more predictable."

"Let *him* tell the story," Tina said. She plucked the item from Mom's fist. I saw that it was a folded paper. "That's the whole point, remember?"

Bonnie didn't respond. She signalled her resignation by looking away, taking a deep sip from her mug. Tina put the mystery paper on the coffee table and flattened her hand over it before I got a good look.

"You ready?" Tina said.

"You're as bad as she is," I said.

"No need to get nasty," Tina said. She lifted her hand. "Ta-dah."

I recognized it, even folded up. The handwriting was unmistakable; I'd stared at it for so long. I lifted it from the table and unfolded the picture of Father Dupuis dressed in his tuxedo. This one was just as old, but undamaged by water and had been better kept. Creases from the folds latticed the picture with wrinkles. On the back was a version of the same, familiar mash note, unsigned and unaddressed, noting the date and place.

"I haven't seen this one," I said. "Where did you get it?"

"Well, this is it," Bonnie said. "Read it."

"Read it out loud," Tina insisted.

They were staring at me like I was auditioning. Here, the writing was clearer than on the ones in my apartment. No blotches, no smears.

"'My love, I don't know how to write these things. I never did. But these days, I am doing everything different from before. You made that happen. When I think of you, I feel like I can do anything, but it's also like a trap. I can't get out. You were supposed to be in this picture with me, but you're not. I still want you there in that red dress. Will you be in the next photo? We can be trapped together.'"

"Do you see it?" Tina said.

"It's in better shape, but it's the same as the others."

"With one crucial difference," Tina said. "This one was sent."

"We found it in your Nonna's rosary box, the one she always had next to her bed. It was tucked under the lining. I always wondered about it."

"You knew about something and didn't say anything? I find that very hard to believe."

"Very funny, Mr. Comedian," Mom said. "It didn't fit the story, so I always kept it to myself. But when Tina showed me the ones you'd found, well, the pieces came together."

"Dupuis was playing Nonna and Maeve? He was a two-timer? What an asshole."

My sister and my mother exchanged another one of their glances. They looked so similar, with the same knowing, motherly, self-satisfied face. A person agreeing with herself.

"He's not getting it," Tina said.

"Next to the date, Gio," Mom said.

"The town?"

"Not the town. Not Fiona, Ontario," Mom said. "Fiona the person."

"Fiona the grandmother," Tina said. "Granda Footloose."

My sister took the postcard from me and placed it on the table. She put her hands flat over most of the photo, leaving only the head. She started moving her hands closer and closer together, tightening the visible space, swallowing up the top hat, the tie, even the ears, until all I could see was the blurred, teenage face of Maeve O'Hara. I looked up at them, both smug on the loveseat.

"Fuck," I said.

*

BF was wrong. These are love stories, not elegies.

Months passed before I was sure. It was hard to make the case for love when all I had was loss. January, February, March—those were elegiac periods of intense, indulgent misery. I changed nothing in the apartment; I lived in a Polaroid. I thought of BF when I woke up with Funshine Bear under my head, and on the toilet making eye contact with Paul Lynde, and when I dusted the top of the radio. I mostly felt that BF was still alive—out teaching a class or visiting his parents—but then his vicious absence would strike as I contemplated the emptiness of the dishwasher. I'd be lost in a place I knew so well, weeping in front of the Eggstractor, crumpling to the kitchen floor.

Outside, snow blindness. The sun was high and far away, but bright, and turned yards into blaring slabs of white. Wind confronted the windows, rattling them, whistling through. I ignored calls from work, parents, siblings. It was limbo.

I transcribed the recordings BF and I had made together about each of the stories in the book. Then I went through them again, checking my transcriptions line by line to make sure they were correct. I did it a third time before I stopped pretending that I wasn't wallowing in his voice. I gave in. At night, unsleeping, earphones on, I let his quippy sarcasm and insight drill into my brain, create their own neural tunnels—shortcuts to an emotional centre where my thoughts could go and marinate in the hormones of grief. As I drifted off to his voice, to that remembered reality, I'd do my old trick: lift off the narrative rails of facts towards somewhere more vivid. Once there, in a kind of half-sleep, I could hear BF's voice hectoring me to stop procrastinating.

No, no, I reasoned. I needed another day, another week, another year—there was so much left to do. All of Maeve's things still cluttered the apartment. I went through everything, looking for signs of her relationship with Nonna. I took notes, I catalogued every cane and candy dish and postcard. I did research, too, requesting old Toronto phone books and newspaper microfiches at the library in search of the Orange Cat. I wanted it to be a queer bar—a place of refuge in a hostile time. I found a few mentions to fuel my imagination. Five men were arrested on the property for indecency. Its liquor license was revoked in 1938. The Orange Cat closed for good at the beginning of World War Two, demonized as "iniquity hidden in plain sight." There was a picture of a door with a small round window, but no signage. Nothing about the Kitten Ball.

Theories were tenuous, but abounded. I shared them with BF, talking into the air as though he were in the next room. All I got back was the echo of what he'd always told me, what was there again and again in the transcripts: keep going.

His ghost and I reached an agreement. When the day came—when *this* day came—I would get on with it. Every Montrealer knows the day in question. It arrives in late March or early April, and reminds us that we are still alive. It declares that it is suddenly, sloppily, spring. The snow decomposes, turns into globs of slush and rushes of meltwater that surge in rivulets to find the sewers.

The wind, after months of enmity, switches sides. It's now our ally. Balmy, it plays in the bare maple branches and blesses us all. It's not objectively warm, but who cares? Montrealers are out, skimpily dressed, the down and wool abandoned, having snowball fights in T-shirts. A winter's worth of dog walks thaws, and the city smells of shit, and it is the greatest smell in the world.

We change when the weather shifts; we don't have a choice. It's why Montreal is interesting and Florida is not. And it's why I pack my bag with notes and transcripts and laptop and float through the city to the Second Cup in the Gay Village. I want a bucket of watery coffee that I can sip for hours. I want open windows. I want to be surrounded by homosexuality. I want to get cruised, but not seriously, just lazily, unobtrusively. Enough to get used to it again. Enough to boost my ego.

On the laptop, I load up insomnia.doc—that file name unchanged in nearly two decades—and zip to my last entry: Papa Zap stung by a bee. I take out the five pictures of Maeve in her tuxedo. The first four are pulpy and water-damaged; the last one is worn and creased, fondled and admired by Grandma Footloose, kept and cherished, hated and demonized.

My fingers hover above the keyboard. I stare into my existing sentences, picking out individual words: "bee," "ankle," "espresso," "grandfather," "Canada," "Fiona." BF believed I wanted to say something about death. Maybe I do, maybe I did, maybe I will. But only if it's considered in relation to love. I want life to be considered in relation to love. Bee, ankle, espresso, grandfather, Canada, Fiona—consider them all in relation to love. I need an ending that doesn't die with BF, an ending in which the last of the characters get the love they deserve. And they are not only loved, but beloved. Everyone should be pursued, at least once, with desire. I will give that to Nonna and Aunt Maeve, knowing that you can't keep love forever, even if you deserve it. Even if everyone deserves it. I will make a love story to end my love stories.

This is it:

9
This Is It

Our Lady of Victory was shabby then, even shabbier than it is now. Fiona was in the Communion line and could feel the planks sag a little under the soles of her hand-me-down Oxfords. She stepped on the lines between the boards. If she distributed her weight, the wood wouldn't crack. She wouldn't cause a scene by being swallowed by the floor and landing in the basement. No one else in the line was so cautious, which made it all the more likely that it would happen to her.

Near the altar, the Communion line split. The women went right, to get the Eucharist placed on their tongue by Father Greene. Fiona hated this part, stepping close to him, the sudden heat of his body, his ghoulish face bending to her, breath tickling her face. And then the intimacy of opening her mouth and presenting her tongue. When the altar boy lifted the silver plate to her chin, it reminded her of being at the doctor—a cold instrument approaching her body.

It could be worse; she could be a man. They stepped right to get their wafer, but also had to take a sip of wine. She thought of all them drinking from the same goblet, the residue of their mouths on the rim swallowed by the next man, then the next, and the next. The men received the blood from Mr. Dupuis. He was still "mister" then because he was a seminary student who had yet to take the Orders. Fiona's sister, Val, often commented that she wished she could be in the men's line so that she could get close to him. Val fantasized that he might abandon his priestly ambitions and marry her. Fiona had been informed that Mr. Dupuis was handsome, but found him gangly and wan. Her opinions were the opposite of Val's; she didn't find his looks admirable, but rather the choice he had made, giving his whole life to God. Not that she had any intention of becoming a nun, but she was jealous of how Mr. Dupuis's life would soon have permanent answers.

Once she had taken the Eucharist, Fiona glided around the side of the room with her head down and her hands folded, faking solemnity. God's always watching, but He's paying extra attention at Mass. She never closed her eyes all the way. She wanted to scan the crowd. She assumed everybody did this, watched their neighbours while cloaked in propriety. Perhaps the suitor was there. Her father said he'd introduce her to a man he knew from the Canadian-Italian Club, but was teasingly secretive about it. The man could be anyone, anyone she didn't recognize. These people were all familiar—all save one family of redheads in the last row. Among them was a woman with freckled cheeks, looking bored. She sat while everyone else was on their knees. She wore no gloves, so she was able to run a thumbnail across the pew in front of her, scratching blackened wax off the wood. She held the gunk to her eye, approved of it, and flicked it at her younger sister.

Filthy, Fiona thought, though she wished she could do that to Val sometimes. Teach her a lesson.

The sister was unaffected by the attack. Twelve, maybe thirteen, the girl knelt with conviction, head up, mouthing a prayer to the ceiling. Her dress was from a different era—a yellow flapper frock with brocade on the chest—and it stood out from her family's palette of navies and greys. She wore lipstick and too many barrettes.

Fiona kept watching the girls after she took her position next to the back exit, where she'd soon collect the hymnals and jingle the donation boxes at the departing parishioners. From here, she saw the whole family. Even in this congregation of drinking problems and hand-me-downs and sewn moth-holes and underfed faces, the clan stood out for their grubbiness. Fiona sized up their economy of clothing. The elder sister was in slacks that were bunchy and cinched into folds at the waist; inherited, Fiona assumed, from one of the adjacent brothers. The pants were grey, as was her blouse. Perhaps it had belonged to the family's matriarch, who leaned forward into a prayer-knot of fingers, nearly asleep, thankful for a moment's rest. The father was a giant, scratching away at a scalp that shone between combed-over bristles of orange hair. They were all redheads of varying intensity. Irish, Fiona thought.

The redheads were the last to go for Communion. They approached the altar, splitting right and left, men and women. The wax-flicker was last, the mustard girl ahead of her. They'd clasped hands, one reaching back, the other ahead, as if for strength, as if they knew they were being judged and needed to get through it. The younger sister stepped into the wrong line, with the men, and the older one yanked her, corrected her. She pulled back, toppling her sister. Maybe she didn't know her strength.

"Why?" the child whispered, just loud enough to pierce the calm. Heads raised. Then she said it again, clear as a bell. And then again, this time a scream. "Why, I *can*. I can!"

The mood in the parish shifted, felt unstable. The mustard girl stamped one foot—a grimy loafer, formerly white—to make her point, whatever it was. The older sister made a hugging gesture, a shushing sound, but the younger one was too quick. She dodged, grasped the chalice from Mr. Dupuis, and slurped back the contents. The child's eyes were wide and pleased and wild above the rim. The elder sister attempted to abort this heresy, gripping her sister's wrist and twisting. Fiona could see the whole thing, straight down the main aisle, but missed the flying wine until it registered as seeping patches on Mr. Dupuis's white cloak. Father Greene approached them with admonishing tones, but neither sister seemed to notice. The elder was focused on the younger, who was wriggling and gasping until her sister's embrace calmed her enough that Mass might end.

*

The sacristy was the only room in Fiona's life that didn't reek of penury. Home smelled of boiled clothes and onions scalded in bacon drippings, and, when the wind was wrong, the outhouse and the grey-water pond up the hill. School had a bouquet of cheap soap and unwashed hair. The Saint Vincent de Paul Thrift Shop, where she volunteered, had the musty whiff of used clothes. Even the rest of the church reminded Fiona of low-class grotesqueries, with its odours of feet and cheap red wine cut by the smouldering wood chips Father Greene snuck into the censer to stretch out the myrrh supply.

But the sacristy smelled of luxury. The cabinets exuded cedar tones, ingrained so deep in the wood that it would be emitted for generations. There was lavender in the laundry soap. If she was alone, Fiona would stick her head in the closet and inhale it off the altar linens, chasubles, albs, stoles, maniples, and Lenten veils—all glorious, rich English words Fiona had been eager to memorize and associate with the smell. And there was Mr. Dupuis's pipe smoke, too, and old books, and the sharp lemon cream used to polish the Communion plates.

The odours embraced her after Mass as she opened the door and pushed in the cart of hymnals. The donation boxes were on top, ringing with coinage. She opened them with the key Mr. Dupuis had given her. There was a two-dollar bill buried in the copper and nickel. Before she'd volunteered to count the offertory cash, she'd never seen such wealth. Like everything in the room, the money smelled of things that would never be hers.

The approach of voices made her stand straight. Mr. Dupuis was one, but the other she couldn't place. Husky, but young. When the door swung open, Fiona was shocked to see the girls who had caused the commotion during Mass. Mr. Dupuis pointed with his pipe for them to stand with their backs to the wall.

"Everyone's chattering about the farm girls now, aren't they?" Mr. Dupuis said.

"You don't know a thing about it," the elder sister said. "So stop bumping your gums."

"I know more than you can fathom, young lady."

"I ain't that young."

"Old enough to know better, then?"

"Know better than you."

"We'll see about that, won't we?"

"Who's the princess?" The elder sister pointed at Fiona. She had a power that extended from her voice and from every bit of her stout body, even her finger. Fiona was unsure if she should be insulted or pleased.

"This is one of our intrepid volunteers, isn't it?" Mr. Dupuis said.

"Well, is it or isn't it?"

"It is," Mr. Dupuis said. "This is Miss Ripo, from one of our parish's most devoted families. Isn't that right, Miss Ripo?"

Fiona nodded. She'd have to speak to these creatures, and a familiar panic started up in her. Her accent would be evident, a give-away of everything embarrassing about her. Family, education, geography. Italians lived in the same place, at the top of the hill—the bad hill—in plywood houses with dirt paths to the outhouses. Everybody knew that, even these farm girls.

"Good to meet you. Maeve! And this here's Dot. We're being kept against our will."

"It's no less than you deserve, is it? After causing such a disruption?"

"Are you really a princess?" Dot asked, slurring a little on the S-sounds.

Fiona shook her head. The girl stared up at her with the wild eyes from earlier, when she was in prayer, looking for God in the rafters.

"I am!" she said.

"Oh yeah, Dot's a real Irish princess. One day she'll rule over the pubs and potatoes and pregnancies. Ha!"

"You have some mouth on you, don't you, Miss O'Hara? Let's

see how much you like talking to the Communion plates. Miss Ripo, will you be so kind as to show these ladies how to polish? The bells, too? And candle holders? That should teach you." Mr. Dupuis puffed on his pipe. "Shouldn't it?"

"It should," Maeve said. "But it won't."

"And why is that?"

"I told ya. You don't know a thing about Dot here."

"I know plenty. If you don't want to cause problems for your family at your new parish, you'll find a way to keep your noses clean," Dupuis said into the well of his pipe. Seeing it unlit, he banged the thing on the heel of his shoe, depositing ash on the floorboards. "Ladies."

In the silence after he left, Fiona got the dustpan and swept up the ash.

"Can't he clean up after himself?"

"No," Fiona said. "Yes."

"You know any other words?" Maeve said. Fiona turned from them and retrieved the polish and metalware from the cupboards. "Yes or no?"

"I can show you. How to shine the things, I can show you."

"She speaks! Hear that Dot?"

"She doesn't *sound* like a princess." The younger one, possibly drunk, was running her fingers along the books packed on the shelves, repeating the bumping sound with her mouth.

"This one's an Italian princess, I can tell."

"How?" Fiona said. She could feel the burn of her cheeks turning red. "You can tell. How?"

"You've got the hair of Valentino."

"That's a man," Fiona said.

"*And* he's dead," Dot said.

"Can I show you how to do this?"

"Probably," Maeve said.

"Get your sister over? She does it too."

"Nah."

"But she drank the wine. She did."

"Dot's Dot," Maeve said. "Give me the lesson. Never was a very good student, though."

Fiona demonstrated how to apply the lemon cream in circles with a scrap of cloth. Maeve took over, rubbing the plate with aggressive squiggles. Fiona forced her eyes towards the pennies. She resumed her tally, but kept losing count, distracted by Dot, who was talking to herself as she flipped through a large book, pretending she was reading it. Maeve was unsettling, too, staring at Fiona and not the work. She was doing a poor job. Mr. Dupuis would be in a state over it.

"How about you, anyway?" Maeve said.

"Me? What about me?" Fiona said.

"I don't know. Tell me something."

"I'm seventeen."

Maeve let out a whistle. "Ripe on the vine."

"What?"

"I said you're ripe. Wouldn't you say so, Dot?"

"Oh sure."

"What does it mean?" Fiona said.

"Means you're ready to be picked. Means the boys must be all over you."

"They're not."

"Flies on shit, I bet."

"Filthy. That's filthy."

"Just us girls here."

"God's listening."

"Nah. He'd be bored to tears if he were." Maeve tossed the metal disc onto the table and picked up another. "But yeah, 'filthy' is on the money. We're not welcome back at the farm church. They think we're filthy up there! You know Sacred Heart? Up on Highway 6? They got mighty sick of Dot, I'll tell you. Ma thought we'd better come into town for Mass. Ruin all the churches in town, that's our plan."

Fiona wanted to ask what Dot had done to get them banished from a church like Sacred Heart, one of the few places she used as a comparison to feel superior. People from the farm church often shopped at the thrift store, swearing and rough. The clothes donations that came in from Sacred Heart often had to be thrown away, they were so dirty or threadbare. Once, a box of flea-specked coats had to be burned in the alley.

"Hated it there, anyhow, didn't we Dot?"

"It was boring," Dot said.

"Show me the church that isn't," Maeve said. "Now we're here. God knows for how long. The priest hasn't taken much of a shine to us."

"He's not a priest. Not yet."

"Can't say it matters much." Maeve knocked a fist on the table. "What's your family like? What's *your* problem? You might think ours is Dot, but it's not."

"What is it?"

"Hooch," Dot yelled from her chair. She'd dropped the book to the floor and was now bouncing on the seat's cushion.

"That's right. Hooch and money. Too much of one, not enough of the other. Ha!"

"Do you talk this way to everyone?"

"What way?"

"This way. The blunt way."

"She does," Dot said.

"It's filthy," Fiona said.

"Who doesn't want to be filthy?"

"Most girls."

"I'm no girl. I'm nineteen. I got a job and everything. More than I can say for most people. Bet your daddy doesn't even have a job."

It was true. He didn't.

"You took a job?"

"You bet."

"But men need them. Girls don't."

"I'm a woman. Pay attention."

"You don't act like one."

"You wanna teach me that, too?"

"Good luck," Dot said.

"I'm beyond teaching, I'd say," Maeve said. "You are who you are."

"That would be a shame," Fiona said.

"You don't want to be who you are?"

"For you, I meant."

Maeve shrugged. She was working on a candlestick now, attacking it. "You in school?"

"Of course."

"Where's that?"

"Where we live, there's no school."

"Where's *that*?" Maeve said.

"We live on the hill."

"Ah, with the Italians. You like it?"

"It's poor. It's where the poor people live," Fiona said. "Twenty-one blocks, I walk to school."

"Twenty-one?"

"I count them."

"Keep walking them. If you hate it, keep walking. School'll get you out."

"Get me out? That's a man's job, too."

"Nah."

"If I'm lucky, a man."

"Lucky? Who wouldn't want you? You do whatever you're told. Look at you with all those coins. Bet you never stole a penny."

"Of course not."

Fiona smiled and regretted it. She often had non-sequitur reactions to things, accepting compliments when she shouldn't. The strangest notions flattered her. Outward signs of ego made her feel unappealing, but she wanted Maeve to say more about her, make more observations. At least I could never be more of an ordeal than these two, Fiona thought.

"And you're poor, too. So good on ya," Maeve said.

"I bet you're lying. Lying about not wanting a husband."

"Who'd have me? Who'd want all this?" Maeve pretended to be a starlet, running hands down the sides of her torso and bringing them up to grope her own breasts, bouncing them. Fiona felt dainty by comparison.

"That's filthy," Fiona said.

"You like that word, eh? Filthy?" Maeve said. "Bodies *aren't* filthy. They're hilarious."

Dot rang the consecration bells, declaring them fun. The sound of the six chimes, gripped to their brass grid, sent a chill through Fiona. A holy sound made playful. It seemed like a sin.

"Tell her to stop," Fiona said.

"Can't you?"

"Mr. Dupuis, he'll hear."

"So?" Maeve squinted at her. "You worry too much."

Dot rang the bells again, as if confirming the fact.

"You don't mind?" Fiona said. "Calling attention to yourself. You don't care?"

"Nah."

"No one likes a show-off."

"Sure they do. Gives them something to yak about." She reached over anyhow and placed her hands on the bells so Dot couldn't lift them again.

"You never let me do anything. You're so *cruel* to me," Dot said. "Isn't she cruel?"

"The bells are going to scare off the princess's husband," Maeve said and winked at Fiona.

"Your sister's right. You are cruel."

"Nah, nah," Maeve said. "I just know better than to count on a man. I got too many men as it is. Brothers, cousins. You want one of them? I'm selling 'em cheap."

"I'm too poor even for your men," Fiona said. "And I'm Italian."

"We're Irish, which is worse."

"You know, then. You know what it's like. These things, they add up," Fiona said. "They add up to nothing."

"Oh, they're something." Maeve had stopped polishing. She was slouched deep in the chair, nodding. "I got something. I put up with worse than you, and I still know I got something. No one wants me. No one'll want Dot. Who cares?"

"You care," Fiona said. She broke the stare they were sharing. "Doesn't matter much, what you think."

"Nope!" Maeve said. She smiled a slice of grey teeth in her bulbous face. "Now you're getting it."

*

"Do you speak English?" Fiona said in Italian.

"English." The suitor swept a hand through the air, wiping away the whole English language. He was portly and gruff. "The grocer? Italian. The butcher? Italian. The girls? Italian. The priest? Who cares!"

The two men shared a laugh. Fiona thought her father was overdoing it, slapping Alberto on the back and chuckling too loud. His performance was making Val nervous. She trembled as she filled the men's glasses with wine. She and Fiona were performing too, after all. They took their cue from how Papa had bellowed for them to get dressed and come to the kitchen to meet "someone." They had to sit on their bench at the table, side-by-side, and be compared. Fiona didn't want to think this way, but there was no avoiding it. She thought of herself in counterpoint to her sister and accentuated the features that would set her apart. Her youth, her propriety. She'd chosen her meekest dress and had pulled her hair back in a sober braid. She nodded at the man, though he was in denim overalls and a T-shirt and smelled of the dump.

Both men did. Ammonia and spoiled fish. That stench always signalled the arrival of some new thing in the house, like wood slats for the windows or rolls of vinyl to cover the dirt floor. Today it was a sheet of corrugated metal. The men had left it outside, leaning on the wall and partially blocking the kitchen window.

It reduced the sunlight to a single fat beam, discernible because dust moved through it, driftingly at first, but wildly whenever Papa gave one of his arm gestures.

"The priest, he's Irish," Fiona said. "Father Greene."

"Not my priest. Mine's a monseigneur," Alberto said. Fiona loved that word. "Novak. Some Polack from Toronto."

"Alberto goes to the Basilica," Papa said. "Does their gardens."

"I love the Basicilia," Fiona said.

She'd been in the town's other Catholic church a few times to pick up donations for the thrift shop. The walls were stone, cold in summer and warm in the winter. She believed there were more bills in the collection plates—certainly no copper—and that they were given without a second thought. The men were clean, dapper, bearded; the women wore dresses with silver buttons and narrow waists. They were thin because they chose to be; hungry as part of a strategy, not out of necessity. It was easier for them to serve their families; they had food and ice delivery, tailors, carpeting, plumbing. Even cars.

"I do the gardens at the university, too," Alberto said.

"Honest work," her father said. "Alberto works with his hands, right in the earth. *Honest* work."

"What's it like?" Fiona asked.

"Dirty, but good. Regular. Money comes in."

"And the Basilica?" she said.

"Full of pricks. Too dressed up, too much English." One of his eyes tended to close from the drink, and the asymmetry was unsettling. Fiona thought of Maeve's men, the drunks, and wondered if they were like Alberto.

"And the women?"

"Nothing to them. They're like sticks. I'll take you girls some time. You can see for yourself."

"Sounds like a date," Papa said.

Fiona would feel like an imposter there; her and her sister fidgeting in their re-sewn clothes from the thrift store. She started thinking through her wardrobe, thinking of what they could wear on such an occasion. Many of their dresses may have been donated by Basilica families. It would be embarrassing to have them recognized on a pair of Italian girls from the hill.

"Alberto here was kind enough to help me bring the metal from the trash pile." Papa clapped the suitor on the shoulder again. The sunbeam went wild with dust.

"It was nothing."

"Strong as an ox, this one. *Strong*. Least I could do was offer him some wine, introduce him to my girls. They're brought up right, Alberto. Not like some of them." Her father pointed all around to indicate the other Italians on the hill, the ones with kids that ran wild, rarely bathed, and indulged stray cats. "Calabrians—right here in our backyard! Filthy houses, insolent children. They never said it'd be like this. *Never.*"

"They never told me," Alberto said. "I think about it all the time, the old village, Biletto. Beautiful place. People who knew who they were."

"They *knew*," her father confirmed. "Alberto is the best card player at the CIC. I've seen him bring down all the greats. Deluca, Mazzani. All the greats!"

These were her father's *paisans* from the Canadian-Italian Club near the base of the hill. Fiona had been once, when her mother had gone into labour and had sent Fiona down to collect Papa. She'd been in the room only thirty seconds—her father, overjoyed, raced her back in the snow to watch his son being born—but she'd memorized the details. A square room choked with cigarette smoke, with six round tables and two dozen Italian men laughing into each other's faces, telling stories of Italy. It was aggressive and loud and jovial, with Briscola cards slapping onto plastic tablecloths. She slipped Alberto into the scene: a revered card player in his undershirt, a bachelor trying to make an impression on men with daughters. A new and wild animal from Biletto, a town sixty miles down the road from where her own parents and Val were born.

"Biletto was glorious. And full of Zappacostas! A place where that name means something."

"Tell them of your brothers! Val, fill our guest's glass. He tells the most magnificent story of his brothers."

"We sired boys, my family. My brothers had boys and boys! One of them, we call The Kingmaker. Ask anyone from Biletto, they'll tell you. Zappacosta men are everywhere."

"My girls want sons."

"Very much," Val said.

"Only sons," Fiona said, and it was true. They'll know how to make money and how to care for women, she thought. They'll never speak Italian. They'll sound Canadian.

"Nothing wrong with girls, though. This is the smartest girl you'll ever meet, right here in front of you. *Right here*," their father said. He beamed out a huge, open smile and bent down close to Alberto's shoulder, shooting a flattened hand across the table, from the suitor's eye to Fiona's face, like he was giving a stranger directions. The dust swooped along behind. "Marks like you've never seen! And it's not only English or whatever. It's math, Alberto. That's the kind of girl I bring up in this house. *Right here*."

"In geography, Val got an A," Fiona said.

"Girls back home don't care about marks, don't get marks," Alberto said. "Another thing I miss."

"Don't go thinking that way, son. Don't do it. Marry a shrewd girl and she'll solve all your problems for you. Shrewd and pious. Tits and faces, they sag after a while. Brains and belief will get you where you want to be."

Brains and belief; shrewd and pious; tits and faces. Alberto's face wrinkled up as he considered these priorities. Her father stood straight and nodded his pride towards his daughters. They'd heard this speech before. He used it to buck them up, to keep their mother from being discouraged.

"Take it from a man who knows. *Brains and belief*."

*

There were sixteen roads on the hill now. Fiona used to walk them with Val, arm in arm. In warmer weather, the sun would blast the girls as they walked to school in the morning. The outhouses would not yet stink in the heat. The sisters said hi to wives who hung from windows, leaning on folded towels placed over the sills. The neighbours called them *gemelle*, twins, even though they weren't, and shouted greetings in different dialects. In winter, the windows were closed, but Fiona and Val waved to the wives beyond the panes, all in great wool garments to protect themselves from the Canadian cold.

Now that Val had graduated, Fiona walked alone with her head down, past the clapboard shacks she no longer saw, waving at nobody. The streets were narrow and muddy, made for horses that passed more and more rarely. Everyone walked on the hill now. Even the knife sharpener had given up his animal. He dragged his heavy whetstone-on-wheels behind him, ringing his bell. The streets all gathered to one long, fat stretch of trampled dirt that funnelled Italians from the sixteen streets towards the neighbourhood's only exit. This stretch of road gave onto Laurier Street, which sat on the other side of a seam where the dirt turned to asphalt, where Fiona and her countrymen passed from one reality to another, from Italian to Canadian, from wooden buildings to stone ones, from garlic to tarragon, from penury to mere hard luck.

"I found you!"

The Italians looked up, brown eyes searching for an English voice. Fiona lifted her chin from where it rested on her books, which she held to her chest over the bleach-reeking white blouse of her school uniform. Laurier Street was still asleep ahead of her. Periodic dandelions grew where the sidewalk met the buildings. At the far end of the street rose the other hill, the wealthy one, crowned with its Basilica.

A single vehicle sat in front of the Imperial Bank of Canada. It was the iceman's truck, black and sooty, with a hearse-like rear to accommodate its cargo. From the driver's side, a figure was waving to the river of Italians.

"I found you!" It was Maeve. "Come on, princess, I won't eat you."

Her eyes had relentless focus, green scopes that locked onto Fiona as she approached. Her face was tough, but babyish and smiling below a handkerchief. She was neither pretty nor handsome; she operated outside of those categories. The thick arms, the splatter of freckles, the wide visage—she was unafraid to blare them out to the world, turn the wattage up and let people make of it whatever they wanted.

"You're here," Fiona said.

"Yep. Only place in town where you're sure to find a WOP if you're looking for one," Maeve said. Fiona had to look up to see her in the driver's seat. Her arm rested in a V outside the window. "I'm taking you to school. All aboard!"

Fiona had never been in a car. She thought of vehicles as giant insects that cruised the streets, unconcerned with humanity—or at least the kind of humanity she occupied. When she was younger, she didn't understand that humans controlled the vehicles. She thought they moved of their own accord and dropped people wherever the cars desired. She knew better now, but never shed that sense of awe about them. She could climb inside a car and it would take her away to different circumstances, ones that she would strive to understand.

"I should walk," Fiona said.

"Should you now?"

"I walk every day."

"Not today," Maeve said. She was grinning down at Fiona, eyebrows up and inviting. Fiona held her books to her chest and came around the front of the truck. It was important to look as though she was hesitating, still making up her mind. When Maeve opened the passenger door, Fiona could see into the truck's maw. Maeve seemed small and scrappy in there. She was in a black jumpsuit, its canvas rolled up at the wrists and ankles to fit her. The steering wheel was huge, the cabin spacious.

"You waiting for a written invitation?"

"I'm not sure."

"Do you know how to get in? Ever been in a truck before?"

"Of course."

"You grab that strap there and yank yourself in. Alley oop!"

Fiona did, landing on the bench seat and bumping her nose against the back of it, then scrambling the rest of the way in, one hand on her kilt to keep it from opening.

Maeve laughed. "You got there in the end."

"You didn't help."

"Ah, you didn't need it."

Fiona righted herself. The interior of the truck stank of pine chips and damp rot. There were curls of wood on the floor and dashboard. Behind the seat was a darkened compartment with soaked wool blankets in a mound.

"The ice, where is it?"

"All over town," Maeve said. She was adjusting levers that made the whole truck shake. "Delivered this morning. On time, every block."

"It's still morning."

"Maybe for you," she said. She stuck an arm out in front of Fiona's chest and did something with her feet. The vehicle shook and moved backwards, flinging Fiona into Maeve's arm. Fiona gripped it, pulling it to herself for security.

"Sure, you've been in a truck before," Maeve said. "I gotcha good."

The truck jolted into the street, Maeve signalling the turn with her arm out the window. The motion of the truck was like nothing Fiona had ever experienced. She was higher than the sidewalk. Out the window, all the places she had memorized appeared shrunken. The perspective was disorienting. A higher plane.

"You delivered all the ice?"

"Yep."

"And you do it all alone?"

"Sometimes I got Dot with me. She's not much help with the ice, in her fancy duds, but she keeps me company. Dot's real special, you know. Sure you noticed. Marches to her own beat. Follows me around like a puppy."

"That's sweet."

"Gotta keep her outside the loo when I crap. Snow or sun, she's there at the outhouse door, making sure I didn't fall in."

"It's a phase, I'm sure."

"Phase my ass. See, Dot's afraid I'll disappear. And I don't mean run away. She thinks that if she doesn't watch me—poof!" Maeve said, and threw her hands off the steering wheel. "I'd turn to dust and blow away. Can you imagine? A woman like me turning to dust?"

"You are quite sturdy."

"Sturdy as stone!" Maeve said. "Tough as tar."

"More determined, I'd say."

"Determined? Determined as—"

"A donkey?"

"Hardy as a horse."

"Forceful as a falcon?"

"Now you're getting it," Maeve said.

"Robust as Roosevelt?"

"Stubborn as syphilis."

Fiona was concentrating on further jokes, and had forgotten she was in the truck until it took a turn and sent Fiona sliding along the seat, right into Maeve, whose body was solid and hot.

"You did that on purpose," Fiona said.

"Gotta loosen you up somehow, girl."

Fiona was flushed. She readjusted her skirt again in case it had crept up. "I'm not used to the motion."

"You get the hang of it," Maeve said. "I've only been driving the thing two months. Starting to love this old behemoth."

"You got in and you could drive it right away?"

"Nah. Brother taught me."

"That was kind of him."

"JJ's a prig," Maeve said. "A prig and an ass."

"Do you like anybody?"

"Oh sure. But that one, JJ, he's got a yellow streak right down his back."

Maeve explained how her eldest brother used to be the iceman, but had quit so he could go marry "some floozy" in the States. There was a violent argument in their house. The family needed the money from his job, so Maeve volunteered to take over.

"A brother getting married, that's a blessing."

"You'd think so, wouldn't you? But not around my house. No sirree. We never even met her—she's just another Irish girl. 'Ain't enough redheads around here for you to fuck?' That's what my father said. He's right, too. Too many of us kicking around without a pot to piss in. Breeding like bugs."

"That's cruel."

"That's the Gospel according to Maeve," she said. "You gotta just *do* things sometimes. Look at my farmhouse. Bank wanted to grab it back. Family laughed at me, but I hauled ice, I got paid, and we kept it. It's a shitbox, but we kept it. No wonder Dot's afraid to be there by herself. She shouldn't worry about me turning to dust, but that place? Ha! Stiff wind could scatter it to the fields." Maeve bounced in her seat, pleased at her own joke. Fiona felt it at her end, a little bump of motion in the springs. "Got walls?"

"What?"

"At your house. Got walls?"

"Oh," Fiona said. Outside were the brick houses that she saw every day, now sliding past at a rapid clip. She never thought of it before, but they were full of walls. "Sort of."

"What does that mean?"

"It means we have things that are like walls, in some places."

"Things?"

"Like bedsheets instead of doors."

"Yeah, us too."

They were rolling up the wealthy hill now, towards the Basilica. This was one of the only places in town where the Basilica couldn't see Fiona, and Fiona couldn't see it. She anticipated it, though, as she did every morning. When walking, the church revealed itself in inches—cross, steeple, bells, roof—but in the truck it scrolled up quickly from the horizon. Fiona asked Maeve if she'd ever been inside.

"Never seen a reason to. Our Lady of Victory is fancy enough for the O'Haras. Way fancier than the farm church. Gotta be Rockefeller to go to the Basilica."

"I've been inside, to pick up the clothes donated to St. Vincent de Paul. It's full of pretty things."

"All those pretty ladies wouldn't spit on me if I were on fire."

"I mean the windows and the statues. They're not *that* pretty, those white ladies."

"We're as white as any of them."

"My mother, she calls them the *donne bianche*. But she means *white* white. Rich white," Fiona said. "I always ask, 'Would they be pretty with brown eyes?' That's how you know someone is really pretty. If they can have eyes like mine, and still be pretty."

Maeve looked over at Fiona as the truck was stopped at a corner. "Nah, that's dumb," she said. "I could have no eyes at all, and none of them would ever notice me."

When they pulled up to the girls' entrance to the school, Fiona felt nauseated.

"Dizzy, eh?"

"A bit."

"That's the Maeve effect. Ha!" she bounced again on the seat. The wave of energy rolled over to Fiona. She thought she might throw up, but overcame it with several swallows.

"Thank you for bringing me."

"Enjoy it! It loses its lustre before too long," Maeve said. "And so do I. Ha!"

✷

Alberto came to the Ripos' house twice more. On the first visit, he collected Val and walked her to town, where they sat on a bench near the Great War monument. Val came back full of details, stories Alberto had told her about the army, digging trenches in Sicily. The man sounded heroic, in Val's rendition, for this service to Italy. "The greater good" was how she put it to Fiona that evening as they bathed their brothers in the kitchen basin.

"He was probably digging latrines," Fiona said in English, so their parents couldn't understand. "Trying to brag for you."

"Men are allowed to brag about things they've done. They can't help it."

"You're making excuses for him already. You're not even engaged yet."

"You think that we'll get engaged?"

"How would I know?"

"You can help me, you know."

"Be a cold fish?"

"Act prim and better than him," Val said. "Be yourself."

"I'll do my best."

"He's what I'd hoped for."

"You like him. Why?"

"Why don't you?"

"I don't know," Fiona said.

On Alberto's second visit, when it was Fiona's turn to walk with him, her father received him at the door with a handshake and booming laugh, dumping praise on the man for having braved the slop of the hill after a rain shower. Alberto himself was well groomed but damp thanks to the lingering moisture of the downpour. Fiona registered the pink rash on his face, outlining where the humidity had attacked his freshly shaven skin. He was wet in the armpits of his jacket, too, and around his low hairline.

Since she'd met Maeve, Fiona had been paying close attention to bodies. She would be sorting clothing at the thrift store and be distracted by Mrs. Schmidt's corpulence as she flipped through the racks. She needed something to fit over her rolls of flesh, which Fiona pictured as mounds of dough in hot summer, softening and falling in fleshy ridges. The young nuns at school, bodies locked away under habits, ramming yardsticks at irregular verbs, jumped naked into Fiona's mind. Taught, white, emaciated poles with pointy breasts. Mr. Dupuis was ropey and narrow under his vestments, skin thin on his ribs, his fat having melted away on one of his bike rides around the town. The physique of a sapling.

And here was Alberto, sweaty and short. A normal man squashed on both ends by the hands of God, creating a harder, compact version, solid as a brick wall, hairy as an ape.

Her father gave Alberto a quarter to pay for Cokes in town, but Fiona suggested they remain on the hill. She was testing his mettle. They skirted the sewer pool, where the residents disposed of grey water and washed items against ridged boards. A soapy scum rimmed the pond and the water had taken on a white cloudiness interrupted here and there by diapers. Whatever they once contained fermented stinkily in the spring air.

Alberto mentioned none of this. He mopped his brow, wrinkled his nose, but kept walking, guiding Fiona along the dirt paths.

"Have you ever been in a car?" Fiona said. She rode in the ice truck most mornings now. Maeve would be there, in front of the Imperial Bank, hanging her arm out the window, smelling of wood chips. Fiona had gotten used to the motion of the ride and knew when to reach for the strap and when to punctuate the conversation by letting herself slide along the seat into Maeve, making the two of them giggle. She'd grown to appreciate the elevated point of view. She felt elevated throughout other parts of her life, too, imagining the scratched kitchen table, the classroom, and the thrift store as though she floated above them.

"A car?" Alberto said. "I bet you think the answer's no, coming from a man like me. But I did it once, back in the village. I knew people. The big people in town! The doctor, the grocer, the mayor.

Once, I had to be taken to another town for medicine, and the grocer took me in his car. I knew I'd have a car myself one day. The speed! I think of it still. Is that what you want? A car?"

"The medicine, why did you need it?" Fiona said.

"I'd been bitten," Alberto said.

"What bit you?" Fiona said. "A horse? A dog?"

"No—"

"A wolf? Another man?" Fiona said. "A woman?"

"A bee," he said. His face, already red from the walk, reddened further. "My body can't take the bee's poison. But I don't let it stop me."

For a moment, Fiona liked this man. A beast who could be taken down by a bug. And he could have lied—she'd invited him to, with her list of animals—but he didn't. His body had seemed so uninviting, cloddish, but now seemed vulnerable. She smiled at him for the first time.

"And yet you're a gardener?" Fiona said.

He shrugged. "I'm not afraid."

To prove it, he described his journey on the ship from Naples to Halifax. Every Italian man in town had this story. He was the only one who didn't get sick in the rocking waves; he had to help with fuel and safety; he had to push the weaker passengers to do their part. "Girly boys," Alberto explained. "They put the whole ship in danger."

"How did you push them?" Fiona said.

"Not for a girl's ears." He showed her his fist, where hair encircled the knuckles. "But they're men now."

"I see."

"Learned it in the army," he said.

And sure enough, he told her of Sicily and the trenches, just as he'd told Val.

"I could've gone to Africa. That would've been something," Alberto continued. "Teach those darkies a thing or two."

"So why didn't you?" Fiona said. "If you're so brave?"

Alberto stopped walking. He looked at her with a blank face, as though she'd guessed a secret.

"I genuinely want to know," she said and smiled for a second time.

"Monsters."

"Monsters?"

"We were monsters," he said. They did not continue walking. He seemed unable to tell his story and move at the same time. He spoke of a friend, Cosimo, who had gone to Africa with the army and returned blind and scarred, unable to care for himself. Alberto described the man's melted skin and directionless eyes.

"This. This is why I left."

"For your friend, I'm sorry," Fiona said, feeling guilty that she'd teased him. "I can help you write to him, if you'd like."

"I don't need help," he said, downshifting back to his gruff demeanour.

"I would only write down what you wanted."

"I got nothing to say."

They never bought Cokes.

*

In the ice truck, they laughed at him. Fiona described the hairs trying to escape out the back of Alberto's collar; his wooing of Papa; the dirt crescents under his fingernails; his stammering dialect; his frustrated English words; his military career digging shitholes; his choice to be a gardener, despite being allergic to bee stings; the furious dance he did when one landed on his neck, arms swiping, face a livid pink, as he choked out Italian swear words; his explanation afterwards about how the bugs spied, carried diseases, conspired against him.

"A real piece of work," Maeve said. "You could write a book of these stories."

"Not that he could read it," Fiona said.

"Ha!" Maeve said. "What passes for men in this town. Different in the cities, I'll tell you."

Maeve often spoke of cities, Toronto and Hamilton, where she had spent some weekends.

"My mother says the men there, they're filthy," Fiona said.

"Oh, it's all filthy down there, alright. Grime everywhere, lots of factory smoke. It goes everywhere, that stuff. But who cares? When you walk down the street, no one knows who you are," Maeve said. "And when I walk into a place, I've picked it—*me*. When I see the people I know, it's because I picked them—*me*."

"Everything, it's up to you."

"Imagine that! Imagine that, Fiona from Fiona."

Fiona easily imagined it. The thought of being unknown became one of her new preoccupations. The city, the city—she thought of it like that, in duplicate, to give it lyricism and importance. Toronto bustled out there, full of English and strangers, a place where something new might happen to her. She thought of its streets steeped in smoke, an urban moor, from which figures emerged, looked at her, looked away, and disappeared back into the cloud. They had nothing to say to her. She didn't know them; they didn't know her. She was unwatched.

Torontonians all smoked, too. The city smelled like the CIC and the sacristy, like adults. There were pipes, cigarettes, incense, but also new smells, industry and exhaust, combustion and oil. The city was unknown, but there was a place for her in it, the way there was a place for Maeve. More and more, Fiona wanted to think of herself the way Maeve thought of herself, as a unit that operated independently from the town, from the church, from her family—from everything.

Except Dot, of course. The younger O'Hara had started to interest Fiona as well. Dot often rode with them, telling wild stories about the adventures she would have one day, or recounting the plots of *Showboat*, *Swing Time,* and other films that she and Maeve had snuck into through the emergency exits at the Famous Players on Exhibition Street. They always arrived at a different point in the story, so Dot had to put the chronology together herself, often grafting a narrative chunk of one film onto another, but still somehow making sense of it, her brain stitching the plots together in ways that made Fiona laugh.

"We only get the endings of things," Maeve said. "We see what everyone else in the cinema has been hoping for, but have no idea why."

Fiona also had new reasons to look forward to church. Where she was once reverent, she now felt giddy, hoping to speed through confession and Mass so she could get to the sacristy, where the O'Hara girls continued to volunteer.

Mr. Dupuis had taken a liking to Maeve, having reinterpreted the woman's gruffness as a kind of no-nonsense productivity. He put her in charge of stuffing and sealing the invitations to his ordainment Mass in July. She'd read out the names of each person on the guest list, and the three of them would come up with a whole backstory for them. Mr. and Mrs. Carr? Underweight pensioners saving up to buy a Packard to make good on their surname. Josef B. Buttenhaus? A German fairy tale villain who lived in a castle made of buttons. Sister Caroline Lavinsky? A nun leading a secret life as a burlesque performer in the city. She took out her breasts for money.

Wicked stories came easily when she was with Maeve. Fiona felt guilty afterward, but it never stopped her from telling them. She developed a system of atonement. For every cruel thing she said, she made up for it with a kind gesture—one she knew that God could see. She went through the penny box at the thrift store to find all the postcards of Canada, then laid them out for Alberto on the kitchen table. He could pick from among the places he had never been. Rocky Mountains, Toronto City Hall, Burrard Bridge. Alberto laboured over the choice. When Fiona asked why—"Your friend, he's blind, no?"—her suitor said that Cosimo's brother, the doctor, would see it and read it and judge it. Fiona did not know why that mattered and did not ask, but understood that Alberto was trying to make an impression. He was trying to seem like something he wasn't. Fiona appreciated that.

The letters to Biletto were unsentimental. They contained descriptions of the weather, the disappointing wine, the CIC, and gossip about people Fiona did not know. They always asked after Cosimo's health. Fiona would sit opposite Alberto at the kitchen table and stiffen her back, trying to look professional. A Toronto secretary, perhaps, adding words to Alberto's dictation to sweeten it, to humanize it. She considered adding cruel things, things Maeve might say, but never had the nerve to turn a good deed bad.

Once the note was done, Fiona blotted it and gave it to Alberto to sign. It was the only thing he could do with a pen, and he never failed to admire his shaky scribble, *Alberto Zappacosta*, under Fiona's confident script.

They walked to the mailbox together, slid the thing in. She pictured a scarred, blind, pitiable man in Italy pawing for the mail, desperate for this dispatch, thanking God for it. And upon hearing this, God would make Fiona's guilt a little lighter.

*

The plan was Maeve's. She explained it on the last morning of classes as they drove through the town, saying she said she was sick of hearing Fiona "bump her gums" about the city.

"Let's just go," she said. "I can show you off."

"But my parents."

"Sod 'em."

For someone who cared so little about what others thought of her, Maeve had a flair for the underhanded. Fiona would tell her parents that she was going to the O'Haras' farm to give a sewing lesson. Her parents had a blind spot for Maeve, approving of her because she was someone they'd met at church, and on whom Fiona was having such a positive impact. The farmhouse was far, so Fiona was to say that she'd go there by bike. It would take hours to make the trip and conduct the lesson. Plenty of time to get to and from Toronto.

"I don't have a bike," Fiona said. "I used to ride Val's, but it broke."

"That's the beauty of it," Maeve said. "We'll get Mr. Dupuis's bike. He'll back us up."

As Maeve described the plan, Fiona knew that she'd go through with it. She also knew the scheme was dishonest, so she planned her atonement. This was a sin she could never confess to Father Greene, so she'd get her penance at the Basilica, with the Polack priest, a stranger who wouldn't know her voice. Alberto would take her; it wouldn't seem suspicious.

At noon on Saturday, Fiona collected the bike from the residence at Our Lady of Victory. Mr. Dupuis bit on his pipe so he could lower the seat with a wrench. He gave her directions, pointing the pipe to indicate the turns and streets that would take her to the O'Haras' farm. "Merciful work you're doing with those girls. God knows they need it, don't they?"

She followed the first half of his directions, stopping at the town limit, where she looked around for another soul. Seeing none, she pushed the bike off the road and into the bushes until she reached the appointed place, just shy of the highway, where the road curved on both sides creating a blind spot. She didn't dare move for fear she'd be noticed but was ready to burst out the minute she heard the ice truck.

It was the first truly hot day of summer. She sweated into her city outfit, an olive shirt-dress with a long skirt and black buttons she'd rescued from an old coat. The dress was wool, intended for winter, Christmas and New Year's Masses, not for standing with a man's bicycle in dense bushes. Her joints hurt from gripping the handlebars so tightly. She vowed only to move her eyes, which she trained on her hands. Tendons moved over her knuckles, under her skin. She could feel the weight of her makeup, the tightness of her stockings, and the pull of her hair up into its bun, where it was stabbed with pins.

At the toot of the truck's horn, impatience blasted her from the shrubs.

"You ready?"

"Quite."

"*Quite*," Maeve said, lifting the bike into the ice hold. "Oo la la."

At first, there were nothing but trees on either side of the truck, with a periodic intersection at a dirt road. The wind through the window felt stinging and cool on Fiona's face and she didn't dare pull the glass shut against this new sensation. They ate the fried zucchini blossoms that Fiona had prepared, wrapped in wax paper, and snuck out of the house.

"That's what I like about you. Always thinking," Maeve said, taking a snack from Fiona. "What the bugger are they?

"*Fiori di zucca.*"

"That mean heaven? 'Cause they look like shit, but taste like heaven."

"They're just fried flowers."

"What'll you people think of next?"

Maeve jabbered with her mouth full as the trees gave way to tobacco fields and a giant sky. It added to Fiona's anticipation, listening to Maeve's histories of the roads and farms, places where there'd been accidents, explanations of the Mennonites' horse-drawn carts. Fiona waved at them as the ice truck passed. Maeve said that their horses look happier than they do. The lake appeared, and its fresh smell cut through the humidity. It was vast and calm, different from how lakes were depicted in books.

Toronto was not the smoky, haunted labyrinth Fiona had envisioned. The air was clear, and she could see stone buildings lining the streets as they zipped into the core along the lake. They parked the truck on Dundas Street and continued on foot. Fiona remarked on the street names. King, Queen, Edward, Victoria. "Like home, the streets. They're the same."

"Thank God they're not," Maeve said. "Alike in name only."

Fiona kept turning her head. Maeve said it was a riot, watching her "take it all in"—but Fiona wasn't taking it all in. She was looking for people from home, worried that they'd recognize her, tell on her. Even along Yonge Street, where they saw the ghostliest people of their visit, Fiona scanned the gaunt faces for flickers of familiarity. They were clustered around the entrances to churches and storefronts. They had grimy hands and torn clothes.

"Missions," Maeve explained. "For the broke, for the bums. We're lucky where we are, I'll tell ya."

Never had it occurred to Fiona that she might be lucky, that the hill, the swamp, the outhouse, and the sheets over the doorframes might be the trappings of an easier life. She felt the grit between her shoe and the pavement, and imagined sleeping on it. Urine was in the air, yeasty to the point of tasting it.

"Who helps them?"

"People like you, people who fry up flowers for auto trips," Maeve said. "People *like* you, but *not* you. I wouldn't allow it. One helping hand, and these bastards would nab you. Take everything you got, virtue included."

Fiona crossed her arms over her chest. She wished she had her shield of school books. In a few weeks, after exams, she'd have no books at all, nothing to cling to. School would be over. And what then? Could she be one of these women on the Toronto streets? They weren't as smartly dressed as she had hoped, and Torontonians had a sinister edge. They seemed distracted, uncaring. One pinched face after another passed by them as they walked to City Hall, where they waited for the bells in the clocktower to ring 6:00 p.m. They did not sound very different from the bells at the Basilica.

The sun had been swallowed by clouds, but the city felt hotter, stickier. Fiona regretted the wool dress. She suggested they walk back to the truck.

"But the city's just about to get going."

"My parents, they'll be suspicious if I'm out past dark."

"Come on, Fee. It's happy hour. Get happy."

"I'm happy enough."

"Nah. I got something to cheer you up," Maeve said. "Maybe cool you down."

"In the truck?"

"Nah."

She showed Fiona into an empty diner. The air was stewy. Three ceiling fans spun over banquettes. Fiona expected them to take a seat, but Maeve led her towards the back of the place, along a counter lined with stools. Next to a bank of diminished pies, two waitresses in sky-blue pinafore uniforms eyed them without greetings or smiles.

A tall woman in jeans and white T-shirt emerged from a phone booth as they approached it. She looked a bit shocked. Her worried eyes scanned Fiona and Maeve, then shot forward. She had no makeup, no jewellery, and made a clomping noise with her boots as she trundled past, leaving a wake of perfumed air. Lemons and musk. Maeve guided Fiona into the phone booth. The trapped heat reminded her of confession. Posh whiffs of the woman's perfume mixed with the odour of sweat and the libraryish funk of the phone book. Maeve was brushing up against her as she fished for coins in the pockets of her slacks, and dialled a memorized number, acting as though Fiona wasn't crammed next to her. But Maeve felt very present to Fiona. In her nervousness, Fiona leaned forward little by little, until she could feel her friend's reassuring back on her chest.

Maeve whispered into the receiver the names of places, streets, people, even animals. All in conspiratorial tones.

Fiona thought of the truck, parked a few blocks away, and wondered if she wanted to get in it. The city, the city—it was not what she'd expected, but she still wanted it. Perhaps it was more conquerable as a disappointment, as a real place. No one knew her here, but she couldn't erase the sense that everyone was paying attention to her, noting her movements, her differences. God, too, was watching, concerned with why she was there. Only Maeve didn't judge her. It wasn't until this moment in the phone booth, sealed off and pressed together, that the two of them felt apart from the world. The space was hot and tight, but it was theirs.

Fiona could feel her heart in her chest. This was the sensation she thought the city would provide, and here, finally, it presented itself.

Maeve opened the folding door. Cool air rushed in. On Fiona's skin, it felt bracing, and she was so dizzy and unsure on their way back through the banquettes that she grabbed Maeve's arm to steady herself.

"That's right," one of the waitresses said. "You keep right on going. Right on out that door."

"I wouldn't stay here if you were Garbo herself," Maeve said.

The waitresses' makeup was thick and blue at the eyes, bubble-gummy on the cheeks. It made them look like cartoon owls, spinning their heads, scowling, making sure Fiona and Maeve left the diner. A familiar shame shot through Fiona, though for the first time, she couldn't trace it to a cause.

"A pair of perfect bitches," Maeve said, once they were outside. She leaned on the window of the diner, feet planted to the sidewalk. The heat hadn't broken, but the wind had picked up, blowing air down the tunnel of buildings. Rain was coming; Fiona could smell it in the gusts. The sun was somewhere, as there was still light around, but it was diffuse, filtered by low clouds. The buildings were flat and grey.

"Should we get to the truck?" Fiona said.

"Nah," Maeve said. "Get a load of these two."

A pair of men were walking towards them. They wore similar charcoal-coloured suits, both with wide shoulders and two sets of buttons and purple ties. Their hair was slicked back in the same way, oily with severe parts, though one was dark-haired and the other was blonde.

"Mincing sods," Maeve said.

"What did you call me?" the shorter one, with the black hair, said.

"You heard me."

"We're passing fine," he said.

"Passing like a locomotive," Maeve said. "So loud I'm deaf."

"The *cruelty*!" the man said. He enunciated each syllable, singing the word up and down. He had a way of speaking that involved his whole face. His eyes disappeared behind fluttering eyelids as words left his mouth. "Don't leave me unloved, you ravishing animal!"

The man embraced Maeve. Fiona looked on in disbelief. Her instinct was to leap forward and protect Maeve from this intimacy. It was the kind of affection she assumed Maeve hated, but apparently not because she accepted a loud smack of kiss on both her cheeks.

"Who's the wife?" the man said, looking at Fiona.

"This here's Fiona."

"Fiona!" the man sang. "Enchantress!"

The waitresses are watching, Fiona thought.

"I'm Saul. And allow me to introduce my associate, Cash. Mr. Jeremy Cash, Esquire."

"Esquire my ass," Maeve said.

"How do you do?" the taller, blond man said. He had the well-bred creamy skin of a British boy, pinkening in reaction to his associate's behaviour. Fiona saw man-boys like him loitering in front of the Anglican church on Sundays, dressed in similar suits and seeming composed, otherworldly. Not knowing what else to do before this kind of Protestant pseudo-royalty, Fiona bowed her head to him.

"The formality!" Saul said. "From what kindergarten did you pluck this one?"

"What?" Fiona said.

"Maeve's *always* shopping in the kid's section."

"You're one to talk, nancy."

"Who's Nancy?" Fiona said.

"I was thinking the same thing," Cash said.

"They both is," Maeve said unhelpfully.

There were instructions, directions. Fiona and Maeve couldn't be seen together for the next few minutes. They were each assigned a man, and were to take turns walking around the corner to a black door. There was a particular knock and the name of the place to memorize. Maeve and Saul were to head off first; Cash and Fiona five minutes later. Perhaps sensing Fiona's unease, Maeve told her it would all make sense shortly.

"Don't go Dot on me," she said. "I'm not turning to dust."

And they were gone—two short, improbable humans with linked arms, disappearing around a corner.

"Five minutes," Cash said. He looked at this watch. "This is the worst part."

Fiona was afraid. She understood that this wasn't a date and that there was no threat from these men. The anxiety was coming from another place; it was the flip-side of the excitement she'd felt on the drive down. It was the now-frightful knowledge that she was not in control of events, that the plan was slippery and open-ended; it made no sense; she was lacking a fundamental understanding that could allow this scene to be the turning point in her story of the day. She wanted that understanding very badly, but even more fiercely, she wanted to appear as though she had it.

"Nice that we can help each other," Cash said.

"Yes."

"Maeve's really something. Saul always said she's a character. She's a real character, isn't she?"

"She's a person of character, if that's what you mean."

"It's not."

"Oh."

"I mean she's a card. A riot. She's memorable."

"She's definitely memorable."

"I met her just the once. We helped each other then, too. Waited right here at the deli." He cocked his head at her baffled visage. "You're a fawn, my dear."

"Thank you."

"I might as well say, as it's important you know a bit beforehand. This place we're going to, she's dying to show it to you, so show a little pluck."

"Me? She talks about me?"

"Indeed. You'll love the Cat. But you can't simply walk in. Not alone. Not two women, either. Or two men. So we pair up. Everyone does it."

"Everyone?"

"Everyone who counts."

Do I count? she thought.

"That's five," Cash said, indicating his gold watch. "Shall we, Miss Fiona?"

Cash put his arm out for her. She took it, seeing no other option. He steadied her shaking hand with his own, saying, "Don't worry, dear. It all gets better." They went around the corner, and the promised door was there. It had a tiny round window. No sign.

Knocking. "The Orange Cat," Cash said to a bearded man who filled the doorframe. His eyes were keen, examining them at length. More watching, she thought. She was keeping a mental record of the people who had seen her: the waitresses, Cash, Saul, the woman in the phone booth. And now this man, who stepped aside and let them into a stairwell lit by a weak lightbulb. The smell of cigarettes and cologne intensified with each step of the descent, as did music—big, swinging music. For some reason, Fiona pictured the main room at the Canadian-Italian Club, as if she'd get to the bottom of the stairs and Alberto would be there, cackling over cards with her father and a bunch of Italian men in unbuttoned shirts.

What she found instead was more like the reception room after Mass. The men were clustered on one side of the room, while the women stayed on the other. It was a makeshift tavern with a dozen circular tables made from what appeared to be huge, empty, industrial spools. The floor was concrete and littered with cigarette butts and peanut shells. A haze of smoke lingered in the air, thin clouds in the room's stratosphere, lit by candles. They were on every table, rammed into wine bottles coated with the drippings of their predecessors. Fiona identified the music as

Count Bassie, brassy stuff Mr. Dupuis sometimes played in the sacristy. A bar had been fashioned out of wooden crates and was staffed by an elaborately made-up woman in an emerald gown. The low ceiling, striped with ducts and pipes, flattened the din of chatter and music, as though it were all happening in Fiona's head. The space had promise, comfort, fun. It had vibrancy and laughter. It was not Our Lady of Victory, or the CIC, but Fiona saw that it shared something with those places. A relaxation. The sense that the people recognized something of themselves in each other. They weren't Catholic or Italian, but possessed the ease of being with their own, the comfort of knowing that what made you different made you the same.

Maeve was waiting at the bottom of the stairs, holding a beer bottle, tapping her foot to the beat.

"Not bad, eh?" she said.

"It is what it is," Cash said. "I'll hand you back now, Miss Fiona. I hope I made all this a little easier on you. Have a wonderful evening." He pulled his mouth into a thin shape approximating a smile before walking off to join the men.

Maeve pointed her O'Keefe's Ale to the nearest table, where three women sat, all smoking. "Come meet the girls."

Ingrid and Sarah introduced themselves with handshakes. Both wore sleek black blouses that looked more expensive than anything Fiona owned. The third woman, introduced by Maeve as Bridgewater, was the tall goddess who'd emerged from the phone booth earlier, leaving behind her citrus funk. They were the kind of women she'd imagined populating Toronto. Finally, they were here. She added each to her mental list of people who had witnessed her forbidden presence.

When Maeve went to obtain drinks, the women stared at Fiona. She avoided their eyes by playing with a cardboard coaster, examining the drawing on it. A woman leaned on a skinny arm, gloved to the elbow, hair pulled back into a bun, lips coy and big. She faced a man in a tuxedo, hair also slicked back, face also coy, only with a manicured moustache. They looked ready to kiss, but perhaps hesitating because of the cat depicted in the triangle formed by their arms. It was an advertisement for the Orange Cat. "Kitten Ball. August 7, 1937. Formal attire."

"A ball," Fiona said. "They do balls here."

"Every August," Ingrid said. "They're grand. Remember last year?"

"Partially," Bridgewater said. "Everyone dressed to the nines."

"Even Maeve?" Fiona said.

"Even Mae," Sarah said, nodding.

"I've never seen her at the dances back home," Fiona said. "We have dances. No balls."

"You can dance any old time, honey," Bridgewater said. "But this is another level."

"Maybe Mae will take you."

"Hey, your wife wants to go to the Kitty Ball this year," Sarah said to Maeve, who was returning with a beer and a glass of red wine, which she handed to Fiona. The stem and bulb were dotted with white bits, and the rim was haunted by a previous customer's lipstick. She turned the glass around, looking for the clearest section, and sipped with minimum contact.

"Does she now?" Maeve said.

"It's grand, they say," Fiona said.

"Ha! It's in this hovel," Maeve said. "It's as grand as the dump."

"Oh, it's a blast," Ingrid said.

"Lipstick on a pig," Maeve said.

"Sounds like your type," Sarah said.

"But I guess it's a thing we could do," Maeve said.

"That's as close to a yes that you'll get from this one," Bridgewater said. "So take it."

Fiona's brain shifted to the logistics. Another fake sewing lesson, another borrowed bike. And what "formal attire" would she wear?

"So! You're Fiona from Fiona?" Ingrid said. "You're famous."

"Am I?"

"According to Mae," Sarah said.

"How'd you get a name like that?" Ingrid said.

"My parents, they named me after the town."

"Thank god. Other than Mae's company, I didn't think there was a reason to pity you," Bridgewater said.

"There's her dress sense," Ingrid offered.

"She's passing better than you ever could," Bridgewater said.

"Fee doesn't have to pass," Maeve said. "Fee just *is*."

"If you say so," Ingrid said.

"Don't listen to these jackasses," Maeve said. "They're just saying you look like a girl. Like any old girl on the street."

"I'd say she looks better than that," Bridgewater said. "I'd say she looks better than any wife. I'd say she's twice as pretty as anyone in here."

"You would?" said Fiona.

"I *would*, honey. I would if I didn't think Mae would pull my hair out."

"Damn right," Maeve said.

"Very protective of her wives, our Mae." Bridgewater was being protective, too, holding her blond hair to her shoulder as she leaned in to light a cigarette off the candle. Fiona couldn't tell if she was protecting it from the flame or from Maeve. Exhaling, creating a polluting mist around her face, Bridgewater said, "You don't have a clue what a wife is, do you, honey?"

Fiona said, "A woman who is married," but she knew she was wrong. In the Orange Cat, she was wrong.

"A woman who can do an imitation of that," Ingrid said.

"With the hair and nails," Bridgewater said.

"With the makeup," Sarah said.

"With the purse," Ingrid said. "And whatever that is you're wearing."

"But it's more than that," Bridgewater said.

"It's the way," Maeve said. "It's the way you go about it."

"Do everything Maeve's not doing," Sarah said. "And you're halfway there."

Maeve didn't object. She smiled at her beer in its squat bottle, the same dimensions as her. Fiona concentrated on the wine. It was making her thoughts swim. She was used to having it with food, diluted with water.

"If you do that, they can't get you," Ingrid said.

"They" were the people out "there"—the police, the bosses, the men. This was explained; the need to "steer clear" and "tone it down." Men got it worse, the table agreed.

"Some of them can't help themselves," Ingrid said.

"Mincing sods," Maeve said.

Fiona thought of Saul and Cash. And of the men on Alberto's boat from Naples, the men who were not yet men, so they had to be made into men by other men—men like Alberto. It occurred to her that there was a whole other reality beyond hers, a map of the same geography where the names and places were the same, but meant something else entirely.

"Sodomites," Fiona said. "Sods are sodomites."

"Now she's getting it," Maeve said.

"Like in the Bible?"

They laughed

"Let's hope not," Ingrid said.

"It's a sin," Fiona said.

"Ain't everything these days," Maeve said.

"But sodomites, they can only be men."

They all laughed again. Fiona squinted in the dark, in the smoke. She did not know what to make of this information. The conversation moved around her. Her face felt as though it were full of blood. She was hot from the wine.

Bridgewater called Saul over.

"Ah, leave *her* out of it," Maeve said.

"No, let's ask her," Bridgewater said. "Honey, Fee here says only men can be sodomites."

"God says," Fiona clarified.

"Praise the Lord," Saul said, lids fluttering. The whites of his eyeballs flickered. "God's not often right, but He's right about that."

"And you're one?"

"Indeed."

"But it's filthy."

"Only if you're lucky."

More drinks appeared. The evening melted into itself. All this sin around, but no one seemed to mind. For them, other things were sins. The women spoke of politics and the police. Fiona followed it in fits. Everything they said had a taint of sophistication, and it made her feel grown-up to be in its presence. At the Kitten Ball this room would be transformed, the peanut shells swept up. There would be paper streamers around the ceiling pipes, the music would be turned up, the wine would be better. She wanted to wear a gown like the one from *Anne of Green Gables*, which she'd often described to Maeve, who had not yet read the book. She'd keep her eye out at St. Vincent de Paul for something approximating that primrose dress with puffed sleeves. She'd be noticed, commented on, and, for once, she'd want to be.

At 8 p.m. the music changed. The men and women took it as a cue, standing from the tables and helping one another clear the furniture to the margins of the room.

"Dancing," Maeve said, handing Fiona her latest beer and the bowl of peanuts, then dragging their table aside with one hand on the candle to keep it from falling. She became the forewoman of this small operation, ordering the others to pile chairs atop other chairs, barking precautions about the ashtrays, the drinks—to her, this was the main event, not the dancing, which was starting up around them, the women paired up with each other. The notion of swaying with Maeve's fingers on her hips, of the two of them in coordination, appealed to Fiona. Here, it was sanctioned. Here was outside of reality, she thought—or rather, this was outside of that other reality. There were zones of realness, levels of realness, and it was bewildering that they existed in such shocking proximity.

"Best we go, then," Fiona said

"Nah," Maeve said, clapping dust from her hands.

"It'll be dark before long."

The bartender flipped a record and dropped the needle.

"One song, Fee."

Fiona protested, even as they were already moving together to a flighty clarinet. She'd danced with Val and her mother before, at weddings, but this was a different sort of motion. Maeve was a terrible dancer, with her stubby hands on Fiona's hips and feet never leaving the floor. They moved uncomplicatedly, shifting their weight from one foot to the other. There was a heat in the gap between them, pouring up over Fiona's face. Their height difference meant Fiona had to look down at Maeve, whose green eyes flashed vulnerability from the newness of the movement. Maeve was unsure for once. She smelled of beer and wood chips. It didn't feel as though they could get closer, but they did. Fiona felt Maeve's curves press into her flesh, her body making room. A hand moved to Fiona's back. Maeve's red floss of hair tickled Fiona's nose. Maeve tipped her head back, showing her entire face, moony and white, with round cheeks and a hungry underbite. Fiona dug her fingers into Maeve's shoulders and could feel a nervousness there, in the muscle—a slight rumble, like the early signs of a volcano's eruption. And that's what Fiona wanted. An eruption. Something destructive and hot; beautiful and unavoidable. The surging of molten material that could no longer be contained.

This is it.

It felt real, all of it; and if it did, maybe it was. What if it was? What if it was not sealed off in some room of permission? If it was real, then it was visible—visible from heaven; the contents of her desire were visible; what was about to happen was visible. That familiar shame started to stir in her, an awareness of offence, a mechanical trigger of responsibility. You got yourself here, Fiona thought. You did it. You made it possible. You made the arrangements. You lied. You're at risk. This can't be undone.

The song ended; their movement ended. The possibility that had opened up now closed on a final chord. My grandmother stepped back. Air came between them.

"Next time," Maeve said.

Fiona looked at her in horror. She pictured the truck, the highway, the hill, and home.

"It'll be getting dark," Fiona said.

"Yeah," Maeve said.

It took all her power, but Fiona pretended to sleep the whole drive back. The journey seemed interminable, the seconds took hours, marked with each pump of the windshield wipers.

*

For the next two weeks, Fiona's eyes scanned the roads for the ice truck. She kept thinking she saw it. Each time, she was possessed by relief and disappointment when she realized it was the hearse from Chéhab and Sons Funeral Home. It had similar dimensions, it was gleaming and black. Mr. Chéhab had recently acquired it and sent it through the town when it was not officially dispatched as an advertisement for his modern funeral home. Show-off, Fiona thought.

Both Sundays, she went to the Basilica for Mass. It was easy now to accept Alberto's offers to accompany her. It turned out the women at the Basilica were nothing like the women at the Orange Cat. They were like the women at her own church, only they wore mink collars in the summertime. Fiona knew Maeve wasn't among them. The fancier crowd was helpful in reimagining herself as a person who hadn't gone to Toronto, hadn't gone to the Orange Cat. Disclosing her sinful departure in confession did not give her the clean feeling she usually felt after the sacrament. This different priest, the rumoured Polack, had given her two rosaries as penance—a cost that seemed scandalously insufficient for the scale of her transgressions. At the Basilica, the clothes were more expensive, but the absolution was cheap.

Getting away with it made Fiona feel worse. When they'd arrived from Toronto, Maeve had dropped her at the bottom of the hill. At the moment of farewell, Fiona had been grateful for the bike and the rain. She'd held the bike between their bodies, like a shield, as they'd said a hurried goodbye at the rear door of the truck, getting soaked. Her wool dress had been heavy, her makeup had been smeared. She'd managed a "thanks" before turning her attention to the river of mud that had, just that morning, been a dirt road leading to her home. There'd been no riding the bike up the hill. She'd had to push it. And when she'd gotten home, Alberto had been there, drunk with her father, and they'd both had such concern for her muddy clothes and soaked hair, that she'd simply accepted it and had gone to her room with a towel.

Deprivation was the real punishment. Classes were over; there were no truck rides across town. The time without Maeve tore at Fiona's nature. It was the abrupt cancellation of a favourite habit, leaving Maeve intensely absent. Fiona dove deep into her studies and wrote her exams and graduated. She saw Alberto. Each day felt like an accomplishment, a step away from the dance floor, a step closer to the altar, but she was still walking backwards, facing forever towards the dance floor, her point of departure. Grandma Footloose would walk that way until the day she died in the room off the landing in my parents' house.

The Holy Orders of Mr. Dupuis, after which he would be Father Dupuis, landed on the first Sunday of July. Fiona left home before her family to help with the event. She walked through the clear, bright morning towards Our Lady of Victory with a tin box that was rusting at the corners. It was full of almond biscuits she and her mother had rolled out the night before.

This return to her old parish was inevitable. Mr. Dupuis had asked her months ago to assist in the ceremony, to bear witness and carry bread as the offering. If the O'Haras were to arrive, she knew she would not be alone with Maeve, amid the bustle of the celebration.

Inside, the church was empty and clean. Fiona headed for the basement kitchen to lay out the refreshments. She smelled coffee. Not her parents' espresso, but the Canadian kind, with chicory, brewed every Sunday in the church's two-gallon boiler. Fiona usually prepared it before Mass, and by the end of the service it would be sweet and burnt and thick. When she approached the open door of the kitchen, she saw Maeve adjusting the boiler's lid, facing away from her, wearing her Sunday clothes—the bunchy grey trousers, the faded blouse—which Fiona had once thought shabby, then endearing, and now alien.

"Hi."

"There she is," Maeve said and turned around. "Those the cookies?"

"Yes."

Maeve took the tin from her, coming close. She popped the lid off and helped herself to one. "Italians don't know cookies," she said, the mulchy proof visible in her mouth.

"You don't seem angry."

"Nah. Don't you worry about that."

"You don't know what I'm talking about."

"'Course I know."

"I don't think so."

"It was your first time. It gets better." She handed the tin back to Fiona. "Why don't you find a plate for those bricks? I'll get going on the tea."

Fiona dropped the tin on the counter with a bang, and said, "It's filthy, I think."

"Do you now?"

"It was a trick. That's what I think."

"Well, I guess you gotta," Maeve said. She heaved the kettle onto the stove.

"You don't feel bad?"

"Not even a bit."

"We lied to a priest."

"Ain't a priest yet. Give it an hour. Ha!"

"I don't want anything to do with it."

"Want all you want. You already have something to do with it. You are it."

"I don't want to lie to people, just so I can drink and smoke in a room somewhere."

Maeve shrugged, lit a match, ignited a blue wave of flame under the kettle. "Some people, they gotta lie most of their lives so they can sit in that room."

"It's wrong."

"It's the only room where they don't lie. You'll see."

She blew out the match and acrid smoke filled Fiona's sinuses. Upstairs, people were arriving, squeaking the floorboards. Maybe they'd fall through. Maybe they'd all crash into the kitchen and everyone would die, but at least nothing further would happen between her and Maeve.

Maeve picked up an Eaton's bag from out of sight, behind the cooker. It was made of black, stiff paper; the ribbon handles and logo were golden. She pulled out a dress of red velour, with puffed sleeves and fine white lace details around the cuffs and neck.

"It's not the exact pink you wanted, but it looks close enough to me. There are shoes, too," Maeve said. "You know, for the ball."

August 7.

"I don't know what you mean," Fiona said.

"You're spooked."

Fiona wanted to put her body in the dress. She wanted to be seen in it. She wanted to be seen.

"Take it," Maeve said. She stuffed the dress back into the bag and held it out to Fiona, who did not take it. "It's OK to be scared, Fee. But please don't be a coward."

But she was. She was a coward.

*

Years later, Nonna went to confession. This was right as the scandal was breaking. Roberto had arrived in Canada, and though Fiona had claimed he was a nephew, his true identity had made it into Father Dupuis's sermon. Bonnie hadn't yet been sent to clean the wine jugs in the cellar, but Nonna was pregnant with her last son.

Our Lady of Victory had been modernized since Nonna's and Aunt Maeve's confrontation in its basement. There was a new floor and abstract stained-glass windows made with chunks of colour. The confessionals were still the same, though. The three cages of waxy gumwood sat behind the altar, each connected to the next by an iron lattice through which sins were sent and atonements returned.

Locked inside, Nonna heard murmuring. A high and squeaky voice first, followed by the deeper rumble of Father Dupuis's instructions and blessing. Holy feedback, God eavesdropping. She placed a hand on her stomach, felt for the baby's kick, and waited for the window to slide open. It was a particular kind of dread, this. Kneeling, waiting for her turn to unload wrongdoing. Nonna rehearsed what she might say. Her catalogue of envies, her disingenuous moments, her anger. There was a lot of anger lately, seething but concealed. The arrival of Roberto had driven a permanent anger into her. He had turned her home into a crucible where God mocked her in every square inch.

This man, this other woman's son, had been lied to. Roberto had grown up believing that his father had died of a bee sting before the war. He couldn't be blamed for wanting to find Alberto once he learned the truth. Roberto wasn't guilty of anything; she knew that, and yet he'd become one of the primary targets of her anger. She had too much of it for only Alberto. She was ashamed of it, but it had to go somewhere, to someone.

The window slid open. There was Father Dupuis, unlit pipe in his mouth, visage separated into diamonds by the sticks of iron.

"Bless me father for I have sinned."

He took the pipe from his mouth.

"Fiona, it's good to see you've finally come."

"It's been twelve days since my last confession."

"Twelve days, is it? Twelve long days?"

"I didn't want to show my face, not here."

"The parish has been burning with this, hasn't it?"

"Gossips."

"Not a sin, gossiping," he said. "But Alberto himself has stopped coming. Is he going to the Basilica?"

"Who cares about him?"

"The Lord. And the Lord will deal with him. And with you, won't He?"

"It feels like He already has."

"I fear not yet, not fully," he said. She registered that he was shaking his head. "When did you know, Fiona?"

The pipe went back into his teeth with a click, the cue for her to chronicle her sins.

"When the boy arrived from Italy," she said. "I swear it."

"So all these months, with Alberto's so-called nephew in your home, you've been lying?"

"Yes."

"To me, to your children?"

"Yes."

"To the parish?"

"Yes," she said. "I confess all that. But the sin in the middle of this, it's not mine."

"Fiona. You married another woman's husband."

"I didn't. Or, at least, I didn't know I did."

"Didn't you?"

"No."

"You had no suspicion?"

She had wondered about the money. Nonna did their accounts, and Papa Zap had her set aside $15 every month, switch it to lire, and mail it expensively to an address in Biletto. The money was for Alberto's brother, The Kingmaker, who was poor and had many sons, but whom Nonna had never met. That was what she'd been told; that was what she had never questioned.

There were many people to ask, too. Fiona was full of immigrants from Biletto who could give her insight, but they never did, neither prompted nor unprompted. They all kept Alberto's secret.

"And now you see where you've landed, don't you? This is nothing short of a scandal."

"Father, I'm sorry. But it's my family's business. Ours and God's."

"And what if it had never been revealed? What then? This sin, this depravity, would have continued—on and on, no? How many more orphans would have to be born?"

She touched her stomach.

"Everyone knows now. Even I had to learn of this from a parishioner. And if I hadn't? Why, the lie would have festered."

"Yes."

"And God would have seen. Best if everyone sees. It's no less than you deserve, is it?"

"No."

"When Miss O'Hara told me, I didn't believe it. You were never one I worried about, Fiona. I always prayed for you. Every time you lost one of your boys, I asked God why. Well, we know now, don't we?"

"Miss O'Hara?"

"She's the one who came to me about this sin. She even asked for leniency on your behalf. She begged for it. I was shocked. I'd never seen Miss O'Hara show a hint of affection for anyone but Dot. But it is God she should ask for compassion, isn't it?"

"How did Maeve know?"

"It doesn't matter, does it?"

"Very much. It matters very much."

"She heard it from the young man himself. This Roberto. They work at the car plant together, don't they?"

Nonna could picture it. Maeve in her greasy GM overalls seeking out Roberto in the assembly room, Buicks on the line, one chassis after another, under the tentacles of cords and ropes required to make them whole. The hiss and grumble of tools.

Men sniggering and chattering around their work. Maeve was supposed to be elsewhere, starting a shift, but she'd made a habit of passing through the assembly room to see Roberto. He was her only source of information about Nonna.

Maeve must have groomed him for weeks. She observed him at first, then welcomed him, then asked about his crossing, then his family, then his father. Nonna imagined Maeve pushing him for details about arguments and bedtimes and noises heard through the walls. She did this enough to learn about Nonna's life, about her children, her house, and her marriage. Roberto's halting English was an advantage for her. Her questions were darting and confusing—but then she landed a simple one, blunt and clear, and he jumped on it, proud of his comprehension. And this unexpected piece of information falls out of him. And Maeve felt what? Finally, closeness to Nonna? A secret they shared? It was a rekindling of their specialness, a joy that leapt through the years, from the Orange Cat to the GM plant to the confessional. A secret knowledge. A truth.

"Father—"

"Yes?"

"—is God mocking me?"

"God is not cruel, Fiona. Perhaps he has sent you this Roberto as a gift?"

"A gift!"

"He is the closest you can have to a son."

"I am carrying a son."

"Maybe you are carrying a boy. Maybe. But no matter what, that child's part of your penance. He's no son." Father Dupuis bit his pipe. "Of course, you can never lie with Alberto again."

Nonna let a pause fill the confessional. She bowed her head and covered her mouth. It was a performance. She pretended to be crying, not concealing a grimace of relief.

"He won't permit that. I'm his wife."

"You were never his wife in the eyes of God. You've been his whore," he said. "Haven't you?"

"Never."

She would have to sleep in the room off the kitchen—but wait, no; she can't send Roberto to sleep with the girls. She would have to go to the attic herself. Every night.

"Child, you have to admit these things. I know you will do what's right. You will feel it, that it's right."

"What? What will feel right?"

"Live with him. Live with Alberto, but as brother and sister. Care for your girls."

"The girls, they're innocent."

"In a way, perhaps."

"Even God must think so! They haven't done anything," Nonna said. "And their children, too. It's not their sin. Why should they pay?"

"They don't have to. And they won't, if you're being honest now."

"I am telling the truth, Father. All of this—this *misery*—must count. It must be worth something."

"Then make it worth something. Do your penance. You know that you can't ever marry now. To God, you and your children will remain forgiven as long as this sin doesn't continue. Don't let the sin go on, Fiona. Choose instead to live in grace."

"I did that already."

He chuckled.

"Father, I did. I made that choice. I stayed. I lived in what you call grace."

"You didn't, child. You will now."

"I have been. I always have been. It was always there, but I stayed anyway."

"It?"

"Yes."

She did not lie, but she did not elaborate further.

FAMILY TREE

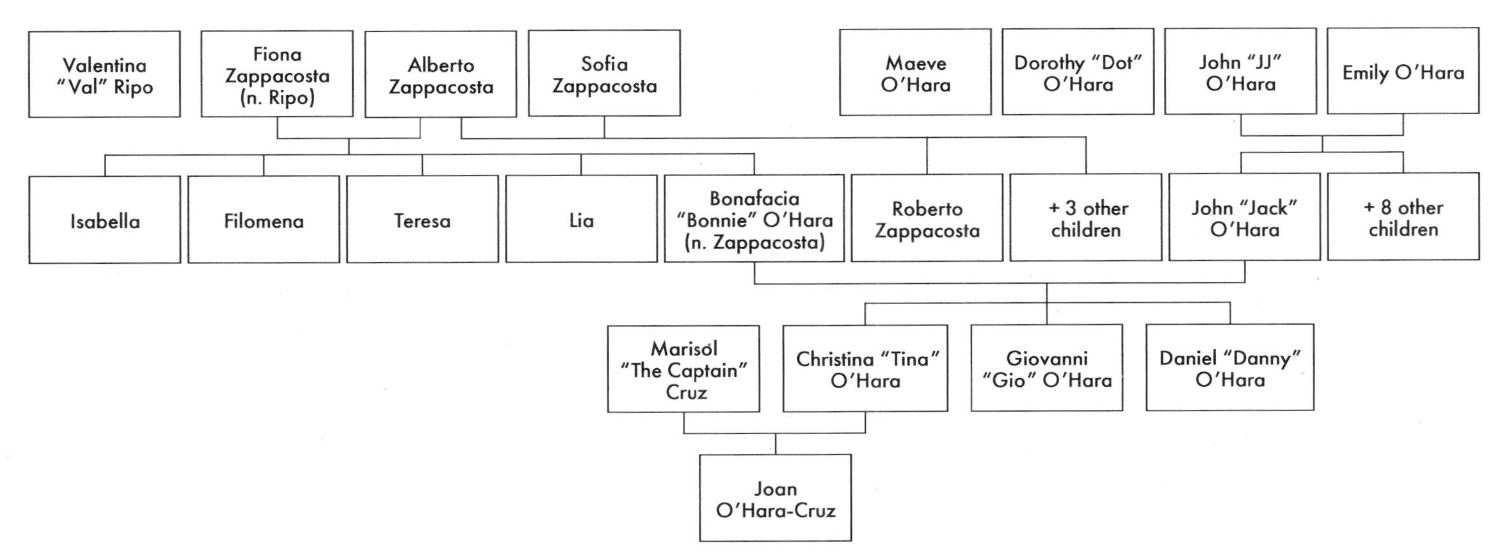

Valentina "Val" Ripo
Fiona Zappacosta (n. Ripo)
Alberto Zappacosta
Sofia Zappacosta
Maeve O'Hara
Dorothy "Dot" O'Hara
John "JJ" O'Hara
Emily O'Hara
Isabella
Filomena
Teresa
Lia
Bonafacia "Bonnie" O'Hara (n. Zappacosta)
Roberto Zappacosta
+ 3 other children
John "Jack" O'Hara
+ 8 other children
Marisol "The Captain" Cruz
Christina "Tina" O'Hara
Giovanni "Gio" O'Hara
Daniel "Danny" O'Hara
Joan O'Hara-Cruz

Selected stories or excerpts in this book first appeared in the following:

"Aliens" (2020) in *Grain*; "Our Lady of Victory" (2020) in *Big Fiction*; "This Is It" as "Toronto, 1937" (2021) in *Here and Now: An Anthology of Queer Italian-Canadian Writing*; "The Last Son" as "Lucky" (2023) in *The New Quarterly*.

Acknowledgements

I am forever indebted to the early readers who helped this book take shape and provided the kind of feedback every writer needs: Christopher DiRaddo, Christopher Ellis, Ted Gideonse, Carl Krause, Matthew Murphy, Matthew J. Trafford, Jennifer Warren, Ilana Weitzman, and Randlyn Zinn. Extra thanks to Frank Smith, who had to endure several drafts. I also want to thank Kalle Oskari Mattila, Hugh Ryan, K.R. Byggdin, and Daniel Allen Cox for their advice on the publishing process, as well as my enduring friends Suna Cristall for designing the family tree and Derek Aubichon for his contributions to BF's playlist. I am much obliged to Macke Prinz, the café that kept me caffeinated enough to write most of this book. Thanks to Catharina de Bakker and Keith Cadieux at Enfield & Wizenty for seeing something in this work.

And, of course, I deeply appreciate my family for decades of love, support, Euchre, and laughs.

BF's playlist, What Becomes a Legend Most, is available on Spotify and YouTube.

MATTHEW FOX is the author of the story collection *Cities of Weather*. He grew up in Ontario, before moving to Montreal, London and New York, where he received his MFA in Creative Writing from The New School. His work has appeared in *Grain*, *The New Quarterly*, *Big Fiction*, *Toronto Life* and *Maisonneuve*. He currently lives in Berlin.

ALI FAISAL ZAIDI